I0522606

SHADOWHEIST

SHADOWHEIST

MORE TALES FROM
THE WORLD OF SPELLMONGER

SPELLMONGER SERIES

Spellmonger, Book 1
Warmage, Book 2
The Spellmonger's Honeymoon: A Spellmonger Novella, Book 2.5
Magelord, Book 3
Knights Magi, Book 4
High Mage, Book 5
Journeymage, Book 6
Enchanter, Book 7
Court Wizard, Book 8
Shadowmage, Book 9
Necromancer, Book 10
Thaumaturge, Book 11
The Road to Sevendor: A Spellmonger Anthology, Book 11.5
Arcanist, Book 12
The Wizards of Sevendor, Book 12.5
Footwizard, Book 13

SPELLMONGER CADET SERIES

Hawkmaiden, Book 1
Hawklady, Book 2
Sky Rider, Book 3

SPELLMONGER: LEGACY AND SECRETS

Shadowplay, Book 1

SHADOWHEIST

SPELLMONGER: LEGACY AND SECRETS BOOK 2

TERRY MANCOUR

EMILY BURCH HARRIS

Podium

Dedicated to my late aunt,
Chris Brown Jackson
who constantly encouraged me to read at every possible opportunity.
She knew where my Talent was.

—Terry

Dedicated to two women who greatly encouraged and influenced
my imagination and my writing,
Marilyn Ezzel *and* **BJ Heibel**.

—Emily

CONTENTS

THE PALOMAR TEMPLE
AND THE
VILLAGE OF EJECTA

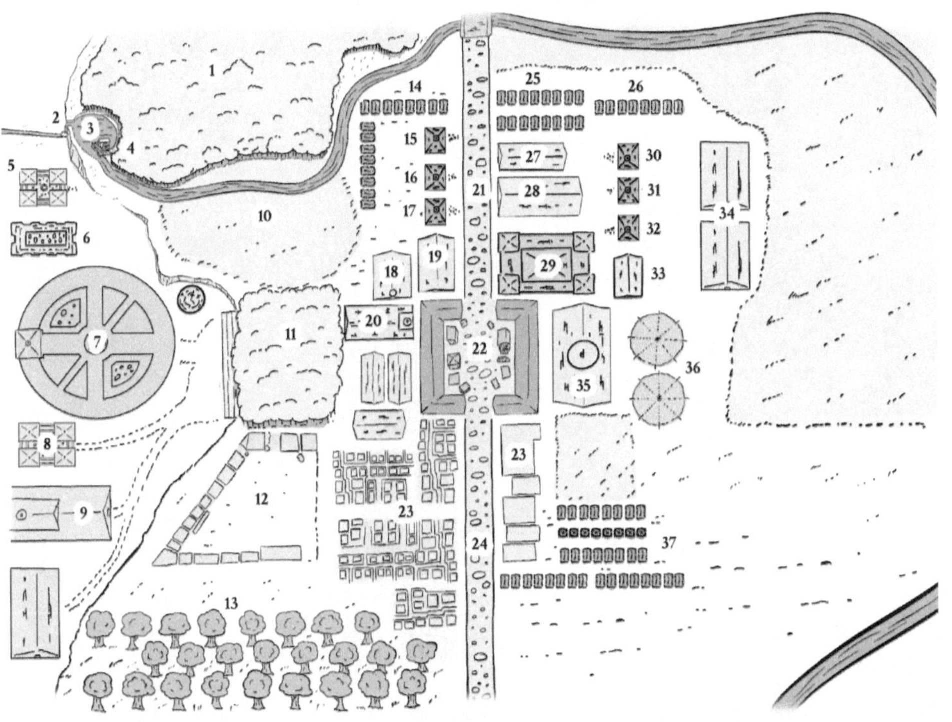

1. TEMPLE FOREST
2. WATERFALL
3. OLD MILL
4. NEW MILL
5. CARTOGRAPHY
6. SCRIPTORUM
7. TEMPLE
8. ARCHIVES
9. CLOISTER
10. TEMPLE MEADOW
11. TOWER WOOD
12. EJECTA COMMONS
13. ORCHARDS

14. DUSKBROTHERS COTS
15. STELLER HALL
16. ZODIAC HALL
17. ADASTRA HALL
18. HALL OF MOONS
19. HALL OF DAWN
20. CHAPEL OF STARS
21. TWILIGHT STREET
22. MARKET SQUARE
23. SHOPS
24. EJECTA HIGH STREET
25. LAY WORKERS COTS

26. GUEST HOUSES
27. PLANETARY HALL
28. NOCTURN HALL
29. PRIORY
30. HORIZON HALL
31. ZENITH HALL
32. NADIR HALL
33. PRIORY ANNEX
34. STOREHOUSES
35. EJECTA MANOR HALL
36. GRANARY
37. PEASANTS COTTAGES

MAP BY LEAH ZINK

SHADOWHEIST

CHAPTER ONE

A LONG CARRIAGE RIDE

The tree of House Furtius has many branches, family members, and scions, and it shall bear diverse fruits: some with the Talent of Darkness and some without. All are Furtiusi, first and foremost, and their loyalties lie with the House whether they have been gifted with Talent or not. Mundane and arcane alike are united. They shall help us continue our unique legacy.

*—from **The Shield of Darkness**, written by Kiera the Great*

"Darkness, Attie, this . . . this is so unfair!" Gatina said in disgust. As the carriage rocked back and forth down the bumpy road, Gatina fumed in quiet outrage, arms folded tightly across her chest. She never thought that Mother would send her away. It was unthinkable . . . but it had happened. It was as if her friend Marga had seen the future when she had joked about it a few weeks before in Falas.

Gatina had considered the idea highly unlikely, but there she was, in an enclosed coach headed away from home. The chill of the early summer air skated across her skin, making her shiver as a gust of wind blew into the carriage. Her father, Hance, was disguised as a hired coachman driving the team. She blamed him as much as Mother for the sudden and unexpected change in her life.

Her brother, Atopol, sat on the bench across from her, watching out the window, while Gatina bit her lip and suffered the torrent of dark thoughts running through her head. As usual, Atopol didn't seem the least bit disturbed by the sudden announcement of their departure. And that irritated her even more.

Earlier that morning in Cysgodol Hall, he had watched her in silence from the foot of her bed while she ruthlessly emptied her wardrobe, tossing items onto the bed in a fit of anger, shock, and resolution. She had made a production of stomping back and forth, which was very unladylike, unusually emotional, and just plain loud. It was so out of character for her that she knew he found it entertaining.

And she found that infuriating.

She knew the announcement of their parents' decision to send them both to Palomar Abbey for the foreseeable future had taken him by surprise, as well, but he had not reacted so forcefully at the news. Indeed, he had accepted it with grace, not voicing a word of dissent. She recalled watching his quietly amused face as she had closed her wardrobe door with a final, violent slam and thrown the final few gowns onto the bed. It had frustrated her to witness his smirk. *Why wasn't he as upset as she was about this?*

The long carriage ride had done nothing to dissuade her from being upset, nor had it tempered her irritation with her brother. And it had not rattled her big brother's calm demeanor one bit. They had ridden in silence for hours now, but she could not stand it one moment longer.

"This is some sort of punishment, isn't it?" she demanded, suddenly. Atopol looked up. His smirk was still there. And that irritated her.

"I did warn you that Mother would not be happy about your unauthorized heist," he answered, gently but loud enough to be heard over the crunch of the horses' hooves and the rumble of the wagon wheels. He sounded perfectly reasonable, which was grating. She knew he was baiting her, waiting for a reaction. The closed carriage allowed for a normal conversation, especially with Mother's added magical touches, which included spells to discourage eavesdroppers and to muffle outside noises.

So, she just stared through the crack in the window, after giving him a stony stare. He was supposed to be on her side, after all.

"Gat? I know you can hear me." It wasn't that she couldn't hear his soft voice it was that she didn't want to answer.

Gatina was quiet and withdrawn, brooding about her exile and thinking about what to say, how she could best explain herself again and keep this awful punishment from happening. They weren't even in proper disguises or traveling under proper aliases, though they did not look as they naturally did. Her striking white hair, a legacy of her family's unusual nature, was covered by a brown wig, and her violet eyes had been darkened to a hazel by magic, as had her brother's. Atopol's white hair, though, had been dyed a jet black. It gave him a swarthy look. But neither of them had true aliases yet. It was as if their parents were rushing them off into the wilderness without even a plan. She could think of no better reason than to punish her for her deeds in Falas Town.

Attie sighed. He wasn't even willing to argue with her. She took a deep breath and exhaled so hard that her hair blew off of her face.

"I *know*," she admitted with a sullen stare. "But she already yelled at me about that. I had thought she had forgiven me."

"Forgiven, not forgotten." Atopol chuckled. "Telling family secrets to outsiders is generally frowned upon in a family of professional thieves. It puts us all in danger, especially now. You should have known better," he reproved.

"I *do* know better, I really do. But Marga's my best friend. They are my friends. Do you know what that feels like? To have friends? To be in a position to help your friends?" she asked him, her eyes now boring into his. Gatina did not quite have the penetrating stare that her mother had perfected, but she was working on it. She hoped to play on her brother's emotions.

Like her, he had grown up surrounded only by their family and a few trusted retainers, insulated from the real world on a remote country estate. They had learned only recently about the reasons for that, and their unusual hair and eyes, and a good number of other things that most children did not have to contend with. That was part of their complicated legacy from House Furtius. Their mutual apprenticeships to their parents were another.

"Friends are nice," he conceded, "but they don't take precedence over the family rules," he reminded her. "You could have gotten me killed. Or others."

"I didn't know what Father had you doing. Mother didn't even know you were there, for that matter. I did not want to mess up our missions. I just went on instinct. But I didn't think Mother would send me away to an *abbey* for that! Everything turned out all right, after all. Don't you think that's a bit of an overreaction?" she demanded with another exasperated sigh.

"It's not meant as a punishment, Gat," Atopol assured her, gently. "Our family has sent their children to Palomar Abbey for more than a century now. It has nothing to do with your insubordination and ignoring the rules. Mother might still be angry, but that's not why she's doing this."

"But everything turned out all right!" she objected.

"Do you think that Mother thinks that's an excuse?" he snorted, as he removed a book from his bag. "You broke the rules. You can't break the rules, even when it turns out all right."

That was what had really stung her pride. Gatina had been working her first mission in Falas, the capital, during the chaotic time after the Duke and Duchess's assassinations. House Furtius had secretly moved to counter the attempt of Count Vichetral of Rhemes to seize power, and had employed every member in assisting—including her and Atopol. As a family of magically Talented thieves, the House had used its skills and resources adeptly, which included sending her on her first mission for the House.

She had infiltrated a band of street orphans by disguising herself as one of them and then befriending them. It was all part of her greater mission in the big city. Mother had instructed her to gain access to the Brotherhood of the Rat, a ruthless gang of thugs that was working with the usurper, Count Vichetral, in the new regime. The goal was to gain access to the Brotherhood's ways and learn information about the cutthroats that could help the greater effort against Vichetral and his cronies.

She had done well, Gatina knew. She'd made friends amongst the Nits, as the orphans were known, especially with a girl named Marga. And she had used her alias as a Nit to run errands for the Brotherhood of the Rats, for coin, of course. That had given her access to what had gotten her into trouble—the loot.

Without Mother's approval, Gatina had stolen from the Brotherhood not once but twice. And then when Marga had been taken prisoner by the gang because she was mistaken for Gatina's alias, Lissa the Mouse, Gatina had rescued the poor girl. She *had* to. But she had acted alone, without asking permission.

Worse—according to her parents—she had revealed too much about herself and her secretive family to the street orphan. And that led to House Furtius taking Marga under their protection and arranging for her service in the Temple of Trygg. Gatina had also gone off the mission plan to help a young noble pay off a debt to the Brotherhood, which had further imperiled the entire effort. So, she had, technically, broken the rules of the House and the instructions of her mistress, her mother.

When you were a newly apprenticed thief, at the very beginning of her complicated training, that was frowned upon by the family of thieves of which you were a part. But Mother should have expected that. Gatina felt that her behavior was entirely predictable, considering she had chosen her working name—"Kitten of Night"—largely because she was as curious and as fearless as a kitten.

Fortunately, Gatina had found a way to salvage the entire mission, not just hers. They had saved scores of hostages to the new regime's power, innocent people who might even prove useful against Count Vichetral in the future. Even her friend Marga. But Mother seemed to think that Gatina was far too impetuous for her own good. Just like a kitten.

Atopol sighed. "Gat, we both know Mother and Father didn't send you—and me—away because of Falas." Again, he waited to see if she would react. She gave him an annoyed look. "We need more training," he emphasized. "More education. Most young nobles go to some sort of temple school. The Temples of Trygg, Ishi, Duin, and Luin run theirs all year long. This one is just a bit . . . unusual."

Gatina grunted and stared out the window. She had heard her brother, but she was still not in the mood to talk to him, or anyone else, right then. So, she didn't.

Instead, she thought about the deck of blank cards in her satchel. That was something she'd been instructed to pack, along with her working blacks and her thieving tools, all safely tucked into a hidden compartment in the special case. But the cards were a new project.

She was responsible for making her own set of the family cards, just as everyone on both sides of the family had to do. Most magically Talented Coastlord families had something similar, a deck of cards that represented their lore and their ideals. Their use went back all the way to the Later Magocracy, when the magi ruled the world. Now they were a dearly held custom by the descendants of the magelords who became Coastlords in Alshar. The deck of cards was part teaching device and part inspirational tool, a means of quietly communicating important elements of a family's history and lore to the next generation without attracting the attention of the hated Royal Censorate of Magic. They were also supposed to advise and suggest wisdom to those who employed them. She considered the card known as OPPORTUNITY and wondered if she was seeing this unfair and punishing exile in the proper light.

Because she knew Atopol was correct: most noble families sent their children to one of the many temple schools in the duchy for education and instruction beyond what private tutors could provide. Sometimes it was just a few weeks at Trygg's temple, she knew, or a summer at Luin's temple school. The Narasi-descended Vale Lords preferred Ishi and Duin to educate their young nobles, and the Sea Lords in the coastal havens had their own version, under their strange religion.

It wasn't a punishment, her reason told her; it was just a part of growing up. And Mother and Father *had* sent their private tutors away shortly after the Ducal assassinations.

But the idea of sitting in a temple, learning a bunch of poetics or mathematics or natural history or whatever it was the Saganites wanted to teach her, sounded so absolutely boring that it *felt* like punishment. Especially after Falas . . . and the four weeks she and her family had spent quietly looting the manor houses and treasuries of the usurpers afterward.

Gatina had tried not to be upset and hurt by her parents' decision . . . but she was. She did not want to listen to Attie, especially when he sounded so reasonable. It suited her better to be mad.

So, she ignored him. He finally shrugged and pulled a book out of his own satchel—it was not one she had seen before in the family library. It was a history of Sea Lord families. But she couldn't bring herself to ask where he'd found it. She wanted to brood in silence. And the carriage bumped along at a steady pace.

But her passionate feeling of betrayal would not let her brood in silence for long.

"I don't see how this *isn't* a punishment," she insisted, finally. "It seems to me, Attie, that Mother and Father certainly decided *very* quickly to send us away."

Atopol looked up from his book. In characteristic Gatina fashion, she had picked up the conversation from their last statement as if no time had passed. Thankfully, her brother followed suit instead of reproving her.

Gatina continued. "This is the first they've ever mentioned going to school. At an abbey. And it was *very* sudden. And that decision was made immediately after our time in Falas, during which, I admit, I behaved in a manner that Mother did not approve. I took an opportunity or two and acted in the best interests of the mission . . . eventually. And now I'm going to be locked away in an abbey for months for a few minor little mistakes." She glanced at her big brother, looking for a reaction. "What else should I think?"

She was trying to be persuasive to her very reasonable brother. If she could get him to agree with her and be on her side, she would feel vindicated in her anger. And less irritated, maybe. Atopol always seemed to have a sensible perspective on things, which irritated her eleven-year-old soul, but if he agreed with her that their parents were being unusually punitive by sending them off to an abbey school, she would at least feel vindicated.

Patiently, Attie closed his book and set it on the tiny folding table between them. He studied Gatina for a moment before speaking. The road had smoothed, and the jostling had lessened as the horses found a rhythm in their pacing. He leaned forward on his cushioned bench, placing his arms out across the folding table around his book, as he tried his best to avoid patronizing his sister with his response. It was at that moment that she saw how much more like their father he was becoming, in both appearance and his mannerisms.

"Gat, your actions in Falas were selfish, in my opinion." She winced at his assessment, but she did not speak. "By acting as you did, you not only endangered your mission but also all of the missions." He paused to gauge her emotions. She was calm, but that could change quickly. She made a point of keeping quiet instead of reacting. He would call a reaction emotional, she knew, and dismiss it out of hand.

"That being said, your actions and your compassion for others helped to salvage the House's main objective—as I understand it—while also helping to rescue a considerable number of almost-hostages and find them a place to hide. I honestly do not think Mother or Father are sending you to Palomar Abbey because of your actions in Falas. Not in the least bit. I think they are sending you and me—yes, us—to the abbey for other reasons. Falas is just not *safe* for us right now," he reminded her. "We're involved in a conspiracy against Count Vichetral, who is diligently searching for traitors and supporters of the old regime. Lingering in Falas, where we've just plundered the estates of four of his biggest supporters to support our conspiracy, is not a terribly wise idea. Besides, everyone has to go to school eventually," he reasoned.

Gatina considered her brother. Matching his gaze with her own, which could be both intimidating and unnerving to those not used to such seriousness, especially from younger people, she quietly considered his statement for a moment. She stifled the desire to scream at him passionately and answered him as reasonably as possible, using her training to regulate both her breathing and her voice.

Perhaps her best tactic was to appear to concede, she decided.

"I can see your point, Attie. I suppose it's not really a punishment. I also understand that Mother and Father may need us away for the foreseeable future. Four heists from four estates owned by vassals and supporters of the same *person of interest* might draw the wrong type of attention," she admitted.

Indeed, the whirlwind round of heists her family had conducted had been one of the most exciting and fascinating things she had ever done. Seeing her parents—both master thieves—in action while they also guided her and her brother through the various ways to steal a place blind had given her valuable insight into the family business . . . which made her sudden exile all the more difficult. She was *good* at stealing, she knew, and she loved the challenge of doing it without getting caught. Giving that up for the prospect of school—of all things!—just seemed completely unfair.

"So, maybe they are sending us away for safekeeping." Atopol smiled and settled back into his seat, relieved, she could tell.

"Or maybe we are going on another mission, and they just haven't told us," she proposed. "What do you think, Attie?"

Atopol sighed. "I think I know a kitten who is entirely too eager to get into trouble, when she should know when to curl into a ball and stay quiet. Falas is dangerous now. Home is not as dangerous, but Mother and Father won't be there often, I suspect, with their work for the conspiracy. But that doesn't mean we'll be bored, I think. From what Father said, we are being sent to Palomar Abbey for both safekeeping and training while the hornet's nest we stirred up last month has a chance to die down."

"Do you really think we caused that much trouble?" Gatina asked, amused at the thought. "It was only four little estates, after all."

"Gat, we stole more than five *thousand* ounces of gold and silver and plenty of priceless heirlooms and art that are likely worth more than that," Atopol snorted. "Enough to fund the efforts of the conspiracy for months. Each of those nobles will be complaining bitterly to the new regime about it. Vichetral will know that they are connected, since they were so close together, and he'll know his enemies are behind it, since each of the nobles is a very public supporter of the new regime. The four heists will, of course, draw all sorts of attention, and not only from Count Vichetral. He will have his guards looking for anyone he thinks was capable of such a feat. He may even bring on a few rogue Censors if he suspects magic was involved."

Gatina flinched at the mention of the dreaded Censors. She had often heard her parents warn them of the enforcers of the Bans.

The Censors from the Royal Censorate of Magic, Gatina knew, were despised and feared by everyone with any ounce of *rajira*. Censors were magi who policed other magi. In her mind, she imagined them to be similar to the Town Watchmen she had seen in Falas but for magi instead of people without Talent. They were regulators of the ancient Bans on Magic, one of the few institutions left from the original Narasi invasion. They answered to no higher authority than themselves. And they didn't just take you to the magistrate; they were empowered to convict and punish as well as investigate.

She had heard her parents talk about them in the past and knew the history from her own private lessons with her mother. Mother had explained that the Royal Censorate of Magic employed magi called Censors to enforce the Bans on Magic. The Censors were zealots, Mother had lectured, obsessed with policing magical use and ability. They had the support of the nonmagical nobility and were used as a means of keeping the magi—especially those magi descended from the magelords of the Imperial Magocracy, like she was.

Censors were incredibly dangerous, her parents had emphasized. They used all sorts of spells to enforce the Bans. They were difficult to bribe, impossible to overrule, and enjoyed complete immunity from the civil authorities, all in the name of "protecting" mundane people against illegal and unethical magic. The Bans were one reason why House Furtius was never properly registered. While not explicitly illegal, shadowmagic was frowned upon, after all.

"But Father has placed so many pieces on the board, in so many different locations, I doubt the Count will know where to look," Atopol continued, hopefully, as he tapped the book. "Confusion is as good as darkness to hide something. And not being around to get caught because you're masquerading as someone else entirely in a new temple school seems like a good way to avoid detection."

"That, too, makes sense," Gatina admitted, coolly. "How do you keep from getting depressed about it, though? I can hardly stand the idea of hiding out studying the stars when there are heists I could be planning!" She shifted in her seat, bothered once more by the unfair situation in which she found herself. Not even the prospect of the Censorate investigating concerned her. A group of Talented men hunting hedgewitches did not frighten her, despite Mother's lectures.

"I see it as an opportunity," her brother said, simply. "As a way to keep my mind occupied as well as preparing myself for the future. I'm excited by the possibilities, if you want me to be honest."

"Yes, but you're always reading books!" Gatina snorted. "They're good, in their way, I suppose, but it's no substitute for learning things by doing things. What's that one about?" she asked, curious but also dismissive of her brother's interests.

"I am reading about the Sea Lords and their havens in Enultramar, and their contributions to Alshar. It's fascinating, really—the Sea Lords ruled the coasts for a century before the Magocracy sent our Coastlord ancestors here, and they have an entirely different society. You should read this too. I will be finished tonight. I think you will find it very useful, regardless of what Mother and Father have planned for us."

It actually did sound interesting, but Gatina didn't want to admit that to him. She didn't get the chance. Before Gatina could pursue her line of questioning, Hance had stopped the carriage for their late luncheon.

Of course, the man driving the team looked nothing like her father—his white hair was covered under a wig, and he was dressed in clothes far below his station, as a common coachman would appear. When he walked, it was with a pronounced stoop, and his gait was completely different from her father's normal decidedly graceful and purposeful steps.

Father parked the carriage under a lonely grove of trees near the side of the road. The foliage provided brilliant shades of green overhead and an abundance of shade from the bright sunlight, which was ideal, as she and Atopol had been riding in a darkened carriage for hours. Her father had unhitched the team and tied the two brown working horses to a tree, where they had fresh tall grass to graze upon to complement their oats and water.

Gatina found the lovely day a bit irritating, considering her mood. The three members of House Furtius shared a meal of watered wine, boiled eggs, a bit of cheese, and delicious apple tarts while sitting on a wool blanket. It occurred to Gatina that it might be the last good meal she would have for a while. Drella, the family's cook who had been part of the household since Hance was born, had prepared the meal, and she had added their favorite tarts for both Atopol and Gatina because she wanted to make sure they had something tasty to eat before they were forced to depend on food from the abbey. Ecclesiastical fare was filling but also known to be lacking in flavor.

"I think you'll like the abbey," Hance suggested while they ate. "I went to school there when I was your age. Most of our family undertook the Saganite Mysteries. You'll be taught all sorts of things—mathematics, literature, history, philosophy, and, of course, astronomy. The Saganites are master astronomers," he added. "They study the stars and watch them in their courses."

"Why in the name of Darkness would anyone bother to do that?" Gatina asked as she nibbled her tart. She really could not think of anything more useless and boring than that, with the possible exception of needlework.

"Because that's how ships navigate the open seas, for one thing," Atopol supplied, tapping his book. "The Sea Lords were good at it, but it took the Saganites from the Magocracy to establish the charts and such for truly accurate navigation. It allowed them to win several key battles back in history."

"Palomar Abbey was established in Alshar even before the Sea Lords colonized the coasts," Hance agreed, his unfamiliar face looking thoughtful. "It dates back to the very beginning of humanity's existence on Callidore. It's not a large or popular temple, but it is well distinguished among the clergy and noted for its academic rigor. You'll learn many useful things there . . . and plenty of useless things as well.

"But the most important lesson to learn is how to portray yourself as clergy," he continued, in a more serious tone. "In our business, that can be an extremely useful thing. The clergy are exempt from many rules and laws, and the Saganites have special regulations that even other clergy don't enjoy. They have often proven useful in our endeavors."

"I've never really heard of them before," Gatina admitted.

"They're fairly obscure," agreed her father. "Unlike the larger, flashier temples, the Saganites keep to themselves and are generally quiet about their liturgies. Their devotion to the stars necessitates that they honor the darkness of night—something I think you'll agree suits our family business. Our House has patronized them for centuries now, as much as any other temple. And part of the reason for that is that there are things you can learn at Palomar Abbey that you simply can't learn anywhere else."

"So, we *will* be getting more training!" Atopol grinned. Gatina shot him a dirty look.

"Oh, you'll be continuing your training for the House along with your regular temple studies—at which you will be expected to excel. But you will have to do it all in disguise," he reminded them. "The temple is aware of the special relationship that we enjoy with it, and the senior clergy will be aware that some of their students are not what they seem, but you must attend to your aliases religiously—pardon the pun—while you are at the abbey."

After eating the last of the apple tarts, Hance continued to explain to them the details of their new lives, particularly their new aliases. He handed them each a leaf of parchment with the details of their new identities written upon them.

"Cat, you will be called Lord Dain of Newmarket in northern Falas, the middle son of a family of Coastlord merchants who has opted to learn astronomy and has a calling to the stars. You are to be quiet, studious, and constantly reading. Dark hair and a persistent squint," he suggested. That did seem to play into Atopol's natural talents, Gatina had to admit.

"And Kitten, you will now become Maid Avorrita of Dentran, the bucktoothed, befreckled youngest daughter of a minor Coastlord family from southern Falas. Intellectually bright but socially awkward. Kind of dull would be best. And you will be Lord Dain's distant cousin, in case you have to consult with him."

"That sounds . . . completely boring," Gatina groaned as she took the parchment.

"It's supposed to be. The goal is to not attract too much attention. Any attention, if you can help it," their father reminded her.

Gatina and Atopol sat up straighter as Father explained the details to them.

"Now, it is imperative that you remain in your alias at all times unless you are with me or the abbot, who is the only member of the Saganites who will know your true identity. He's my uncle, actually. There will be others who understand that there are clandestine pupils at the abbey, but you are to stick to character constantly and not reveal yourselves. Consider it a test of your abilities. Do you understand?" Hance pointedly looked at both of his children. Gatina restrained herself from asking the many questions she had and simply nodded. "Good. This is an important exercise. I want you to create an alias based on the bit of truths you read on the parchment. But the details of each character will be up to you. You'll have to maintain them, after all.

"Remember, it is easier, as Kiera the Great has suggested, to remain as close to the truth as possible in regard to your alias. In fact, these identities will hopefully be of use to you for years to come. Cat, yours will be a little easier than Kitten's. Newmarket is also a real village, and the noble House you claim to come from is real, if minor, so you will have to study to be prepared to answer any questions about it. And they do have a history of magic, since they are Coastlords. Not a great one, but it has come up in the past." After Atopol nodded his understanding, Hance turned his attention to Gatina.

"In your case, Kitten, the fictitious noble household of Dentran has been cultivated as the source of useful aliases for House Furtius for years. In fact, I have used the House Dentran alias myself, in my youth. There are records of Dentran nobles with magical Talent, even full adepts. All of those are your Furtiusi ancestors in disguise. That will be how we explain it if your *rajira* comes on this summer," he explained.

Gatina smiled for the first time, finally excited by the thought of this trip, she realized. She had desperately wanted her *rajira* to finally emerge, the way her brother's had the last year. Indeed, she was eager for the power to perform magic the way her parents did, and didn't even mind the prospect of study. The things she could do with magic . . .

Her father saw her expression and caught her in a stare. Gatina tried to force a blank expression on her face. "Cat, if you would take over the driving duties, I will assist with Kitten's disguise and give further *specialized* instruction on her mission to your sister."

While Atopol tended to the horses, Hance opened a satchel and removed several jars, setting them on the blanket. Gatina remembered the last time she had seen a satchel and jars of this sort—in Falas before Cousin Huguenin used leeches to dye her hair. Instead of speaking, she watched as he gently lifted a velvet pouch from the bag.

"While wigs and dyes and cosmetics are useful to change your appearance, there are special prosthetics that can be used to distract attention from who you really are. In this case, this is how we will alter the appearance of your teeth," he explained.

He opened the pouch and slid out two parchment-thin metal trays shaped like a crescent. "These are pliable and will be coated in a special mixture of beeswax that I will use to model a set of false teeth that will fit over your front teeth for you to create Avorrita's bucktoothed appearance," her father explained. "It will take a little getting used to, especially speaking and chewing. I don't think this will be as unpleasant as your hair experience, Kitten, but it will require a bit of patience."

Gatina nodded and watched. Her father mixed three heaping spoonsful of a sweet-smelling powder with a beige paste and a warm lump of wax and then smeared the mixture onto one of the metal appliances using a small brush. Once he was satisfied with the mixture's consistency, he nodded.

"This is the part that requires your patience. And a bit of stillness. I will place this over your top teeth. Then we must press it up, as far as we can, to get a good impression. And then we must wait a few long moments for the impression to set. Do you understand?" Gatina nodded, wondering why there was not a spell for this. Hance saw her expression and gave her a sympathetic smile. "Unfortunately, Kitten, there are some circumstances where magic is of little help. This is one of those."

Gatina sighed, then helped her father position the tray in her mouth and around her upper teeth. The sensation of the metal was odd. It didn't hurt, but the tray was cold enough to send a chill down her spine. The taste of the mixture was neither good nor bad. It reminded her of unbaked bread dough. The texture was chalky and waxy at the same time. She nearly gagged as they worked to adjust the tray around her front teeth. The mixture squished out and covered her tongue, causing her to cough.

"I think it would be easier and more comfortable for you if you lay back. We can exert more pressure, which will lead to a better impression" Hance explained.

Gatina did as her father suggested. As it dried, the mixture stuck to her tongue. Hance continued to explain the process while she tried not to cough. "This is the first step in creating Avorrita's false teeth. When this is removed, we will allow it to dry. Then, I will use wax that hardens over time to sculpt the gums and add the false teeth. Sculpture was one of the classes I took when I was a student at Palomar Abbey," he added. "Terribly useful, sculpture is."

After what felt like an eternity, but was only a quarter-hour, Hance gently pried the device from Gatina's teeth and removed it from her mouth with a loud *pop*. There was a chalky residue in her mouth that made her forget all about the delicious tart she'd had—in fact, it seemed to be mocking it.

"You may want to rinse," he suggested, handing her a cup. She did, feeling a sense of relief.

"Once it dries, this will be your mouth appliance," he announced. "And that is where magic can expedite the process. I was able to procure a powder from one of our most-trusted adepts. That is one of the many ways to speed the drying." He held up a small vial and carefully shook a small amount of the fine powder over the impression of her teeth. "While I apply the potion, you can help. Knead this wax so that it becomes pliable." He handed her a small wad of wax wrapped in parchment.

"You took sculpture class?" Gatina asked, finally able to speak. She removed the wax and began to knead it.

"Indeed I did. And it's a good thing. You can do a lot of things with a bit of wax or clay and a knack for sculpture. I can copy keys or create keys. I can fabricate all sorts of things. And I can make false teeth, too," he said. "The impression is dry."

She watched, fascinated, as he worked using what she supposed were artisan tools—thin wire, small brushes, tiny knives, and several long needles of various sizes and widths. When he looked at her, Gatina handed him the now very soft and warm wax. He pushed it into place in the front four upper teeth.

"This is the medium I am using to craft your teeth," he explained. "These wires will help secure the false teeth in place. When I'm done, they should be able to pop in and be held firmly." He bent the wire to create a frame while the wax hardened in the mold. "It will be uncomfortable at first, but you will adjust to the fit and the feeling. You can take it out to sleep, of course."

When the wax had hardened, also sped by the potion, he pried the teeth from the tray. He removed another jar, he explained, to give color to the teeth. The needles were used to add texture. "No teeth are perfectly smooth," he explained. "This helps craft the illusion and it adds depth to the appearance. And this helps create your gumline."

"And you learned this at Palomar?" she asked, intrigued.

"I learned a great many things at the abbey," her father agreed. "My classes in art enriched my experience. The library there is filled with ancient knowledge. The Coastlord Houses have used it as a quiet repository for their archives and secrets, if you know where to look. And there are plenty of masters of all sorts of obscure and useful crafts lurking around the temple. Do not dismiss the possibilities, Gatina. A good thief—and a good mage—always embraces the chance to learn a new skill, a new discipline, or an obscure bit of knowledge that might make the difference someday," he counseled.

Gatina nodded thoughtfully and felt the influence of her father's words. They seemed to dash her reluctance to the disruption in her life and assure her of the value of a Palomar Abbey education. OPPORTUNITY, she suddenly knew, would surround her at the abbey. She just had to recognize it, as her father had done with his art class.

HANCE TOOK ATOPOL'S SEAT ACROSS FROM GATINA IN THE CARRIAGE AFTER he'd helped Atopol hitch the team back up. They continued north. And her father continued his instruction.

"This is a nice change from being up there," he sighed, pointing toward where Atopol sat in the coachman's seat. "I even have a cushion! Less chance that I'll eat bugs, too." Gatina laughed and relaxed, some of her earlier tension forgotten. Her father's easy nature was like magic. "I think you'll enjoy Palomar more than you suspect," he added.

"You really went to school there?" she asked, skeptically, her voice sounding odd with the dental device in place. His enthusiasm for the place was a surprise to her. In her experience, Father wasn't particularly interested in the stars. The darkness, yes, but not the points of light that shone through it at night.

"It's family tradition. Your great-uncle Handrig was my father's youngest brother," Hance explained. "He and I both came to the abbey about the same time, and he remains as one of the holy Starbrothers, as he had no talent for thieving or magic. But he supports the House as much as any. Indeed, he's become the abbot of the place. But we both started out as Nocturns. I loved coming to Palomar for summers when I was a boy," he recalled. "It was a magical place and a magical time before I had *rajira*—or girls—to distract me." Hance sighed fondly at the memory and considered his precocious and currently odd-looking daughter. "You are carrying on a family tradition by coming here, Gat. It's not a punishment. There's no place in the duchies like Palomar. Maybe you'll discover a hidden talent, as I did."

As persuasive as he was, Gatina could not resist one last attempt at dissuasion. "But don't you think I can learn a lot more from you and Mother, Daddy? We learned so much from you on those heists!" Gatina knew using the familiar word *Daddy* instead of the more formal *Father* sometimes worked to her advantage. But, she discovered, not this time.

"It's a greater opportunity, Kitten," Father said calmly and patiently, his eyes shining with a promise of mischief. "We can teach you some of what you need, but there is a place for more-formalized instruction. I promise you: this is not about punishment. You and your brother are being sent to a safe place where you can be instructed in more than what your former tutors or your mother and I can teach you, especially now with the Rebel Counts positioning themselves to take power in Alshar," he said. "It's just not safe for you in Falas or even Cysgodol Hall now. You and Atopol would have visited either way, eventually. It's tradition," he emphasized. "And it's not all bad. You'll have new friends—or Maid Avorrita will. You'll learn some interesting things, and not all about the stars. We'll be working on some specialized techniques—swordplay, lock-picking, stealth, all sorts of things."

"You mean you'll be there too?" she asked, surprised.

"Only in the background," he answered. "And only upon occasion. I will be portraying an honest servant . . . and pursuing my own investigations and missions," he added, cryptically. "I will be known as Dareth, an ignorant, illiterate manservant of Newmarket hired to the abbey for the summer. That should be enough cover to disguise my efforts. And that way, I can keep an eye on you both without arousing any suspicion. There is much happening in Alshar now that the Duke has been killed. Ejecta is actually ideally positioned for my purposes. Being close enough to Falas to hear news yet far away enough to avoid suspicion is of benefit to the conspiracy, right now. Your mother is away at the coast on her own tasks. But at least for the summer, I'll be around, though you must never become familiar with me in public," he advised her.

"So, what is *my* mission?" she asked, curiously. "Besides studying stars and staying in my alias?"

"You should learn the history of the abbey and why Maid Avorrita of Dentran is attending to her education there, of course," Hance said. "As you are aware, children of noble and merchant classes are often sent to temple schools for both their basic education and the possibility that they will take holy orders. If they have *rajira*, they can even get some elementary, Censorate-approved training there without inviting suspicion. Some of the Talented actually do take holy orders and become monks or nuns for the temple. That, of course, is not the goal for you. But education is the goal for dull little Maid Avorrita of House Dentran. As for more rigorous duties, I will let you know if you are required to do anything beyond that, at the proper time."

"So, how did our House form this . . . alliance with the Saganites?" she asked, after thinking about the matter for a moment. "It seems an odd pairing."

"But useful," her father insisted. "House Furtius's connection with the Saganites and Palomar Abbey dates back hundreds of years. Your great-uncle Handrig will doubtlessly go into greater detail about it at the proper time, if he sees value to it.

"But consider this. One reason the partnership has been so gratifying is very simple: it has allowed our family to evade the Censors by being right under their noses, should they visit the abbey. We hide in plain sight, just as you and Atopol will be doing. You do not need to attract attention. You need to become the entirely unremarkable Avorrita. Keep your lips sealed and your eyes open. Since the Duke's death, I expect there will be plenty of gossip amongst the petty nobility for you to hear. Listen to all of it, carefully, so that we can identify which families are in favor of Count Vichetral and which are still loyal to the Ducal House . . . and might be open to assisting our efforts."

Gatina nodded resolutely in agreement, drawing a smile from her father.

"It really won't be that bad," he assured her. "The temple is situated in the village of Ejecta, which is a quaint and sleepy little hamlet. You may even be able to spend some free time there." As they rode on, he explained the abbey's hierarchy. "There are three levels of priests and priestesses among the Saganites, each with distinct liturgical duties and distinguished by their clothing: Nightbrothers, Duskbrothers, and Nocturns. Of course, Nightsisters and Dusksisters for the women. You are to be trained as a Nocturn."

He went on for two more hours about the history of Palomar Abbey and the village of Ejecta as well as important details about the Saganite Order. He also reminded her that the Censorate had been harassing Coastlord families for centuries, and that the abbey offered some protection from that.

By the time Hance had replaced Atopol in the coachman's seat, her head was spinning with those details. And by the time they arrived at Ejecta, in the early evening, she was starting to get tired.

But she perked up when they arrived at the ecclesiastic estate. It was sheltered from prying eyes by a dense and lush forest of pine, oak, and cherry trees, as well as a tall hedge of cedar and hemlock. Rhododendron trees encircled the estate's main house of the complex, she saw as they rode past the stately old manor. *Abbey*, she corrected herself. The great temple was a reminder of that and could be seen in the distance, looming on the edge of the cliff on a great rocky outcropping, framed between two small waterfalls. It was quite lovely, she decided.

Gatina realized that she needed to stop thinking of Palomar as an estate; it was an abbey, and it would be her home for the foreseeable future. Despite her misgivings and her skepticism about the reasons for that, Gatina—*No, no, no, Maid Avorrita of Dentran,* she corrected herself—would do her best to learn to be a Saganite Nocturn . . . at least well enough to fake it. There was a certain challenge in that, she conceded to herself. And she knew she would do her duty.

CHAPTER TWO

A NEW ALIAS

<hr>

The success of our House depends upon the establishment of convincing disguises. Cultivating an alias is essential to moving through society without being noted or noticed. Often it requires the suppression of our natural impulses and reactions, which requires adept control of our emotions. Only actors and poets approach the level of mastery a Furtiusi requires when it comes to adopting a second identity.

*— from **The Shield of Darkness**,*
written by Kiera the Great

THE YARD IN FRONT OF THE TEMPLE'S GRAND HALL WAS FILLED WITH ARRIVing carriages and wains from all over Alshar as students arrived. Gatina felt a tide of excitement rising within her as she watched one carriage after another pull up and haphazardly begin unloading baggage and children in the temple yard. Gray-clad Dusksisters with wads of parchment in hand tried their best to keep order, Gatina saw through the carriage window, but there was a lot of quiet confusion and restrained chaos in the effort. She was intrigued by all the children, who appeared to greet the occasion with a mixture of excitement and dread.

Footmen and coachmen argued with the temple servants on just where and when the baggage should be delivered, while harried-looking nuns and monks tried to keep track of the growing number of confused-looking students that were congregating around the yard.

Their own carriage lurched to a halt as her father asked for direction, his voice and accent humble and of lowly station to suit his appearance. Gatina did not hear the response of the monk who spoke with him, but after a few moments, the coach lurched forward again. It took a few moments for it to find an acceptable place to finally halt.

Gatina began to rise and open the carriage door, eager to plunge into her new alias. Atopol's hand stopped her.

"You are in disguise, Kitten," he reminded her in a quiet voice, "and we are in the abbey's carriage. You must allow Father to play his part in this ruse. He is a manservant. We are nobility. He will open the door when the time is proper."

She nodded, disappointed. To occupy her mind, Gatina drew back the curtain farther, curious to see all she could from the carriage. The first thing her eyes found was a glorious garden alive with pink and red flowers arranged along a low stone fence. But what was inside that fence drew her attention immediately away from the flowers. She spied an impressive vegetable garden that could easily have fed the Nits in Falas for an entire year. Row after row of climbing beans, tomatoes ready to burst on their vines, cucumbers, onions, garlic shoots, squashes, and other green, red, and orange vegetables she had never seen before filled the lush-looking garden.

A familiar flutter—a mixture of adrenaline from the excitement and the curiosity of the unknown—welled up inside her as she felt the carriage shift when Father jumped from the coachman's seat and began unloading their luggage.

"You remember your new name?" her brother prompted her. Gatina made a face. Of course she did. They had been practicing their aliases for hours now. Every time her tongue wandered over the new teeth in her head, she was reminded that she was no longer Gatina anna Furtius, Kitten of Night.

"Maid Avorrita, the dull daughter of House Dentran," she answered, affecting the accent of the rural nobility. "When shall we be able to depart, Cousin? I have to pee," she added.

"So do I," Atopol—no, Lord Dain of Newmarket, she reminded herself—admitted. It really was not difficult to make the switch, as Atopol looked nothing like himself now. Gone were the distinctive white hair and lopsided grin, to be replaced by dark hair and an overly serious expression more suited to his alias. He had changed into a dark green velvet doublet and black hose, replacing the gray-and-black outfit he had started the journey with. His violet eyes, like hers, were now a bland shade of hazel, the effect achieved with a simple spell her father had cast on them both. The spell would have to be renewed every few days, else it would fade, she knew, and until she achieved her *rajira* and learned it, she would have to rely on her father's magic to maintain it.

She, too, had transformed herself before they'd arrived. Her plum-colored traveling gown was a bit more formally cut than the one she'd set out with, and the freckles she'd painstakingly painted on her face around her nose were also subject to a spell that would keep them from rubbing off lightly. Her own white hair was now covered by a mousey brown wig and utterly plain under her wimple. She was dreading dying it later, but Father was insistent.

Most annoying, however, were the artificial teeth that fitted over her natural incisors. She traced her tongue over them, still trying to become accustomed to the feel. They bulged out and made her appear buck-toothed. While it took a lot of getting used to, it also provided a constant reminder that she was no longer Gatina of House Furtius, Kitten of Night, but plain old Maid Avorrita of no place special.

They waited patiently until Father—no, Dareth—finished unloading the luggage then jostled open the carriage door with some attempt at ceremony.

Gatina was standing before Lord Dain could say anything. She daintily paused at the door before taking her father's hand, and she stepped out onto the ladder, her magically colored hazel eyes drinking in everything.

The neatly tended village of Ejecta was laid out in front of her, with well-built stately temple halls dominating the main avenue and smaller cottages spread out behind. There were short walls separating the yards from the street and many more decorations than she was used to in the plain old farm villages back home. The folk of Ejecta were clearly proud of their association with the abbey; many of the signs and decorations had a motif of moons and stars.

But her eyes were drawn to the great tower on the cliffs overhead and the pretty double waterfall she had longed to see ever since she had heard her father speak of it. It seemed to mimic the great twin falls of Falas Town in miniature, she decided, though both sets tumbled down the same great escarpment. The waterfalls fell from the heights high up on the cliff from either side of the abbey's tall, magnificently domed temple, which she saw dominated the view from the village. Everywhere you went in Ejecta, she realized, that tower loomed above like the stars themselves. In the heat of the day, she imagined how delicious that cold water would taste, especially after being in the carriage for so long.

As Dareth the manservant offered her his hand, she accepted it to help her down. It was entirely unnecessary, of course—there were only two steps she could have leaped down—but she was a noblewoman, and ladies accepted such assistance as a matter of course whether it was needed or not, just as Mother had lectured her to do.

The three of them stood there, looking around, until a gray-clad nun not too much older than Gatina came over to them, a sheaf of parchment in hand. Gatina waited while Dareth announced both of their names to the nun, who found them on the rolls she had been provided. When they were properly checked in, she directed them to where the abbot was standing and overseeing the chaos—although to Gatina's eye he mostly ignored it.

"Abbot Handrig, I present Lord Dain of Newmarket and Maid Avorrita of Dentran," Dareth announced loudly in his loutish voice. "They are to be admitted to the temple for instruction and service!"

The monk did not look considerably older than her father, but he was balding, Gatina saw. Her father must have made some special sign to him, because the man's bored expression changed. There was a hint of recognition in his eyes, she could see.

"Ah, yes! I've been awaiting the arrival of our special new students," he said, suddenly staring at them both with interest. "A billion blessings upon you both. It is always a treat for the youths of your *House* to take lessons at Palomar," he assured them. He paused and checked a scroll he had tucked under his arm. "Lord Dain, you have been assigned to Adastra Hall. That's the large one over there," he said, pointing to a stately building of brick. "Maid Avorrita, you shall be in the Hall of Moons with the noblewomen. You will find it across the road," he indicated, "the one with the red brick and the hedges. Pray report to your halls before the evening bell. There will be a ceremony this evening. Your luggage will be brought to your quarters. And do not be late," he warned. "We prize punctuality at Palomar. The stars wait for no man," he quoted.

"That's our great-uncle?" Atopol asked in a low voice, after they had left the monk's presence and headed back to the coach. "He doesn't look like you at all!"

"He's a fine fellow, really," their father agreed, also speaking quietly. "But he takes his duties seriously. If you have need of something and I am not available, you can bring it to his attention. Handrig will help. But do not do so lightly—he will protect the House, but he has duties to the temple to consider." Hance ushered the children toward the village shops, glancing around at the crowded courtyard.

"It will take them some time to get all of this chaos straightened out. Remember, I have business to attend to first, after I return the team and carriage to the stable," he said, quietly. "The two of you have a few moments to explore and stretch your legs. Take a moment to look through the shops, if you'd like. And you will find a noble's privy over there," he added, nodding to a small building near the street where there was a short cue forming.

He slipped them each a silver coin, then turned and headed back toward the carriage. Gatina kept her eyes on her father until he disappeared. She knew he could use his *rajira* to vanish, but in this case, there was no magic involved. A carriage's arrival had kicked up a cloud of dust. By the time the dust settled, her father was gone.

In the line for the privy, she began to follow Atopol's example and shifted into her alias as best she could. She was third behind two other girls. She noticed, unsurprised, that the boys' line moved faster. Instead of finding that aggravating, she allowed herself to listen to the older girls talking in front of her.

From their demeanor, they were quietly gossiping. Her instinct was proven right as soon as they began to speak, quietly, about the threats in Falas. Their accents and mannerisms were decidedly Coastlord. That meant, she knew, they may be of Talented lineage.

"What will that mean for us?" the girl closest to her said, barely above a whisper. "My father is worried sick about the situation in Falas. He's concerned that Palomar is too close to the capital. He considered sending me elsewhere, but Mother convinced him the abbey would be safest. He was one of the Duke's men," she explained in a hushed whisper.

The other girl turned slightly to answer, allowing Gatina a moment's glance at her face—well, half of it. Her raven hair peeked from her wimple before it tumbled out and covered her green eyes. "My family was loyal, too. My father hates Vichetral and all Rhemesmen. It means we must be careful in all we do and say," she advised sagely before it was her turn at the privy.

AFTER ATTENDING TO THEIR ABLUTIONS, GATINA AND ATOPOL practiced their disguises as they slowly walked to the village proper. Their exploration of Ejecta's high street did not take long, for there was little enough to see. Most of the shops were involved in trades specific to the temple—parchment merchants, ink makers, a glassblower, a tailor who specialized in ecclesiastic clothes. There were two different booksellers, however, and the two of them enjoyed prowling through the shelves of the tiny shops. One was fundamentally oriented toward religious materials, but the other had a surprisingly wide range of topics. There was also a confectioner's shop, which surprised Gatina and delighted her brother.

Atopol busied himself looking through the store's selection of sweets both mundane and exotic, which included breads, hard candies, honeyed fruits, sugar cubes, and a variety of cakes. Her brother had always had a sweet tooth. She had no need nor desire for sweets, preferring fresh apples to much of anything else, unless that anything was one of Drella's baked pies. And it would be Darkness only knew how long until she had another of those, she thought.

Gatina instead watched the traffic on the street, including the number of students, servants, and footmen who were in Ejecta for the start of classes. She wondered how deserted the streets would be in a few days' time, after the visiting families left. Or what the village was like on Market Day. She hoped it was busy. She missed the bustle of Falas. And the bartering on the streets with the vendors.

Seeing all of the strangers in this strange place elicited a pang of homesickness, which surprised her. This place was tiny, compared to the grand capital of Falas. It wasn't much larger than the villages near Cysgodol Hall with which she was familiar. But somehow Ejecta made her feel oddly out of place in a way no other place had. Gatina recognized that feeling, wondering which of her cards might connect to that. After a moment, she decided on DISCRETION because she was a stranger in a strange village with a new alias. She had to protect both her identity and her House. And, she knew, those secrets must be kept under lock and key.

Vexed by her new assignment, though less frustrated than she had been earlier, Gatina resigned herself to shopping. And eavesdropping. She could not help it, and she did not see it as rude as much as an important part of her training—or, at least, that was what she told herself.

A pair of noble matrons who had indulgently led their younger children to the sweets shop before they returned to their estates were loudly whispering about the news from Falas. It was news that Gatina already knew, of course, thanks to House Furtius's growing network of spies, but it had only reached Ejecta that morning. Gatina found it fascinating to overhear how Count Vichetral's sudden usurpation of the duchy's government was being seen by the folk of Alshar.

"That Count from Rhemes is in charge now, since the poor Duke died in battle away north," one of the noblewomen confided to the other. "There's a bad bit of business going on in Falas. He's executed some ministers—and clergy!" she added, scandalized. "Can you imagine? My sister sent me a letter about it. Soldiers in the streets, riots, arrests, fighting . . . she says Vichetral is hunting down anyone who was in the good graces of the poor Duke and Duchess now, may Trygg's grace bless their souls."

Her friend nodded, clearly disapproving of the development. "It's shameful. The man is insidious. He's brought half his army to the capital to keep order, he says. It's said that he's even got the bloody Censors interrogating everyone," the second woman said, her hushed voice tinged with anger. "They can use their magic to tell if someone is lying," she informed her friend, authoritatively. "My cousin married a resident adept; she knows," she said, with confidence.

"Even nonmagical folk?" her friend asked, in disbelief. Two more noblewomen, apparently acquaintances of the first two, joined the gossip.

"*Every*one," she emphasized. "It's part of the new order, apparently." She looked around the room, likely, Gatina reasoned, to see if anyone of importance was within earshot. Only Atopol and herself were within earshot. Two young people—mere children—would not register as a threat to this woman, Gatina figured. She tried her best to look bored and uninteresting.

"And it's not just Falas," she continued, insistently, clearly enjoying being the source of the news. "He's sending his men all up and down the Mandros River, to every large estate and small town, to find out any who might betray him and his cronies. He wants to be the Duke in all but name, and he's sparing no coin to rule us. You know how vicious those Rhemes folk are. I've heard the Censors were even to come *here*."

The woman's companion gasped, hand to her chest in dramatic fashion. "Ejecta? Why would they come *here*? There's nothing to see here except the stars," she said, shocked.

"My sister says all abbeys and temples are to be . . . *inspected*," she pronounced, distastefully. "Supposedly, they're looking for agents of Castal, but I suspect they're just trying to clobber any opposition after the clergy of Falas objected."

"Rebellions often start in temples," one of the other women related.

"Vichetral is the rebel!" the other new woman snarled. "Not honest folk who supported Duke Lenguin! He's just using this as an opportunity to seize power he should never have gotten. My husband says he's always coveted the coronet. Blaming Castal for this mess is just convenient for him. But now he's in Falas, and it will take Duin the Destroyer to pry him out, he says!"

Gatina shifted her focus to this new, younger woman who spoke so passionately about the political strife. She apparently understood what was happening and how real the threat at hand was, Gatina realized. She took a moment to memorize her face, her accent, and her appearance. It was good practice, she knew. And, whether the woman was Talented or not, Gatina knew an ally when she heard one.

"Careful of what you say!" the first woman hissed in a low voice. "It may not be prudent to . . . get political," she said with a swallow. "He had more than a score of ministers and clergy executed like common thieves in front of the palace. If he has spies about . . ." she said, trailing off and looking around worriedly at the other passersby on the high street.

"In a sweets shop?" snorted one of the others, skeptically.

As interesting as the conversation was, Gatina turned away when her brother tugged on her elbow. She knew her information was both more accurate and more recent than theirs, and she wanted to shop for art supplies so she could properly work on her cards. She knew all about the executions, too. She'd been in Falas at the time. Count Vichetral had demonstrated he would endure no objection to his seizure of power and the palace itself. His viciousness was one of the reasons that the conspiracy had been formed against him.

Atopol held the door for his sister as they left the shop, his mouth full of cake.

"What did you buy?" Gatina asked, nodding toward his purchase, which was tucked gingerly under his arm. He smiled.

"Enough candy to get me through the month," he confided, proudly. "Apparently, they only let us out of the temple grounds infrequently, and candy is at a premium in the dormitories. It will help me study," he insisted.

"As if you need anything to help you study," she snorted. Atopol was always a good student under his tutors. He rarely had to be told anything more than once. "But I suppose it will help you seem more bookish.

'Affecting a distinctive habit provides the opportunity for misdirection in the formation of an alias,'" she said, quoting a passage from Kiera's *Shield of Darkness*, the family's fundamental history. "I suppose I should cultivate some 'distinctive habits' for Avorrita. Something other than candy," she said, wrinkling her nose at the thought. "Anything but needlework," she added, nodding across the street at a tiny shop with a large wooden needle on its sign. "Needlework is entirely boring, and it seems to be the favorite topic of conversation among girls."

Her brother laughed at her expressive rejection of the art. "It always does. You just lack the patience. Find something you can do that won't bore you, then."

"Perhaps painting," she decided, as they came to a stationer's shop— one of three little spots on the street where ink, parchment, brushes, quills, and other tools of the clergy could be purchased. "Wait here; I'll only be a moment."

Gatina took slightly longer than a moment, but she was quick. Soon she had her own parcel filled with tiny bottles of ink, quill pens, and some charcoal pencils. She was pleased by the purchase, and it gave her some idea of just who her new alias was to be. Someone who was preoccupied with art and not a thief in training who was acting as a spy for a grand conspiracy.

That thought reminded her of what she heard, and she realized she should relay it to her brother as they made their way back to the temple yard.

"I . . . I overheard some gossip in the sweets shop," she informed him quietly. "The usual outrage over the palace. People are not happy about that. But they also mentioned the Censors. Vichetral is allied with them, apparently. They're using them to determine who is loyal to the new order and who is not. And they may come here," she added, with special intensity.

"Here? To Palomar?" Atopol said in surprise. "Why would they do that?"

"To intimidate the clergy, most likely," Gatina guessed. "And the Coastlord nobility." Gatina suppressed a shudder.

The Coastlords were descended from the nobility of the old Magocracy, when powerful magi from Merwyn, in the east, had conquered the Sea Lords and settled the Coastlands of Alshar. While only a small percentage of their descendants possessed *rajira*—the Talent and ability to practice magic—the subsequent Narasi Conquest of Alshar had brought the Royal Censorate of Magic to the duchy to quell the rebellious Coastlords who bristled at the rule of the barbarians. They had brutalized the Coastlords for decades before settling into a largely regulatory role, ensuring that the magi were heavily restricted in the magic that they could use and paid a price in social and legal affairs for it.

It was all very complicated, Gatina knew, but the sight of the black-and-white checkered cloaks the Censors wore as a symbol of their order still sent a shiver down the spine of any family with a history of *rajira*. The thought deeply troubled her.

"Maybe sending us to Palomar Abbey wasn't the best idea," she offered.

They walked back to the abbey grounds in silence, making their way toward the stable, where they expected their father to be lurking.

"So, do you think you have your alias memorized?" Atopol asked, as they neared the temple yard. "Remember, you must remain hidden in plain sight. Use your training. And remember that you are not you; right now, you are a Nocturn named . . ."

"Yes, yes, I know," Gatina said, as she realized she was still thinking like a professional thief in training and not a dull noble girl. She closed her eyes, took a deep breath, and subtly shifted the way she moved and composed her facial expressions. When Gatina opened her eyes, she had become Avorrita. "I am Maid Avorrita of Dentran," she said, her voice low and soft. "I am just newly arrived here in Ejecta with my cousin Dain, whom I've barely met before, to begin my studies at Palomar Abbey and possibly find a husband." She then poked Attie in the arm and said, in her normal voice, "I'm not an oaf, dear brother. Cousin," she corrected self-consciously.

Atopol sighed. "No, but like a kitten, you are easily distracted and often take on more than you can handle in your enthusiasm. Don't worry; I'm still trying to master this Dain of Newmarket fellow in my head. He's smart," he reflected, "but a bit shallow, I think. He listens more than he speaks and he's uncomfortable being the center of attention."

"Avorrita is always daydreaming," Gatina nodded. "Slow-witted and dull but friendly. More concerned about how things affect her than the greater story around her. And a bit shallow, as well—likely a family trait," she teased.

"We should fit right in with these fellows, then," Atopol chuckled as they passed a boisterous group of young students headed into the village.

None of them looked particularly bright or aware. "Remember, you barely know me and don't entirely understand just how we are related."

"Agreed," she nodded. Gatina stopped and turned to face her brother. "There will doubtlessly be some questions about that. A good opportunity to display my dullness."

"I think those will abound," Atopol chuckled. "Oh! That's the bell for the evening services, I think," he said as a great brass bell clanged from the top of one of the halls. "That's the signal we should return to the yard and find our rooming assignments. I suppose we'll have to explore the rest of the village later."

"It won't take too long," Gatina agreed, looking back over her shoulder at the small high street. "This place is smaller than most neighborhoods in Falas Town."

From the shops to the village's Market Square, which she imagined would be packed on Market Day, there wasn't much to see in Ejecta, she realized. Apart from the few specialized shops and the abbey, it was just like any other village. Quiet. Tranquil. Insular. Filled with people concerned with their daily lives, not the politics and problems of the greater world. That was the kind of person Avorrita was, she realized. Self-absorbed and self-centered. That should be an easy-enough role to play.

FROM THE MOMENT GATINA AND THE OTHER CHILDREN WERE USHERED INTO the Nocturn Hall of the temple for initiation, she knew she had arrived at a place steeped in mystery and lore. Every icon and decoration said as much.

There was a gorgeously painted fresco on the high-domed ceiling depicting the night sky, a field of glittering stars on a field of jet, supported by a range of fanciful-looking beings around the edges. The triangle-shaped cloud she knew was the Void was portrayed in a magnificent purple on the southern side of the dome. A complicated-looking . . . sculpture, she decided, featuring a number of gilded spheres of various hues was hung from the ceiling by wires. The altar on the northern side of the chamber was an extravagant wooden affair stained black with gilded accents depicting stars and little circles, ovals, and fanciful bursts, and was installed on a raised dais that allowed the clergy to be seen from anywhere in the room. There was no idol or depiction of Sagan, the minor god responsible for the celestial world. That was interesting to note.

This was unlike the abbey where Sister Karia and her friend Marga had lived in Falas; that was a Tryggite-run order, whose holy nuns were devoted to the Mother Goddess. That was an orphanage and filled with the laughter, singing, and squeals of children and ornamented with mosaics depicting the various stages of feminine life. Palomar Abbey, under the Saganite Order, was different in far more than decoration, she realized. There was no noise. Everyone spoke in whispered tones and maintained silence in the presence of the sanctuary. It was serene. It was peaceful. It was . . . boring.

To occupy her mind while waiting for someone to take charge, Gatina observed her surroundings with a professional eye. The Great Hall, she noticed, was intimidating and not a place she could imagine engaging in frivolous behavior or fits of laughter. The smooth marble floor was as black as a starless night, the walls were dark-paneled wood, and the drapes were a heavy black velvet, thick enough to block even the brightest light from outside casting judgment on the Saganite Order's obscure doings, nor the slightest whisper of their liturgy from being overheard.

The Great Hall's main double doors were massive, large enough for the grandest carriage to pass through, made of wood but also framed on the inside with brass and quilted with black velvet, Gatina saw, that was thick enough to dampen any noise from the vestibule outside. She suspected that the metal had been enchanted to keep out unwanted or unnecessary distraction more than a defense against raiders. The floors were well-polished enough to show a reflection of the multitude of candle sconces. The black-robed Nightbrother who served as door warden motioned them inside to the celestial sanctuary.

"The others are in here," he told them, smiling serenely through his beard. "The Nocturn Initiation will begin shortly. Pray be silent until you are bidden to answer," he said by rote.

The priest led the children to the Great Hall, where they had been divided into groups by gender at a long banquet-style table—girls on one side, boys on the other—and then sorted by the Saganite Order's classification. Gatina quietly shuffled into the herd of whispering children. There were other monks—Duskbrothers, she recalled—clad in long gray robes. Gatina guessed they were the older students, already entered into the lay order, who were congregating behind them.

A dour-looking nun in a gray habit waited until she received a signal from the rear of the temple before she addressed them all in a loud, practiced voice.

"A billion blessings upon you, and welcome to Palomar Abbey," she began, her voice loud and clear in the quiet sanctuary. "I am Duskmother Luya, and I am in charge of the summer's term and will be guiding and ordering you through the mysteries of the celestial spheres," she said, her tone high and reverent as she gestured toward the ceiling. "This is known as an orrery," she said, gesturing upward to the spheres. "It matches the much larger one in the temple above. It represents the exact position of the planets around our sun at this very moment. Under the night's sky, the entire Cosmos may be glimpsed, and if one understands the mysteries of the heavens, that Cosmos can be understood in part.

"Our goal as Saganites is to arm you with the education to achieve that understanding," she declared. "Some of you will end your affiliation with the Nocturns after your final initiation; some will stay all year. Some will continue to study and take holy orders with the Nightbrothers or the Duskbrothers. The Cosmos alone knows what lies in your futures, but by completing the mysteries—and the education implicit with that—you will be entered into the company of sages and scholars who have fathomed the deepest questions on the universe. The greatest minds of ages past were once simple Nocturns when they began. Noble or clergy, there is *no* greater glory than that!" she promised, with absolute conviction.

Gatina had her doubts about that. She could think of several things more glorious than staring blankly at the stars.

"I envy you the adventure that awaits you," Duskmother Luya continued. "You shall learn the stars and constellations by their proper names, the habits of the planets and the moons as if you were neighbors. You will come to understand the elegant mathematics that keeps the stars in their courses. You will discover the great powers of the Sacred Cosmos and how they act on us, each in their way. You shall learn the mysteries of light and darkness, of gravity and space, the intricate dance of formula and form that comprise . . . *everything!*" she finished in a dramatic—and, to Gatina's ear, oft-practiced—whisper.

But then her demeanor changed. Gone was the dramatic and mysterious tone. It shifted as she turned to matters *far* more serious—the rules.

"During your tenure here at Palomar, there are many expectations you shall fulfill. Particularly expectations of propriety and behavior befitting your station. You will have rules you must adhere to that your group brothers and sisters will explain to you . . . and let me assure you, the abbot will brook *no* foolishness," she warned. "Believe me, he has *billions* of ways to make you reflect on your misbehavior. Pray to the stars you avoid them.

"Now," she said, her expression relaxing, "when you hear your name called, please gather with the Nightsister or Duskbrother to whom you have been assigned and don your new habit. This garment signifies you as a Nocturn. You shall wear it at all times while you are in Palomar, and also if you are sent to study outside of the abbey. Your normal clothes shall be put away for the duration of the term and shall not be worn even when you are between duties. You may wear them again after the Midsummer initiation and not before. Then you will be taken to your assigned halls, where you will begin initial instruction and learn the scope of your duties and studies. Sister Anka? Will you begin?" she asked one of her fellow gray-clad nuns, who had a thick sheaf of parchment.

One by one, the nun called out the name of an attendant and four or five names, alternating between boys and girls. Gatina heard Dain of Newmarket called in the third group of boys. Gatina almost missed hearing her own name—her new name, her alias—and guiltily went forward to collect her bundle from Nightsister Nimandi along with four other maidens.

The tall, thin nun seemed cheerful enough despite her somber black habit as she led the girls back into the recesses of the hall into a private chamber, where they were bidden to strip off their traveling clothes and pull on the short, heavy gray woolen habits over their heads. Each was equipped with a cowl and a linen underdress. While they dressed, the priestess looked on and lectured them.

"I am Nightsister Nimandi, and you have been assigned to the Hall of Moons, or simply Moon Hall, second floor, second chamber. I shall be the one who will guide you and instruct you for the next few days as the Initiation continues. I shall teach you the ways of our abbey, our customs and liturgy, and prepare you for classes with the esteemed faculty of Palomar. If you have questions or problems, please come to me—quietly!—and I will tend to them."

She continued to instruct the girls about the various halls, laboratories, and workshops around Ejecta, general rules for their behavior as Nocturns, as well as how the girls would eat, sleep, and tend to their daily needs. The young nun had evidently given this lecture many times.

Once in her group, Gatina stood with the others, listening and observing the girls' mannerisms as they changed their clothes and prepared to go to the Moon Hall. Unsurprisingly, Gatina found that the girls were stand-offish and awkward in this novel situation. There were some nervous giggles, whispers, and the occasional groan as they pulled on their new clothes and tried to adjust to the unfamiliar clerical habits. They weren't particularly uncomfortable, Gatina noted, but they were not as fine or smooth as the usual gowns to which the noble maidens were accustomed. The habit was, she knew, much nicer than what she wore in her alias as an orphan.

"Girls," Nightsister Nimandi continued, when they were finally dressed, "Nocturns, before I lead you to your dormitory in a few moments, I would like you to introduce yourselves and determine a schedule for tonight and tomorrow's chores."

"Chores?" one of the girls asked, as if she had never heard the word before. "Isn't that for the servants?" There was a horrified expression on her face under the gray hood of the habit.

"While the abbey does employ a variety of servants," sighed the nun, "their duties are more . . . institutional in nature. As a means of instilling a good work ethic and a sense of dedication to your studies and devotions, the Nocturns are required to do some service, upkeep, and maintenance duties every day," she informed them.

Gatina saw a few shocked expressions within her group. She noted them with interest.

"This is not the Temple of Ishi in Inmar, girls," Sister Nimandi continued. "The cook at the Hall of the Moons is very good, and she will prepare your meals. But you will assist in that process. You must serve dinner tonight and do the washing-up of your dishes. Tomorrow morning, at daybreak, you will gather eggs, milk the cows, tend the gardens, and prepare the dining chamber before the morning meal. And there will be both daily and weekly chores to follow: laundry, sweeping, that sort of thing. Do not worry—all chores are divided equally among the classes. Whatever our rank outside the abbey, whether we are Coastlords, Sea Lords or Vale Lords, Imperial or Narasi, we all wear the same habit," she said, fingering the hem of her own.

"Now let us hear your names and lineages and get that out of the way," she continued in a businesslike manner. "Let's start with you," she said, pointing toward an Imperial-looking girl—the one who had been shocked at the idea of chores. The girl nodded, cleared her throat, and looked around at the others.

"I am Maid Leonna, of House Baskley," she said, proudly, as if everyone should know that House. "I am from Baskley Manor in the south of County Falas, of course." There was an undeniable air of superiority that Leonna bore, as if she were addressing servants, not fellow Nocturns. It immediately put the group on edge, Gatina noted.

"I'm Maid Dina of Vorone," the next girl said, her speech somewhat accented with a Sea Lord lilt that belied her Wilderlands origin. A dark blond lock of hair had escaped from her hood. She was tall and carried herself confidently, as if she were used to such awkward situations. She seemed a little older than anyone else in the group. "But my mother's folk hail from Ganivet."

"Isn't that a Sea Lord holding?" Leonna asked, a dark eyebrow rising skeptically. The Coastlord girl was clearly bothered by Maid Dina. That was interesting, Gatina thought.

"An old and distinguished one," agreed Dina evenly as her eyes narrowed.

That brought a grunt of disapproval from Sister Nimandi, who flicked her eyes to the next girl. "Wine merchants . . . since before the Magocracy. Who is next?"

"Maid Arryn of . . . of Raida," the next girl said, hesitantly. Though Raida was also near the coast, she had the complexion and features of a Vale Lord, complete with the blue-green eyes. Her hair was far blonder than Dina's, Gatina could see, far lighter and curlier than the Imperial girl's.

"And now a *Narasi?*" sneered Leonna in mock surprise as she rolled her eyes. "Do we invite horses to chapel next?"

"*Nocturn!*" Sister Nimandi objected sharply. "Palomar Abbey welcomes all to our Mysteries, regardless of House or station or ancestry. A curious mind and a sharp intellect are all that is required." She flicked her eyes toward Gatina.

"I'm, uh, Maid Avorrita of House Dentran," Gatina said, trying to sound both proud and anxious. She didn't add anything else. She found Avorrita did not want to say more than was necessary.

"And I am Maid Mathilde of Bothaire," the last girl said. She was only slightly taller than Gatina but had a quietly commanding presence. Her dark eyes and hair told her out as of Imperial stock, pure Coastlord if she had to guess, and her nose was as straight as an arrow. She looked like the pictures in the old books about the Imperial Magocracy. Indeed, the girl's glance at Avorrita for support confirmed that to her mind.

"Very well, girls," Sister Nimandi said, when the introductions were concluded. "Henceforth, for the remainder of your stay at the abbey, as you are novitiates you shall not be known as maidens, but as Nocturn Initiates or just Nocturns. No patronymics, no listing of Houses, no distinctions due to ancestry or birth. It is against the rules of the abbey. Understood? Excellent. Now follow me—*quietly!*"

Sister Nimandi did not wait for a response. She turned and marched away while the girls newly under her charge looked at each other with concern, confusion, and dismay. A brisk snap of the nun's fingers and a stern expression quickly got them in line behind her. Sister Nimandi paused near a group of older girls, senior Nocturns, who were snickering uncontrollably over the dismay and awkward bearing of the newcomers.

"Girls!" she chided harshly, "I expect you recall your own initiations last year. And I expect you to provide an example of proper decorum in our Great Hall!" Her voice echoed in the room, which had a high, vaulted ceiling that seemed to drink in the noise. "Nocturn Illana, you shrieked aloud when you found out you were to be sent to the milking sheds for the first time, if I remember correctly. I expect better of you now. You are *far* too old to act like novices," she scolded as the senior Nocturns struggled to control themselves. Sister Nimandi breezed by them, giving another snap to summon the Initiates.

The girls dutifully followed, five sets of eyes boring into the back of the nun's head as she walked brusquely back through the sanctuary and into the Great Hall, leaving her new charges to follow, dumbfounded but obedient.

Gatina, who ordinarily might speak her mind in such a situation, had decided that Maid Avorrita of Dentran—no, Nocturn Avorrita, she reminded herself—was shy until she became friends with people. She let her tongue feel along the bumpy edge of the false teeth she wore to appear bucktoothed. That and the magical freckles and her now-unremarkable eyes and hair, both shades of brown, kept her appearance from being distinctive. Betraying that by drawing attention to herself too early would not be in character. Instead, the disguise worked to hide in plain sight, much as her alias as Lissa the Mouse had.

Nocturn Avorrita, she practiced in her mind, over and over again, as she dutifully followed the nun with the others out the Great Hall and into the yard.

It was twilight now, and from within a nearby chapel, the sound of the Saganite Vespers being sung filled the early summer air. She inhaled deeply, appreciating the new smells that lingered there. She tried to leave Gatina behind in the Great Hall and invest herself fully in the alias of Nocturn Avorrita. She had to discover who this new girl in her mind was, what she liked, and what she hated; what she feared and what she took joy in. There were thousands of details to discover. It would be a challenge, but the Kitten of Night delighted in such things.

CHAPTER THREE

BLESSED DARKNESS

As glorious as the sun, our star, is to behold, its brightness obscures the Mysteries of the Cosmos with its brilliance. Only when we are crossed by the sacred Terminator into Night can the Blessed Darkness reveal what the light in its brightness conceals.

—*from the* **Book of Nocturns**
Saganite Litany

THE HALL OF MOONS WOULD HAVE SEEMED AN IMPOSING STRUCTURE IN THE abbey if it hadn't been among more-impressive architectural company. There were many such buildings at the abbey, but the place was still quite impressive to Gatina's admittedly novice professional eye. She regarded the place for a moment with the eye of a thief.

It was built to four stories out of well-cut yellowish limestone blocks, and the high-peaked roof was sheathed in sturdy-looking terra cotta tiles—much easier to dash across than mere thatch, Gatina noted. The windows were wide and possessed handsome wooden shutters, painted black and gray, iron gratings, and a few were even glazed with lozenges of murky glass. That was a significant demonstration of the wealthy largesse that had been bestowed on the abbey over the years.

The old brick hall seemed to have a number of wide windows and small verandas supported by elaborate latticework. Despite the iron gratings that could be swung into place at night to protect the virtue of the Nocturns within, Gatina realized just how little security was in place at the Hall of Moons.

Why, she realized, if you opened each grate on the first and second floor, they would provide almost a ladder straight to the third floor. And despite the imposing double wooden doors that guarded the hall's main room, she could see at least three other entrances on

the ground floor that lacked any special measures to keep intruders—
or thieves—out.

A handsomely painted sign outside the main entrance showed a large white disc with a much smaller green disc set within and proclaimed in Narasi and Old High Perwynese that this was the Hall of the Moons, or simply Moon Hall.

Nightsister Nimandi opened the door to the hall with some ceremony and ushered her charges past the buttery and pantry and into a spacious central chamber that was far cozier than the Great Hall of the Nocturn Hall. The furnishings were simple but well made, and the tapestries (displaying, of course, each of the constellations of the night's sky, the planets, and the moons) were of good quality. There were several other small groups of initiate Nocturns shuffling from place to place, each guided by a Nightsister or Dusksister who was giving them their own tour of the hall.

"This way, Nocturns!" Sister Nimandi urged as she opened a door to a narrow stairwell leading up. "This is the second sleeping chamber in the hall. Each bedchamber has a separate stairway, to avoid any unnecessary disturbance of the other sisters in other groups. You will find there are duties that are required at all hours of the day and the Blessed Darkness, and we value our sleep!"

"*These* are our quarters?" Gatina heard one of the girls ahead of her whisper to another. "They're so dark and gloomy!"

"I'm sure there are tapers," another whispered doubtfully. "I can't see in the dark." Gatina suppressed a snort. There was still enough light to read by, even in the stairwell.

"Your belongings were taken to the room already," the nun continued when she reached the top of the stairs. "You also have your wardrobe bundle. One additional habit and wimple, plus several days of undergarments, are waiting on your beds, which have been assigned." Gatina wondered if the nun ever took a breath. "Your belongings are minimal, of course, as you were instructed to bring but one change of clothing. Those, along with what you are wearing now, will be placed in the wardrobe."

"Only . . . two sets of clothing?" Leonna asked, critically.

"As of this moment, you are novitiates with no need of the material world. All of your needs will be met by the order." She paused to open a door, which she held open as she ushered the girls inside. "Welcome to your new home."

The room was not at all what Gatina had imagined. From the gasps of the other girls, it wasn't what they had expected, either.

"You'll notice a few differences from what you are probably used to." Sister Nimandi said, almost apologetically. "It is still half an hour until the supper bell, so take the time to get acquainted and put your things away, wash up, and take care of any personal matters. I remind you that punctuality is demanded of Nocturns," she warned. "Do not be tardy. The stars wait for no man . . . nor maid," she added.

To her surprise, the small chamber at the head of the stairs was crowded with six large boxes, like elaborate crates. She wasn't the only one surprised. Several of the girls gasped.

"Where are the beds?" demanded one of the girls—Arryn, Gatina remembered.

"These are your beds," Sister Nimandi assured them, opening a small door—more like a cupboard—in the side of the crate-like box. "These are box beds. They help keep the sunlight out of your eyes so that you can rest during the day if you draw night duties. They also keep the noise down. Sleep is vitally important to your studies."

"We're to sleep in boxes?" Dina asked, skeptically.

"You'll get used to it faster than you realize," assured the nun. "Now, your luggage has been brought up by the servants, but you should put your things away in the drawers under the beds. The privy is in that cupboard there," she indicated, pointing to a narrow door at the end of the small chamber. "Don't forget to sort out an order for chores. I would not recommend leaving that task to me," she warned. "Supper will be served shortly downstairs, at the sixth bell. We'll be explaining the daily schedule there. And do not be tardy. Those bells are loud enough to be heard even in your box beds." She returned downstairs, after that, and left the girls to their tasks.

"This . . . is *awful!*" complained one of the girls, staring balefully at her box bed.

"No one said clerical life was supposed to be fun," Dina said wistfully as she opened the tiny door to her box bed and set her satchel on the thin tick within. There was a thin sheet folded on it and a sparse-looking pillow. "Indeed, that is the point, isn't it?"

"This is *not* acceptable," Leonna pronounced after the nun had left the girls to sort their belongings. "What does she mean? Where is the bed? Is this a *joke?*" She turned to find her large travel chest sitting beside the first box bed with a number of other pieces of luggage, far more baggage than any of the other girls. She turned and gestured dismissively at the box bed assigned to her. "This is not a bed. It's a *coffin.*"

She sat on her chest with a soft thump. Gatina imagined that Leonna's chest contained more frilly and frivolous dresses, shoes, and other things she would not need at the abbey. She realized, quickly, that Leonna was not finished with her performance. The girl had buried her head in her hands and had begun to weep, her quiet sobs shaking the chest.

"Well, it's best to get ourselves sorted and settled," Dina suggested to the others, ignoring the weeping maid. "We'll give her some space to adjust."

Arryn, it seemed, was agitated after Leonna's emotional outburst, Gatina noticed. Gatina looked back at the weeping Coastlord maid, to find her glaring at Arryn's back through her tears, as if she blamed her—or someone, *anyone*—for her misery. She filed it away as simple distress and pettiness, and began to look for her satchel among the sleep boxes.

As she considered the giant wooden bed as if it were an intricate puzzle, Gatina tilted her head side to side far enough to cause her wimple to slide off—and nearly her wig. She removed it carefully and casually. Her hair wig was in place, and she was in her dormitory so, she reasoned, she could let go of the societal standards in such a private setting. She studied the bed box, scanning from side to side and top to bottom, looking for hinges and seams in the woodwork. She knew that there were, of course, hinges, else it would not open.

She recalled the secret doorways back home at Cysgodol Hall. Those used recessed hinges. She assumed these beds used those, too. Using her fingers, she felt along the long bottom of the bed box frame until her right index finger tripped over a latch. Using her finger, she pressed down, and the latch released, and she slowly opened the bed's door as if it were the top to a giant jewelry box. She smiled, impressed by the clever design.

It was different, certainly, from what she had imagined. The room itself was fine. The space was long and narrow, the natural stone-and-daub hue in stark contrast to the mahogany bed boxes and wardrobes. Narrow windows were set high in the walls, nearly to the ceiling, which was tall, probably at least twelve feet high. This allowed for a bit of light and a breeze, which would be a good thing on warmer days. And each bed box seemed to give the girls their own space within the narrow portion of the sleeping boxes perpendicular to the exterior wall providing a simple screen to allow for a tiny desk, with a plain wash basin and ewer on top of it, and dressing area, complete with a curtain that could serve as a door. Not exactly a room, but not a cell, either.

She was about to start unpacking when Leonna stopped her weeping, cleared her throat, and made an announcement to the chamber.

"I suppose I will have to endure this horrible bed. However, there are limits! House Baskley has commanded the affairs of our lands for three hundred years," she said loudly. Leonna addressed them with a cloud of resentment in her voice.

"We are *unused* to menial tasks. I did *not* come here to do chores like a drudge, even if the rules insist on it. I will pay you in silver coin to do mine for me."

Gatina was shocked at the girl's blatant—and tellingly early—disregard for the Saganite rules. Leonna's pride was clear, as was her inclination to dominate the group with her status. But it ran counter to the rites of the mysteries Palomar Abbey was to teach them. She was tempted to speak against her, even though she doubted that Avorrita would have had the courage to challenge the prideful girl.

Before she could speak, another girl. Dina, did.

"I have a question for you, Nocturn Leonna: why *did* you come here?"

The tall girl looked sharply at Leonna, who was clearly not accustomed to being spoken to in such a direct manner—particularly by a girl of Wilderlands descent. Indeed, Leonna seemed to possess every bit of the Old Imperial prejudice against the Narasi and Sea Lord nobility that had plagued Alshar for four centuries. It took all of Gatina's restraint to maintain her composure and not speak up in support of Dina, even though Avorrita was clearly from an Imperial line.

To her delight, Dina did not shrink from Leonna's stare, nor did she relent. "I mean no disrespect, Nocturn Leonna, but surely you realized that as clergy, chores would be part of the duties."

Gatina remembered seeing them before they had changed into their habits. Her mother had trained her to observe how someone dressed and draw certain conclusions based on their clothing. It was often the fastest means to judge the social position, wealth, and status of someone you wanted to rob or manipulate in some way. The two girls had been dressed similarly in current fashions popular with the nobility, straight from Falas, before Count Vichetral had seized power. But there had been some telling differences.

Leonna had worn a cornflower-blue traveling dress of fine Gilmoran cotton, she recalled, hemmed with white ribbons, cloth-covered buttons, and matching blue shoes of suede. Her dark Imperial hair had been covered with a stylish velvet hat that matched her dress perfectly. She had displayed plenty of jewelry—multiple rings, necklaces, and silver bracelets that she had reluctantly and resentfully put away when issued her habit. Nothing really worth stealing, of course, but Gatina guessed that she had not realized that, in addition to chores, there would be such a plain and undistinctive uniform involved.

Dina, by contrast, had worn an emerald-green gown of good wool over a long yellow cotton shift, a style popular last summer when the late Duke and Duchess had traveled to the Wilderlands to the summer capital. Dina had worn short boots stained a darker green. She'd complemented it with a simple starched white wimple, but her stray dark blond curls seemed to perpetually peek out to tickle her bright blue eyes. She'd worn one simple golden pendant and one ring, Gatina remembered—far less ostentatious than the Imperial girl.

Now that they wore the same habit, it was harder to distinguish them. Dina was a few inches taller than Leonna and was far more developed, as the modest dress strained to contain her chest. But they seemed equally imposing, despite the differences.

"How dare you talk to me in such a manner!" Leonna said, scowling, as she squared off against the northern girl. "Why am I here? I came here to complete my education and consider holy orders if I decide not to marry. Of course, I will likely attract a good husband after my education, but men of quality prefer a wife who understands scholarly matters, it's said in my House. But what of yours? Who do you think you are, then? House Baskley has held our lands for centuries, and I certainly deserve to be here. You? What is a poor Sea Lord maid from the wilderness doing in an ancient Imperial temple? Here on charity, no doubt!" she snorted.

A social challenge, Gatina realized, to Dina's upbringing and her family's wealth. *Interesting and catty,* she thought, while she tried to keep Avorrita's face fearful and surprised at the outburst. *It's not the Rat Orphans' kind of challenge. No one is likely to get stabbed, but it could get vicious. And be entertaining.*

"Oh, you're from the provinces? I hail from Vorone, the Summer Capital," Dina replied, coolly, her Wilderlands accent becoming more pronounced, "where my father is the Court Vintner. Our House procures the fine wines produced for the Ducal Palace and hosts tournaments and entertainments for Their Graces and their court," she explained, "He also directs trade between Enultramar and the Wilderlands. My mother, of course, comes from the prestigious maritime House Amazar, in Ganivet." Dina assessed the other maiden calmly.

But the Wilderlands girl was not finished. "Not as glorious a profession as *farming*, perhaps . . . but my father feels I have the intellect to master the Mysteries of Sagan. That is why I am here," she said, pointedly. Then she shifted her focus to another girl. "And how about you?"

Dina did not direct her question directly to Leonna, which further infuriated the girl, who realized she had been dismissed by the Wilderlands girl in favor of someone else. But it was interesting to know why each of them had come to the odd little abbey. It was the Narasi girl from the south, Gatina saw.

"Me? Oh, yes. I am Arryn," the blond girl reminded them, flustered. She took a settling breath before continuing. "My father is a counting man who works at the counting house of the merchant House of Frelesta. He's good with figures. As am I," she admitted, almost sounding guilty about it.

Leonna snorted. "I wasn't aware the Narasi valued counting, beyond horses. Or had any head for it. Certainly not a Narasi noble." The venomous comment hit, and Arryn's pale complexion turned bright pink in embarrassment.

"My . . . my father is a commoner," Arryn said, uncomfortably.

"A commoner? A *Narasi* commoner?" Leonna almost shrieked. "Here? I was led to believe that this was a quality temple!" she said disdainfully. Then she gave Arryn what Gatina guessed was a sympathetic look. "But I suppose that does mean you need the coin. Honestly, I will pay you to do my chores." Arryn looked away toward the door, her face burning red in embarrassment as if Sister Nimandi might return and set things right.

Gatina couldn't take any more of the mean-spirited Leonna, though she enjoyed a good social scrap. "I am Avorrita of Dentran. A Coastlord, not that it matters. I am here to gain an education, not a husband. And I thought we were here to learn the Mysteries, not brag about our ancestry." Gatina made it a point to draw out the words of that statement, taking the time and care to look Leonna directly in the eyes before looking away. She also decided that finding a husband was not one of Avorrita's interests. Leonna met the glare and plastered a less-than-genuine smile on her lips.

"Well, I suppose we are," Leonna agreed, in a sarcastic tone.

Gatina turned to the fifth girl and said, "It's your turn, I think," she said, gently.

The final girl had been wearing a burgundy gown with matching slippers before she had received her habit, Gatina recalled. She had dark, almost black hair, and pure Imperial features. She nodded.

"I am Mathilde. My father is a merchant in Bothaire. I suppose that I, too, am here to get my education before I am married off to another merchant house. I truly am interested in the stars." She smiled sadly. "And I miss my dog."

The five girls looked at each other, taking stock of each other after the squabble. The silence became awkward as they sized each other up.

Before Gatina could speak, Dina finally sighed and said, "It's certainly nice to be out of the carriage and to meet you all, Nocturns. As for chores, I am no stranger to working. My mother instilled a strong work ethic in my brothers and myself." She looked at each girl briefly. "I would prefer to do the kitchen chores, if that is acceptable to you. And I would not suggest that anyone pay anyone else to take their assigned work. No matter whose lineage is eldest, or what husbands or livelihoods we hope to find, we're supposed to be equal in status during the Mysteries. So, no buying off your chores. I imagine that Sister Nimandi would find that idea a violation of the spirit of the abbey's rule." Her gaze lingered overlong on Leonna as she said it, her meaning clear: she would not stand for Leonna bullying anyone in such a way.

In that one instant, as each of them declared which chores they would prefer, Gatina realized that the social pecking order among the group had been established. Dina would be their leader, the dominant voice of reason in the group, and based on the sour look on Leonna's face, it was an unwelcome surprise to at least one of their group. No doubt there would continue to be a struggle between the two dominant Nocturns, but Dina's forthright manner and her unwillingness to bend to the Imperial girl's whim were clear to all.

Nightsister Nimandi returned ten minutes later to find the girls talking quietly among themselves as they finished unpacking their luggage. She smiled.

"Good, good, it's nice to see everyone getting along. And important. For the next several weeks, you will all be working together, and I think you'll find that talking pleasantly is better than arguing about chores," she said, astutely guessing what the first discussion had been about. "The supper bell will sound in a moment, but if you are all ready, it is best that we get there early. Afterwards, we will gather in the Chapel of the Stars for Vespers and an address by the abbot. And do keep up," she said over her shoulder as the girls rushed to fall in line behind her and be within earshot.

"I hate this place already," Gatina heard Leonna mutter from behind her.

It wasn't that terrible, Gatina reflected, remembering how her orphaned friends in Falas lived on the street. And while it might have been her unusual nature, she found the idea of a sleeping box to be intriguing, for some reason.

———

THE DINING CHAMBER OF MOON HALL QUICKLY BECAME CROWDED AFTER Gatina's group arrived and took their seats on the long wooden benches. Nocturns from the other bedchambers came in, and, surprisingly, several groups of boys from Adastra Hall, which apparently did not have a dining chamber of its own. It was interesting to see how loud the volume of chatter became when they arrived; boys seemed naturally louder than the girls, she reflected. But the nuns quickly got things under control until the blessing was said and the food was brought in from the kitchen.

The meal was simple—roasted fish, tubers, carrots, and sweet bread served with a light, fruity wine, which had, of course, been watered—and surprisingly delicious despite the reputation ecclesiastic institutions had for plain fare, Gatina noted as she ate. Not nearly as good as Drella's back home, of course, but tasty and filling.

Of course, Leonna began complaining about it at once.

The Nocturns of each group were seated together. All three floors, as well as one floor of Adastra Hall, took meals together, she realized, with all five of the girls from her chamber seated on one side of the table across from one of the boys' groups from Adastra Hall. Conversation was not discouraged, but it was never allowed to become overly loud. The talk amongst the Nocturn Initiates ranged from criticism of the food and polite inquiries about homes to confusion about the lessons and a heated debate about the sleeping arrangements and lessons at night.

"I simply will not sleep in a coffin," Leonna said, still very much upset by the beds provided to the Nocturns. "I cannot believe we are being subjected to such treatment! It's unbecoming. And in . . . poor taste," she decided, looking around the table for support. Of course, she had moderated her behavior in the presence of the boys, but the Coastlord girl clearly still wanted to complain.

"You'll get used to it. My brother is a Nightbrother now," offered a boy whose name Gatina had not heard. "He said they still sleep in those. It's better for daytime sleeping, he says," the boy said between enthusiastic bites of his sweet bread. "He also said that the food is pretty good here, compared to other temples," he added, spilling a crumb from his mouth while he chewed around his words.

Gatina smiled; she liked this boy, poor manners or no. "Anyway, you get used to the box beds," he assured Leonna.

That did little to mollify the girl, but Dina quickly steered the conversation away from complaints and toward the sad state of political affairs since the shocking deaths of the Duke and Duchess. Gatina quickly was able to identify which of her peers were in favor of Count Vichetral seizing power and those who were opposed. Dina was in the latter camp, unsurprisingly, and while Leonna had little opinion on the matter, she seemed to favor the Count's actions. The others had no opinion at all or had not heard enough of the news to form one. That was also good to know.

As the meal drew to a close, Sister Nimandi stood to address the Nocturns in her group. "Once you have finished your supper, line up and we will walk to the Chapel of Stars together for the abbot's blessing. Tonight, at least, the kitchen drudges will clear the dishes away and attend to washing-up. Starting tomorrow, that will be your responsibility."

The gravel path between the residence halls and the Chapel of Stars was well worn from years of traffic, which was fortunate because the night was falling fast and a few of the girls were nervous about walking without a torch to guide them. But the Order worked in the Blessed Darkness, not light, the nun had explained as she led them across the grounds. She clarified the significance of the gathering along the way.

"This is where you will meet Abbot Handrig and be assigned your initial class schedule for the next season. Our schedules change with the stars, just as do the seasons," the nun informed them as they walked. All five of the girls had clustered around her on this trip rather than following in a line, so that they could better hear her. "Then you will take your oaths and learn a few important bits of liturgy before the Nightbrothers ascend to the tower, where they will be starting their work for the evening. All night duties will begin for Nocturns tomorrow night, so be certain to learn your schedule and know what time you need to be where. The Timemaster will keep you prompt," she assured them.

Gatina understood they would sometimes be working at night, as her father had explained that to her. She was actually looking forward to being on the nighttime schedule. That was when thieves traditionally worked, after all, so she was used to such hours. It would be a relief to work and sleep when everyone else was doing the same. The nun ushered the five Nocturns inside the chapel and directed them up the center aisle to the pews closest to the chancel, near the altar where the priests and priestess would soon stand. The chamber was filling up rapidly as other Nocturn halls arrived from supper.

The chapel was larger and taller than Gatina had imagined from its exterior appearance. She relaxed, watched, and waited for the night's activities to begin. After a bell brought them to silence, a door opened at the rear of the chapel, and she heard heavier footsteps and the swishing of robes. A number of priests and priestess arrived, each announced with the ringing of bells. Everyone stood when the nuns prompted.

The abbot wore a white vestment over his black habit, and the priestess a white veil over hers. Both walked to the altar, where they knelt for a moment in silent prayer, before turning and uttering a benediction in unison:

"Heavenly Stars, we ask your eternal blessings on these new Nocturn Initiates and ask that you keep them as steady and faithful to your ways as your course through the zodiac. May your manifold light shine bright to offer them guidance, always. May your Blessed Darkness bring them peace. A billion blessings be upon you."

"Billions and billions," the rest of the clergy responded by rote, in unison.

Abbot Handrig spoke first, his voice strong enough to fill the entire chamber. His resemblance to her father was strong, Gatina noted, especially in the eyes, though his were brown and not lavender. He was a large man, she realized, taller than she initially thought, well fed and well muscled, Gatina judged as he addressed them. A far cry from the typical idea of an ascetic monk.

"I am Abbot Handrig, and this is Duskmother Luya, whom some of you have met. We bid you welcome to Palomar Abbey."

"And to the Saganite Order," the priestess said. "Tonight, your calling and your education begin in earnest. We know this will be time well spent."

"Education and service are fundamental to our Order's success," the abbot agreed, and launched into a long speech about the history and importance of the abbey in Alshari life.

Gatina halfheartedly listened to the pair talk about duty, determination, the stars, and success. In truth, she paid little attention to most of it. Saganite service was not her goal there, and she affected an expression of rapt attention while her mind wandered other places.

She wondered where her father was and what adventures her mother might be having. She thought about her friends in Falas and the dreadful state of the capital. She wondered where Atopol was and if he was as bored by the service as she—until she recognized him in his disguise as Dain two rows ahead of her. She caught Atopol's eyes, hoping her gaze expressed that very question. But he shook his head and turned back toward the droning abbot as he finished his introduction and began the Vespers service.

Gatina became possessed during the liturgy with a sudden and deep desire to see her father. She couldn't easily look at the ceiling, she knew, but the next two times the participants were directed to stand in prayer, she chanced a glance over her shoulder to scan the audience for him. It was of no use. He wasn't there.

She stifled the urge to go look for him. That would damage her alias, she knew, and she was resolved to perform her family's assigned tasks flawlessly on this mission. Duty and determination would order her steps during this time, she vowed. She would make her father and mother proud—even if they weren't there to witness it.

"I now place you under your holy lay orders," the abbot finally said, gesturing for them to rise and repeat the oath that would bind them to the Saganite Order for the next few months.

"In the name of the sacred stars, the holy moons, and the Blessed Darkness I swear to hold the Mysteries of Sagan separate from the mortal world of men . . . learn them with diligence . . . practice them with precision . . . adhere to the sacred liturgy and the rightful order of the abbey . . . and solemnly obey my superiors in the order in all things and in all ways . . . until I am released from my vow or the stars fall from the sky."

Gatina repeated the oath with the others in the chapel, mentally excepting herself from certain portions of it. This was Avorrita's oath, not hers, she rationalized. Her true loyalty lay with her House and her family, not the abbey or even the stars.

"Now for a bit of housekeeping," Duskmother Luya announced, after the abbot's final blessing. "Unlike most clerical orders, our day begins here, at Vespers in the Chapel of Stars, not at dawn. Tomorrow after Vespers some of you will be directed to chores, tasks, or classes according to the Timemaster's schedule. There is to be *no* deviation from the Timemaster's schedule," she insisted, with emphasis. The priestess's sharp words jarred Gatina from her daydreams.

"Nocturns, your primary classroom is the Hall of Dawn, near the front of the Market Square," the priestess said. "Though, as your lessons progress, you will visit other classrooms, laboratories, and workshops as directed. Your hall sisters will have a complete listing of this schedule, which will vary to accommodate the number of Initiates this year. They will explain your duties to you in a moment.

"Sworn Nocturns, please remain seated when the Initiates are dismissed for the evening, and you will be given your specific assignments. Now, Initiates, go with a billion blessings on your heads, my dears," she finally concluded, "and get some good sleep tonight. It will be the last one you enjoy for many weeks," she promised, with a smile.

With that, the abbot brought the service to a conclusion, and they were dismissed.

Nightsister Nimandi took only a few moments to gather her group in front of the chapel and explain their duties before they returned to Moon Hall. The stars were already shining overhead, Gatina saw.

"Now that you are official members of the Nocturn Order, it is time to learn your responsibilities. In addition to your studies, which will commence in the morning, you are tasked with housekeeping chores and assisting both Duskbrothers and Nightbrothers in their sacred duties.

"The Duskbrothers and Nightbrothers frequently require aid in the various Saganite rites. You might run errands or work to finish tasks in the Archives, the Scriptorium, the Chapel, or Clockworks, all of which I will show you shortly. In rare cases you may be assigned to the Holy Temple," she added, glancing up at the imposing tower overhead. "That is considered a high honor, usually reserved only for Sworn Nocturns . . . but occasionally an Initiate will be named for the privilege. I was, when I was an Initiate," she bragged as she gazed at each of them, as if judging their abilities to be effective novitiates.

"Why aren't you a Dusksister?" Arryn asked, suddenly.

"It is traditional for Nightbrothers and Sisters to spend at least a few terms helping out with the Initiates and the Sworn Nocturns as part of our calling," Sister Nimandi explained patiently. "Usually, a Nocturn's vows leave them in service of the temple for two years before they accept higher orders. It is supposed to aid our lecturing and increase our humility," she said with a skeptical smile.

"It is important that you learn how to complete the basic skills needed for survival in addition to your education, as well as help with the upkeep of the abbey. Several of you shared your chore preference. I have assigned the remaining duties. Arryn, you will clear and clean the dishes tomorrow. Leonna will report to the chicken coop. Dina, you will be in the kitchen. Avorrita, you're to go to the vegetable garden. And Mathilde is assigned to the laundry. Most of your first day will be instructional, so pay attention. The following week, everyone transits to the next position. Is that clear? Are there any questions?" the nun asked.

The novitiates said nothing, though Gatina heard Leonna sigh in frustration over her assignment. Sister Nimandi continued. "While our day begins with Vespers, you are expected to attend Lauds in the morning and subsequent services during the day, chores and lessons permitting. Our primary classroom will be the Hall of Dawn, which is out these doors to the right, the second building on the left, just before you get to Twilight Street. Now let's get back to Moon Hall and prepare to retire while the stars are still fresh in the sky. Believe me, you're going to need every precious minute of sleep," she assured with a knowing look.

Soon, but not soon enough, based upon the yawns among the girls, they returned to their bedchamber and confronted their box beds. Unlike Leonna, Gatina smiled in satisfaction as the opened door revealed a bed, already made, inside.

She climbed in atop the plain quilt spread out on the fresh straw tick and examined the box bed's interior while trying to ignore the cries of dismay and complaint from the other Nocturns.

It really wasn't that bad, she realized. The linens were not scratchy, which was a relief, she thought. The quilt was soft, if plain, and the feather pillow was almost luxurious under her head. The Saganites took their sleeping seriously.

The box bed was like a miniature bedchamber, she saw. There was a tiny lamp on a hook behind her head that held a taper lamp, she noted, as well as a number of little drawers and shelves. Looking up at the ceiling of the bed, she saw the familiar double moons painted onto the black ceiling of the box bed.

She easily identified the Triangle and two of the other constellations of the zodiac, but the others were a mystery; she quickly realized how little she really knew about the Saganite Order's blessed stars.

The footboard wall was also black, but it featured a shelf large enough for books, she saw, and there was a slatted wooden grate that allowed fresh air into the bed without permitting light. There was another above her head. The wall opposite the door was painted with a map of the duchy transited by strange lines. It was similar to the maps in her parents' library she was familiar with but with some distinct differences she did not yet understand. It was a good reference point, she realized, as she looked back to the bed's ceiling, although she could see how it might inspire homesickness.

Gatina noticed two woven rope straps just above her head. When she sat up to grab one, she discovered how heavy the door was and realized why there were two ropes. Stretching her reach for the second rope, Gatina gave both a tug and the door closed silently. Counterweights, she realized with a smile.

She settled back onto her bed, took out her prosthetic and laid it aside, and peered into the darkness, which was complete. As Darkness was her patron, it did not bother her in the least. Despite the dismay she heard her fellow Nocturns express about the beds, she found it peaceful. It did not take long for the Blessed Darkness to lull her to sleep.

CHAPTER FOUR

ABBEY LIFE

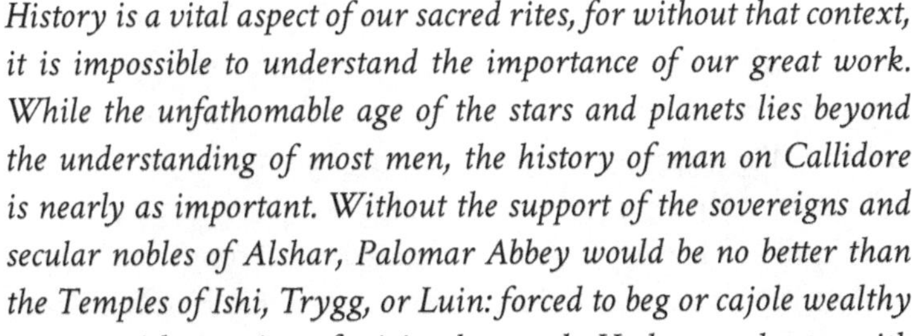

*History is a vital aspect of our sacred rites, for without that context,
it is impossible to understand the importance of our great work.
While the unfathomable age of the stars and planets lies beyond
the understanding of most men, the history of man on Callidore
is nearly as important. Without the support of the sovereigns and
secular nobles of Alshar, Palomar Abbey would be no better than
the Temples of Ishi, Trygg, or Luin: forced to beg or cajole wealthy
patrons with promises of spiritual rewards. Under our charter with
the Dukes of Alshar, we are able to avoid most of that awkward
discussion and ensure that we can devote ourselves to the sacred
mission of understanding the Cosmos.*

*— from **The Litany of the Cosmos***

GATINA WAS AWAKENED THE NEXT MORNING BY A SHARP KNOCK ON THE
outside of her bed box, a noise loud enough to startle her from her sleep.
It took a few moments for her to reorient herself in the dark, enclosed
space, but she quickly recalled her circumstance and the personality she
was supposed to display. She was Avorrita today.

It took but a moment for her to shove the false teeth over her normal
ones, slap her wimple on her head, and struggle through the small cabinet
door and out into the dormitory. Some of the girls were already groaning
and complaining about the early hour—the eastern sky was just beginning to lighten through the high windows. Others were hurriedly using
the privy or splashing water from the basins on their faces. All the while,
Sister Nimandi lectured them in a cheerful voice about the day ahead.

"First breakfast, then chores, then we will join with another cell and
repair to the Rectory before going to the Hall of Dawn for your first lessons," she informed them, as she wandered the room to help various girls

with their habits or give them some encouragement as they got ready. "That will begin with a brief interview with the Rector for placement. The first bell will be shortly," she reminded them, "and then we will meet with Dusksister Franda at the second bell to assess your talents and abilities, to properly place you in the rites. We must be in our proper places and correct classrooms by the third bell. The stars wait for no man," she quoted.

That was to become a familiar refrain to Avorrita's ears at Palomar Abbey.

Over breakfast, she did her best to keep quiet, eat, and listen to the chatter of the Sworn Nocturns and Dusksisters, who were far more animated at this hour than the poor Initiates. She realized that keeping her mouth closed while chewing was not only ladylike but was also necessary to keep her dental device from slipping out and falling into her porridge. She discovered a surprising amount about Palomar in a short time as a result of her eavesdropping.

Gatina quickly learned the complicated hierarchy that ran Palomar Abbey's daily operations. As abbot, her great-uncle Handrig was technically in charge of the entire place, of course, but he largely kept to the temple, on the cliffs above, where he oversaw the rites of observation and recording—the abbey's primary function. His authority in Ejecta was actually delegated to three important officials: the Night Prior, the Day Prior, and the Timemaster. All other officials reported to those three, she figured out.

The Night Prior, surprisingly, was the senior of the three, and was second only to the abbot himself in rank. He was given the responsibility for the abbey's main purposes of observing and charting the stars, recording their positions in the archives, and overseeing the advanced work of the monks and nuns. He was regularly seen running up and down the cliffs at twilight as he managed his complicated and complex duties.

The Day Prior, by contrast, was charged with administering the staff that kept the grounds and facilities of the abbey functioning, oversaw the storehouses and kitchens, and maintained the lucrative guest houses the abbey rented out to visiting nobility and fellow clergy—the sorts of mundane housekeeping that every large ecclesiastic settlement required. She was the actual master of the Nocturns, both Initiates and Sworn, and responsible for their learning the fundamental rites.

The Timemaster's function was a bit different from either of them, Gatina discovered. The sage-looking monk who held that title was responsible for keeping the number of complicated clocks at the abbey functioning and accurate. He was also charged with ringing the bells that kept the abbey's great number of workers, lay and clerical alike, promptly on their assigned tasks. The Timemaster was in charge of scheduling . . . everything, and his small but studious staff regularly booked work parties, classes, deliveries, and special events as well as the complex nocturnal rites that were the abbey's liturgy. All such occurrences had to be made with his knowledge and permission, lest the complicated clockwork nature of the abbey fail.

Reporting to the Timemaster was the Rector, Dusksister Franda, with whom Gatina met the very first day at the abbey. The middle-aged nun had invited each of the female novitiates into her chamber in turn and interviewed them to assess their native abilities and determine which classes they should be assigned to during their tenure.

One of the other cells from Moon Hall joined them after chores, and while the two nuns who guided them chatted, they were led over to the stately brick building of the Hall of Dawn.

The ten Nocturns looked around the teaching hall with curiosity while the second bell tolled. Its walls were covered with paintings of various stars and planets, their names and courses indicated in an elegant-looking script in Old High Perwynese, the language of the original Magocracy, as well as Narasi. The windows there were also glazed but were largely clear, not stained except at the corners where occasionally a whimsical portrayal of some celestial object or event was portrayed. The Nocturns were quietly led to a chamber on the second floor, where they were directed to wait for their names to be called by the Rector's assistant.

She looked around the cluttered chamber while she waited, trying to see it through dull Avorrita's eyes—books, charts, diagrams, slates, a large abacus, models of things she had no idea about were crammed onto shelves and tables. The spacious room was divided into four quarters in which different topics would be covered, she reasoned.

Each quarter had a learning area. Two had long tables and benches, one had large floor pillows, and the other had pallets positioned on the floor. Gatina looked at the ceiling and noticed a much-larger version of the celestial painting in her sleeping box. While there was a certain order to the mess, it was clear that the Rectory was a place for storage as much as for administration and training. It almost looked like she imagined a wizard's workshop would appear. Gatina wondered how a true magical academy would contend with such clutter.

She'd always been curious about the famed magical academies in Castal and Wenshar, and the many in distant Merwyn. They were the subject of much family history—after all, Kiera the Great had famously attended Varshi Academy in Vore before she took up the art of thieving, according to the lore.

She remembered those academies were only for those with a strong full measure of *rajira*, people destined to become professional magi—spellmongers, resident adepts, seamagi, or other specialties. Inarion and Alar Academies catered to specific gifts, from what she understood. There at Palomar Abbey, she could expect much less emphasis on magic; the temple was for those training to study the stars, with only a few students who might possess magical Talent taught just enough about their emerging powers to keep them from hurting themselves and others.

Both her mother and father had family members who had attended Inarion Academy, a long time before. Inarion was in Castal, and that was firmly within the new kingdom of Castalshar, King Rard's realm, now. Gatina had no idea why Alshar lacked a comparable school when so many Coastlord families continued to have high levels of *rajira*. Beyond elementary training, Alshari magi either became apprenticed to a competent master or went to Inarion or, if their families could afford it, distant Alar Academy in Wenshar. Either academy was seen as a worthy goal.

"Initiate . . . Avorrita?" the aide finally called, startling Gatina from her reverie. She leaped to her feet awkwardly, just as she expected a real Avorrita would, and shyly scuttled into the inner chamber, where the dour-looking Sister Franda was awaiting her behind a battered trestle table piled high with parchment, inkpots, and well-worn quills.

After a terse introduction, Sister Franda began administering her examination for placement. Gatina was asked to read aloud several times, write her name and several sentences on a slate, and figure several appallingly simple mathematics questions. Only toward the end did the questions become more difficult, until there was a string of them that she discovered she could not answer. Sister Franda quickly determined that Gatina—no, Maid Avorrita of Dentran, she corrected herself—could read and write, and knew her numbers. Initiate Avorrita also showed off her abilities with addition and subtraction to the nun's satisfaction.

"Well, your tutors did well by you, Avorrita," the old nun grunted, as she looked over the simple problems she'd given the girl. "And your hand is steady enough, though it could be fairer. We may well keep you out of embroidery class and flower arranging and see if you cannot master the intricacies of mathematics, poetics, and history," she concluded as she referred to a scrap of parchment with Avorrita's name on it. "Those are morning classes. Afternoons will be assigned special study, according to your aptitude and our need. I see you're a legacy to the Order of Nocturns . . ." she said, her eyes flicking up from the parchment in front of her.

"My father was a Nocturn," Avorrita assured her. "My family has always been honored to attend Palomar Abbey," she added enthusiastically.

"So it says. And a fair contributor to the abbey's estate. Therefore, you are designated a special student. I've been advised that your afternoon classes will be more . . . select. You will have special lessons after luncheon, in consideration of your lineage and likely receipt of *rajira*: Exercise, Lore, and Practicum."

"What are those?" Avorrita asked dully.

"Whatever your tutors decide," the nun said, unhelpfully. "Exercise usually includes some archery, some games—croquet and badminton, I'd suspect. Lore is up to the instructor, as is Practicum. For serious students, this often involves learning the higher rites," she explained. "For others . . . well, the tutor usually attempts to find something the student excels at, some practical skill like copying or ink-making, and sets them to mastery over the subject.

"Of course, that is if you don't gain *rajira*," she added, cautiously. "Should you be granted the Talent, your afternoons would involve basic instruction in the arcane arts. We're licensed for that," she declared defensively. "Every year, a few students gain their *rajira* here. Mostly Coastlords, but sometimes even a few of the Narasi or Sea Lords. Those students wear a small green crescent-moon pendant. Non-Talented students wear a white crescent. Has your House any history of *rajira*?" she asked curiously.

"My great-uncle was a practical adept in Torine," Gatina lied convincingly. "But he died a few years ago. And my second cousin was a seamage who ran away with a common Narasi mariner—oh, what a scandal!" Avorrita said, shaking her head in delighted horror at the story.

"It happens in the best of families," the nun nodded, sympathetically. "Well, at Palomar Abbey we cast no shame on those who gain their Talent. If that should happen, then you will be given what instruction we are permitted to by the Bans, and then recommended for apprenticeship or entry into a proper magical academy. But I wouldn't worry about it," the mature nun assured her. "It happens to only a very few."

"Some of the girls in my group are expecting it," Gatina offered.

"Of course they are!" snorted the nun. "Likely the Coastlords, such as yourself. Everyone wants the Talent, but few understand the great burden it can be. Believe me, I've seen generations of young things such as yourself pine away because they didn't get their *rajira* when they got their monthlies. They all have dreams of being great adepts, or court wizards, or more. They don't even mind giving up their titles under the Bans on Magic, if it means they can practice the art. They'd be far better served to do something truly useful, like pursue the sacred study of the nighttime sky."

"Studying the sky is important?" Avorrita asked, skeptically.

"Oh, Blessed Night, yes!" Sister Franda chuckled. "Without the work we do here in Palomar Abbey, Alshar's ships wouldn't be able to navigate anywhere beyond sight of the coastlines. We track the tides and chart the stars they steer by. It is our primary purpose now. So, whatever happens in the capital, whoever is in charge, they will need us. It's not just about religion. Without us, the fleets would fail. Not even the seamagi are as accurate as we are when it comes to such things."

"I've never met a seamage," Gatina admitted truthfully.

"They are as subtle and obscure as all magi," the nun informed her. "Occasionally, one of our Talented students goes on to study their arts. But nothing is better for navigation than an accurate map and sky chart. The merchant fleets depend on those. Which means they depend on *us*. Magi," she continued, shaking her head and frowning, before beginning to rant. "Everyone wants to be a mage. The reality? It's a hard life, full of study and oversight by those checkered-cloaked Censors, always worrying about breaking some obscure rule and ending up fined, imprisoned, or worse. You lose your title, you lose your lands, and you lose your social standing in most cases. There is no guarantee of a position, there's little security, and there's always suspicion . . . particularly among the Narasi.

"If you are fortunate, you won't have *rajira* emerge and upset your life. And things are about to get worse for the magi in Alshar," the nun warned in a hoarse whisper. "Now that Count Vichetral is in control of Falas, you can count on it. He suspects them of plotting rebellion against him, it is said. He's already approved the recruitment of a whole troop of Censors to help him . . . rule," she said, her eyes narrowing critically.

"Count Vichetral. I've heard of him," Avorrita nodded, forcing her eyes open wide in recognition.

"Many have," agreed the nun. "He's one of the leading gentlemen in the Duchy . . . and now he controls it. Or he's trying to. We've been flooded with students since he seized power. Duke Lenguin had strong support amongst the Coastlords, of course, and many fear retribution for their loyalty to the Ducal House now. They want their children safely tucked away at temple while there are troubles at home. Politics!" Sister Franda spat. "We do our best to steer clear of it, at Palomar Abbey, but now . . . Well, that is a discussion for another day. I've already gone on too long with you, Nocturn . . . What was your name, again?" she asked, confused.

"Avorrita," Gatina supplied. It was almost becoming automatic.

"Avorrita, that's right. Well, Nocturn Avorrita, I urge you to apply yourself to your studies whether you gain your Talent or not. Either way, you will find it useful in your life. And perhaps you will discover a calling to pursue the higher purpose of sacred astronomy." She made a note on one of the pieces of parchment and handed it to her. "There's your schedule—show it to your instructors. Now you are dismissed. Go with a billion blessings," she added absently.

"Billions and billions," Gatina responded dully, and left.

―――――――――

AVORRITA'S LESSONS STARTED AT ONCE, WITH HER FIRST CLASS IN HISTORY, along with the rest of her cell. They followed Nightsister Nimandi across the grounds to a large chamber in the Hall of Dawn, where three other groups were already gathered. The Hall of Dawn was located beside her dormitory, Moon Hall.

Gatina sighed and let the growing personality of Avorrita overtake her. She was there to be a novice nun, after all, not a thief. Avorrita was awkward, she knew, a sheltered petty noblewoman only recently come from her family's provincial estates for the first time. That part was easy, she reflected as she mounted the stairs. She was, after all, only recently herself come from her family's provincial estate. The best lies had an element of truth in them, she knew.

But then there were differences. Avorrita stumbled, Gatina decided, mumbled, and sometimes blurted out inappropriate things that Gatina might not ever do. She wasn't terribly bright but had a good heart. And she did nothing remarkably well. A completely average, normal girl who was the furthest thing away from an apprentice thief.

By the time she made the door, the transformation was complete. She felt Avorrita's bland personality fall upon her shoulders like an undyed cloak. The Nocturn who met them at the door barely glanced at her as she showed her into the teaching chamber of the hall. That was where Sister Nimandi turned them over to Dusksister Amora, a plump, middle-aged nun whose chins spilled out of her wimple like a waterfall.

"Nocturns, please gather around," Sister Amora called, clapping her hands to get their attention. "Find a seat and pray pay attention to today's most important lesson," she called in a melodious voice.

When everyone was seated at one of the tables, the Dusksister motioned for quiet before she began addressing them.

"Welcome to the Hall of Dawn, your educational home for the next season. Our first lesson begins now and concerns the history of this abbey. If you feel the need to take down notes, materials can be found here." She pointed to a cabinet built into the wall under the bank of tall, wide windows that let the morning light shine brightly through the chamber.

"As you are no doubt aware, the temple performs its most sacred rites under the Blessed Darkness of night," she began, smoothly. "Why is that? You," she said, indicating a girl from the other group. "Please state your name before you answer, Nocturn," she added.

"I am Nocturn Calmisa. We work at night because that is when the stars can be seen," the girl said hesitantly but matter-of-factly. "By reasoning, we must sleep during the day to be rested for the night."

The nun clapped, beaming at the girl, who seemed to find the attention unwarranted. "Very good, Nocturn Calmisa. Judging from some of your faces, this lifestyle has come as a surprise, yes?" There were a few nods and some murmurs. "I promise you this: your parents were told of our rules. They do take a bit of getting used to, but you will adapt quickly enough, just as generations of other Nocturns have. Maybe you did not hear them when they spoke of this to you?" There was a chorus of nervous laughter. "Don't worry, Nocturns. I will explain our routines and rules as we discuss the history of the temple.

"While many of you know something about our sacred rites and our purpose, you may be surprised to learn that Palomar Abbey isn't just an ancient and distinguished temple . . . It is, in fact, the oldest temple in Alshar, predating not just the Magocracy and the rise of the Coastlords but even the arrival of the first Sea Lord ships from Cormeer. Long before the first castles were raised on the Great Bay, Palomar had already been built by our ancient ancestors and was in use. Indeed, with a few small exceptions, Palomar has been in continuous use since the very first days of human life on Callidore. Since we first emerged from the Void, as legend has it.

"Why did the ancients choose this place to construct the temple?" she asked, rhetorically, her eyes scanning her captive students. "After all, this is a remote and obscure location, even today. In antiquity, it was considered even more remote. And it was not agriculture that attracted the first Saganites here. This location has long been sought after because of the water in those two pretty little waterfalls that fall unceasingly from the escarpment. Water brings life," she said, "but it also brings death. But that is not why the temple was built on that big, looming rock overhead.

"It is far more likely, according to our most ancient records, that the latitude of the site and its geological stability was why the first blocks were laid here. We are near enough to the equator of this world to allow observations of the entire zodiac—that is, the plane through which the planets move on their courses. While locations in Farise and beyond might have been even more advantageous, the number of earthquakes and the poor weather near the oceans was thought to hamper our work. The position of the temple on the escarpment—and, more, the exceedingly large, rocky cliff face—provided a great deal of stability. The mild and temperate climate allowed year-round observations without interruption, save for a few rainy weeks in spring and autumn."

Avorrita started to shift in her seat. She wasn't used to long lectures—her tutors and her parents were usually concise with their lessons . . . and her backside was already falling asleep. But still, the nun persisted in telling the glorious history of Palomar Abbey. And her voice was not helping Avorrita's focus.

"In those earliest of days, before the Inundation of Perwyn, the Later Magocracy, and the Narasi Conquest, the first Saganite clergy were already dutifully making their observations, though many of those records have been lost. There were a few local tribes who practiced horticulture and agriculture, and the relationship between temple and the local estates was good.

"But after the first archmage took his throne in distant Perwyn, things began to . . . decline," she related with practiced sadness. "Order fell out of fashion. The local tribes became belligerent and forgot their ancient duties to the temple. Our location was so fragile, in the early years, lifetimes ago, that we were forced to seek the protection and cooperation from the tribal warlords who eventually came to rule this area. Their lands stretched from beyond the great rock above all the way to the famous double waterfalls of Falas.

"When the Sea Lords established their havens in the Great Bay, they largely ignored the temple. A few demanded tribute, but they eschewed the importance of the work we did and relied upon their own seamagi to help them navigate. Then, when the Coastlords first arrived, they briefly took the ancient structure of the temple as a fortress. You have only been in the temple a short time, but you no doubt saw how tall and imposing it is." Sister Amora looked at the students for an agreement, and seeing it, she continued. "The structure predates most, if not all other temples in the duchy."

"Why is the tower of the temple so . . . odd-looking?" ventured Mathilde after raising her hand. "It doesn't look like a regular tower. A castle tower," she corrected. Mathilde's question surprised Gatina, who was relieved that someone had asked, because she wanted to know, but also knew that asking was not in character for Avorrita.

"Your name, Nocturn?" Sister Amora asked, her eyebrows raised.

"Uh, Nocturn Mathilde," Gatina's chambermate answered, blushing.

"You have a good eye, Nocturn Mathilde," the nun nodded. "The temple was never built for defense. It was constructed to rise above the petty conflicts of man and place us closer to the sacred stars. The ancients once had an impressively complicated mechanism installed there, one which allowed them to discern the stars and planets with breathtaking clarity, legend has it. Indeed, there are portions of the temple that we have no idea what purpose they served, they are so ancient. The Great Telescope was one of them. Though, sadly, that great engine was destroyed a few centuries after its founding, the metal roof atop the tower can still swing open and allow for our less-sophisticated observations. Still important," Sister Amora insisted, "but not nearly as detailed as we once were capable of.

"But after the Inundation of Perwyn and the rise of the Second Magocracy," she continued, referring to distant Merwyn on the map behind her, "the archmage and his court sent new settlers to Alshar. Magi and men of great learning. They found the abbey still hard at work at our observations, and, recognizing the value of our observations for maritime trade, they invested heavily in the temple and its clergy. That was a golden age for the abbey," she said, smiling at the thought. "Indeed, you can still find inscriptions and records in the abbey's archives written in Old High Perwynese, the ancient language of the Magocracy and the Archmage."

"What about the village?" asked a girl from the other cell. "Nocturn Avica," she added, belatedly. "Does the abbot hold the village in fief?"

The nun smiled. "Ejecta is as old as the temple itself," she answered. "The village is under our abbot's control, and it is ruled from the mountain"—she pointed behind the cluster of Nocturns—"all the way to the edge of Ejecta. Our ancient charter from the archmage states that explicitly. And that is very important, Nocturns. Do you know why?"

Gatina did not know the answer, so even if Avorrita had wanted to speak up, she couldn't. Nobody answered, so the nun continued. "It's important because it means that this abbey—all abbeys, actually—is exempt from taxes, tributes, and scutage. When the Narasi came, the Count of Falas and later the Dukes of Alshar reaffirmed that charter word for word. And that means what?" She looked around expectantly as her words sank in, and another student from the other group raised her hand.

"Nocturn Olavala. It means that we are untouchable, right?" she asked, nervously.

"Perhaps *untouchable* is too strong a word," Sister Amora chuckled. "We still fall under all applicable Ducal laws as well as the laws of the Counts of Falas. But your point is well made," the nun agreed. "By our charter, the temple is sacrosanct, even more so than other temples. Our libraries, our classrooms, our relics, your belongings, the villagers' belongings and crops are all exempt from being taken by the Duke—would that we had one," she said, quietly frowning as she acknowledged the recent political turmoil in the duchy. "In light of our important contributions to the maritime fleet and other matters, Palomar Abbey has by tradition and right a number of unusual privileges, some of which stretch back centuries before there even was a duchy."

"I am Nocturn Leonna. What about Count Vichetral?" asked Leonna curiously. "Will he still allow the abbey to work?" It seemed as much a challenge as a question.

"The temple and the abbot pride ourselves on being able to work with anyone," the nun frowned. "We don't have the resources or holdings that often attract the attention of ambitious nobles, and our liturgy is considered obscure and pointless by many of the nobility.

"Of course, should the Duke or his court request our assistance, we would provide it. And if Count Vichetral serves to lead the duchy during this dark time, we will, of course, do what we must to support his regime. It is always wise to cooperate, and that is a very good first lesson for your first day as Nocturns. Cooperation. I bid you to keep that in mind as you consider the chores and studies ahead of you. The abbey has always cooperated with . . . those in power to ensure our divine mission is uninterrupted by mere politics. This policy was first begun by Nightfather Hansmeyer, the third abbot of record, when he ceded the lands to the south of Ejecta—temporarily—to the tribal warlords. Those were restored to us under the protection of the first Count of Falas, as the Magocracy laid claim to Alshar . . ."

Sister Amora continued to lecture in a well-practiced tone that told Avorrita that she'd spoken these words many times in the past and was exceedingly comfortable with them. Alas, that did little to spark her interest—at times, the nun's voice seemed to drone, lulling Avorrita closer to closing her eyes even when Amora was saying something interesting. She was already familiar with the exciting period of history when the Coastlords first arrived in Alshar—her ancestors, including Kiera the Great, were among them, and they were a prominent part of her family history.

But the boring recitation of a number of counts and then dukes, abbots, and abbesses was hardly riveting to Avorrita's dull mind, no matter how important they had been to the temple's history.

Instead, her imagination wandered to the actual temple site. That was fascinating to her. The little mountain upon which the famed abbey was perched was unlike any other she had seen. Instead of a fairly graceful conic shape, as a mountain should be, the entire thing seemed out of place on the relatively flat edge of the great escarpment, as if a giant had hurled some massive stone to land there.

The cliff rose above the village for six hundred feet, slightly overhanging the base by a goodly amount, she recalled. The summit was crowned with the ancient tower, a broad cylinder of stone that rose five stories to a gentle hemisphere cap constructed entirely of metal—which dated to the very earliest days of the place, as Sister Amora had helpfully supplied. A winding switchback path was cut into the face of the rock of the escarpment that led up to the unusual mountain.

Gatina had a great desire to ascend to the very tallest height of the place and look out over the lands below. More, she was intensely curious about the legendary store of books and archives in the temple proper that her father had mentioned. What secrets were hidden in the dusty recesses of the place? What ancient legacies lingered in the dark corners of the antiquated temple? She could not wait to explore it.

That was unlikely anytime soon, she knew. It was rare, from what she'd heard, for any Nocturn Initiate to be invited up to the great tower, much less allowed to prowl its inner recesses, searching for lost lore. That was a privilege largely reserved for Sworn Nocturns who had committed to taking oaths to become Nightbrothers or Nightsisters in their own right. The very smartest and most dedicated to the Mysteries of Sagan. Not curious kittens or nosy thieves.

She would have to be patient, she knew, as Sister Amora concluded her lecture with the late Duke Lenguin's gift of a fifty-acre estate to the abbey around the time she was born. She could do that, she knew. Indeed, if Avorrita could endure more lectures like this, then Gatina could bide her time before she pillaged the tower of its ancient knowledge.

Indeed, she reflected as she and the other girls filed out of the chamber and headed for the mathematics room, the prospect of exploring might be the only thing that kept her sane.

CHAPTER FIVE

LESSONS

Mathematics is the language of understanding the nature of the Cosmos. From the simple matter of counting to the most abstract and obscure formulas, knowledge of mathematics is essential to peer beyond the veil of ignorance and glimpse the fundamental underpinnings of the universe. It separates us from the animals, glorifies the human intellect, and gives us kinship with the very gods.

*— from **The Litany of the Cosmos***

"Usually, a Nocturn's vows leave them in service of the temple for two years."

Sister Nimandi's words haunted Avorrita as she struggled to solve the difficult math equation assigned to her and her fellow Nocturn Initiates. The idea that she might be consigned to a sea of mathematics for that long suddenly sounded horrific. She was very glad she would not be taking up such permanent service in the Saganite Order.

She had no *idea* how much math was actually involved in star-casting. She also had not realized how terrible she was at math. Simple arithmetic was one thing; she could count money or figure a percentage, and she was passingly familiar with multiplication and division. Gatina had been confident in her abilities when she first sat down in the chamber.

That confidence was gone after the second problem. Indeed, when the aging Dusksister Lestine began to explain some of the more advanced concepts and gave the girls examples to work through, Avorrita realized that there was far more to mathematics than what Gatina was familiar with. The groans and grunts of exasperation around her indicated that she wasn't the only one whose illusions were being shattered by the steady march of numbers Sister Lestine was hurling at them.

Frustrated, she used her hand to wipe yet another wrong answer off her slate. The dust caught her off guard and caused her to have a sneezing fit—nearly dislodging the dental prosthetic in her mouth—which disrupted the other Nocturns and brought the nun's focus to her.

Dusksister Lestine had been at the temple since she was a girl, she had revealed at the beginning of the class. From her wizened appearance and creaky old voice, Gatina guessed that she'd arrived sometime around the ancient temple's founding.

"Nocturn Avorrita, would you care to show us your progress on the equation?" the elderly nun asked, mistaking Gatina's frustration as a sign of completion. She felt everyone's eyes on her as she flushed under her fake freckles with embarrassment. *If only I could vanish in plain sight like Father,* she thought.

"No, Sister Lestine, I am not ready to share," she admitted guiltily. "Not until I get it right. I am finding this to be much more difficult than I thought it would be." Indeed, she had no answer on her slate. To their credit, her classmates did not laugh, which made her feel a little less anxious. She saw that very few of them had solved the problem.

The nun clucked her tongue as she looked over Gatina's shoulder at the string of numbers and symbols. "Don't worry, girl. I've beaten these equations into generations of heads over the years. I see you have been through several iterations, Nocturn Avorrita. It sounds as if you are not the only one having difficulties. Why don't you try your work on the large slate? Let's just see where you became derailed, shall we?"

Avorrita swallowed hard, her anxiety growing. The nun wanted her to work the equation again, but this time in front of the class. Avorrita looked up at her, hoping that her eyes conveyed her lack of desire to do that, but the nun pointed at the big slate insistently. There was no escape.

Avorrita stood. The slate board loomed in front of her. Once there, she prayed to Darkness that the answer would magically come to her as she slowly wrote out the equation. Sadly, the Darkness did not oblige.

She was frustrated. Gatina had never been confused by mathematical problems before. In fact, at home and with her tutors, mathematics was not a challenging subject. Usually, though, those problems involved figuring things she could imagine easily, like coins or chickens or the distance to an open window. Not mere abstractions and meaningless numbers that didn't represent anything she could determine. Her only solace was that she could blame the fault on dull Avorrita, for whom such struggles were entirely in character, and not her own personality. She realized that it wasn't much of a relief, as Gatina wanted to do well by her House and her alias, and this problem presented what felt like an insurmountable obstacle. And both Gatina and Avorrita were becoming increasingly embarrassed by the lack of understanding.

After a few minutes, when the solution still had not appeared, the old nun sighed. "Nocturn Avorrita is clearly stumped. Does *anyone* have any idea of the answer?" she asked skeptically. Gatina was surprised to see Arryn hesitantly raise her hand. "Nocturn . . . Arryn, is it? Would you care to give this a try?"

"I would, please," the Narasi girl said quietly but confidently as she stood to answer. Leonna gave a skeptical snort as Sister Lestine motioned her to the front and handed her a piece of chalk. Before Arryn began the solution, the girl studied the problem for a moment and then began to aggressively mark down her answer while describing her reasoning. She wrote three quick notes beside the equation and then smoothly explained how to solve three components of the question. In a moment, it was clear to everyone that she had solved it and exactly how she had arrived at the correct answer.

Sister Lestine clapped her hands. "Glorious!" the old nun praised in her creaky voice. "Nocturns, you will soon learn just how important these equations are to understanding the Cosmos. Each of these variables stands for a particular physical property. And you will learn them . . . in time. With practice. But it appears as if someone has some talent with mathematics," she said, nodding at Arryn with a smile. You had a good tutor, I take it?"

"My father taught me, Sister," Arryn admitted. "He's a counting man." That produced another derisive snort from Leonna, which made Arryn wince. While a respectable profession, Gatina knew, keeping accounts was not considered high-status by the nobility in general. Not like Dina's family wine business, which was considered quite respectable. Leonna's attitude toward such a livelihood was all too common in Coastlords, she realized. The old nun shot her a dark look before turning back to Arryn.

"This equation is far beyond mere accounts, Arryn. You have arrived at the correct answer. Do the rest of you follow her reasoning? No? Nocturn Arryn, please again explain your work to the class." Avorrita listened carefully, fascinated by how Arryn came to the answer. It seemed obvious, the way that the Narasi girl explained it.

Avorrita thanked the Blessed Darkness when the temple bell finally rang to end the grueling class. Her palms were sweaty, and she was trembling at the mental effort as she gathered her things and joined the other girls as they left the chamber. It did not seem so casual and inviting now.

She was surprised as she followed the other girls of her group when she recognized her brother moving in the other direction. A flick of his head caught her eye, and she paused, lingering for a moment in the crowded corridor.

"Enjoying your lessons, cousin?" he asked, as he scribbled something on his own slate.

"Nocturn Avorrita has no head for numbers, I'm finding," Gatina confessed.

"And Nocturn Dain is a boor who knows far too much history," Atopol said cheerfully as he showed her the slate. He had scrawled what looked like a random doodle around the edge of it. She only saw it for a moment, but she took the meaning instantly.

It was one of the family codes, a *katkea* which was a simple replacement code. In this one, Atopol had replaced vowels with numbers, so that, she saw to her chagrin, it resembled another mathematics equation. But it was much easier to solve.

CONTACTED SHADOW ABOUT CENSORATE COMING HERE, it read.

Gatina nodded almost imperceptibly, but Atopol saw it. *Shadow* was their father's name-of-art.

"At least the food is decent and the chores are light," he continued as he quietly wiped the message away with his sleeve. "Are the other girls treating you well?"

"We're ... still getting introduced," Gatina acknowledged diplomatically.

"Off to mathematics now," he said eagerly as he pushed past her to catch up with his group. "A billion blessings upon you, Nocturn!"

"Who was that?" Dina asked, suspiciously, when Gatina did likewise.

"My cousin Dain," she said with a shrug, slipping more fully into her alias. "He just wanted to check on me."

"He's . . . handsome," Mathilde suggested hesitantly as her eyes flicked down the corridor at Atopol's retreating form. Dina's smirk showed her agreement . . . and Gatina suddenly felt awkward. She couldn't have her cell mates liking her brother, even in disguise. That was unacceptable.

"He's a hopeless boor," Avorrita assured them. "All he cares about are books and bragging about the books he's read. He tells bad jokes. Clumsy, too," she added, just to discourage them all from any further interest. The last thing she needed was too much entanglement of Atopol's alias with hers.

The tactic failed. "He is still handsome. Is he from a good family?" Mathilde asked, raising an eyebrow.

"Good enough, I suppose," Avorrita shrugged. "It depends on how you measure such things. And I'm *quite* done with numbers for the day," she assured.

———

THE LAST CLASS OF THE MORNING WAS CALLED POETICS, BUT IT LARGELY concerned the rites and rituals of the temple as well as the litany used by the monks and nuns. The Nightbrother who taught the class, Brother Marus, was a stern-looking, clean-shaven man whose black habit and gray hair made him look all the more somber as he lectured. Nor did he have the patience of her previous teachers, expecting the students to absorb the volume of information he recited at once.

There was a lot to learn—the forms of address, the blessings, prayers, and order of daily services seemed easy enough to pick up, to Gatina's mind, but then things became more complicated when the subject of the temple's study was introduced.

The names and numbers of the planets (some of which were invisible to the naked eye, the monk insisted), the size and color of the sun and the two moons, their distances from the surface of Callidore (an unimaginable number, to Gatina's reckoning), and the differences between the various rocks and comets that flew between them.

She found particularly difficult the common names of the constellations of stars in the Sacred Zodiac that provided the guide against which the planets were charted—the Necklace, the Sickle, the Anchor, the Leviathan, the Telescope, the Octopus, the Crab, the Ring, the Hook, the Cat, the Arch, and the Ship—as well as their preferred names in Old High Perwynese.

Brother Marus used a long rod to point to each of them in turn as he explained where they were and what they looked like—though many of them did not seem to look at all like the things they were named for. Worse, they were only a dozen of scores of other constellations in the sky, she learned. But the zodiac constellations were important, the monk insisted, and had to be learned by heart—in order—so that the positions of the moons and the planets could be accurately tracked against them across the sky.

"As Nocturns, you will learn all of these in this class," Brother Marus assured them, despite the confused looks on their faces, "as well as the physical sciences, reading and literature, history, and religious history. Each constellation has a story, a bit of lore about it, to help you remember them. But remember them you will. Indeed, you will be required to recite them back to any Dusksister or Nightbrother on command, and be tested at your initiation at Midsummer," he said, sternly. "Failure to repeat them accurately can lead to *remedial* instruction, if necessary." The way he said the word, it was clear to all that such instruction would not be pleasant.

"In addition, you will learn to identify the directions—north, south, east, and west—with a glance at the sky. You will learn the intricacies and importance of keeping time, for the night sky is the clockwork of the gods.

"And, yes, you will learn a few things about the gods themselves—not the mindless uttering of prayer and hymn," he said, waving his hands dismissively, "or the myths and lore in the litanies of all the temples, but the nature of the Divine in regards to the fundamental nature of the Sacred Cosmos: the forces that keep the planets on their courses and your feet on the ground; the lightning creeping across the sky and the light of the sun; the secret powers that bind matter together and weave it into everything from a grain of sand to the mind of the mightiest leviathan. We are all related, for we are all composed of starstuff.

"Those are the important elements of the Divine. Not prayers in temples—even in our august institution—not blind belief and ignorant faith, not rite, ritual, or sacrifice. The gods, my dear Nocturns, dwell within the atomi of the Cosmos. Within sacred light and Blessed Darkness. And within the hearts, souls, and, most importantly, the *minds* of everyone in this chamber. The secrets of the Cosmos and the minds of the gods will both be laid bare to you, should you persist in your studies."

Gatina could not wait to start *those* lessons. Brother Marus might seem stern, she reflected, but he had a quiet passion and a sincere enthusiasm for his subject that was contagious. She had rarely considered such lofty matters, of course—she'd been far too preoccupied with practical matters, like learning to steal and mastering an alias.

But there was something special—sacred, even—about the passionate lecture. She had no doubt of the monk's desire to understand the universe and teach others what he'd learned. His enthusiasm was contagious. Her other teachers were clearly competent, to her reckoning—Sisters Lestine and Amora were knowledgeable about their subjects, even intent upon them. But neither showed the passion and enthusiasm that Brother Marus displayed. She found herself excited about poetics far more than she expected . . . and far beyond how she felt about history and especially mathematics.

"This day seems long already, and we haven't even had luncheon!" complained Leonna when the bell signaling the end of class finally rang. "I can't believe I stayed awake during that dull lecture—all those stars! All those words!" she said with a snort of disgust. "It all sounds like a lot of mystical superstition to me."

"Afternoons should prove more enjoyable," Mathilde commented with a shrug, ignoring Leonna's dismissive conclusion. "Those are supposed to be more active classes, the ones that are tailored to our interests and abilities."

"Which means we'll all end up playing badminton or lawn bowling in good weather and chess or backgammon in the rain," suggested Arryn, frowning. "Or, worse, needlework! I got quite enough of that sort of thing back in Raida. I want to do more than that."

"From what I understand, we won't be wasting our time on idle amusements," warned Dina. "The afternoons are given over to practical skills, I've heard. I'm curious about that myself," she admitted. "What, precisely, do they consider practical? Archery?" she asked eagerly. "I've always enjoyed that!"

"It changes from week to week," reminded Leonna with a frown. "Our illustrious house sister is to make the initial determinations. It will be up to Nimandi to decide what wretched activity we're forced to learn. So, she's who you will want to bribe if you want to escape flower arranging or painting," the Coastlord girl assured them.

"I quite like painting," Avorrita objected quietly. Which was quite in character with her alias, Gatina was certain. But she hoped Sister Nimandi would include climbing in her activities. Sitting still for so long was irritating, and nothing promised her more joy and recreation than scaling a wall or tree. The Tower Wood, which provided a buffer from the Palomar Temple and the rest of the property, had some gloriously tall trees peeking over the roofs of the temple complex, and she wanted to climb them. Gatina could only imagine the views. Of course, they would never allow her to climb the great tower of the temple itself, but that did not stop her from suddenly wanting to, very badly.

Sister Nimandi gathered them up a moment later, leading them out to the courtyard where several trestle tables had been set by the temple's cooks for luncheon. The aroma of fresh-baked meat pies filled the air, and Gatina noticed that there were tea, lemonade, and weak ale available on one table as Sister Nimandi pulled her charges into a knot around her. The nun politely inquired about their classes and patiently heard their complaints (largely from Leonna, Avorrita noted), addressing a few matters before she released them to eat.

"Nocturns, after you dine, you have a few hours to rest and tend to your studies before Third Bell. At that time, you will be sent to your afternoon activities until Fifth Bell. We will gather again at the house before Twilight Vespers, when you will have your first night devotions," she informed them. "And I remind you, there is to be no . . . *fraternization* with the male Nocturns," she said, biting her lip. "Being away at Temple often leads to some impetuous souls to consider breaking their schedules for such . . . explorations. The Darkness conceals many secrets—but the temple does *not* tolerate certain activities. We will ensure that rules are enforced, and we will strive to provide guidance and support as you navigate your first season at Palomar Abbey."

That produced some snorts and giggles amongst her group, Avorrita noted. It also suggested that there had already been some incident. She couldn't imagine sneaking out of the hall to meet some boy. Sneaking out to climb a tower or steal something valuable, certainly, but a *boy*? The idea produced a wry smile on her lips but there were those in her group she could well imagine might be tempted.

The nun scanned their faces, then nodded. "I think I've got a good cell of Nocturns here," she praised them. "I'm sure there won't be *any* trouble with such a bright and clever assembly. Now go eat," she encouraged. "And rest when you can. If you think you're tired now, just wait a week!"

CHAPTER SIX

THE TWO TORCHES

Every light creates shadow, be it the light of the sun or light from a simple taper. A single light reveals the shape of those things in its path. Bear a torch in the darkness and you discern your own form on the ground below. Bear two torches, and while the light is brighter, the shadows multiply and confuse the mind and the soul.
— *from **The Litany of the Cosmos***

A WEEK LATER, GATINA HAD A VERY FINE APPRECIATION FOR SISTER NIMANDI'S prediction. She was *exhausted.*

In the long week that she had been at Palomar Abbey, Avorrita had busied herself with mastering the schedule of classes, the demanding mental work, the reading, and the devotions required for a Nocturn Initiate. She had seen her brother only twice in that time, passing in the corridors or briefly at luncheon, and barely had time to speak with him. She hadn't seen her father even once, in his disguise, and she wondered daily what he was busy with. Surely, she reasoned, he would not be wasting his time with the drudge work to which his alias was suited.

Her days had settled into a rigorously predictable pattern after that first week. Between classes, meals, and services, she and the other girls in her group—and in the greater hall—got to know each other a bit better. She developed a genuine appreciation and affection for a few—she had come to quite admire Dina, the northern girl, for her forthright nature and willingness to challenge Leonna's high-handed manner. Arryn had revealed herself to be very insightful and learned, despite her shy presentation. Mathilde was a deep thinker—a plotter and planner, in Gatina's mind—whose mind was always grinding away on something. But though she seemed aloof, she never failed to have a kind word for Avorrita.

And even Leonna, to Avorrita's surprise, was not entirely awful. Once the Coastlord girl's initial complaints had settled into predictable grumbles and she had put aside any idea of changing the institutions of the abbey to suit her convenience, Leonna appeared to settle down herself. She still complained quite a bit, of course—that was clearly in her nature—but she became less vicious with her mates as she realized she needed to depend on them and their good will. After a week, she had largely found Nocturns in other cells to direct her ire toward instead.

There was little news from outside the abbey, Gatina realized as she celebrated her first week at Palomar. After the bulk of the new Nocturns had arrived, there was little traffic between the remote estate and the rest of the world beyond the occasional pilgrim. That meant Gatina had little information about what was going on in Falas, what Count Vichetral was up to, and how the conspiracy was faring against him.

That was both a good and bad thing, she decided: hiding at Palomar provided excellent cover for her family because it was obscure and remote, but it also insulated them from the pulse of political events, and she was hungry for news. About the only development she was aware of was the abbot journeying to Falas for a great ecclesiastic meeting, in the wake of the vile executions amongst the senior clergy that Vichetral had ordered.

It was frustrating, not knowing, but it was also good to practice patience, she told herself unhelpfully. A good thief stayed hidden until the right moment, she reasoned, and then moved decisively. She was safe in the shadows now. But bearing two separate and very different personalities in her head at the same time was challenging. It was like bearing two torches, and she had to be aware of both at all times.

If Gatina was frustrated, Nocturn Avorrita was industrious, throwing herself into the comforting routine of the Timemaster's bells. The Saganites prayed a lot—at rising, at midnight, at three hours past midnight, and just before dawn. Learning the clockwork of services provided a rigorous regularity to her life: greeting the sunrise at Lauds services in the hall's garden, the Hour of the Sun every day at noon, the Vespers of Twilight as the sunset began, Nonces at the ninth bell, when the first stars appeared in the sky, and Matins at midnight.

Each had a liturgy and hymn reflecting on the meaning of the change of hour and the endless rotation of the world under the sky. Nocturn Avorrita quite enjoyed the simple devotions between chores, work, and other activities. They provided a predictable structure for her day.

Gatina, the Kitten of Night, on the other hand, found them pointless and usually boring. Even her afternoon activities were getting tiresome. She'd spent three days at the butts, practicing archery, which she had found gratifying, but then had been turned over to an elderly Dusksister for painting lessons when Sister Nimandi discovered her sketching in her box bed. Now she was using watercolors to depict flowers from the gardens. That wasn't something the Kitten of Night was pleased by. Nocturn Avorrita, however, found the lessons helpful and soothing. Gatina realized, however, that she might be able to work on her cards during that activity.

She had, of course, maintained her alias religiously for the last week. Avorrita was quiet, dull, and introspective, and she dutifully played her role—though she was desperately eager to indulge in some kind of adventure. She had long since given up her feelings of frustration, accepting that what would be at the temple would simply be. But she resented the timing of events. There were revolution and rebellion going on in Alshar, and she was stuck at a quiet, boring old temple in the countryside.

It wasn't always easy. History was boring. Math was hard and growing harder. And Leonna was insufferable sometimes. After one week, Gatina was very much ready to lock her into her sleeping box. She was pleasantly surprised that Nocturn Avorrita largely approved of the idea.

But, thankfully, Gatina thought Avorrita had blended in as a Nocturn so far. She had attended her classes and temple devotions, and she had worked every morning and evening in the garden as her chore. She was entirely unremarkable, merely one girl amongst many.

The garden, she quickly discovered, was one of the more enjoyable chores compared to doing laundry, milking cows, or gathering eggs. Though it involved a lot of hard work, she found gardening to be both educational and rewarding, which surprised her. She didn't mind the hard work, and she liked to learn about the various crops, which included all manner of tubers and root vegetables, carrots, and kale. There was something fascinating about seeing the vegetable you picked in the morning wind up in the evening's meal. And working at night, when it was cooler, was a much more pleasant experience than being on the streets of Falas as a nit. But it still made her tired.

Nightbrother Henri, who supervised the garden, had explained that the vegetables the students were caring for would be used in meals, preserved, and stockpiled throughout the coming winter to feed not only those at the abbey but also the occasional pilgrim or visitor. The abbey also traded vegetables for meat and other produce with local vendors, including Lindule Hall, which he said was the closest estate—about five miles away—and had the best cattle. Another estate of note, he said, was Sunidal Manor, locally famous for its orchards. He promised their apples and fruit were better than anything the students in his charge had ever tasted. Brother Henri also said that the best grains came from the Great Vale and listed out the three estates above the escarpment where Palomar got its bread.

Gatina was intrigued that a temple devoted to studying the stars employed such an earthy man; in an abbey full of starwatchers, Brother Henri was nothing if not practical.

"Just because we study stars does not mean we should get lost in them," he lectured the Nocturns on their first day at the gardens. "Our minds cannot contemplate the Sacred Cosmos when our bellies are empty and our eyes are starved of pleasure."

He had a point, Avorrita realized as she got to work pulling weeds. All that hard work made her hungry, too. It was a different type of hunger from the physical training and sword play, and it was a different type of muscle soreness she felt every night when she tumbled into her box bed, too. She was so hungry sometimes that she thought about swiping a stray carrot and stashing it in her habit to eat later, but she didn't.

She wasn't a nit anymore, after all. She was a Nocturn Initiate who was quite well fed. The work, however, was rewarding. She would miss the gardens when she was rotated into another chore.

Complaints about chores were the most common form of evening entertainment around the table, she discovered, and it had fallen into a predictable pattern. Usually led by a loud and vociferous complaint from Leonna, and then a wry remark from Dina, followed by sniping by the others; only mathematics received more discussion as a grievance. From what the other girls had said, the other chores were not nearly as enjoyable, and Avorrita was happy to have been chosen for the garden and not laundry duty, which Arryn found particularly distasteful, as it involved mending torn habits and scrubbing soiled underclothes.

Nearly every night, the girls' discussion about chores had quickly descended into arguing about who was better from a social class standing, who had a more distinguished lineage and more honorable ancestors, and which of Alshar's various cultures was superior in standing. Avorrita found that argument tiresome and simply volunteered for the garden again when asked her preference.

"That is so *typical* of your type!" Leonna had hissed at her when she finally gave her opinion. Avorrita leveled her blank gaze, sizing up the dark-haired girl, unsure what she meant. "Oh, pretend you don't know," the girl continued, irritated. "You provincial families seem to delight in playing in the dirt!"

Maid Avorrita of Dentran kept her cool, but Gatina seethed inside. She reconsidered locking Leonna inside her bed box. Before she was able to formulate a calm reply, Dina interjected.

"Your family farms the land, just as hers does!" the northern girl reminded her.

"Our family owns our estates; we don't work them," objected Leonna. "Our *peasants* farm."

"How do you know they're doing it right, if you don't know how to farm, then?" Avorrita asked, slowly.

The question caught Leonna by surprise. "What? Because the harvest comes in, of course. And then the peasants pay their rents. It's not our business to know how they produce."

"So, without your peasants, you'd starve," chuckled Arryn as she folded away her clothes fresh from the laundry.

"Someone has to grow the food," Leonna dismissed. "And someone has to own the land. It's bad enough we have to pay to have it farmed. But Father says that the Council of Counts may have a solution for that," she grinned. "He says that he favors returning to the practice of agricultural indentures. That would save us a lot of money," she assured.

"Agricultural indentures . . . Do you mean *slavery?*" Dina asked, appalled.

"It would be less expensive than paying peasants to do it," she assured them. "You just pay for them once, and then you just feed them. After that, the work gets done for free."

"That's barbaric!" Arryn gasped. "The Dukes forbid the practice of slavery!"

"It would save a lot of coin," Leonna insisted. "All the gentry think so. The Dukes of Alshar were shortsighted when they banned the practice. If our ships take prisoners at sea, what else should we do with them until their ransoms are paid?" she asked, as if it was the simplest equation in the world.

"And without the money you pay your peasants for their labor, how will they pay their rents for their land?" challenged Dina.

"That is not our problem," Leonna said, shaking her head. "They will pay or they will be put out. They can work for each other, or take in the laundry, or whatever they need to do, if they want to keep living on our lands."

"Slavery," Arryn said, shaking her head sadly. "That's . . . That's . . ."

"It's simple economics," Leonna said. "And it would be good for Alshar. That's what the Coastlord gentry believes, anyway. It's only pragmatic to use captives in labor. Perhaps the Narasi have some simplistic ideas about such things, but the Coastlords aren't nearly as idealistic. Neither are the Sea Lords," she added, glaring at Arryn. "The smart ones, anyhow," she added, her eyes narrowing accusingly at the girl who claimed half of that lineage.

That made Arryn blush. Gatina was aware of the torrid history of slaveholding in Alshar—it had been the subject of an entire day's lesson in Sister Amora's class that week. The Sea Lords had begun the practice by indenturing sailors taken aboard prizes at sea if they could not arrange a ransom. The Coastlords had institutionalized the practice, however, and had once held thousands of slaves to work their fields and orchards during the Later Magocracy. Only after the Narasi barbarians had arrived and pressed their claim on Alshar had they eventually forbidden the practice and freed those held in bondage for generations.

"The smart Sea Lords realized they were being taken advantage of by the Coastlord merchants, and wisely stayed out of trade in human bondage," Arryn said evenly.

"And the Narasi Vale Lords were smart enough to ban the trade altogether," Dina agreed with a sniff.

"My folk have never supported it," added Avorrita with a shrug. "We've always supported our peasants. They are more like family than tenants, back home." That wasn't far from the truth—her father had always had a good relationship with his tenants back at Cysgodol Hall. But that only seemed to inflame Leonna more.

"The provincial petty nobles of the Coastlands used to know how to respect the leadership of the gentry about such policies!" she said, her nostrils flaring. "Instead of dogging our heels for favors and position!"

She looked at the pretty girl, wondering how someone so lovely could be so ugly and full of anger. Gatina wanted to slap her face. Avorrita shrank back, her eyes wide.

"Why . . . I've never asked you for anything!" Avorrita protested. "Nor my family! Why would we?" she snorted. "There's nothing you have that we can't find better elsewhere!"

That didn't dissuade the Coastlord girl. Leonna sniffed, drawing her head up and back from Avorrita, as though she had caught a whiff of the sewer in Falas. "You know, your freckles are unbecoming, there's something wrong with your eyes, and your teeth look weird," the girl said, her voice low, nearly a whisper. "I would bet my dowry that your family is not as lordly as you pretend. All of you downriver types are the same, just taking advantage of the rest of us. I *refuse* to allow you to take advantage of me." The final sentence was issued as a challenge, not a dare or statement of fact.

Leonna's response took Avorrita aback. She wasn't sure, at that moment, what it had meant or from where it had come. *What triggered that?* she thought, mystified by the attack. She knew she had to respond quickly, lest she lose an opportunity to both prove herself capable and defend herself in the future. Avorrita might be dull, but she was not to be cowed by such pettiness.

"I beg your pardon?" Avorrita answered. "I do not know what you mean, but I do not appreciate your tone or your intention. When have I *ever* given cause to think that I would take advantage of you? And for *what?* The chores? We all have to help earn our keep and the chores are how we do that. Someday, you might need to know how to weed a garden," she proposed, reasonably enough.

"I assure you I shall marry well enough to ensure that I never have to weed a garden!" Leonna huffed. "Perhaps *you* will need to, with a face like that, but—"

"That is *quite* enough!" Dina exploded, her eyes flashing angrily as she confronted the girl. "No one wants to take advantage of you, Leonna! In fact, I think most of us don't want to associate with you much at all! The way you complain, the way you treat us all, the way you act like you're better than the rest of us—"

"Isn't that obvious?" Leonna shot back harshly as she turned toward the northern girl. "I have been raised with the very best tutors, enjoying the highest society, and to appreciate the finest elements of culture . . . not something a *Narasi* would understand, of course," she said, with an arrogant toss of her head. "Be honest with yourselves: you all envy me for that," she concluded. "You enrich yourselves by my presence here. Someday you will brag about it. *That* is how you take advantage of me!"

"Yes, our lives are all improved by your presence!" Mathilde said with a sarcastic roll of her eyes. It was unusual for the quiet girl to speak so forthrightly, but Leonna's tantrum had clearly upset her as much as everyone else. "All you have done since you came here is complain, insult us all, brag about your Imperial heritage, and act as if we're less than servants. No one cares about the great Coastlord House you are from," she pronounced acidly. "In fact, you reflect poorly on your lineage by your behavior. I pity your future husband for what he will have to endure," she added, her eyes narrowed. It was clear that the prediction stung Leonna.

"You are all just jealous!" Leonna spat, whirling on the girl. "You cannot stand that I am making you look so poorly, and so you contrive to attack me and talk behind my back!"

"I'm *quite* comfortable saying what I think to your face," Dina assured her coolly. "Consider it a fault of my barbaric Narasi bluntness. We have an unfortunate reputation for plain speaking," she reminded her. "Perhaps we just aren't as subtle as Coastlords. But we do strive to be polite while we're pointing out what a simply *awful* person you are, at least!"

"I agree, Leonna," Arryn said, before Leonna could respond. "I am the oldest of five children and the only girl. I've never even heard my little brothers talk to someone in such a manner! In the eyes of the Saganite Order, we are supposed to be sisters. I've never had a sister, but this is not how sisters act, at least to my mind." Arryn paused to look at the other girls, who nodded in agreement. "Perhaps your vaunted ancestry and upbringing never concerned such matters, but your behavior has been appalling. You owe Avorrita an apology. You owe us all an apology. This is neither the place nor the time for your misplaced anger, as not one of us here has wrought that on you! Coastlord or Sea Lord, Narasi or Imperial, propriety demands an apology for that kind of nastiness."

A chorus and nods of agreement led Leonna to finally reconsider her position. In the face of a consensus against her, she was forced to relent. It gave Avorrita a tiny thrill of victory when the Coastlord girl finally took a deep breath and did just that, though her jaw was set and her teeth were clenched as she delivered the carefully worded, barely acceptable apology before stomping off.

Gatina doubted the sincerity of her words, of course. If it hadn't been for the overwhelming social pressure and the willingness of the rest of the girls to stand up to her, she had no doubt that Leonna would have continued her abuse indefinitely. While Avorrita accepted her apology at face value like a lady of breeding should . . . Gatina wanted to grab the insufferable girl by the hair and smash her face into the nearest box bed or push her down a well or something, which might be awkward to explain.

It was difficult bearing two such torches, but she managed. That was a small victory.

But she had learned something valuable: Leonna's outburst had revealed the willingness of some to accept the reinstitution of slavery. She wondered about the girl's other politics and whether Leonna and her family, therefore, supported the vile Count Vichetral. If so, Gatina thought, the girl very much might need to be locked into her sleeping box.

In any case, she would be keeping a close eye on Leonna, she decided. She doubted the girl could be trustworthy. Her vicious nature and her high opinion of herself seemed to mask some other problem, Gatina figured, and it raised an alarm in her mind.

Not that Avorrita bothered with that sort of suspicion. Her demure alias was quite content to let Leonna get away with such behavior as long as it wasn't directed at her. Avorrita was dull and wanted to get along with everybody. It took a lot of effort to suppress Gatina's more violent impulses.

But the conflict had reminded her of something important: *her eyes.* When the Coastlord girl pointed out the flaws in her features, she had mentioned how her eyes looked funny . . . and she wasn't wrong about that, at least. Gatina realized that the spell that concealed her violet eye color was fading. She knew she had to seek out her father, in whatever disguise he was wearing, and get him to refresh the enchantment before she attracted more attention. She could not bear two torches of her identity if she suddenly showed up to breakfast with purple eyes. People would talk . . . and Leonna most of all.

She wanted to dismiss the girl's unreasonable and unpleasant attitude toward her and the others, and she was tempted to do just that. Avorrita did not seek any trouble.

But Gatina knew better. She recalled her mother's voice in her head, reminding her to never underestimate anyone. Particularly someone who was so quick to judge and take offense at . . . well, everything. Mother would urge caution with someone like that.

She was soon borne out. While she was more polite on the surface, after the argument, Leonna began shifting the focus of her aggravation from the Saganite Order to Avorrita and Dina, making both girls the target of her quiet rage without crossing the frontier into such open hostility once again. Leonna didn't overtly challenge either of them anymore, but her comments were universally unfriendly and frequently unkind in the worst way.

The only good thing that arose from it was the feeling among the other girls that they were united on at least one topic: Leonna was awful. Perhaps it was not the foundation of some mystic sisterhood, but it did help bind them into a friendship.

CHAPTER SEVEN

THE MYSTERIOUS ARCH

*In antiquity, the Sagan Institute was founded to provide a haven
for those called to the sacred study of the Blessed Darkness and the
eternal heavens above. In their wisdom they chose to build Palomar
Abbey as a place of refuge and observation of our ancestors, the
sacred stars, from whom all things are descended. For, as Sagan
declared, we are all made of starstuff, and every fragment of our
being was once forged in the belly of a star. Our observations of the
heavens are truly just our celestial souls peering back at the billions
of blazing ancestors of the Sacred Cosmos.*

*— from **The Litany of the Cosmos***

"What's that?" Avorrita asked Nightbrother Henri as she lugged
a basket of cuttings to the far end of the garden. This portion was too
close to the cliff face to get enough sun for most things, the monk had
explained, but there were plenty of vegetables that preferred less sunlight
and more shade.

The thing that had attracted Gatina's attention wasn't a natural part
of the cliff, however; it seemed to be some sort of square stone arch set
within the natural rock, at least ten feet high and twice that across. There
were two lintels a foot wide on each side, supporting a thick slab that
protruded slightly from the rock. The entire thing was covered with vines
and foliage to the point where if she had been standing next to it, she
likely wouldn't have noticed, but from this distance it was clearer that the
structure was artificial . . . and woefully out of place.

"That, Nocturn, is a remnant of the abbey's founding," the old monk
explained patiently as he paused on the garden path. "You have a good eye.
It's been here since the beginning, according to the lore. No one knows why
it was built or what it was used for, but it's at least as old as the temple," he

said, glancing toward the tower looming overhead. "It's one of the ways we know about our founding. The inscription is clear enough," he added.

"Inscription?" she asked as the other girls filed through the garden with hoes and baskets, so enrapt in their conversations that they hadn't even seen the arch. "There's an inscription?"

"In Old High Perwynese, of course," nodded Brother Henri. "A simple one. It reads THE SAGAN INSTITUTE. That's an old Perwynese word for *temple*," he added. "That's how we know the place has been run continuously for all of these centuries."

Avorrita nodded and studied the arch more carefully. Yes, she decided, she did see some sort of faint writing carved out of the rock, but it was so old and weathered that it wasn't clear enough to read. It did add something to the garden, though, she decided. Like those fake ancient ruins some Coastlords had installed on their grounds to make believe that they were living on some ancient remnant of Imperial civilization, it lent a bit of mystery to the place.

But there was more to the arch than met the eye, Gatina knew instinctively. Indeed, the certain sense that she'd possessed since childhood was bothered by the arch. Since she was a little girl, Gatina had been able to sense the presence of metals—all sorts of metals—just by proximity. It had helped to make her an adept thief and promised a stronger *rajira* to come. Most of the time, she didn't even realize she was doing it, until something unusual came along that challenged her senses.

That strange ability was screaming at her now. There was *metal* behind the earth and foliage under the arch, she knew with certainty. A great gob of metal, some sort of iron . . . or steel. Or perhaps something more exotic—she could not determine its exact composition, but she had no doubts that there was a lot of metal buried just inches away under the accumulated soil and foliage under the arch.

"Are there any more of these . . . arches?" she asked curiously, desperately trying to sound like a provincial simpleton.

"Oh, the abbey holds a few old mysteries," assured the gardener with a chuckle that was pregnant with meaning. "The Ancients often had a peculiar way of looking at things. They built things for which we have no understanding now. I'm sure they were important in their time, but a lot of the unimportant things were lost over the years. That thing was built there before the very first archmage took power in Perwyn," he reminded her. "A lot of things have happened in the world since then."

Gatina shuddered involuntarily at the thought. This place had been centuries old when her illustrious ancestor, Kiera the Great, had come to Alshar from Vore. It was there when the first Sea Lords had built their havens along the Great Bay. It had been old when the Coastlords had established the Counties of Falas and Rhemes. It had been old when the Narasi had conquered the Magocracy and elevated the first Duke of Alshar. The feeling of age seemed to permeate the soil there in Ejecta.

"How has it survived?" Avorrita wondered, aloud.

"Because no one thought to destroy it—even if they could," chuckled Henri. "The abbey has either been too important to attempt its destruction . . . or believed it too unimportant to bother with. I only hope that continues to hold true," he added with a troubled note to his voice.

"What do you mean?" Avorrita asked, because it was the kind of dumb question dull Avorrita would ask.

Brother Henri considered thoughtfully, choosing his words carefully. "The new Council of Counts in Falas that has risen since the Duke died is . . . not entirely popular with some folk," the monk explained with a critical sigh. "With quite a few folk, actually. That rascal Vichetral is moving against that opposition. He's brought his soldiers from Rhemes," he supplied grimly. "And worse. Don't be surprised if we have visitors appear here at the abbey."

"Pilgrims?" Avorrita asked, confused.

"No, lass. Not pilgrims . . . Royal Censors," he warned, softly.

Avorrita's eyes got big. It was one thing to hear such rumors in the streets and shops of Ejecta from the gossip of innocent noblewomen; it was quite another to hear it from the lips of one of the abbey's clergy.

"Censors? Why would they come here?" Gatina asked breathlessly.

"Ostensibly, to oversee the training of the Talented students and ensure that all of our parchment is in order. But their real purpose can only be guessed at."

"And what would you guess, Brother?" she probed.

Henri looked around and cleared his throat nervously. "They're looking for . . . spies. *Traitors.* The children of families who oppose the Council of Counts. Loyalists to the late Duke and Duchess. And general troublemakers. It's rather stupid, actually. The abbey doesn't get involved in politics. The stars are weighty-enough matters for our attention." Though the monk spoke with calm assurance, Avorrita could tell by his voice that there was room for some doubt about that. She was starting to suspect that no one would be able to avoid getting involved in politics, with what was going on in Falas. People, institutions, and even the temples would be forced to take sides eventually, she guessed.

"What happens if they come?" she asked, her voice just above a whisper.

"We . . . we will contend with it," the old monk said, reluctantly. "That is all we can do. The abbot will cooperate as much as he can, as long as they do not interfere with the Great Work. I've heard him say that himself when he spoke of the potential of their visit."

"They wouldn't dare disturb the holy temple!" Gatina said in Avorrita's naïve voice.

In truth, she knew the Censorate would dare to interfere with anything they chose. She had heard enough tales about the checkered-cloaked regulators from the family's histories to understand that. The Censorate was not answerable to *anyone*, not even the Five Dukes. Their order predated the Five Duchies and was, by tradition, established by the Narasi king who had led the Conquest. Even after he had died without naming an heir, four centuries earlier, the Censorate he founded had maintained his royal authority in their business. No duke could override that.

That meant that they could go where they wished with impunity, and they could arrest anyone suspected of violating the Bans on Magic at a whim. They could imprison them, try them in a Censorate court, and even execute them—or burn the magic out of their brains with spells that sometimes left their victims mere imbeciles afterward.

"They would be hard pressed to," admitted Henri with a grunt. "Our temple is not as powerful as the Huinites or the Tryggites, nor nearly as large and wealthy, but we are essential to Alshar's dominance of the seas. Interfering with us would harm that work and therefore the merchant fleets. The Council of Counts would be foolish to do that. If we do not deliver an accurate ephemeris table and other charts to the duchy on time, then navigating through the Straits of Sinjar and beyond is nearly impossible. But," he continued with a sad sigh, "that doesn't mean they won't try. Don't worry, little Nocturn; the temple will protect all who study here. You need not worry about such serious matters. Ah! The bell! Time for you to head to your lessons," he said, taking the basket from her. "Try to put all of this out of your mind. You have more important matters to consider."

Of course, Gatina did not stop thinking about the Censorate's possible visit. Indeed, the idea haunted her throughout her classes that morning. Her family would be in danger if they came—as would many others.

She'd heard other rumors, of course. The girls gossiped incessantly during and between classes, at meals, and at chores. And Gatina was very good at overhearing conversations to which she was not party. It was the only way she could get any news, as unreliable as it was.

Some of it she could discount as false on the surface, of course. There were wild tales about rebellions and revolts in Rhemes and among the northern Vale Lords that were clearly fabricated or exaggerated. Count Vichetral ruled Rhemes with an iron fist, and most of the Narasi who farmed the great plains above the escarpment were largely uninterested in politics that did not affect their own fiefs. Farisian pirates had not invaded the Great Bay, either, she was certain, and there were likely no goblins lurking in the shadows up and down the great Mandros River. That was just silly.

But other bits of news struck her as more likely: that Duke Rard of Castal had declared himself king, and he had expelled the Royal Censorate from the lands he controlled. That one she heard from more than one source, and it matched what she'd learned in Falas in the spring. The backwoods spellmonger who advised the Castali Duke had insisted on it, apparently. Even the Censor General had given up his cloak to take service with the new king, it was said. Many of those Censors who stayed true to their order and their oaths were taking refuge in Alshar, with Count Vichetral, who refused to part ways with four hundred years of tradition. Especially if it served his purposes.

Gatina could not imagine a world where she and her family did not have to worry about the Censorate. They had been considered a necessary evil for so long that they were part of the culture of Alshar, like Sea Lord corsairs and the criminal gangs that dominated the wharfs of the Great Bay.

As descendants of the Imperial Magocracy, the Coastlord families had always been a favorite target of the Censors. It was part of the Narasi Dukes' effort to suppress the powerful nobility of the coasts and the noble houses who produced so many magi who could be used against them. In the early days of the duchy, she knew, plenty of Coastlords had led revolts against Narasi rule. Usually they ended badly, with the leaders executed or fled to Farise and the last shred of the Magocracy left in the world.

But now Farise was in the hands of Castal and Remere, and that remnant of the ancient world was lost forever. Raising a rebellion now against Count Vichetral and his henchmen would be difficult, if not impossible. That did not stop her from contemplating how it could be done.

Such thoughts plagued her until her poetics class, when the lecture from Brother Marus about the movement of the sacred planets was so engaging that she nearly forgot about her earlier obsession. Afterward, it wasn't until luncheon that her mind returned to the matter . . . just in time to be distracted yet again by her brother at luncheon.

"Greetings, Nocturns!" Dain said in an overly enthusiastic manner as he approached the small knot of girls dining together under a tree on bread, butter, bacon, and hard-boiled eggs. Avorrita flinched convincingly as he did so, pretending to be embarrassed by the interruption. "May I borrow Nocturn Avorrita for a few moments? I've had some news from home I wanted to share with my dear cousin."

"News?" Gatina asked skeptically as she pulled herself to her feet.

"What sort of news?" probed Leonna suspiciously. "Is she being sent away?"

"No, no, nothing like that," assured Atopol in his disguise. "Family news, is all. Do you mind?"

"Take her," Leonna said, dismissively. "She's barely spoken a word all morning. Perhaps you'll give her something worth talking about."

With a backward glance at the Coastlord girl, Gatina dutifully followed Atopol as he casually strolled through the crowded courtyard to a tree at the far end of the garden.

"What is this about, then?" she murmured as she followed.

"Just as I said, news," her brother replied, cheerfully. "News and a spell. For your eyes," he reminded her. "They're starting to look terribly purple. Has anyone noticed?"

"Just a bit," Gatina admitted. "I've been waiting for . . ."

"I know," Atopol said quietly, as they were safely out of earshot. "He's been preoccupied, I'm afraid. I saw him two days ago, briefly, and he gave me an update. It was all terribly mysterious, of course, but he's been working."

"On a heist?" she asked in a voice just above a whisper. Her heart raced with excitement at the possibility.

"Shockingly, he did not spare me the details," chuckled her brother. "He said we'll learn in due time. But he did bother to teach me the spell for our eyes. It's actually not complicated, once you understand a few basic rules of photomancy. Here," he said, taking her by the shoulders and directing her to stand next to the tree in front of him. She waited patiently as he closed his own eyes—which were perfectly brown—and then opened them as he whispered a word or phrase she did not understand. There was the slight tingling around her eyelids that she'd come to associate with the spell that disguised her violet eyes.

"There," he said with a sigh. "I did it! Not a trace of your true color. I wasn't sure it would work," he confessed.

"You weren't?" she asked, surprised.

"I've only been studying magic for a year," he reminded her, "and not exactly formally. But Shadow thought this was an easy enough enchantment for me to try. How does it feel?"

"Like it normally does," she decided. "They're a little itchy, but that usually passes quickly."

"That's the thaumaturgic field around . . . Well, no need to get into all that," he said, interrupting himself. "You'll learn about that soon enough if your *rajira* arrives. Any signs of that?" he asked hopefully.

Gatina considered. "Well, this morning, I was in the far part of the gardens and noticed a big stone arch built into the cliff. Something the ancients left behind. I could sense an awful lot of metal under the soil that covered the inside of it. Like the entire thing was made of iron or steel. It was strong."

"That is interesting—both the arch and your reaction to it. Then perhaps your quickening isn't too far off," he concluded. "How about your . . . your . . ."

"My *monthlies?*" she supplied with a small grin as her brother struggled with such a delicate topic. "Nothing yet. But you shall be the first I inform," she declared with a wicked look in her tingling eye. Most men were squeamish and embarrassed about that sort of thing, and Gatina was enough of a little sister to take a bit of delight in that weakness.

"Ugh! No need for that! I was just curious. In any case, I really do have a bit of news from home. Mother is alive and well and working in Falas now, her task at the Great Bay completed, according to Shadow. She sends her love and says she is proud of us both."

"What is she doing back in Falas Town?" Gatina asked, curious.

"I think she's working with our cousin Huguenin, from something Shadow said, but I can't confirm it. Things are apparently heating up at the palace, however."

"Rebellion?" she asked hopefully.

Atopol made a face. "Wouldn't that be nice? No, the Counts have been busy. New emergency decrees, new lists of persons wanted for questioning, new edicts proscribing certain violations of law, that sort of thing. There have been a lot of protests. They've arrested hundreds in Falas Town now, mostly for questioning over their loyalties. One of the boys in my group says his father is a prisoner now. They're looking at everyone. Particularly anyone with a connection to Castal."

"We don't have any connections to Castal," Gatina pointed out.

"Not officially," agreed Atopol. "It's just an excuse to intimidate anyone who is thinking about rising up against Vichetral. There is speculation that he is going to declare himself Duke eventually, but he's not ready for that yet, according to Shadow. But he has extended an invitation to the Censorate," he added, his brow furrowed with worry.

"I just heard that from Brother Henri," Gatina confirmed with a solemn nod.

"Rard expelled them. There are an awful lot of Censors from Castal that are coming here as a result. Vichetral pledged to keep the Bans up, in defiance of Rard's decree, as a way of establishing his legitimacy. That's bad news. Shadow believes that he's using them to help control the duchy and keep any secret Coastlord conspiracies of magi from becoming active." There was a twinkle of amusement in his eye as he said it.

"When will he learn that such things are base rumors or folklore?" Gatina nodded sarcastically. That response was what the Shadow Council promoted in public to hide their very real conspiracy against the Council of Counts. Denying the conspiracy they were actively promoting cast doubts on Vichetral's legitimacy.

"The nobility are often willing to believe all manner of unlikely tales, if it helps support them in power," Atopol agreed with a smirk. "Still, it is best that we're wary."

Gatina suddenly frowned. "We may have cause to be," she said worriedly. "I got confirmation this morning from Brother Henri that they may well be coming *here*—to the abbey where we're supposed to be hiding in safety. The abbot is worried since he returned from Falas Town," she added.

"Everyone with any sense is worried," he sighed. "It's a worrying time. But don't let that disturb you. Just cling to your alias, don't change your story, and hope it doesn't happen in the first place," Atopol counseled. "If it makes you feel better, Shadow said he might have some work for you, soon."

"Really?" Gatina asked hopefully. "That would be *lovely*. Especially if it keeps me from doing math. I'm starting to *hate* numbers," she confided.

"It only gets worse as the lessons go on," he reflected thoughtfully. "You'll get the hang of it. It will get easier once you actually start applying what you've learned. At least, it did for me. I was always confused until I could see what the point of all of it was. Once it becomes useful, it makes more sense," he reasoned.

"I'm not certain if it will ever make sense to me," she replied, shaking her head, discouraged. "My mind has not yet grasped the concept of mixing numbers and letters in mathematical equations. Codes make sense. This type of math does not . . . yet. But some real work would be welcome. I'm starting to really get *bored*," she confessed, letting Avorrita's persona slip away for a moment.

"Me, too," Atopol agreed with a grin. "I mean, I'm learning some interesting things, and the fellows in my group are all fine, for the most part, but . . . well, I couldn't stand it anymore the other night. I snuck out in my working clothes and took a stroll along the rooftops, just to get some practice in." He looked a bit guilty about that, she noted.

Gatina's newly renewed brown eyes bulged. "Dain! You *didn't*! You could get caught!"

Atopol snorted. "Me? Not likely. Not *here*. People go outside at night all the time. Indeed, the biggest challenge is that there are so darn many people awake at night in Ejecta that there's a risk of bumping into someone. But that kept me on my toes. You should try it sometime," he encouraged. "It was refreshing to get into my working blacks once again."

"It's going to be a little harder for me," Gatina decided. "The sisters tend to jealously guard the virtue of the Nocturns. Hence the metal grates on the windows. Not that that would stop me, of course, but it does make things complicated. Besides, I value my sleep more now that I have to get up at odd hours for services and such. But a midnight stroll across the rooftops *would* be lovely. Or just climbing something."

"Like that?" Atopol asked, looking up at the temple tower looming over the village. "I told Shadow that I was surprised you hadn't scaled it yet."

"I'm waiting for a special occasion," she assured him. "If I do it now, I won't have anything to look forward to later."

"I suppose that's one way to look at it. Is there anything else you need?" he asked, concerned. "Anyone giving you any problems?"

"Nothing I cannot handle. The other girls are . . . well, they're being girls, but I can contend with that. Or meek little Avorrita can. There's only one who is really irritating. The only thing I really need is an alibi for why we're talking so long. What's our story? They're going to want to know what all the secretive 'family business' was about."

"How about a distant cousin who's getting married unexpectedly?" he proposed. "That certainly counts as sensitive family business. Say, a Cousin Margine? A dowager who finally landed an aging country knight?"

"That might work," she nodded. "Any convincing details?"

"She has two little dogs that won't stop barking," he decided. "We met her once at another relative's wedding. She was fat, annoying, and no one ever thought she'd get married because of her little dogs."

"I like it," Gatina grinned. "Completely believable, too. Everyone gossips about that sort of thing. Just to let you know, there is some speculation about *you* among my group. Some think you are passing attractive. Your disguise, that is. If they knew how horrifically ugly you really were . . ."

"Thank the Darkness for my skills with makeup and magic, then," he chuckled. "But they think I'm attractive? Really?" he asked, with more interest than Gatina expected. Why would he care what a gaggle of girls thought about him, after all?

"I assured them that you were a fatuous boor who couldn't say three words without talking about yourself and how smart you are," she assured him.

"Best keep the lie close to the truth." Atopol nodded sagely. "But that's . . . interesting. Which ones think that? The pretty Imperial girl who wanted to send you away?"

Gatina made a face. "Leonna? She's horrid; believe me. She's the one I was talking about. Just awful and not at all nice."

"But she's pretty," Atopol pointed out. As if that made up for her glaring character faults.

"They're *all* pretty except for me," Gatina dismissed. "But she is shopping for a husband, if you're interested. I'm sure she comes with a nice dowry. And she'd make your life miserable if you wed."

"Well, as tempting as that might be, you know the family rule: boys marry the best female thieves they can find," he said with a discouraged sigh.

"And girls marry the best wizards they can find," sighed Gatina in return. "In a land where wizards are suppressed and demeaned. I'm sure I'll be a maid as long as our fictitious Cousin Margine. Only, I'll have cats, not dogs."

Atopol was good enough to escort her back to the others before he departed for his afternoon activities. Then the idiot made a point of lightly flirting with Leonna, just to irritate Gatina, she was certain. Thankfully, he stayed completely in character. He was as boorish as a dandy, and he bragged about his superior intellect three times before he finally took his leave.

"That conversation looked intense," Dina noted casually as she lay back in the soft grass. The next bell would ring soon, summoning them to their afternoon classes.

"Were you spying on us?" Avorrita asked, surprised.

"Not spying, just watching," Mathilde suggested with a smirk. "Your cousin is tall, isn't he?" she asked casually.

"He's . . . I suppose." Gatina shrugged. "Compared to me, he is. I never really thought about it. And the news really wasn't much. Just some news about a relative of ours who is unexpectedly getting married in the autumn, apparently."

"Oh!" Arryn asked, her eyes flashing at the hint of scandal. "Is she . . ."

"She's old, she's fat, and she has the two most annoying little dogs you've ever seen," snorted Gatina in Avorrita's best voice. "We've only met her once, at someone else's wedding. No one ever thought she'd be wed. But some half-blind old country knight made a proposal, so there you are."

"That just proves that Ishi puts someone in the world for everyone," Dina said dreamily. "Even if you are old and fat. That should give you some hope, Leonna," she said, digging at the Coastlord girl.

"My father is already receiving some offers for my hand, thank you!" Leonna said, acidly. "Quite a few, actually. He hasn't even set a dowry yet. In fact, I may be betrothed by next year. There are plenty of handsome young knights interested in an alliance with our House. And a comely maiden," she added, as if it were obvious.

"I'm sure your dowry has nothing to do with it, and they are all enamored of your engaging personality and reputation for being agreeable," Arryn suggested sarcastically. That earned her an irritated glare from the Coastlord girl.

"Oh, stop it!" sighed Mathilde, who was clearly irritated by the pointless sniping. "Leonna *is* a beautiful girl. And rich. And well bred. I'm certain she'll get plenty of offers for her hand. And a beautiful wedding," she added.

"As I said, Ishi put someone in the world for everyone. Every pot has its lid, my mother says," Dina explained.

"Actually, my cousin Dain was asking about 'the pretty Coastlord girl' just a moment ago," admitted Gatina, feeling wicked for revealing it. It might inflate Leonna's already-gigantic opinion of herself, but it also presented an unusual opportunity for teasing her.

"Really?" Leonna asked, sitting up on her elbows. "He thinks I'm pretty?"

"Everyone thinks you're pretty, Nocturn," Dina groaned. "At least until you start talking. Then they start looking elsewhere, I imagine."

"And so what if he does? You cannot *possibly* be considering my cousin!" objected Gatina, making Avorrita gasp in disbelief. "He's not a bold warrior or a landholder. Or deaf. Or stupid. Besides, he's so . . . so *boring!*"

"And likely not nearly rich enough to entertain a serious offer," considered Leonna, with a calculating expression on her face. "He is not unattractive, of course—it's hard to tell you two are even related, to be honest—but the rural gentry rarely have the kind of wealth necessary to ally themselves with the great Houses. He's likely to become a clerk, perhaps, or a counting man. Or take holy orders here and spend his life staring at the stars until he's old and blind. Or, worse, develop *rajira* and have to become a practicing adept or something. I prefer a man of action," she said with exaggerated maturity.

"You're *thirteen years old*," Dina said, rolling her eyes. "You're too young to know what kind of man you prefer. And if you did, you'd likely be wrong and regret the choice. My father would never marry me off without my enthusiastic assent. He wants me to be happy, first and foremost."

"You Narasi have odd ideas about marriage," sneered Leonna. "You don't understand how it should be used to build a base of power and security for a great House."

"We understand that it's a way to become miserable and hate your life if you choose the wrong husband," Dina replied, her eyes narrowing. "Marrying for love is just as valid as marrying for treasure, rank, and position. More so, if you believe Ishi's priestesses."

From there the discussion devolved into idle speculation about the institution of marriage and the different perspectives the various cultures had on it. Coastlords, of course, saw it as an opportunity for political alliances. Sea Lords viewed matrimony as a means of gaining economic advantage. The Narasi lauded marriage as a fulfillment of love in song and story—often when it went horribly wrong.

Gatina mostly kept quiet about it, which suited her Avorrita persona just fine. Avorrita wasn't particularly attractive, particularly rich, or particularly important, by design. Speculating about what kind of husband she might end up with was just depressing. Taking holy orders might have been preferable for the plain-looking, quiet girl to a miserable marriage to a man much older than Avorrita just to advance her family's status and wealth.

But she did wonder about her own family's rules on the matter. While they were not concerned in the slightest with rank or position, and certainly not with wealth, they were as stringent as any Coastlord family's.

Kiera herself had laid them down centuries earlier as a means of improving the fortunes and skills of the greatest magical thieves in the Five Duchies. Boys married adept female thieves, regardless of class or status. Girls married wizard adepts who were subtle enough to keep the family's great store of secrets and add to them.

Intellectually, Gatina understood the reasoning for the rules. Like the other Coastlord Houses, the goal was to improve the fortunes of the House, after their manner. Selecting among the best magi and thieves for husbands and wives made sense from that detached perspective. Otherwise, the great legacy of House Furtius would fade eventually, and someday someone might actually get caught . . . or, worse, be better at the trade than they were.

But another part of her was deeply suspicious of the custom. It wasn't so bad for her—there were plenty of wizards in the world, after all, and she was sure she could find one, somewhere, that she could stand to marry without plotting to slay him. But for Atopol, the odds were stacked against him. Thieving tended to be a male-dominated trade, from what she understood. There were few female thieves that were more than pickpockets or blatant opportunists. Finding one who was skilled enough to be considered as a bride seemed impossible.

But, then, her father had met her mother in the middle of a heist, she reasoned. While she hadn't been exactly a professional at the time, she had demonstrated enough skill to warrant his noticing her. Thank the Darkness she had been as passionate and intelligent as even Kiera the Great could ask for, else neither she nor Atopol would have been born.

It gave her a lot to think about, until the bell rang and she reluctantly headed off to painting class.

CHAPTER EIGHT

A CONVERSATION WITH SHADOW

The Rose represents DUTY and LEGACY to my House and my Art. I have begun to craft my personal deck of cards and have chosen the Ace of Ships as the first attempt. While I am unhappy with the artwork, so far, it does depict a maiden on the deck of a ship bearing a rose, a token of duty well-respected in my family. Kiera first came to Alshar from Vore bearing a rose from her beloved, legend says, along with a charge to establish the House here in the west and see it prosper. It is with a significant amount of reflection as to what DUTY and LEGACY mean, both to me and my House, that I compose this card. I may well start again from the beginning, as I am unhappy with the result, so far, though I've made progress. DUTY demands that I complete it. LEGACY insists that I finish it as perfectly as possible. But drawing roses is damn hard.
— from Gatina's Heist Journal,
Palomar Abbey

GATINA WAS GRATIFIED AND EXCITED AT THE NEWS THAT HER FATHER MIGHT have some "work" for her, and not a little intrigued. She knew that Shadow had business in this part of the duchy while his children were being educated at the temple school, but she had figured that it likely involved more spy work and information gathering for the conspiracy than actual thieving. But she truly didn't care what the task was. The prospect of getting away from the abbey—and Leonna—for a few days was enticing to her imagination. She figured that within the week, he might make contact with her and give her some details.

But the very next morning, she unexpectedly spotted the shuffling figure of Dareth making his way across the abbey grounds, pushing a wheelbarrow. She nearly did a double take and just barely caught herself before indulging in something so suspicious. After all, there were hundreds of servants at the abbey. Taking undue notice of one in particular would be out of place for dull Avorrita.

Instead, she lowered her eyes and then very carefully glanced up, catching sight of her disguised father from the corner of her eye. She saw him make a sign with his hand as he scratched his chest through his sweat-stained tunic. He wanted to meet, it indicated.

Gatina's heart began to race as she quietly broke away from the group as they trudged along to class and began walking into Ejecta village proper. It wasn't uncommon for Nocturns to have an errand in the village, after all, and the temple was not so strict as to insist on absolute obedience to their prescribed schedules. She might be going to the shrine to Trygg, for instance, to secure supplies, or to pick up a package from a messenger, or to purchase something from the market or one of the shops. As long as she didn't look too suspicious, it was unlikely that anyone would even question her business in the small village.

She didn't look back over her shoulder, of course, but she could hear the wheel behind her, turning loudly in the gravel of the street.

Hance, with his laden wheelbarrow, was following behind her, giving her the space to avoid suspicion. He was well into his own character as he began to whistle a tune that he knew his daughter would recognize, once she heard it—"The River Barge Song," a favorite tune from when she was a child.

At this hour of the morning, there weren't many people on the streets of Ejecta to witness her passage. There were two village goodwives, she guessed by their clothing, on either side of the high street, both headed away from the village's small residential district, likely going to the Market Square. Each carried a basket for shopping. It was still three days from Market Day, but there were always a few stalls open to sell essentials during the week. Neither one gave her a second glance as they moved briskly by. They saw Nocturns all the time, she reasoned, and one lone girl in a habit was hardly worthy of note. She passed the sweets shop, which, she admitted, smelled delightful. She caught the scent of cooling pies, which made her think of old Drella, their cook back home. That made her smile as she continued on her mission.

When she came to the village well, which was mostly deserted at this time of day, she stopped and waited for her father to catch up.

"Good morning, and a billion blessings upon you, Goodman," Gatina said, casually as her father set down the wheelbarrow. "Have you broken your fast yet? I had porridge this morning. *I've always had a fondness for good . . . porridge.*"

Her pause between *good* and *porridge* was key in the expression, a long-time identification code used by House Furtius and its operatives to determine whether or not someone was included in their secrets. Of course, both of them knew that, but Gatina didn't mind showing off under the circumstances. Her father was always testing her.

Her disguised father nodded, then gruffly replied with the answer to the code.

"*My grandmother's porridge was hearty and . . . delicious.*" He paused to allow the certainty of the phrase to register. "But, thankfully, I secured a basket of rolls from the abbey's bakery. Well done, Kitten," he continued in a murmur. "Let's step away from watchful eyes and discuss some business while we walk around the village, shall we?"

He did not look like her father, not at all, but she knew him emotionally. As good as he was at disguise, his mannerisms were a giveaway.

"You're faring well?" he asked as he shoved the wheelbarrow next to the well. "I spoke to your cousin the other day. He thought you might be having difficulties."

"Only boredom, and a little catfighting in the dormitory," she shrugged. "I have an intense desire to climb something, which is far outside of Avorrita's interests. Nothing a kitten can't handle."

Hance's eyes twinkled, but it wasn't the violet to which she was accustomed. These eyes were pale green, thanks to the same spell Atopol had used upon hers. But they did twinkle.

"Very well, Nocturn Avorrita. But let me know if you have real difficulties."

"I'm more concerned about what you've been up to," she said sincerely.

Her father looked around to ensure that no one was watching. Then he cast a silence spell around them, one she had seen Mother use before.

"Dareth, the occasional carter and frequent liaison of a very special group of Talented magi, has been carting things for the abbey . . . among other duties," he explained. "Indeed, I've had to take a load all the way to the capital this week."

"Falas?" she asked, with a little gasp. "What's happening there?"

Her father frowned. "All manner of things, and few of them are good. The public news is that Vichetral and the other counts are heroically responding to the emergency by demanding the return of the Duke's heir from Castal—"

"Anguin, isn't that his name?"

"Yes," her father nodded. "I was there on his name day. And his sisters'. But the demand is a ruse: the last thing that Vichetral wants is a return of the heir. That would ruin his plan. Instead, he is learning who his friends are and who his foes are amongst the nobility and the merchant class. He sees at least two of the other counts as potential rivals. And dozens of barons, merchant companies, and great Houses. Not to mention plenty of temples."

"So, he's not about to announce himself as Duke yet?" she asked.

"No, things are far too tenuous for him to make that mistake. He does not yet have the support he would need to take the coronet. Instead, he's compiling lists of his enemies," her father explained, quietly. "Worse, he's assembling a force to . . . *remove* them. Spies. Informants. Assassins. Soon, he'll begin rounding up entire families to keep a real rebellion from breaking out."

"Cat said one of his cell mates' fathers was already arrested," Gatina provided.

"He's already gotten control of Falas and secured the support of most of the eastern baronies in County Falas along the Mandros River. His associates have secured a great deal of support along the Great Bay. And he has supporters from here to the Narrows in the Great Vale."

"He's also allying with the Censors," Gatina dutifully reported, her own frown growing. "I heard one of the monks speak of it. He said he heard it from the abbot himself."

"We're well aware," her father said, nodding—suddenly, he appeared far more like his alias as Shadow, leader of the conspiracy, than simple Dareth to Gatina. "Your mother discovered—and do not ask for details—that over a hundred of the checkered cloaks have already come down the river, fleeing from the Wilderlands and Gilmora. More are on the way by sea, as Remere banished them and they seek refuge in the west. Even as Rard expelled them, Vichetral's agents were offering them refuge here—for a price: they support his regime and help him control the magi and the Coastlord nobility; he will give them safety and a position in his government."

"Doesn't that violate their charter or something, somehow?" Gatina asked, confused.

"Oh, it's entirely an unofficial offer, of course—the Censorate cannot legally be subordinate to a Duke, much less a count. But the two parties have similar goals and common enemies. They both hate Duke Rard and prefer the law under the Bans on Magic. So, this is a matter of political expediency as much as it is a shift in policy."

"It is said they might be coming here," Gatina reported in a murmur.

"That's unlikely but possible," conceded Hance. "Usually, they don't interfere with places like this, in favor of more important targets. Already, the Censor Captain of Alshar and a few of his lieutenants are working on Vichetral's behalf, under the guise of 'normal' operations and a return to a more rigorous policing of the Bans. But it is little more than a mercenary magical corps, subject to Vichetral personally."

"A magical corps?" Gatina asked curiously.

"Military wizards—warmagi," her father explained. "The Magocracy used them extensively, but after the Conquest they largely fell out of fashion in favor of Narasi cavalry. The Censorate kept them from ever becoming too powerful. It wasn't until the Farisian Campaign against the Doge of Farise and his Mad Mage that they were really used in war again," he explained. "But the Censorate never lost those skills and spells. They've now put them into Vichetral's service, all without technically violating their own rules. And unlike common warmagi, the Censors have little concern about the law outside of how it defends them. Some of them are brutal. All of them are vicious fanatics."

"That doesn't sound good," Gatina said, shaking her head. "Not for the conspiracy, at least."

"It's not," agreed Hance grimly. "Vichetral's mundane spies we can contend with. Magical thugs with no real constraints on how or who they use their spells on . . . that is problematic," he admitted, his expression troubled.

"So, what *are* we doing about it?" she asked, her voice just above a whisper.

"What we have to—and you'll learn only what you must about that," he reminded her. "But hope is not lost. Every mishap hides opportunity. The involvement of the Censorate may actually work in our favor, in the long term.

"In the meantime, we shall continue to do what we have been doing: learning information. Making plans. And taking action when we need to in order to protect our people. That is really all you need to know until you are called upon to help."

"That can't come soon enough," Gatina said sourly, earning a chuckle from her father.

"My curious Kitten, is the abbey not holding your interest?" he teased, amused and concerned but also likely knowing the answer. He opened a wicker hamper in the wheelbarrow, revealing a half dozen fist-sized rolls.

"Prayers are boring, chores are tedious, history grows stale, math is beastly, and this alias feels like a wet cloak with buck teeth," she said, baring the prosthetic she wore to demonstrate. "Running the streets of Falas was exciting. Sometimes, I feel like I'm going to scream if I don't steal something," she revealed.

"At least the food is decent," he said, opening a tiny crock, which proved to be filled with butter. "I will credit you this—you have outlasted both myself and your brother in staying on the grounds before taking a clandestine walkabout of the village." Hance reached for the basket of warm rolls, breaking one, buttering it, and offering half to Gatina. "How are lessons?"

Gatina took the roll and bit into it just as her father asked her the question. She made a face. It smelled better than it tasted. Too much salt in the dough, she theorized. Drella would have thrown them out. But the butter helped.

"Sorry," he said. "I know the food here is not *that* tasty. At least, it didn't use to be very palatable. I think it's gotten a little better than I remember it. But I want you to tell me truthfully, Kitten: how are you really faring at Palomar?"

Gatina took that moment to swallow her bite, take a sip of water from the well's communal dipper, and gather her composure. Her father was inviting a truthful report, complete with complaints and criticism. That was rare, and she felt obligated to take advantage of the opportunity.

"Yes, the food is passable. I have certainly had both better and worse meals. I find the garden work to be enjoyable. I'm growing to dread my turn at the laundry. The abbey grounds are pretty. Painting flowers is boring, though I have worked on a few of my cards. I don't think they're very good yet. The monks and nuns are nice. The Saganites pray a lot, though, and have a lot of odd ideas. Poetics is interesting. And I have discovered that I am very poor at my numbers, at least compared to the other Nocturns." She paused and reflected. She hoped she did not sound ungrateful or like Leonna. But while the Coastlord girl was on her mind . . .

"And there is one girl who is so *mean*." Gatina had not planned to say anything, to anyone, ever, about Leonna and that situation. But her emotions got the best of her. "She is just *awful*, Father. She complains, she insults, she abuses everyone around her. I don't know what to do or say to defuse the situations and the conflict she seems determined to cause without acting out of character.

"Adversity is part of life, Kitten," he said sagely. "How you respond to it builds your character. I believe there is a house rule about it."

Gatina nodded. "Yes, I know there is. It's one thing to read about it, but it's another thing to live it. She seems very focused on northern Alshar's politics but almost in a misguided manner. As if she bears some grudge against the Wilderlands, or just Narasi in general. She doesn't think very highly of Sea Lords, either. Nor lower-status Coastlords."

"I know the type," her father agreed with a wry chuckle. "No doubt her parents thoroughly spoiled her, treating her like a little duchess. I'm guessing she's also unhappy with the monastic life?"

"Deeply," Gatina agreed. "She hates it. But there is no real reason for her to be. She's just *mean*. She's always trying to start a fight over something. Or make someone feel awful about themselves. Anything to dominate everyone around her. Oh, I know that I could easily put her in her place, but that would destroy my alias and draw attention to me." She sighed, staring at the well. "It's very frustrating. I just don't know what to do about her."

"Study her," her father suggested unexpectedly.

"*Study* her?" Gatina blurted out in surprise. "I can barely *stand* her! I'd rather push her head into this well or lock her inside her box bed!"

"*Study* her," Hance repeated firmly. "She sounds awful. Petty. Vindictive. So, study everything about her, every attack, every word she speaks, every ugly expression on her face. Someday, you will need an alias that acts like her," he reminded Gatina. "You will have to cultivate an alias who is just as mean as she is, at some point. It's best that you understand how to do that, and the best teacher is someone who *is* that mean. It will make your alias sound more authentic. Just like with the Censors getting involved, every mishap hides opportunity. Darkness has provided you with an ideal model for you to study. Use it," he urged.

"I can do more, I suppose," Gatina decided with another sigh. "I still don't really understand why you sent us here, of all places." She really didn't, and she was still more than a little upset by it. "Attie seems like he is actually enjoying it," she added accusingly.

"This isn't the most entertaining life, but it is safe. It has always been safe. And never particularly entertaining," Hance confessed. "I was miserable at first, but then my *rajira* arrived. This village is where my training began."

Gatina looked at her father again in surprise.

"Oh, yes, this is where I began my studies—both in class and out. Indeed, where better to learn how to practice magic and operate under the cover of the Blessed Darkness than at an abbey of stargazers who sleep in the day and work in the night? This entire village was my classroom in that. There are places here, hidden places, where such work is done. Secret classrooms, workshops, yes, even a studio for swordplay. Libraries of spellbooks and grimoires. Hidden rooms and staircases to long-forgotten cellars. That sort of thing. You will begin to learn to be a mage here. And you will continue to learn to be a thief.

"But first, you must learn to be a nun," he concluded. He reached for the battered tin dipper and scooped water from the well, then sipped while Gatina absorbed what he had just said.

"It still feels like punishment for what I did in Falas," she said, reluctantly.

Hance chuckled. "Well, Kitten, your mother was rather upset, but had you not undertaken those missions, I doubt that we would have been able to successfully form the conspiracy as quickly as we did.

"Now, I know that your mother explained that you only know what you need to know in order to complete a mission. That is a rule. It keeps everyone safe. But, in certain instances, having a larger picture of the plan is necessary. And that is why I am so glad I lingered in Ejecta, because now I need your help with a mission."

"What kind of mission?" she asked, suddenly eager.

"Remember all of that loot from our spree a few weeks ago?" he asked, cocking his head.

She nodded. There was no way she could ever forget that. The entire family had sat around that pile and toasted the heists with good Bikavar wine once they'd gotten home. It had felt like a great accomplishment, even though the profits were all going to fund the conspiracy against Vichetral. It was one of the most exciting things she'd ever done.

"Well, while the gold and silver are easy enough for us to use," he related, "there were several objects in that hoard that are far more valuable if they aren't melted down. And some that can't be. So . . . we need to turn to a fence."

Gatina nodded. She knew he was speaking of someone who specialized in quietly buying and selling stolen goods. He'd explained that in the past. Mother had also discussed the topic briefly back in Falas Town, but she had not gotten around to practical lessons on the matter.

"Don't we have one in the family?" she asked, suddenly.

"Several," agreed Hance. "But fences specialize, just as thieves do. And sometimes, location matters. If we try to sell this stuff anywhere near Falas, it could be recognized. Some of it is so rare and expensive that only certain kinds of buyers are available for it. So, we have to seek out a very special fence to get rid of it—someone who can pay us and then sell the loot without attracting the attention of the former owners. Or Vichetral's agents."

"You know someone?" she asked, eagerly. "And why do you need my help?"

"I do. A man who lives on an estate not too far away. I've dealt with him twice before, years ago. Under another name, of course. And, despite your mother's inclinations, I think you should go with me, not Cat. I argued that it would be instructive," he conceded. "And I could use the extra set of eyes and ears. Our *friend* in Falas is increasing the pressure on his men, among others, to locate certain items recently stolen from the country estates of his biggest supporters. The sooner we get rid of that loot, the better. Especially if he's getting the Censorate involved. They have ways to track such things: location spells."

Gatina was startled at the idea. "They can *track stolen loot?*" she asked, alarmed.

"They're wizards," he shrugged. "It's not a hard spell," Hance admitted. "Oh, they won't be able to attract the coin, but some of those things we took are quite distinctive, enough to use a spell to find them. You can counter it with certain defenses, but the problem is that there are plenty of different kinds of location spells, and we can't counter all of them indefinitely. If that loot is tracked, it will lead back to the Shadow Council. So . . . we need to get rid of it."

"And you want my help," she said, as much to get his commitment to the mission as to clear up any confusion.

"It should only take a few days to travel and meet him and see what he offers us. I will make the arrangements with the abbey to excuse you.

You may accompany me under the following conditions. First, you must remain in character *at all times.* You must be a traveling Nocturn, on a sacred mission from the abbey, and no one must suspect otherwise." Hance looked intently at Gatina, his eyes conveying the seriousness of the request.

That was easy enough to do, she decided. She nodded in agreement.

"Second, you must return to the abbey immediately after this excursion. There will be no side trips or casual wanderings into strange ruins, rat-infested sewers, or intriguing-looking taverns. Nor may you talk to strangers or try to make friends. That's another good reason to travel as clergy.

"Third, you are observing *only.* There will be no action on your part. You are not to say or do or especially *steal* anything that I don't approve of. And when you do have something to report, you tell me outside, afterwards, when we are alone and unobserved, what you saw, think, and feel."

"I can do that!" she assured him with confidence.

"This might seem like a casual trip, but in truth, there is more danger here than I'm comfortable with, thanks to the political situation. Remember, there is still very much you don't understand. Any action on your part may very well lead to jeopardizing either the mission or our aliases. Do you understand? And agree?"

"I can agree to those terms. When do we start?" Gatina asked eagerly, with a buck-toothed grin.

CHAPTER NINE

BLACK SILK THREAD

Opportunity is a fickle mistress, a slave to Fortune's capricious whim. Sometimes, it's a trap set to ensnare us. Other times, Fortune chances to reveal it to your naked eyes and dares you to seize it. To know one from the other is the height of mastery of our great Art.
— *from **The Shield of Darkness**,*
written by Kiera the Great

GATINA WAITED PATIENTLY FOR TWO DAYS FOR HER FATHER'S SUMMONS, dutifully carrying on with her routine at the abbey. As Avorrita, she had no trouble stumbling through the daily courses, chores, and devotions with the other girls. As Gatina, she was getting increasingly anxious and excited at the prospect of a new mission with her father.

Finally, on the morning of the third day after their meeting at the well, Nightsister Nimandi announced the Nocturns' new assignments over breakfast. While most of the girls in the group were rotated into new chores, as expected, the nun gave special assignments to a few of them.

"Nocturn Arryn, you are to report to Adastra Hall and begin special instruction in mathematics with Nightbrother Cortamar. Nocturn Leonna, you are to report to the Nocturn Hall for special assignment to Dusksister Ardenia. Nocturn Avorrita, you are to report to Nocturn Hall for special assignment for a technical pilgrimage. Please pack a travel bag—you may be gone for a few days."

"A *technical* pilgrimage?" asked Mathilde, confused. "What is that?"

"Occasionally, one of the senior clergy will need to take special observations from a vantage point outside of the abbey proper," the nun explained patiently. "It's traditional for them to be accompanied by a Nocturn or two to assist and observe the procedure for instructional and devotional purposes. They can last anywhere from a day to a week, depending upon the specifics of the observations. Now, whose turn is it to clear away the table?"

Gatina had already packed up her travel bag, of course, including a number of items that most Nocturn Initiates would never have taken concealed in a secret compartment at the bottom of the heavy leather satchel. After bidding farewell to the rest of her group, she trudged the heavy bag across the abbey's grounds to the Hall of Nocturns, where she waited until she was called into Dusksister Diandine's office. A tall, black-robed monk was waiting next to her table.

"Initiate, this is Nightbrother Espus," the old matron introduced with a gesture of her hand. "He is one of our travelers—Nightbrothers who wander the duchy to undertake specialized observations for the temple."

"'Wander' implies a lack of direction, Sister," Espus scolded . . . in her father's voice.

It was slightly deeper in timbre than usual, and he was using an accent she placed as more prominent in the upper Great Vale than the Coastlands or the Great Bay, but there was no doubt in her mind. She nearly startled when she realized who the tall monk was.

His hair, his face, his eyes, even his height had been altered, she saw. He wore a shock of dark hair and a full but neatly trimmed beard now, and his shoulders seemed to be wider. He must have been wearing boots with lifts in them, too, she figured. His eyes were now a pale blue. But there was no mistaking that voice, no matter how he tried to disguise it.

"A billion blessings upon you, Brother," Avorrita said, hesitantly, giving the monk a bow.

"Billions and billions," Brother Espus said automatically. "Can you figure?" he suddenly demanded. "How are you with numbers?"

"I am . . . adequate, Brother," Gatina admitted in Avorrita's timid voice.

"Hmph. We shall see," he said sharply. "And your hand? How is your penmanship?"

"Passably readable, Brother," she assured him, looking down at her feet.

"I see. Are you able to identify the Necklace, the Anchor, and the Crab constellations?"

Gatina knew that she could do that. "I can do that," Avorrita answered, this time with a stronger voice and a glance at Brother Espus's face. "And I know the Triangle is ever in the north," she added.

"Again, we shall see. I don't normally take a Nocturn as an assistant on these errands, but this trip will take me all the way to Inmar, in the north, and a little assistance would be welcome. Ever been there?"

"No, Brother," Avorrita answered, meekly shaking her head. "I've only been to Palomar since I left home."

"You're a scrawny thing," her father said, as he examined her with a stranger's eye. "I expect you don't eat much. Pray to Darkness you don't speak much, either. I value my sleep and don't have time for foolish questions. Have you ever driven a team?"

"N-no, Brother," Avorrita admitted. That produced a grunt from the monk.

"I suppose you can learn, then," he decided.

"Will she do?" asked Sister Diandine asked, impatiently. "If not, I'll have to summon another. That will take time."

"Time I do not have. The stars wait for no man," he reminded her sternly. "She will do . . . or she won't. We shall discover that. Come along, girl—what was your name again?" he prompted.

"Nocturn Avorrita, Brother," Gatina answered.

"Well, Avorrita, get your baggage out to the steps," he said impatiently. "We'll climb the path up to the temple, where we'll secure a carriage. A few days north to Inmar, a night or two making observations and measurements—if the skies cooperate—and then two days back."

"As you wish, Brother," she agreed, hefting her satchel and departing, with a nod toward the nun.

"She's as new as a lamb," she heard the monk complain to Sister Diandine as she left the office.

"All Nocturn Initiates are," Diandine dismissed. "Try keeping to the temple for more than a few days and you might remember that."

Avorrita didn't speak until they crossed the abbey's grounds to the head of the long, winding path that switchbacked up the face of the cliff between the two merry waterfalls. When she was certain they were far beyond earshot, and she was struggling to heft her bag as she climbed the steep path, she finally grunted.

"I thought you had forgotten me," she said accusingly.

"I had to make some preparations," her father explained. "I had to resurrect this old alias, for one thing. Plain old Dareth wasn't adequate for this mission. But we'll be riding hard for two days, mind you, before we even arrive in Inmar."

"We're really going to Inmar? Wouldn't a barge upriver be faster?" she asked skeptically.

"Yes, and far more noticeable," he agreed. "We're trying to obfuscate our movements, remember. The last thing we want to do is attract any undue attention. The abbey's special carriages should avoid that."

Indeed, there was a carriage and a team of horses already awaiting them when they finally made the top of the escarpment. A Sworn Nocturn stableboy held the team steady while they got their baggage aboard, then blessed them as Hance drove the team away and down the road leading north.

Once they were on the road, they relaxed their aliases and became father and daughter once again.

"So . . . *why* are we going to Inmar?" she asked, intrigued. She'd heard of the famous City of Temples, of course, but had little idea what it looked like or how far away it was.

"The fence I know has an estate there. Inmar is a wealthy place, as well as being beautiful. It's famous for its hunting. He doesn't care for the sport himself, but he gets plenty of wealthy customers who summer up there who do. And he can make sales far from the oversight of anyone in Falas. Quietly, of course."

"Does he have a shop or something?" Gatina asked, curiously.

"Oh, no, at his level, he is far beyond keeping a mere shop. He has a noble estate just outside of town and simply throws parties all season. He's known among the upper gentry for the amazing bargains he happens across, and they never ask questions. As a fence, he pays out decently—not the best, not the worst. But he's one of the few fences who has the possibility of reselling some of this loot without arousing suspicion."

"Can you trust him?" Gatina asked, after considering the matter. "Does he know who you really are?" she clarified.

"He doesn't, though I'm certain he suspects. And no, I can't trust him. You can never truly trust any fence to whom you aren't related. They are in an unenviable position: they must have a permanent residence in order to do business. But that puts them in a delicate situation. It means that they're subject to leverage by the authorities, because it's hard for them to move around with all of that stolen inventory. You always have to be careful when dealing with a fence outside of the family. But I trust his greed and his ignorance. I doubt he would even have heard about our recent heists," he assured her.

They spent all morning chatting, with Hance instructing Gatina in all manner of lore about the family and its unique profession. Gatina enjoyed herself immensely, despite how hot and sweaty her nun's habit made her. It was rare that she had an opportunity to discourse with her father alone, in private, for any length of time and she took full advantage of the opportunity.

They made good time, too—it had barely rained in the Great Vale this week, so the road was dry and dusty. While they occasionally passed a peasant on his way to market or a carter delivering goods by wagon, the road was quite deserted of fellow travelers. If avoiding notice was important to Hance, he'd chosen the perfect route to do so.

The weather was perfect, a warm summer's day with only big, friendly clouds in the sky. The gently rolling landscape presented the Great Vale to Gatina in all of its understated fertile beauty, with small groves of trees or fences of rocks and stones separating expansive fields of wheat, barley, maize, and oats, each crop eagerly stretching from the soil toward the sky. Pastures of sheep and cattle grazed contentedly in their pastures at regular intervals. The breeze was gentle, just enough to take the edge off of the worst of the summer's heat. Birds chased each other through the sky, while bees and other insects whirred by on their important errands.

By noon, they had passed through three villages and had come to a fourth. Gatina guessed they were spaced out this way to facilitate the local markets, but it seemed as if each of them had been grown from the same seed, they were so similar in appearance and composition. Still, she found them interesting.

They were built far more simply than the farmhouses in the south that she was familiar with, she noted. Instead of brick or stone, they seemed to be half-timbered structures of wattle-and-daub, their roofs uniformly thatched with the straw that grew so abundantly there. Neither were the streets paved in any of them, the way a Coastlands village of any size would boast.

"The Great Vale is Narasi country," explained her father, as they approached the fourth village. "It has always been one great plain with a few woods here and there. It was deserted and unsettled even during the Magocracy. There was still plenty of uncultivated land in the Coastlands, back then, and our ancestors made more coin growing grapes and fruit and olives and such to make the trip up the escarpment into the Great Vale.

"But the Narasi lords preferred grain farming to horticulture. Their grain god, Huin the Tiller, compelled them to look for better, dryer lands for that than could be found on the coast, where the weather is too wet and unpredictable for much grain. Within three generations of the Conquest, most of the good lands north of the Falls of Falas had been claimed by some tawny-haired knight or another. It's better horse and cattle country, too," he added as they passed by a corral with a couple of the big beasts within. "You know how the Narasi love their horses."

"So, why are the Coastlords so at odds with the Narasi?" she asked, though she suspected the answer.

"The very same reason the Sea Lords are usually at odds with the Coastlords. They resented the invaders, the way that all conquered peoples do," he reflected. "The magi and the Coastlords had ruled over Alshar as counts of the Magocracy for three centuries before the Narasi came along. They had the havens under control, a booming trade in wine, olives, and hemp, and were making plenty of money under the Imperial rule.

"When the Narasi came with the first Duke of Alshar, they resisted. But the magi had lost much of their power by then, and the Censors were powerful warmagi—mostly Wenshari turncoats who would rather work for the Narasi barbarians than bow to the Imperial authority of Remere."

"So, what happened with all of those wizards, then?" she asked, curious.

Hance shrugged. "Some capitulated and accepted the Bans on Magic and continued life as best they could. Those who couldn't bring themselves to do that fled to Farise, which resisted Narasi rule for another four centuries. Others hid themselves and strove to strike back at the invaders. That's what House Furtius did. There was a century where the Narasi Dukes were facing a magical insurgency for a while. Our ancestors were part of that," he added, proudly.

"They stole from the Narasi?" she asked, interested in that side of history.

"Oh, we stole them *blind*," Hance chuckled. "It's all in the detailed history books. Kiera the Great's twin grandsons, Hengerot and Langerot, were raiding the strongholds of Narasi horselords from the Great Bay to the Great Narrows for decades. Famous couple of thieves, those. Hengerot fell to his death at eighty when he scaled one of the temple towers in Inmar," he reported with pride. "Langerot died peacefully at his estates in Rhemes a year later. Between the two of them, it's estimated they stole over a hundred thousand ounces of gold, according to their heist journals."

"That's . . . that's a *lot* of gold," admitted Gatina, whose studies in mathematics had given her a new appreciation of just how big a number that was.

"Enough to buy estates, ships, and influence at the Ducal Court," her father agreed. "If Kiera laid the foundation of our House in Alshar, Hengerot and Langerot built the first few floors. Let's stop for luncheon," he proposed, as they came to the hedgework at the edge of the village. "There's a tavern here that has good lamb stew this time of year, if I recall correctly. And I need to water the team," he added.

"Will I have time to look around?" Gatina asked, curious.

"A little," her father conceded. "I don't want to tarry too long, but the horses need a little rest before we press on. There are a few shops herein . . . I think the place is called Estapool. But don't steal anything," he cautioned. "As prosperous as this village is, it is far below our standards."

Estapool was not much larger than the village she was familiar with back home in the Falas countryside. It wasn't on a river, she knew, so it sprawled evenly out from the central market, which boasted a chapel to Huin on one side of the square and a small temple to Trygg on the other. A line of tiny shops had sprung up in between.

While Hance tended the team, Gatina stretched her legs and began wandering from shop to shop. The people of Estapool were a little taller and had lighter hair and complexions than the peasants she was used to back home, but otherwise they behaved the same. The Vale folk were largely Narasi stock, she realized, not the darker Imperial blood of the south.

She was uncomfortable, at first, with the amount of deference the local folk seemed to pay her. She was unused to people bowing to her respectfully and seeking her blessing. It was a little exciting, she decided, to enjoy that kind of position and authority even if the ignorant farmers and shopkeepers didn't realize that she was still just a novitiate. They couldn't tell the difference between a Nocturn Initiate and a Nightfather, she figured. They just saw the habit and acted respectfully. One of the shopkeepers even gave her a free biscuit after she delivered a mumbled blessing.

Though Estapool was a sleepy little village, it was a little larger than the first three they'd passed through, and it was a crossroad as well. Twenty miles or so west was the mighty Mandros River, while to the east were mile after mile of abundant farmlands that sent their surplus wheat and barley through the village on its way to larger markets. There was a lot of artisan traffic, too, she noted, and the occasional merchant wagon or packtrader making their way east to west, or north to south. There was no sign of the strife and conflict infecting Falas and the Coastlands that she could see.

That is, until she spotted three men in very distinctive black-and-white checkered cloaks and her blood froze in her veins.

Royal Censors. *There.*

The three men were also wearing leather armor under their cloaks, she noted as her heart pounded in her chest. They wore snugly fitting iron helmets over cloth coifs. They carried themselves as warriors as they dismounted their horses, and she could see the distinctive swords they wore over their shoulders—mageblades, she recalled. The chosen weapon of warmagi. Heavier by far than her slender shadowblade and often enchanted with spells to give them advantage in battle. They were businesslike in their demeanor, and they were clearly intent on something. One held the horses while two others entered one of the shops.

Gatina couldn't help herself. She followed them.

She hadn't intended to. The smart thing to do would be to slink away into shadow, make herself unobtrusive, and remain unseen. But she could not stop herself. After so many recent conversations about the Censorate, to stumble upon three of them there, in the middle of nowhere, seemed just too convenient not to take advantage of. OPPORTUNITY, she realized.

Gatina was smart about it, of course; she waited a decent interval before deciding to enter the shop, walking in Avorrita's inelegant gait. She passed right by the man holding the horses and gave him a glance and a shy, buck-toothed smile before she headed into the shop behind them.

It wasn't much of a shop. In Falas, she would have passed right by it without noticing it. Two stories, tall and narrow, with the merchant likely living on the floor above. There was only one window to let the light in, so there was a bit of gloom. The place sold notions and sundries—mostly thread and yarn, and some needles and pins. There were bolts of cloth rolled up in the center of the floor toward the front and a thick pair of shears on a rope nearby. Baskets of thread and yarn, empty spools and knitting needles of bone or horn lined the walls. More cloth was suspended from the rafters to keep it out of the way.

A middle-aged man with a scraggly beard and a well-stained apron lingered in the back, where he seemed frozen at the unusual sight of the two big Censors. His eyes were wide with surprise. Apparently, he did not get many men as customers, much less Royal Censors.

The two were talking animatedly among themselves and just loud enough for her to hear *"about Falas"* and that caught her attention immediately. It also invited further investigation, however foolhardy that was.

She made herself as tiny as a kitten and as quiet as a mouse as she eased closer to them while earnestly trying to avoid looking as if she was doing so. She willed her body to become invisible, as she had seen her father do so many times, or at least unnoticeable. She gently eased down to her knees and pretended to study the baskets of thread stored on the bottom of a shelf. From this vantage point, she could study the men's feet and hear their conversation as the sound bounced off the wooden floor.

Both men wore sturdy boots meant for riding—or kicking in doors—not working fields. She had seen many of these types of shoes in Falas on the feet of guardsmen and soldiers during the riots.

She could hear them speak more clearly from there, too, she found.

"—three hundred miles through the gravel wastes for *this*!" one of the men was complaining. "We get to ride dusty roads while the captains ride south in comfort on a river barge like proper gentlemen. And for what? I didn't figure I would be chasing down unregistered hedgewitches and harassing village spellmongers when I came to Alshar. I could do that in Castal!"

"You do as you're ordered." The other man shrugged as he studied a shelf of spools. "You know how we left Castal. What did you think we'd be doing?"

"Organizing to overthrow that upstart Duke!" snorted the first man. "You can't just start calling yourself king and throwing the Order out like that. There need to be consequences."

"You can if you have a whopping big army and a commander who's a traitor," the second man said as he pushed the spools around. "Calm yourself, Corporal. We'll see to Rard in time. Until then, we do as ordered. Captain Nargus wants every footwizard in Alshar crapping themselves when they think of us, every adept too afraid of the Order to even think about stirring up a rebellion. Captain Stefan is intent on his investigations. That's how the Count wants it, and right now we do what the Count wants. You!" he said, strongly, as he pointed toward the clerk. "Do you have any strong black thread? Really strong," he emphasized. "Not this linen; it's as thin as a whisker. Cotton? Strong cotton?"

"Silk, m'lord?" asked the merchant as he dug around in a basket. "I've got some strong black silk here."

"Do I look like I can afford silk?" the Censor asked, irritated.

"It's not Unstaran, m'lord; it's from the Shattered Isles. Half the price," he assured. "Strong enough to fish with, and black as night!"

"You'd look good in silk," the first man jibed.

"Shut up," the first man said casually. "Strong enough to keep this cloak together for another week?"

"Oh, aye, m'lord," the merchant agreed enthusiastically. "We use it for stays and boning, for the ladies—and girdles for gentlemen, of course. Nothing better, nothing better."

"Oh, fine, give me six yards of it," the Censor snorted, fingering his torn cloak. "A footwizard tried to get away and yanked on this one so hard, the seam split. I won't be able to get a new one made 'til we get to Falas. Pissed me off so much, we hung the scoundrel," he said with a hollow laugh.

The merchant swallowed hard at the casual mention of an execution. "Half price, m'lord," he assured, enthusiastically nodding his head like a bobbing chicken as he nervously wound the requested length around a small wooden spool. "That's near to my cost. Always looking to help out the authorities."

"That's good thinking, now that the Counts rule Alshar," the second man advised. "Vichetral keeps the Bans rigorously. He's dedicated to the law. And we are always about. If you hear tell of any stray witches, you let us know at our station in Cumray. Or any other strangeness."

"Oh, there isn't so much as a dowser in twenty miles of Estapool, m'lord," the merchant insisted, as he presented the spool to the Censor with some ceremony.

"How about talk against Count Vichetral?" asked the second man, raising an eyebrow.

"Who, m'lord? I don't know any nobles beyond Baron Ridden, I'm afraid. No counts or such. Of course, the Duke and Duchess, bless their poor souls. But no counts. Why?" he asked, confused.

"Never mind," dismissed the Censor, eyeing the man critically. "It's above your station. You don't look the type to start a rebellion, I suppose."

"Would you like a needle with that, m'lord? A thimble?" he asked, his voice shaking a bit.

"I've got my own sewing kit, just no black thread," the Censor dismissed with a growl. "How much?"

"Two pennies, m'lord," the man said apologetically. It took a moment for the Censor to dig his purse out of his belt and find the coins. "You said you hung a footwizard, m'lords?" the merchant asked hesitantly.

"Two days ago, up in Inmar," agreed the second man. "Found a pair of 'em. Put a lot of practical adepts to the question, too. We found much was out of order. Seems like you folk have gone slack, when it comes to the Bans," he observed. "We'll soon set that to rights. Captain Nargus has charge of this entire county now, and there's more of us coming. And Captain Stefan is always on the hunt for mischief."

Gatina waited until the men completed their transaction and left before she presented a half-spool of red linen and a pretty copper thimble to the merchant along with two silver pennies. The man looked entirely disturbed.

"Who were *they?*" she asked hesitantly, as Avorrita would have. "Soldiers?"

"Wizards . . . and soldiers. Enforcers. Censors, they're called, Sister," he said, shaking his head. "Never seen 'em up close before. They make sure the magi stick to the straight and narrow way. Not men to cross, not at all. They can kill you with a glance, so it's said. And no one will do anything about it."

"If you're a wizard," she said, glancing over her shoulder toward the door.

"Well, hard to tell if you are or aren't if you're hanging from a tree by a noose, isn't it?" he pointed out with a snort.

"I . . . suppose it is," Gatina agreed. Indeed, she hadn't really thought about the kind of power the Censors had. "A billion blessings upon you," she added as she took her purchases and left. The Censors were already gone when she went outside. She was rather relieved at that.

She hurried back to the tavern, where her father was already sitting on a bench outside with a bowl of stew. Gatina sat down beside him and tried to calm herself. It was late for luncheon, and there wasn't anyone within earshot.

"Brother, I just saw—" she began.

"I know," Hance said, quietly. "I saw them leave. What were they seeking, I wonder?"

"Thread, actually," Gatina reported. "Black thread. They were just stopping by on their way somewhere else."

"And you had a chance to listen to where, I take it?" he asked.

"Cumray. They report to a Captain Nargus. They're from Castal."

"You picked up quite a bit in a short time," he praised.

"Including how they just hung a footwizard. In Inmar. For *ripping his cloak*," she said, shaking her head slightly at the thought of such a brutal punishment.

"They don't usually resort to that sort of heavy-handed treatment," Hance reflected, his voice far too casual for such a harsh subject.

"Father, I heard what I heard," Gatina insisted, exasperated but struggling to remain calm. She closed her eyes and practiced her breathing technique, which helped to slow her breathing and heart rate, an essential skill for a thief . . . or a spy.

"The Censors are coming for unregulated magi," she insisted. "That's what they said. And they work for—with—the Counts now. They mentioned Vichetral by name. And I don't think they will stop until they've found all of them. They want to control them—us. Or at least Vichetral does." Gatina was absolutely certain the three Censors were fanatics.

"That's what they do, Nocturn," her father said, calmly. "The entire point of the Censorate from its inception was to suppress the magi in the name of regulation. And don't forget that they are magi themselves, each trained not only in warmagic but in special arcane interrogation techniques. Their spells can wring the truth out of a man like water from a dishrag. They promote the most subtle and vicious into their leadership. And they have absolutely no compunctions about their power . . . say, hanging a man out of hand for ripping a cloak."

"Just like the Brotherhood," nodded Gatina. The Brotherhood of the Rat—the criminal gang who controlled the docks and riverports on Count Vichetral's behalf—were filled with thugs who would stab you in the back for a few copper pennies.

"No, they're actually far, far more dangerous," Hance countered, his voice just above a whisper. "You haven't gotten your Talent yet. When you do, you'll understand a bit better. Magic gives them a great advantage over the Brotherhood. And while the Rats are motivated by greed and opportunism, the Censors are more disciplined . . . and more idealistic. That makes them fanatics. That's what they do," he sighed, the slightest bit of frown appearing within his false beard.

"They just came from Inmar," she pointed out uneasily. "Are you sure it's safe to go there now?"

"If they just came from there, then yes, it probably is safe," he decided. "It's rare that there are two Censors in a single county. Three, all together, is significant. If they've already been there, then we'll likely see no more when we arrive. Darkness willing," he said, with a small smile.

CHAPTER TEN

A FENCE IN INMAR

When cultivating a convincing alias, it is best for the thief to work from truths and half-truths rather than fabricate a story. The temptation to employ a lie may seem easy at first, but oft those mistruths bring trouble and complications. Exploiting the trust of others is simple enough, but to do so without arousing suspicion demands that the thief keep the threads of his alias woven tightly together with the strength of truth to support the fiction.

*— from **The Shield of Darkness***
Commentaries

INMAR WAS A BEAUTIFUL CITY—STUNNINGLY BEAUTIFUL, COMPARED TO Falas, Gatina decided, as the carriage rumbled across the neatly cobbled streets. Known as the City of Temples, her father explained, it was the religious capital of the duchy. Every major sect had a temple there . . . and they all boasted beautiful green tiles on their roofs.

Gatina had gasped when she first saw the place in the soft morning sunshine, earning a grin from Hance. The shimmering blue lake in the background seemed to conspire with the delicate marble architecture and the vibrant green rooftops to please the eye.

"I had the same reaction the first time I came here," he chuckled. "It's unlike any other city in Alshar. It's a playground for the upper nobility, wealthy merchants, and senior clergy," he informed her. "Inmar has a bustling commercial quarter, a prosperous artisan class, and a reasonably solid servile class. Plenty of students, artists, and minstrels, too. There are temples, schools, libraries, theaters, hostels, and a number of incredibly fine inns. It's a great place for a thief to holiday in. Or spend loot. Or, in our case, to dispose of some."

Gatina tried to look everywhere at once as they rode through the streets—much broader than the streets in Falas. Indeed, while the capital city was filled with unexpected turns and an almost haphazard layout due to its long and tumultuous history, Inmar seemed completely orderly, with stately stone buildings surrounding the magnificent central square and beautiful statues, fountains, and plazas that seemed to all have been created by the same hand. Falas was chaotic, she decided, but Inmar was sublime.

Hance, still in his guise as Brother Espus, secured a room at a fancy inn called the Duke's Dalliance. It was as different from the inns she'd seen in Falas as the streets were. Indeed, it seemed to be decorated more like a temple or a palace than a simple hostel. While the innkeeper who took their fee raised an eyebrow at the sight of a monk and a novitiate paying for an expensive private room, Brother Espus made a fuss about noise, the thickness of the walls, and his ability to sleep during the daytime to an extent that seemed to justify the high price . . . which he also complained about.

While Gatina carried the baggage up the narrow (but intricately carved) wooden stairs to the gallery that led to their room, Brother Espus disappeared for nearly an hour, leaving poor Nocturn Avorrita to sit in the common room in her habit, shyly mumbling blessings at the departing travelers.

Avorrita was clearly uncomfortable with the situation, of course, but Gatina was drinking in every detail as she waited. Within a few minutes, she established in her mind the composition of the staff, the quality of the clientele, and a goodly bit of neighborhood gossip. Twice, a serving girl only a little older than she shyly brought her a small glass of weak ale, then asked a few awkward questions about the Saganite Order and Avorrita's duties. After that, Gatina was so quiet that most everyone else left her alone.

Gatina found she enjoyed the perceived authority that the gray habit gave her. It really was a superior disguise, as it brought with it all sorts of notions about her—such that she was intensely spiritual, that she had a touch of power about her, and that she was honest by nature. Avorrita, of course, did share some of those traits in Gatina's imagination.

But Gatina was far more concerned about the people coming in and out of the inn and their errands than the mystical nature of the stars or her apparent sanctity. There were many merchants at the Duke's Dalliance, some local and some traveling from long distances to sell their wares to the elite of Inmar.

Gatina guessed one was a jeweler, by the fine leather satchel he kept close to him and the hulking bodyguard who followed him everywhere. Another was a cloth merchant from the south whose cart filled with fine silks and cottons and had just arrived in Inmar. There was another clergyman staying at the inn, too: a high priest of Luin the Lawgiver in a rich black silk robe who seemed to be dead drunk when he arrived. He barely glanced at her as he stumbled up the stairs to his own room.

There were also a number of very beautiful girls in stylish gowns who frequented the inn, as if it were a festival day. Gatina gathered that the Duke's Dalliance was a favored gathering place for the local nobility, as well as travelers, from the casual way the women were greeted by the staff.

By the time Brother Espus returned, Gatina had discovered quite a bit from the casual gossip. While a few of the people in the spacious chamber glanced at her respectfully in passing, after that they ignored her, as if she were another statue. That was another function of a nun's habit, she realized. It provided a kind of invisibility all its own. People saw the robe but not the girl inside it.

It was fascinating, listening to other people's discussions. She was almost annoyed at having to stop once her father came back. But by then, much of the morning traffic had waned, and there were only a few servants left.

"I have sent the message," he said as he sat down beside her. "He is in town, as I expected, and likely to meet with us tonight. But we will have to change clothes," he added, tugging at his own black habit. "And I'll need to 'shave.' He knows me by another name. Hungry? Let's get a few cakes to break our fast before we nap." He raised his hand and summoned the serving girl.

"Which one?" Gatina asked, curiously, after the girl left to fetch some cakes and more ale.

"He knows me as Dronadal, and he knows that's not my real name," Hance explained. "He knows I work out of Falas, sometimes in the cities along the Great Bay, but I stay out of the Great Vale, which makes him more eager to buy. It can be awkward to try to sell someone's stolen goods back to them. That's professionally embarrassing."

"What about me?" Gatina asked, curious.

"I've had companions both times I've used him, so he won't find that unusual. One was your mother," he said, smiling at the memory. "That was an exciting time. But you shall be my new servant girl. He won't ask questions, in any case. He deals with all manner of people in his business, and he knows enough not to ask too many questions he doesn't really want the answer to."

"That seems reasonable," she agreed. "How should I dress?"

"A dark traveling dress over your working blacks," Hance suggested. "You have one?"

"Avorrita arrived in one, if you recall," she reminded him. "I brought it with me. It's plain enough for me to be seen as an artisan's daughter, a prosperous peasant girl, or minor nobility, if I dress it up with a few accessories. The right accessories. Which would be best?"

"I see your mother taught you well," he praised. "And Cousin Huguenin, I suppose. Use the artisan's daughter," Hance decided. "Not too poor, not too rich. And put a dagger in your belt, one that can be easily seen. But don't say a word you don't have to," he reminded her. "The less detail he has, the better."

"I'll just be pleased not to be wearing my buck teeth. Who is this man we're meeting? The more detail *I* have, the better," she reminded him.

"His name is Erad, Lord Erad of Dalefoot. The youngest son of an old Narasi household. His mother was the second wife of his sire, and Imperial. She was of House Morlyan, actually, small but distinguished. And, by all accounts, quite young and pretty at the time. Erad didn't have a chance of inheriting title or estate, but he was ennobled by birth, and he got a small bequest when his father died.

"So, he went to temple school here until his sinecure ran out and he left his studies. But he made a lot of friends while he was there—many, *many* friends. And eventually a small fortune. He's a merchant at heart, despite his pretensions to culture and his noble position. And he's quite charming, almost as much as your cousin Huguenin. He lives at a small estate near town. It's called Lemon's Reach."

"Lemon's Reach?" Gatina asked skeptically. "What kind of name is that?"

Hance chuckled. "Local custom," he explained. "The gentry of Inmar like to call their homes something exotic like that to inspire interesting conversation. Each name has some sort of story behind it, so it's an excuse to talk at parties—of which there are a lot in Inmari society. In this case, Erad has a lemon tree that he's quite fond of. And this is the farthest north anyone has gotten a lemon to grow, so he called his home Lemon's Reach."

"That's a stupid name," Gatina decided after a moment's consideration.

"Just wait until you meet the tree," Hance smiled. "And the man."

———

LEMON'S REACH WAS JUST OUTSIDE OF THE UNWALLED URBAN LIMITS OF Inmar, a small estate on a gentle rise that gave it an excellent view over both the pristine lake and the pretty town. The house itself was no larger than Cysgodol Hall back home, though it was wider than it was tall; there were only two stories to the place.

But what it lacked in space it made up for in opulence. Not even the exterior of the Ducal Palace in Falas or one of the central temples there was as extravagantly appointed as Lemon's Reach. Beyond the gate, the yard was filled with large marble statues and delicate pathways that threaded through the abundant gardens. There was even a fountain in front of the doorway, a wide pink granite bowl that featured not porpoises, clippermen, fish, or even a swan as the centerpiece, as were common in Falas, but a large, gilded lemon the size of her head. Water squirted out of the pointed top and flowed down the golden sides with impossible grace. It looked ridiculous.

They had ridden to the estate on their horses instead of taking the carriage. Gatina could think of several reasons why that was better. Carriages were loud; they required time to prepare and attention to drive. And they made their best speed on the road. A horse could travel cross-country, jump walls, and go much faster than a carriage.

Of course, all that was correct in theory. In truth, Gatina was quite unsteady in the saddle for much of the journey. While she had ridden a few times in the past, she was far from knowledgeable in horsemanship. And she found it disconcerting not being truly in control of where she went.

Thankfully, her rouncy was a gentle mount, and long before they rode up the hill to Lemon's Reach, just after the Blessed Darkness fell, she was riding more steadily in the saddle than when they set out from the Duke's Dalliance.

Along the way, her father had lectured her more about Inmar, its history, and its economy. By the time they came to the ridiculous-looking fountain, she knew a lot more about how and why Inmar was the way it was, and the types and manner of folk who lived and visited here.

"Why don't we live here, then?" she asked as they dismounted.

"It's too easy for a thief to make a living here," he explained. "Oh, you could live as richly as a duke on what you could steal—and some do. But where is the skill in that? Or the challenge? Our House has traditionally avoided working here unless necessary. But the rooftops are an absolute pleasure to run across at night. Now remember: not a word if not necessary," he warned.

A keen-eyed servant came out and took their horses, while another escorted them beyond the stylishly gilded doors and into the luxurious main chamber of the hall. There, smoking a pipe by the tiny fire in an immense fireplace, waited a youngish man with long dark hair, wearing a soft yellow mantle over his doublet. He rose at once when he saw them.

"Dronadal? Dronadal? It really is you!" he said, smiling enthusiastically. "Ishi's beaming smile, it's been years! I thought there had been some mistake when you sent word," the man laughed.

"No mistake," assured her father. He was wearing a dark wig over his close-cropped white hair, and he had removed the fake beard that Brother Espus had worn. He wore a dark blue light cotton mantle draped over a burgundy doublet. He looked younger, somehow, than he did when he was undisguised, and considerably younger than Brother Espus. Though he didn't wear a sword, Gatina was certain he was well armed. The dagger at her belt wasn't the only blade she had brought, either. Dealing with fences could easily go awry, her father had explained, and it was best to be prepared to defend yourself.

"No one has had word of you in years," offered Erad. "I was worried."

"I've just been busy, down in Enultramar," Dronadal shrugged.

"You've been very quiet about it, then," Lord Erad chided. "I hear about everything, and I *never* hear about you. I suppose that's a testament to your craft. But it made me suspect that you were dead or retired."

"Neither," her father insisted. "Just very, very careful. Particularly now," he said pointedly.

"Oh, the Duke and Duchess—I *heard*!" Erad clucked. "Terrible business! And they were just here last spring on their way to Wilderhall. So young," he sighed. "And so sad. They set quite the fashion at court. And she threw *lovely* parties. They will be missed."

"They will," her father said sincerely. "But times have changed. And that presents opportunities."

"You know I adore opportunities," Lord Erad said, smiling even wider. "Wine? A glass for you and your . . ." he asked, finally acknowledging Gatina's presence.

"*Companion* is all you need to know," Hance said in a firm manner.

"Then that is what I will know. Maid Companion? Some wine?"

Gatina nodded. Her father had assured her that it would be fine to accept hospitality from Erad. Indeed, it was expected. Fences had to trust the thieves and buyers that they worked with, and few would trust someone who would not share a drink or a meal with them.

The three retired to a small, cozy chamber toward the rear of the house, one with a window that overlooked the lake. While a servant brought them wine, Erad gossiped about other people—presumably other thieves he and her father both knew, or at least knew of. That, too, was expected, Hance had informed her. Trading news that might be beneficial to both parties was part of the service a fence did. An enterprising thief could often get advice or a good lead on a heist from a reputable fence.

"Now, what have you brought me tonight?" Erad finally asked, after the first cup of wine. "Something from the coast?"

"Some things I picked up from another fellow, actually," her father said, pulling open the satchel he wore around his shoulder. "We were both busy this year, so we swapped a few things, and some of it seemed to be wares you'd be interested in," he said, pulling one small, wrapped bit of loot after another out of the bag and placing them on the small table next to the wine, along with a few books they'd stolen that had some value.

The fence made a point of examining each piece carefully, even using a gazing lens a few times to inspect the details. He began to sort items into piles as he encountered them, and after each inspection he got a faraway look in his eyes for a moment. Gatina watched his expression change from glee to a scowl as, one by one, he assessed the quality and value of the piece.

When they had come to the last piece—a beautifully illuminated book of instruction for the Temple of Ishi, each page gorgeously decorated— Erad sighed.

"It's all quite lovely, and a credit to your—your friend's," he corrected, "abilities. Very high quality. This," he said, indicating the larger of the three piles on the table, "I can work with. I'll give you nineteen hundred gold, all together. This," he said, indicating a smaller pile, "I can't work with. It's terribly good, but I won't have a buyer for it. I don't sell *tekka*," he explained, sympathetically. "It's too distinctive and too difficult to value."

Tekka, Gatina knew, were bits and pieces of things from the time when humans first came to Callidore, centuries ago. She'd seen a few simple pieces, and her parents had described some of the more common types. The wealthy and the nobility liked to collect the things for their age and novelty—sometimes they could do the strangest things—and some of them were quite valuable.

"Understood," nodded Hance, a thief portraying a thief. "I can find other buyers," he shrugged.

"Try Master Inkshed, down in Gavina; he likes that sort of thing," Erad suggested, helpfully. "There's a good market for it in Farise—or, at least, there was. You might not get a good price now. Things have been difficult . . . since the change in regime."

"Vichetral controls most of the ships coming in or out of the Great Bay," Hance agreed. "Not many are bound for Farise now."

"Or anywhere else," Erad agreed, shaking his head. "Vichetral has the entire bay locked down. His pet Sea Lords guard the straits, and his pet Rats control the docks now," he complained. "A pity. I was considering a holiday in Remere."

"Times are challenging," Hance said, nodding. "And the third part?"

"Ah," Erad said, staring at the smallest share of the loot. There were three small items there, all jewelry. "This portion is . . . problematic. I'm tempted to buy it," he admitted, reluctantly, "and would offer you a good price on it—the pieces are beautiful, particularly this ruby pendant that looks like a rose—it's exquisite. And I could easily find a buyer in this town."

"But it's *problematic*," Hance prompted.

"Just so," agreed Erad sympathetically. "You see, I've heard these pieces described in detail, just a few days ago."

"How, *described*?" Hance asked, confused.

"Five days ago, a gentleman came to one of my parties—you remember my parties, don't you, Dronadal? Not one of my larger ones, I admit, but quite cozy. Just a small affair, a few score friends and acquaintances. This gentleman was the only stranger.

"But he seemed to know my business," Erad frowned. "I don't know how he knew, but he made it quite clear that he understood my little hobby. Stefan, his name was. He had a book, you see."

"For sale?" Hance asked.

"Oh, no, it was his and it was not for sale. A notebook," Erad explained. "A notebook full of names and questions. And after asking me if I was acquainted with—oh, he must have asked about twenty, thirty different people, all well-respected nobles and distinguished clergy—he asked if I had come across a number of very specific items. Including a golden looking glass with an anchor design on the back—like this one—a bejeweled perfume bottle with a gilded top in the shape of a nightweb—like this one—and a ruby pendant in the shape of a Matadine rose . . . just . . . like . . . *this* one," he said, tapping the necklace and looking pointedly at her father.

Gatina stifled a gasp. She tried to make her face a mask absent of expression. Hance looked concerned.

"It seems the fellow who traded me these may have attracted some attention," Hance finally said.

"So it appears," Erad said with a nod. "And quite the wrong sort of attention. Of course, I truthfully told him I'd never seen or acquired those things or any of the others he described, and he seemed satisfied with my answer. But of course, I could not make that same claim now, could I?" he asked, an eyebrow raised.

"Who was this man?" Hance asked thoughtfully.

"Not someone I'd like to cross paths with again, truth be told," admitted Erad. "He wasn't the friendly type. More of a military bearing. His name was Stefan, I recall quite clearly. He virtually interrogated my guests after he was done speaking with me, and he pushed the bounds of my hospitality. It was a bit unnerving and not at all conducive to a festive occasion."

"People can be so rude," Hance said carefully.

"Oh, they certainly can. Particularly if they have authority and power. Always avoid authority and power, Dronadal," Erad advised. "It brings nothing but trouble and never the happiness one would expect. It's much better to stay in the corners of the room than dance in the center. It's cozier and more relaxing. And far more fun. Too many people think authority and power will solve their problems, and the unfortunate truth of the matter is that they complicate things entirely, no matter what your intentions might be."

"So, this man works for . . . the Council of Counts," suggested Hance.

"Indirectly," conceded Erad. "At least, that was the implication of his visit to Inmar. And my lovely home. He did not wave a commission under my nose, nor a magistrate's warrant, but he was clear he had the endorsement of authority. And these days, there is only one source of authority in Alshar."

"Vichetral," answered Hance with a sigh.

"Just so. Your friend must have burgled one of his lackeys, because the Count spared no expense to search for these items. He sent Captain Stefan. Nor was that the only errand he was on. He was searching for *people*, too—that list of names I spoke of. A very odd list, containing quite a lot of prominent Coastlords. People I would normally think would cling to Falas, or Vorone, or running their vast estates from their palatial manors. Now, why would this man be looking for those people? And wondering if I—of *all* people—might know them?"

Hance shrugged. "Did you?" he asked.

"Of course I knew some of them—this is Inmar! And I am the most genteel host in Inmar! Half of Enultramar comes here to escape the heat and their wives if they don't want to make the bloody great trek to Vorone. And I inevitably meet them and invite them to one of my parties. And they are almost always intrigued and honored at the invitation.

"So, yes, I had to admit that I knew some of them, albeit poorly, in most cases," Erad said, disconcerted at the thought. "But he wouldn't tell me *why* he wanted to know, and I found that quite disturbing. The list of jewelry was incidental—before you came along and showed this to me. Now I'm trying to establish a connection between the two."

"It is a mysterious situation," Hance agreed, clearly disturbed by the news.

"Isn't it, though? And now my good friend Dronadal arrives in town so soon afterwards—mere days—and presents me with these distinctive pieces. So, forgive me, my friend, but purchasing them would put me in an awkward situation, should the gentleman return."

"Couldn't you just . . . *lie?*" Gatina burst out, earning a sharp look from her father.

"Oh, Maid Companion, a man in my position has to be very careful with the truth," Erad chuckled. "Of course I could lie, but why would I? Lies can trip you up and bring trouble, and I despise trouble as much as I adore opportunity. Lying to your clients will erode your reputation if you are discovered. Much better to not know at all and truthfully confess your ignorance rather than tell a mistruth that might bite your backside unexpectedly later. In the business of stolen goods, a man is only as good as his reputation . . . and no one wants a reputation as a liar. Particularly in this circumstance."

"You've never been questioned by the authorities before?" asked Hance skeptically.

"Oh, of course, the local guardsmen and magistrates frequently ask me things, but they also know not to pry too deeply lest they learn more than they care to about their superiors and their peers in the service of the law," Erad said loftily. "We usually get along quite well. We know the rules. I can withstand a gentle interrogation in most circumstances. These were not most circumstances."

"Because the man worked for Vichetral," Gatina suggested, earning another look from her father. She knew she must do better at remaining silent. But it was challenging in this situation.

"Even that would not concern me, Maid Companion, in most circumstances," admitted the fence. "I'm a clever fellow, after all—a fence has to be, if he is to survive. Yes, I've answered the Duke's own men when they've brought me questions, and managed to do it without lying . . . *too* much. Without evidence to bring before a Lawfather, it's usually fairly simple to avoid any unpleasantness with the courts. But not in this circumstance. The gentleman's attire was sufficient to tell me that. And his means of interrogation."

"Did he strike you?" Hance asked sharply. "Threaten you?"

"Ishi's twinkling eyes, no!" chuckled Erad, without mirth. "Who would hurt a beautiful face like this? No, he put me under a truthtell spell to compel my veracity."

"Ah," said Darandol, nodding. "A wizard, then."

"You understand," agreed Erad. "I told him all I knew, which was little enough. As I said, I'm clever. But it wasn't the spell that had me concerned . . . it was his wardrobe. A *checkered bloody cloak*. His men wore the same livery. That compelled my cooperation more than his magic. And to avoid that detestable situation again, I will—sadly!—have to decline purchasing these three items. If Censor Captain Stefan returns to Lemon's Reach, I do not want to have to answer him again.

"Now, who's ready to see my magnificent lemon tree?" Erad asked, eagerly. "I'll have my man write out a letter of credit to the Temple of Ifnia for this while we do so. This will be quite a treat for you. She's in full fruit right now, and so close to Midsummer," he added conspiratorially. "So, please take care to be *very* respectful of her."

CHAPTER ELEVEN

A DUEL IN A MEADOW

*When forced to fight, fight to win. Bide your time, and then when
the moment arrives to strike, do so without hesitation.*
— *from Gatina's Heist Journal*

THEY DEPARTED INMAR BEFORE DAWN, BACK IN THEIR GUISES AS MONK AND
novitiate. It was a more somber journey than the ride to Inmar had been,
and her father rarely spoke on the first day. He had a thoughtful look on
his face the entire time, the kind that let Gatina know he was thinking—
undoubtedly about the news Lord Erad had given them.

"Censors," he finally said with a sigh, a few hours into the rumbling
journey, "I had not figured on their participation in this struggle. Censors
. . . complicate things."

"More than the Brotherhood of the Rat?" she asked.

"Far more," agreed Hance. "We had anticipated the Rats' working with
Vichetral. They're opportunistic, and they've been trying to infiltrate the
Ducal Court for years. Successfully," he added. "One of the duchess's close
advisors was a senior-level Rat. He was actually blamed for her assassination," he revealed to her. "But the Censorate has always steered well clear
of political entanglements unless they're forced into them. They see themselves as having a higher calling: regulating magic to protect the common
folk from its abuses."

Gatina was familiar with that story—even the Rats in Falas were aware
that Baron Jenerard was their agent in the Alshari court, she knew. He
had been cultivating a relationship with Duchess Enora for years, according to her mother, and it was even whispered that it was his hand that
had ended her life. But the Censorate was still largely a mystery to Gatina.

"Like during the Magocracy," she offered.

"Things weren't as bad during the Magocracy as the Narasi say," her father disagreed. "Especially in Alshar. Oh, the magelords used their powers to their advantage, it's true, but on balance, they weren't any better or worse than any other lords to their people. Just . . . more efficient. But they did use warmagi against the Narasi, during the Conquest, and the Narasi saw a lot of the old prerogatives as abusive. Apparently, it's fairer and more equitable to compel a man with a sword than with a spell. So, when they conquered the Empire, they established the Censorate to control the magi. Or try to."

"But aren't they magi too?" Gatina asked.

"Of course—you need a wizard to control a wizard. Or a well-placed dagger in his back. Unfortunately, the Wenshari magi were willing to work with the Narasi knights to do so. So, we've had four centuries of checkered cloaks to try to keep us in line. Not that it did much good," he said with a small grin. "Many of the magi in the Coastlord families went underground and hid their books and tools. The Censorate in Alshar has mostly been involved in regulating spellmongers and registered adepts, and then arresting rural magi for being unregulated."

"Like that poor footwizard they hung," Gatina recalled.

Hance nodded. "Yes, although they rarely resorted to such arbitrary brutality in the past. Unlicensed witches and footwizards usually get away with a heavy fine at most. They were clerks more than warmagi.

"But with Rard expelling all of the Censors in Castal and Remere—and in the Wilderlands—a lot of them are apparently coming here, like the trio you met on the way. Vichetral has given them safe haven, and in return they have given him and the Council of Counts their service . . . and brutality. And that was something the conspiracy did not foresee," he admitted.

"If it's just some footwizards and hedgewitches, that shouldn't be a problem," Gatina suggested. "Awful and sad, but how will that interfere with . . . whatever it is we're doing?" As soon as she spoke the words, Gatina felt a pang of regret. Nobody deserved that fate. And for tearing a cloak? She could not imagine how such a punishment fit the crime. Or why the man had been so scared. It was unjust.

"Because it won't stay contained to footwizards and hedgewitches," Hance explained. "Vichetral is no fool. He understands the great power and potential advantage of the Censors. And how desperate they are. With Rard eliminating the Bans on Magic in his lands, they have no purpose now. Vichetral is giving them one: strike at the loyalists under the guise of enforcing the Bans. The Censor who came to Lemon's Reach proves that. I suspect that Vichetral is testing them by having them track down that loot. That little book Erad talked about sounds like a record of suspected loyalists to the late Duke. That will be a problem for us."

"What can we do about it?" Gatina asked, concerned.

"What we must," he sighed. "The Censorate can be very effective when they feel their ideology is being challenged. They recruit young magi and shape their perspectives through tradition, power, and indoctrination. Each of them believes that enforcing the Bans is a nearly holy cause. They see themselves as the only protection the mundane folk have from the magical. But now they're just acting like thugs . . . very powerful, dangerous thugs with mageblades and warwands."

Gatina kept quiet when her father stopped speaking. He was clearly disturbed by the development and was using the long ride to sort out his thoughts. She devoutly wished that she could give him some solace, some suggestion of how to counter the dangerous wizards, but nothing clever came to her. This was not the kind of situation where a child's perspective was at all helpful, she suspected.

But she could still ask questions, she reasoned.

"What about the seamagi?" she asked suddenly. "Could they help?"

"The Brethren have never been particularly concerned with the wizards on the land, and the Censorate knows better than to interfere with the seamagi. It's possible we could draw them in to assist us, but that's not necessarily the wisest course of action. Their loyalties tend to stop at the seashore and are complicated on the waves. And they are as dangerous as the Censorate in their way."

"What about . . . Duke Rard?" she asked hesitantly. Invoking the man who was supposedly responsible for Lenguin and Enora's deaths was a touchy subject, she knew, but he had lifted the Bans on Magic and expelled the Censorate. Surely, he might be sympathetic to the cause.

"Duke . . . Rard," her father pronounced with a deep sigh. "Soon to be King Rard. And captor of our duchy's heirs. I'm certain that he's eager to interfere, of course, but if he had the means to do so, he would have acted by now. His wife, Duchess Grendine, is Alshari. She was Duke Lenguin's sister, married off and sent out of the duchy to spare the court her schemes and plots. No, I'm afraid a couple of backwoods spellmongers aren't going to be enough to pry the duchy from the Censorate's grasp. Nor can we look to Farise or Remere for help. There are Censors in Farise now, I'm told—they were quite enthusiastic for its conquest—and the Duke of Remere has thrown his lot in with Rard to form this new kingdom. No, Kitten, we are on our own with this struggle."

He said no more, and Gatina respected his silence until they stopped at noon to feed and water the horses at a ford. There they took some time to eat luncheon in the meadow that led to the river crossing.

The countryside was beautiful in high summer, with wheat fields and forests stretching out over the plains of the Great Vale. The air was thick with the smells of vegetation—not the cool, damp odor she was used to in Falas but a dry, hearty aroma of ripening wheat and barley. She inhaled deeply as she stretched her legs and prepared luncheon. The cheese and bread, fresh fruits, and watered wine had been purchased from the Duke's Dalliance before they left. It was much better than she had expected, though she was still hungry. She wanted something salty, of all things, to eat.

"Do you need some exercise?" her father asked unexpectedly as she was putting away the hamper and blanket after eating.

"You want me to climb something?" she asked hopefully as he began to rummage around the trunk attached to the rear of the carriage.

"No," he said, straightening. He tossed her something, and she caught it automatically. "Take off that heavy habit. It will just slow you down," he advised, as she realized what he had thrown to her.

Her shadowblade.

It was the practice sword she'd carried in Falas on that fateful mission and then on the four heists she'd assisted on in the countryside. Short, straight, slender, with a blade painted a dull black, the edge and point still gleamed just a hint from where she had sharpened it enough to be serviceable.

Hance had his own sword out—not his shadowblade but a long cavalry sword. Straight and double-edged, it was in the Narasi style, a long, heavy-hilted weapon suitable for fighting from horseback.

"Let's see how well you remember your mother's lessons," he said with a small grin. He took a guard position.

Gatina smiled and nodded. She loved swordplay more than climbing. And she was good at it. She took her own guard position.

It was a friendly match, of course, mere sparring and practicing. Hance called out corrections to her stance and grip as they worked through a few exercises, his patient advice providing improvement as their blades clashed. And it became quite apparent to Gatina that though she was good at swordplay, her father was much, much better.

She didn't mind that at all. After weeks of being Avorrita the Dull, the opportunity to be Gatina the Kitten was delicious. There were no stars when there was a sword in her hand, no numbers, no prayers, no aliases, no petty bickering with the other girls in her group. Swordplay simplified things. There was just her, her blade, and her opponent. She vowed to impress her father with what she could do.

Instead, she found that he had an endless list of gentle criticisms about her fighting. He stopped the bout repeatedly to lecture her about what she was doing wrong, what she needed to remember, and what she needed to improve upon. As tempted as she was to get angry about it, she tried to absorb his advice.

"You're fast," he praised, "and you have excellent reflexes, but if your stance is out of line, you're going to get skewered or hacked in two," he said as he made a pass with his blade. "Facing a sword this heavy, all the delicate techniques you have won't help you if your opponent bulls through your guard. Let's try that again."

"I thought the objective was to fight just long enough to find a way to get away," she asked as she resisted the slashes that he threw at her.

"It is," he agreed. "But you may not be able to. So, you should always fight as best you can. When forced to fight, fight to win. Bide your time," he counseled, "and then when the moment arrives to strike, do so without hesitation."

"And I thought thieves weren't supposed to fight," she said as her chest heaved at the effort.

"We're no longer just thieves, Kitten," he said, as he began to circle her. "Check your footwork," he cautioned as she moved to counter. "Once Duke Anguin was killed, things changed. We have to be . . . more. We cannot just let Vichetral and his minions take control over our duchy."

"Why not?" she challenged as she threw an unexpected blow at his waist. Hance neatly parried and pushed around to her left side. "Someone has to rule," she reasoned. As they continued the dance, Gatina became quicker to adjust her footing, sometimes before her father gave direction. She found those moments gratifying.

"And that's what a good many people think," nodded her father. "But I've known Vichetral almost as long as I knew Duke Lenguin. He is a man of limitless ambition. He has coveted the Duke's coronet—and, more importantly, his power—since he was young. *Left foot! Step back on your left foot!*"

Gatina struggled to match her footwork to her father's pace while also listening to his opinion on the current political strife in the duchy. Mother had told her to only fight if necessary. *If you draw your sword, then something has gone horribly wrong,* she had said, Gatina recalled. But what father said changed things, she realized.

"That, alone, would not be a bad thing, necessarily," Hance continued. "Good leaders need some ambition. But it is Vichetral's character and policies that are at issue. He was positioning his men in court to try to remove Anguin when Rard beat him to it. He wants to return Alshar to its glory days, when our Sea Lords were kings of the wave, our merchants as rich as archmagi, and our banner feared at our frontiers. Raise your point higher," he said, and slashed his sword toward her eyes. "Because if you don't, a kitten will lose an ear." He chuckled.

"What policies are we striving against?" she asked, enjoying the discussion as much as the swordplay. It was reassuring to have permission to fight. And it was exhilarating to feel the rush of adrenaline as she sought to keep pace with her father.

"Well, seizing power without authority isn't terribly nice," he pointed out as he reversed his turn and began shifting toward her right side. "Neither is conspiring to kill your sovereign. He has little respect for the temples save as how they can be used for his own purposes."

"He did execute all those priests and abbots," she agreed, dropping her left shoulder as she lunged and then recovered. "So, he's not a godly man."

"But he understands power, Kitten, and that's the problem," her father agreed as he tested her defenses. "Keep your feet in line—Better!"

She quickly adjusted her stance.

"When he struck at the heads of the temples in Falas, he kept the temples cowed against him," Hance explained. "When he invited some of the other counts to join his council—entirely illegal, in my estimation—then he was able to get the strongest lords of the Great Vale and the Coastlands to share his responsibility—and increase his own power. And soon he will go after the Sea Lords in the Great Bay by appealing to their darkest desires. He wants to start slaving again."

"I've heard rumors of that at Palomar," she nodded, and then tried to stab her father in the chest, quickly adjusting her positioning to match his.

He shifted his stance and easily parried the thrust. "They're well founded. The conspiracy is aware of the proposal and how it's likely to secure Vichetral a—temporary—hold over Alshar. He will have appeased the other major powers and made it in their best interest to keep him in power as Duke in all but name. Faster this time! He's hoping that after a few years, people will forget about the Duke's captive heirs and take the coronet for himself. Vichetral wants nothing so badly as being Duke of Alshar. Let's take a break," he suggested, lowering his blade. "You're doing very well," he added, as he leaned against the carriage. "The monastic life hasn't taken a toll on your fitness."

"I work hard in the garden," she admitted, realizing that this was the most exercise she'd had in weeks. She was nearly out of wind, and her thighs ached with the effort. So did her abdomen. Her arms were starting to feel the strain too, and her wrists felt stressed with all the contortions she'd asked them to endure. But her back and her knees hurt the most, probably, she reasoned, from the time spent on horseback.

"I want you to learn how to fight because what we're trying to do is very, very dangerous," he said thoughtfully. "And, in reality, unlikely to succeed anytime soon. Perhaps not in my lifetime," he admitted.

Gatina could not imagine her father not being around. That comment caught her off guard.

"There are only a few of us, and Vichetral moves fast and hard. Thankfully, he has a lot of enemies. Sadly, he's also good at making friends. So, we're likely in for a long, long struggle. One we may ultimately lose," he explained.

"But I will not abide living in a land where men are purchased at market like hogs and cattle. It stains the divine dignity of both the master and the slave. And it ruins the lives of the poor, who cannot compete with slaves. It's the worst sort of exploitation and one that we must always fight against."

"Aren't some peasants serfs?" Gatina asked. "Bondsmen?"

"Yes," admitted her father with a heavy sigh. "They are bound 'features of the land,' along with their first two children. But they have rights and protections under the laws of Huin and Luin," he reminded her. "A serf can sometimes sue to have his bond released by a Lawfather in some cases.

"Nor was Lenguin in favor of serfdom. Indeed, his policies directed the court to diminish the practice. There are many serfs in Rhemes," he said, shaking his head sadly. "That was a point of acrimony between Vichetral and Lenguin. Count Vichetral saw Lenguin's policies against serfdom as attacks on him personally. Vichetral profited from it—and he stands to profit much, much more if he allows the Sea Lords to raid and sell their prisoners at Alshari ports.

"Serfs cannot be bought and sold," he explained, a dark expression coming over his face. "They must remain with the lands they serve. Slaves can be sold at market and then worked to death in the fields and orchards, or worse. Slaves can be worked on the thinnest of rations and starved to death if the owner desires. Slaves can be compelled to fight each other to the death for sport," he revealed. "They can be punished arbitrarily, including cutting off their ears or hands if they do not obey. They can be exploited damnably in ways that punish the free men around them. Slavery invites abuse and cruelty. They are property, not people, and that kind of relationship demeans everyone around it. It steals the lives of the slaves, the souls of the masters, and the ambitions of the common folk."

"Well, we shouldn't let that happen, then," Gatina agreed. She thought of her friends on the streets back in Falas. They were poor—the very poorest—and they were perpetually close to a quick and violent death. But they were free. Free to starve, perhaps, but not forced to starve while they labored in another man's fields.

"No, Kitten, we shouldn't," Hance agreed. "Nor will we. Eventually. Make no mistake: Vichetral is building a strong base of power in Falas. But it is not impregnable yet, and it won't be stable for years. There are plenty of ways we can undermine it if we're clever, quiet, dedicated, and lucky. We have magic. We have stealth. We have wealth. And we know about him, while he can only guess at who we are."

"We do excel at hiding," she agreed.

"That's why that little book Erad spoke of concerns me," he admitted. "We do excel at hiding, but it is easiest to hide if no one is looking for you. Now we know someone is. Vichetral and the Censorate. He has to suspect that his political enemies were responsible for our little larceny holiday. Employing the Censorate to hunt us proves he suspects that it is some group of Coastlords who did it. And the Coastlords produce more magi than the Sea Lords or Vale Lords. So, using the Censorate to track us down suits both of their purposes."

"I don't see how that makes much difference," Gatina shrugged. "We've been hiding from the Censorate for years." She thought of the web of tunnels underneath Falas. It was more than a web, she knew; it was a small city, it seemed. It had served her ancestors for years.

"You sound like your mother," chuckled Hance. "Yes, we have . . . but they have only really pursued our hidden wizards and troves of forbidden magical lore when there was a problem. Now *we* are a problem. The conspiracy includes some of the most powerful adepts in Alshar," he reminded her.

"And we're to fear the Censorate, when we have the most powerful adepts in Alshar on our side?" she countered. She could not imagine the Shadow Council being unable to contend with these Censors. To her mind, they were the equivalent of the Town Watch, only for magi.

"When there are three times as many Censors in Alshar as normal and they have the permission of the Council of Counts to aggressively pursue us, there is reason to be cautious," her father observed.

"There is also reason to take risks, with so much at stake," Gatina considered boldly. "Father, if the Censorate is just arriving here in force, they're going to be strangers to Alshar. And unorganized," she pointed out. "That will make them sloppy."

She remembered how disorganized the Town Watch in Falas was when Vichetral's soldiers arrived. The soldiers were professional, and the Watchmen were sloppy. She had imagined the Censors to be as efficient as the Watchmen, at least until they learned their way around Alshar and its many towns and villages.

"You aren't wrong, Kitten," Hance admitted, "but it's more complicated than that. The Censors excel at investigation the way we excel at hiding. You don't yet understand just what magic can do when it's used in such a way. If the Censors manage to learn the identities of the conspiracy, even just a few of us—Darkness, even *one* of us!—then that could lead to our downfall. In a war such as this, information is as important as spells or swords. We gather information on our enemies before we strike. Now Vichetral is doing the same. The truthtell spell that Lord Erad mentioned . . . *that one spell* could unravel everything."

Gatina considered that. She was starting to understand that aspect of the struggle now—it wasn't all just about stabbing people and stealing their things. Watching how her parents had operated in Falas in the spring had demonstrated just how important knowing things was to getting anything done. And how keeping your enemies from knowing things—even your very existence as their enemy—was important to protecting yourself and taking advantage. The thought of a single spell damaging everything they'd worked for sent a chill down her spine.

But that gave her a thought. "Father, if that book is a danger to us, then could it not also be a help to us?"

Hance considered for a moment. "It sounds as if it might be, if we knew what was in it. Who was in it," he corrected. "It sounds as if Vichetral is hiring the Censorate as a kind of magical spy service. No doubt there are other things in there that could be valuable."

"Then wouldn't it be helpful to have it rather than just destroy it?" she ventured. She imagined all the illicit items the book must contain. And the names. If the families on the list were not part of the Shadow Council, she reasoned, they should be, else they would not be in the book.

"Of course it would, Kitten," he agreed with a sigh, "but we just learned about it. We don't know where it is or who has it. We have to find out those things first. We still have a lot more information to gather before we can formulate a plan around this book."

"It sounds like we're going to steal it," Gatina proposed.

Hance frowned. "You're getting ahead of yourself, Kitten," he reproved.

"It's a book we need," she reasoned, "currently in the hands of very bad men. It desperately needs to be stolen." Gatina was already considering how she could steal the little book. If she were able to find that particular Censor, that is.

"That may be, but that doesn't mean—" he began.

"It's a heist," Gatina said, smiling.

"It's not *your* heist," Hance shot back.

"We have not established that yet," Gatina riposted. "But it *is* a heist."

"It *might* be a heist," her father said, evenly, "or it might be an assassination. Or it might turn into something else again. It's too early—"

"It's a heist," Gatina insisted. "A much more interesting heist than the ones we performed in Falas. That was just for money and loot. This one is for something important—something vital."

"That doesn't mean you're going to be the one to do it!" Hance said sternly. "It's in the possession of the most dangerous warmagi in the world, following the orders of a tyrant with nearly unlimited powers at his command and no accountability for what he can do," he listed patiently. "We don't know who he is, where he is, what defenses he has, and what he knows. There are a thousand—a *billion*," he suddenly grinned, "complicating factors, and any one of them could spoil things in a very dangerous way. Even if it does turn into a heist, it's very unlikely I would send a half-trained apprentice who hasn't completed her studies to do it," he reminded her.

"We know it's in the hands of Captain Stefan, whoever that is," she reminded him.

"Who we know nothing about, save that he is a Censorate investigator," he answered.

Gatina considered. "Kiera the Great would do it," she pointed out.

Hance sighed. "Possibly. Probably," he conceded.

"Mother would do it," Gatina added, a small grin on her lips.

"She would at least try, if it was necessary." Hance sighed.

"Which has already been established," she agreed.

"What is the point of discussing this?" her father asked with a groan.

"I just want to propose that this is a heist," she countered reasonably.

"That is a matter for the Shadow Council to decide," he said, shaking his head.

"And you're the leader of the Council," she reminded him.

"It's more of an administrative position," he said, frowning.

"You can get the Council to decide to go after this book," she reasoned, "and if they do, it will be a *heist*."

"If they do, you probably won't be involved," he reminded her.

"Let's put that aside for now," Gatina said, rolling her eyes defiantly. "If it's a heist, it's going to need thieves, and we're thieves. The best in the world." She was considering how she could pick the pocket of the Censor, reasoning that a Censor would not expect a thief. He would expect a magical attack, not a mundane one.

"*I'm* the best in the world," Hance corrected. "You're just my insolent, half-trained apprentice." He said it sternly, more sternly than she expected. She stared back at him and noted the resolution in his eyes. "Now let's try another round of sparring," he suggested, raising his blade and moving away from the carriage. "We'll have to get back on the road soon."

Gatina took a position and brought her shadowblade into guard.

"It's still a heist," she said, and attacked.

CHAPTER TWELVE

AN ELEMENT OF EARTH

*Fearful times oft lead to calamity, opportunity, and great transfor-
mation. Fear them not! Embrace them! For it is in the Darkness that
we cultivate our finest talents.*

> — *from **The Shield of Darkness**,*
> *written by Kiera the Great*

"You were gone a full week!" Leonna snarled accusingly at breakfast. "You completely missed your whole turn at the laundry!"

"Did I?" Avorrita asked innocently as she spooned honey over her porridge. "I suppose I did."

"Why is that a problem, Leonna?" asked Dina, annoyed. "You didn't
have to take her place."

"Because it's unfair that she gets to skip laundry when the rest of us
have to take a turn!" the Coastlord girl said, her eyes narrow. "If I have to
do it, everyone should have to do it. Instead, she got to go off on a bloody
holiday—and miss classes, too! And devotions!" There was a savage edge
to Leonna's voice today, and she seemed willing to attack anything and
anyone who she deemed was taking advantage of her.

"It wasn't that pleasant," Avorrita defended herself. "I was stuck in a
dark carriage on a bumpy road with a boring old man for more than four
days," she reminded them. "Then I had to stay up all night for two nights
in a row while he stared up at the sky. But the inn was nice," she ventured.
"Good food. And Inmar is very pretty."

"Inmar?" Leonna asked, her eyes wide in outrage. "You got to go to
bloody *Inmar?*"

"The City of Temples!" clapped Arryn, smiling at the thought. "I've
heard it is beautiful. Isn't there a lake there?"

"A big blue one." Avorrita said, nodding. "And yes, the city really is beautiful. Bright green roofs, pink granite, fountains, elegant towers, loads and loads of sculpture. It was very colorful," she reported. "What I got to see of it. Mostly, we only went out at dusk for devotions and observations, and then slept all day. And Brother Espus *snores*," she said, wrinkling her nose at the pretend memory. "He denies it, of course, but it was like sleeping in a room with a thunderstorm."

"Why did *you* get to go?" demanded Leonna. "Why you and not the rest of us?"

"It wasn't a holiday excursion," Avorrita reminded them.

"Special assignments are given to Nocturns either because they've been specially requested or they are chosen at random," Nightsister Nimandi informed them. "I rather suspect the latter in this case. The Nightbrother needed an aide, and Avorrita was selected at the Hall of Nocturns. Just be grateful to the stars that you got to go to Inmar and not some miserable swamp along the Great Bay," she added as she finished her porridge.

"Now, because there are still two days before the chore schedule changes, I'm going to let Avorrita work in the garden instead of the laundry," she announced. "It would be too difficult and disruptive for her to be thrust into that chore when she hasn't been trained. And she looks tired," she added.

That much was true—though Gatina had done her best to hide that fact with cosmetics. Travel was always exhausting, and after hearing about the Censors—not to mention seeing them in person—she hadn't slept well. She also felt more than a little achy and her stomach hurt. Probably from riding horseback and the mediocre traveler's fare she and her father had endured on the trip back. When they had finally returned to the abbey the previous night, she had fallen into bed with her habit still on, she was so tired.

"So," the nun continued, "I'm going to put her back in the garden until the chores change. Brother Henri felt she did some good work there, and she's already familiar with the job."

"But it's *my* turn at the garden!" whined Leonna.

"You will both go," Sister Nimandi decided. "There's plenty to do this time of year, and another pair of hands will be welcome. With Nocturn Mathilde out, our group is lax in our contribution to the abbey. We must not fall behind."

"What happened to Mathilde?" Avorrita asked, concerned.

"You didn't hear?" Nimandi asked, surprised. "Her *rajira* emerged. She's getting special instruction for the next few days. We can't have a newly quickened mage running around the abbey until she understands her powers."

"When did that happen?" Avorrita asked, surprised.

"Three days ago," Dina reported. "She woke up, and every chamber pot and basin in the dormitory was frozen over. It was . . . odd."

"It was disgusting," Arryn added, wrinkling her nose.

"That is actually a pretty common indication of the emergence of *rajira*," Sister Nimandi explained. "It often manifests with elemental magic. She must have an affinity for water, then. Just be glad it wasn't fire—she might have started a blaze in her sleep. It has happened before," she said, frowning to herself at some troubling memory.

"She's very lucky," agreed Dina. "I had hoped that I would be favored by magic. I think that would be exciting."

"I don't!" sneered Leonna. "Think of it—forced to give up your title and live as a commoner? Living like an animal as some mage's apprentice? And you can't own property," she reminded them. "No more than a house. A single house," she emphasized.

"And the Censorate," Avorrita pointed out. "I saw a couple of them on my trip. They were rough-looking fellows."

"Learning magic is difficult," agreed Sister Nimandi. "In some ways harder than learning the stars. I feel fortunate that *rajira* did not come to me in my youth. I've seen many Nocturns who have suffered through it, over the years. Every season, it seems that at least one of my girls achieves her Talent. Some of their experiences were quite unpleasant. It doesn't always come to you peacefully, and for some it can cause great distress. Even after they've learned basic control," she added warningly. "Poor Mathilde has a very difficult journey ahead of her."

"I think it would be fascinating to have the power and learn," Dina mused. "My father and older brother once took me up to the northern plateaus in the Wilderlands where we met a wise old witch, a few years ago. Supposedly the greatest hedgewitch in the north. She could do amazing things! That was before the . . . the invasion, though," she added, her face changing. "I wonder if she survived the goblins."

"Aren't goblins only about four feet tall?" asked Arryn curiously. "That's about my size. How can they be a threat?"

"When there are thousands and thousands of them, they can be devastating," Dina answered somberly. "That's why I was sent south. They're positively infesting the Wilderlands now. They all but took Tudry—that's a little town north of Vorone—and they still threaten the summer capital. Duke Lenguin stopped them from going further, but north of Vorone, they're everywhere. I saw a few before I departed. Vicious killers, all black fur and big eyes," she said, shuddering at the memory.

"Now, don't go filling our heads with terrors on such a lovely morning, Dina," Sister Nimandi scolded. "Remember, there isn't a goblin for hundreds of miles. All of you, off to your chores before the bell. I'll clear away the table. That was poor Mathilde's chore this week."

———

IT WAS GOOD TO BE BACK IN THE GARDEN, IF ONLY FOR A FEW DAYS . . . though Leonna's presence was distracting. The Coastlord girl recited a litany of complaints as she grudgingly weeded under Brother Henri's watchful eye, taking issue with the dirt, the labor, the insects, the heat of the summer sun, the lack of a breeze, the laziness of everyone around her, and everything else except the color of the sky. Avorrita was certain that would be brought up eventually.

Brother Henri endured her with the patience of a monk as he trimmed herbs with a well-honed pair of gardening shears on one row of the garden while the Nocturns were dutifully tending the long, lush rows of tomatoes on another. No doubt he'd seen a hundred girls like her over the years and had apparently found silence the best answer to her endless complaining.

Avorrita was impressed by the stoic way he grunted answers to her questions and ignored her jibes at the abbey. He had already directed the older students on picking ripe tomatoes, cucumbers, and tubers. The kitchens had placed a larger-than-usual order, he had explained when all of the Nocturns had arrived that day, in preparation for the upcoming Midsummer holiday.

Avorrita, on the other hand, was starting to think about suddenly grabbing the garden shears and cutting off all of Leonna's hair.

If nothing else, Leonna's bickering was a good distraction from thinking about the little book the Censors were writing. Gatina had thought of little else since she'd returned from Inmar. While she appreciated her father's concerns and was starting to understand the dangers of the dreaded Censorate, she could not get the idea of stealing that book out of her head.

Leonna's incessant complaining was also reminding her that she was Nocturn Avorrita, quiet, shy, and dull, not Gatina, Kitten of Night, shadowthief apprentice and veteran of six entirely successful heists. The dental appliance helped that transition, as did the heavy gray nun's habit. The garden was a far cry from exotic Inmar, enigmatic fences, brutal Censors, and swordplay in a meadow, but the work did give her a certain serenity as she more fully became Avorrita.

"Take care with those stems, Nocturn!" Brother Henri suddenly said to the Coastlord girl as she was tying tomato plants to wooden stakes. "They are more delicate than you think, and a careless twist can ruin an entire branch. Each branch can bear several fruits, so a heavy hand can ruin weeks of growth and reduce the harvest."

"I think I know how to tie a *bloody knot*!" Leonna fumed as she worked. "Why must we tie them like this, anyway? Aren't they strong enough on their own?"

"The more support they have, the heavier the fruit can be," Brother Henri explained while he watched the girl work. "By tying them thus, we can expose the inner leaves to more sunlight and encourage more flowers to bloom, which leads to more fruit. If they have sufficient water," he added. "But that is all for naught if you manhandle the branches and destroy them. Do be careful!" he reproved.

Avorrita didn't find it too difficult to do the work. There were hundreds of tomato plants in this part of the garden, painstakingly grown from seedlings and carefully cultivated. Already, the rows upon rows of plants were filled with little green fruit, some already producing a hint of red. She found it an opportunity to practice a delicate touch—an important skill for picking locks, swordplay, or thieving in general. It was a challenge, sometimes, to maneuver the stems of the bushy plants away from where they wanted to go and into a shape that would produce more, but it wasn't that much of a challenge. It was annoying to hear Leonna turn such a simple task into a chance to complain.

"I don't see why we need all of these, anyway," Leonna dismissed as her fingers flailed on the vines. "I don't fancy tomatoes; my nurse back home said that they could give you the ague sometimes. And we rarely have them at meals."

"Because they are not ripe yet, Nocturn," Brother Henri answered. "And your nurse was foolish if she believed that old tale. There is nothing unwholesome about tomatoes if you prepare and store them properly.

Some of these will be served fresh, when they are ripe. Some will be dried in the sun and stored—but never in pewter," he cautioned. "This variety is meant for neither fate. The abbey cooks them down into sauce, which you will enjoy later in the year . . . if there are enough fruit left to do so after you've mangled so many. Do be careful!" he said, sternly this time, as he dropped the shears on the ground and went to correct Leonna's abysmal attempt at staking.

"Brother Henri," Avorrita asked quietly as she straightened from the work, her back aching, "how do you get such abundant flowers on these? Back home, the peasants' tomatoes don't seem to grow as richly as these."

"Oh, there are many secrets to cultivating the red fruit," the old monk answered with a chuckle. "A good gardener learns all the mysteries of growing them over the years. Good and frequent watering with good drainage, keeping the soil stirred up around the roots to let some air in, and, of course, ensuring they have the right soil," he explained as he handed Leonna another stake and a bundle of string. "Sunlight, water, and soil—plants need them in the right combination to flourish, even as the planets need mass, spin, gravity, and velocity to stay in their courses. Soil is the most important. Every year, we raid the chicken coops and the dung heaps for the magic ingredients to add to the soil, lest it become tired and worn through use."

Leonna stopped, the stake held limply in her hand, and stared at the next plant in need of tending. There was a horrified expression on her face.

"You mean . . . we're digging around . . . in *poop*?" she asked, dismayed.

"Only the finest poop, Nocturn," Brother Henri explained with a smile. "It has to be mixed in the right proportions with mulch and—"

Gatina never learned what else was added to the soil, because Leonna started wailing like she was being beaten.

"Dear gods, I cannot believe that you expect us to toil at this miserable chore in this unbearable heat amidst so many bugs for so terribly long . . . and now you're telling us that we're wallowing in filth?" she cried, actually producing a tear. "That explains the bloody awful smell, at least! This . . . is . . . barbaric!"

Gatina suppressed a snicker at the girl's discomfort, though her outburst had attracted the attention of all of the other Nocturns working away in the garden. Gatina didn't understand the complaint about the smell—she found it intoxicating and relaxing to be working with the fragrant plants. Nor did she concern herself with the prospect of manure at her feet. She'd swum through a city sewer before; a little chicken poop was hardly a problem for her.

But Leonna seemed distraught at the very thought of it. She stared at her hands as if they were covered in blood, though only a little dirt clung to her dainty fingers.

"I . . . am covered . . . in chicken poop!" she wailed.

"Not entirely," Brother Henri consoled her. "Some of that is horse dung, cow poop, even some poop from the pigsty," he informed her, helpfully.

"We are *all* covered in poop," Avorrita pointed out, showing her own hands—which were far dirtier. "It washes off, Leonna. I promise."

"The filth might wash off, but that does not cleanse the humiliation!" Leonna shot back bitterly, her face stained with tears. "Perhaps you don't mind the stench and the shame of that—you provincial girls know little of polite society—and this mumbling lout seems to revel in it! But I am the product of far better, and I am destined for even greater prospects! I was not raised to be forced to labor in such conditions! I was raised to practice the nobler virtues of society!"

"Such as . . . humility, Nocturn?" Brother Henri asked, his wrinkled eyes narrowing. "That is known as a noble virtue in most polite society."

"Humility is not humiliation!" Leonna stormed at the old monk, dropping the stake as if it were a serpent. For some reason, that activated something within Gatina. A wellspring of rage and defiance burst out of her as the Coastlord girl railed against kind Brother Henri. Avorrita was stunned at the outburst. Gatina was livid. Leonna was so *mean* . . .

Suddenly, the shears that Brother Henri had dropped flew to her hand, unbidden and entirely without physical action on her part. One moment they were on the ground, the next the cool metal of their handle was firmly pressing into her fingers. A wave of emotion swept through her, and her stomach wrenched painfully, as if she herself was being stabbed with the garden shears. There was a heat spreading through her, one she had never felt before. This sensation started at her stomach and inched out along her spine, sending a jolt of fire through her body.

Unfortunately, the unusual occurrence had attracted attention—a lot of attention. Every girl in the garden was staring at her, even as she was staring at Leonna, the blades of the garden shears bright in the morning sun. For a single moment, the girls' eyes locked together, and for a blissful instant there was real fear and confusion in Leonna's eyes, not mere outrage.

"Nocturn?" Brother Henri asked, concerned, as he realized what had happened. "Are you well?"

Avorrita couldn't speak. There was a terrible tearing in her midsection, and she stared at the shears in sudden horror, realizing what had happened. The whole world spun around her as she dropped them . . . and then she fell into the soft, loamy ground, her face pressed into the manure-laden soil. Then all was Blessed Darkness.

———

When Gatina next awoke, instead of the now-familiar ceiling of the box bed in the dormitory she found herself on a far larger, far softer bed that was unmistakably stuffed with feathers, not straw, surrounded by clean white muslin curtains suspended from a sturdy wooden canopy. She looked around in confusion, realizing that something was dreadfully wrong.

There was still a pain in her lower stomach, a gnawing, growling pain that felt like an animal was trying to burrow through her abdomen. She was wracked with aches in her back, in her legs, in her arms, as if she had tumbled down the stairs or been in a particularly grueling sparring match. And everything looked . . . strange.

Her head was swimming with sensation, as if the light beyond the curtains were casting strange shadows around her. But there weren't shadows, exactly, that were confusing her eyes. Things just looked different—more vibrant, more active, somehow. A thrill of alarm washed through her as she struggled to figure out where she was and what had happened to bring her here.

Then she realized something else disturbing. Her dental appliance was missing.

She didn't normally sleep with it, but popping it over her real teeth was the first thing she did when she awoke, before she got out of her box bed. Her tongue confirmed without a doubt that her fake front teeth were not in her mouth. She didn't know where they were. But she did know that losing them exposed her. The buckteeth were an essential part of her Avorrita persona, and without them she risked discovery. She began to panic. She pushed back the blanket that covered her to discover her habit replaced with a sturdy cotton nightdress.

"You're awake!" a strange, mature female voice called from beyond the curtains.

"Y-yes," Gatina said, after a moment's pause. Her senses reeled again, and a wave of nausea passed over her. "Am I . . ."

"You are fine, girl," the sympathetic voice assured her as a gnarled hand pulled back the curtain on one side of the bed. "You just fainted, is all. Well, that wasn't all, of course, but that's why you're here."

"Where?" demanded Gatina.

"You had a bumpy time, my dear," the woman explained, "and you are in the infirmary for a bit of observation. Nothing to be concerned about."

The woman was a nun, of course, but she did not wear the black or gray habit that Gatina had become accustomed to. She wore the soft tan vestments of a Tryggite nun, a much different cut from the Saganites', under a crisp white cotton apron. Her face was wizened under her cowl, but her eyes were bright and kind, and there was a sympathetic smile on her thin lips.

"I am Birthsister Tria," she introduced herself as she pushed all the curtains back, letting in the light from the window. It was twilight, Gatina saw, as the long shadows of dusk extended across the room. The sky outside was orange and purple . . . and seemed oddly strange, even alien. The colors were vibrant, almost humming, and she could feel a kind of pressure from them as the light slowly faded away. It was as if she'd never really seen a sunset before. "I'm from the chapel, in town. They call me in when there is an occasion such as this."

"Such as what? What happened?" Gatina asked

"What do you remember?" the kindly nun asked as she helped Gatina sit up.

The sister adjusted the pillows behind her to help Gatina get more comfortable.

"I remember working in the garden, then . . . it all gets kind of hazy," she admitted, her voice scratchy from sleep. "Now I just feel . . . awful. And strange."

"That's because you finally received Trygg's Blessing," explained Sister Tria. "Nothing to worry about. Your monthlies have come—your first, I'm assuming."

"I . . . I suppose," agreed Gatina, realizing what had happened in the garden. "But why do I feel so odd?"

"Because, like many young Coastlords, you also had your *rajira* emerge with the onset of your menses. *Menarche*, it's called."

"I remember," Gatina nodded. Indeed, she had attended services at the chapel of Trygg back home in Cysgodol where she'd learned about the inevitable Blessing of Trygg—the monthly bleeding that promised children someday when she was wed. The nuns there had explained what it was, what to expect, and how to contend with it when it arose. It was supposed to be a tangible sign of the grace of the mother goddess. It felt, instead, like a punishment. "But why do I feel so *awful?*"

"Your first courses can often be startling," soothed Sister Tria, patting her hand. "They are a Mystery, something that can't be understood until it's experienced. And they do take a toll on your body. It will never be pleasant, but you will get used to it in time.

"But the discomfort is likely compounded by your *rajira* emerging," she continued. "From what Brother Henri told me, you had an unexplained . . . happening just before you fainted."

"I . . . Well, the garden shears," she remembered, "they flew into my hand. I don't know why, but they just flew across the garden—"

"Which is how we know your *rajira* emerged, and while it is an unusual manifestation of magical power, it is not unique. It indicates that you have an affinity to the Greater Element of Earth instead of Water, Fire, or Wind. That's all. But it is unmistakable, and it is conclusive. You have manifested magical Talent. And apparently a strong one, too," she added.

"You know about that?" Gatina asked, surprised.

"I'm a mage, myself, in a small way," Sister Tria admitted. "Fully inspected and registered by the Censorate of Magic. Only, my Talent is just barely present, just enough to cast a few small cantrips. That's why the temple ensured I was posted in Ejecta, to help ease the transition of the young people who present with *rajira*," she explained. "It's helpful to have someone who understands the intricacies of the process. I've helped many a young lass contend with the onset. I understand Nocturn Mathilde is in your group. She was my patient just a few days ago when her own Talent emerged in much the same circumstances. Without the fainting," she added.

"I didn't mean to faint," Gatina confessed.

"Of course you didn't," agreed the nun. "But that sometimes happens in a moment of stress like that. Nothing to be ashamed of. But your *rajira* is why you feel a little extra strange. You are adapting to an entirely new set of sensations as you start to perceive thaumaturgical energies for the first time. It's as alarming as your monthlies sometimes, but you will get used to that as well." She poured Gatina a cup of water and handed it to her. "Did you get hurt in the garden?" the nurse asked, handing Gatina a cup from the bedside table.

"Thank you. No. But my back hurt all day. Then I got dizzy, and I became sick," Gatina said, pausing to take a sip of water. She did not mention her metal attraction and overreaction. This was a temple school, after all, not a magical academy. "My back still hurts." She also realized how tired she was.

The nurse stood and bent down at the bedside table. When she straightened up, she presented Gatina with a basket. "These will help. You have rags, herbal tinctures to help with the cramping, and a few extra undergarments, and a few pearls of scented soap for washing. And, of course, the sachet containing your soiled undergarments. At the end of your first menses, it is traditional to burn them at the altar of the chapel as a devotion to the All-Mother. Courtesy of the Temple of Trygg." The nurse winked at her. She patted Gatina's leg, and before turning away, she said, "You can return to your dormitory when you like. I think it's nearly suppertime. Have you eaten?"

"No, not since breakfast," Gatina admitted.

"Well, you might want to stick to just porridge tonight," Sister Tria suggested. "I've always had a fondness for good . . . porridge," she added lightly.

Gatina could not help herself—her eyes bulged and she stifled a gasp. But she remembered the proper response.

"My grandmother's porridge was hearty and . . . delicious." She gulped.

Sister Tria nodded knowingly. "I thought as much," she sighed. "But you can't be too careful. You might fare better at eating with this," she said, holding out her hand. When she opened her palm, she revealed the dental prosthetic she'd lost. "Then again, you might not."

"Thank you," Gatina whispered, her mind whirring, as she took back the teeth and slipped them over her own. "I was wondering where that was."

"I've been a nun at this shrine for many, many years, my dear," Sister Tria assured. "But long before that, I was a girl from a good Coastlord family, like yourself. A very special family," she emphasized. "I needn't know any details, but it's good to know who your friends are, especially these days. If you ever need anything, please let me know. Now, as soon as you feel up to it, you are released to go back to your dormitory. You'll get further instruction about the change in your schedule soon," she informed her.

"Change in my schedule? For my monthlies?" Gatina asked, confused.

"No, my dear, for you to start your magical training. First with a tutor, and then with the temple's regular introductory class. And then there is your examination to determine the extent of your *rajira*, your registration with the Censorate, and, of course, the notification of your parents. You do have parents, don't you?"

"The last time I checked." Gatina nodded.

"They need to be told . . . although I'm certain they suspected already. You should write to them. But you should be excited," Sister Tria added. "You are about to embark on a magnificent journey. Both toward womanhood and toward being a mage. There's no life quite like it," she assured Gatina as she turned to go.

Gatina sat in silent reflection after the wizened woman left. Her monthlies had started. *Was that why she had had such a bizarre reaction to metals?* she wondered. *And why did it have to feel so . . . miserable?* As comfortable as this bed was, she immediately swung her legs out of the bed and stood up, only to realize just how wobbly and sore she was.

She balanced on the bed for a moment and looked around the infirmary. She saw six beds in total and one other nurse. She was surprised by how large the facility was for such a small abbey. But then Gatina remembered that she had not seen an infirmary in Ejecta Village, and she realized that Palomar Abbey likely provided medical care for the village as well as the temple. Each bed had the same curtains and bedside table. The nurses worked at a large shared desk near the door.

As she gathered her strength, she looked at the foot of the bed. Her clothing was there. She quickly, and cautiously, changed into her clothing, careful to keep herself situated away from anyone's eyes. Once dressed, she gathered the basket and left for her dormitory.

She arrived just as dinner was breaking up, which was fine. Despite Sister Tria's suggestion, she didn't think she could eat. Instead, she quietly went upstairs and put the basket of feminine supplies away in the cupboard under her box bed.

As she did so, she saw the little silk bag under her clothes that held her mother's cards. She should be working on her own, of course, but she hadn't had much time, other than a few sketches in the garden. She found working on her cards there to be inspiring, offering her far more spiritual fulfillment than all of the abbey's devotions. On impulse, she pulled them out and did one of the exercises Mother had shown her: selecting a single card at random to reflect on the momentous events of the day.

It was the Six of Ships: the card known as *Transformation*. It showed a sailing galley cutting its sails and deploying oars. The first thing that came to her mind was the arrival of her *rajira*.

But, she knew, there was more to it than her Talent. Her life was fully transforming now. Before, she never questioned whether she would receive the arcane gift, only when she would receive it. She knew now, though, that it was larger than magic. Now she was transitioning from a girl to a woman, from a child to a mage, from an apprentice to an adept . . . eventually. And, she realized, with the arrival of her *rajira*, Censors would not hesitate to question her.

She sighed, then looked at the card again, realizing something else. *Ships* might indicate travel.

"That's . . . interesting," she whispered to herself.

"What's interesting?" asked a voice from behind her.

Gatina startled—she hadn't realized that anyone else was in the room. She whirled around to see Mathilde standing there, a concerned expression on her face.

"Oh!" Avorrita's voice said as Gatina slipped the persona on like an old pair of slippers. She made the cards disappear. "You startled me."

"They said that you'd gotten Trygg's Blessing and fainted in the garden," the other Nocturn said. "And that you probably had *rajira*."

Avorrita nodded. "It appears that I do. I . . . I don't know exactly what that means, exactly. I wasn't expecting either of them."

"One is inevitable; the other . . . Well, I suppose you just have to figure that out. That's what I'm doing," she said, turning and snatching a parchment from off her bed. "I got this yesterday. You'll probably get one tomorrow, when they get news of what happened."

"What's this?" Avorrita asked, curious, as Mathilde handed her the parchment.

"Your new orders—mine, but yours will be the same," she answered. "I just thought you'd like to know, so you wouldn't be surprised. I don't know what I'm going to do—I spent the last few days getting poked and prodded and asked stupid questions so that they could figure out just how Talented I am. I don't know how I'm going to explain this to my parents," she confessed sadly. "I suddenly miss my dog all the more."

"I suddenly wish I had a dog to miss," agreed Avorrita as she read the notice.

Dear Nocturn Initiate Mathilde,

We have been informed of your possible onset of rajira. *As a result, in accordance with Censorate regulation, you must submit to examination and elementary training in accordance with the Bans on Magic. While this will, unfortunately, have an impact on your current academic and devotional education, in accordance with our charter it is part of Palomar Abbey's duty to ensure that all magically Talented students are adequately examined, tested, and given elementary instruction in their emerging abilities to ensure that you do not pose a danger to yourself, others, or the Abbey.*

In place of lessons this week and for the foreseeable future, you are to report to Nightbrother Heziak at Zenith Hall for additional training in the specific art to which you have been called by the gods. This should not affect your ability to complete the Mysteries of Sagan or your continued education. Your instructors have been made aware of the change in your schedule and will adjust your lessons accordingly.

As is sometimes the case, you may develop only a minor degree of Talent. While this still necessitates registration with the Censorate and the applicable Ducal authorities, as well as subject you to conditions under the Bans on Magic, you will find that the disruption to your life will likewise be minor. In the case that you are judged a strong or extraordinary Talent, you will be given advanced instruction by a competent and qualified tutor to begin your life amongst the magi. It may interest you to know that some Talented magi find the serenity and discipline of the Temple of Sagan to be a refuge from the rigors of secular magic and elect to take holy orders. If this is of interest to you, please inform the inspector, and arrangements will be made to discuss it further. If, however, you display any uncontrollable outbursts of power that the staff cannot control, please know that we are obligated to inform the local Censor, who will take appropriate steps in accordance with the Bans on Magic.

May the stars grant you a billion blessings as you embark on your new journey,

Abbot Handrig

"Darkness!" Avorrita swore as she looked up from the note. "We have to submit to an examination? And . . . the *Censorate?*" she asked in disbelief.

"It's part of being a . . . a mage," Mathilde said. "It sounds so strange to say that about myself."

"I know," groaned Avorrita. "And then to get my monthlies at the same time. I feel like I'm an entirely different person now, and I don't know how to act." She looked at Mathilde carefully. "How are you doing? How does it feel?"

"It's . . . odd," the other girl confessed. "I always knew it was a possibility. That's why I was assigned to this group. We all have a higher-than-normal possibility of *rajira*, thanks to our ancestry. It's part of being a Coastlord, I suppose. But . . . I never really thought it would happen to me."

"Me, either," Avorrita lied. In truth, not one child of House Furtius who was born with the distinctive white hair had failed to get *rajira*, to one degree or another. "I guess we were favored by the gods. Or cursed."

"Which one, though?" Mathilde asked. "What am I going to tell my parents? What is this going to do to our . . . our future?" she asked anxiously.

Gatina considered. Then she grinned weakly. "Well, if it gets us out of mathematics lessons, it can't be entirely bad, can it?"

CHAPTER THIRTEEN

A MYSTERIOUS WOUND

Aspirations of perfection in our Art are misplaced and dangerous. The pursuit of mastery in thieving and magic are about effort and desire, not the pursuit of an elusive and unattainable perfection. There are no perfect thieves, merely those who make more of an effort and desire to succeed where others have failed. A good thief takes those elements and uses them to better himself, his Art, and our House accordingly.

*— from **The Shield of Darkness***
Commentaries

For three long days, Gatina endured Nightbrother Heziak's exhaustive examinations, most of which consisted of her sitting there while the Talented monk cast spells, asked her questions, and made notes on a long scroll of parchment. Occasionally, he would have her try different tasks and record the results. The man looked harried—apparently, there had been a number of emerging magi popping up among the Nocturns, and he was responsible for examining them all. As a result, he was frequently called away to other chambers in Horizon Hall to conduct examinations on other Nocturns, leaving Gatina sitting, bored, waiting for her own to resume.

"It appears you have quite a considerable Talent, Nocturn," Brother Heziak finally sighed as he sanded the ink on the scroll. "Congratulations are in order. I've only had a few of you test this strong this year."

"What does that mean?" Gatina asked, earnestly, in Avorrita's quiet voice.

"It means that you will have to be trained to use your new powers," he said as he rolled up the scroll and wrote her name on the outside. "It also means that you will have to register with the Censorate as a full mage, not merely a sport or residual Talent. You will, sadly, lose your title and ability to own property as well as be subject to other restrictions, but it's not all bad," he suggested. "I've been able to make a good life for myself here with my Talent."

"I'm to be trained . . . here? What about my devotions? My classes?" she asked, trying to sound horrified.

"Oh, you'll get some basic instruction at Palomar, things like how to manifest and use magesight, how to raise and ground your natural arcane energies, some basic thaumaturgical theory, the first two or three staffs of runes, and how to do a few simple cantrips that most magi can manage, but the level and extent of your training will be up to your parents. As I am familiar with your family," he added, referring to Nocturn Avorrita's legacy, "I should imagine some private tutors will be hired.

"Until then, you will report to Sister Tavane in this hall every afternoon after luncheon to begin your introduction to the arcane sciences. And there may be other duties and instruction required of you, depending upon the scope and nature of your developing Talent. Do you have any questions?"

"I . . . I don't really know," Avorrita said honestly. "This is all very confusing. But that means I don't miss mathematics?" she asked, a hint of whine in her voice.

Brother Heziak laughed. "I'm afraid not. You will need that discipline when you start studying deeper magic, in any case. You will find that Saganites often excel at the arcane, thanks to their firm grounding in the Mysteries of Sagan. Now be off," he dismissed. "And a billion blessings on your new life!"

The next few days were hard. In addition to her regular courses, Gatina began to learn the basics of magical theory at a rapid-fire pace. She and a dozen other Nocturns and Initiates crowded into a chamber for hours every afternoon, and as they learned the basics of raising power and manipulating arcane energies, an entirely new set of rules and laws had to be memorized. They also had to demonstrate what they had learned to Nightsister Tavane, who was charged with teaching them.

But Gatina was pleased that she made quick progress. She learned how to manifest magesight, the wizard's ability that allowed her to perceive faint lines of magical force that seemed to be everywhere, to some degree. She learned to meditate quietly and gather power from those energies until it accumulated in her mind enough to be directed. She learned the first sixteen runes that allowed her to transform that power symbolically and channel it to a specific purpose if she could focus her mind properly. And she learned the elements of shaping those forces into symbols and flows, how she could produce some minor effects if she followed the rules.

She studied the *Perinisi*, the laws of magic. She learned the *Perada*, the arcane use of the Lesser Elements in magic. On top of constellations, planets, moons, and the other matters she was learning in the Mysteries, it seemed overwhelming.

But she made progress. Gatina had a quick mind and a sense of understanding about magic, as if she had been just waiting to be introduced to it. Most students struggled with one aspect of the discipline or another, but Gatina seemed to pick them up naturally. And some of it helped her make sense of a lot of things in her life.

Using magesight, for example, she was able to magnify the very smallest of things until she could see them in detail. Or she could see far into the distance as if she were close by. She noticed throbbing lines of arcane power pouring out of the tiny waterfalls that flanked the tower, and the more subtle currents of earth energy the garden seemed to produce and thrive within. Fires were of particular interest with magesight, as the whirling plasma sparkled with incredible intensity and shot bits of elemental energy out to her like sparks.

It was all very exciting, and it was hard to keep to her alias sometimes because of how distracting the new knowledge was. The Mysteries of Sagan were fascinating in their way, but they were mostly passive. The Nightbrothers observed the Sacred Cosmos in the Blessed Darkness, but they couldn't *do* anything about it.

Magi, on the other hand, could take the forces of the universe and bend them to their will in some small ways. That was far more exciting than merely gazing at the stars . . . and taking complicated mathematical notes on the results of your observations.

While she, like the other students, was tempted to explore their newfound powers and knowledge outside of Horizon Hall, they were strongly cautioned against it by the stern Sister Tavane. Such flirtations could invite the attention of the Censorate of Magic, she warned, and should be avoided until they were far deeper into their studies.

"Well, I suppose I'll be apprenticed off now instead of married off." Mathilde sighed as they walked back to their residence after a particularly grueling session. It had been a week since Gatina burned her sachet on

Trygg's altar, and she was feeling much better now. "That's not so bad, I suppose."

"I guess it depends on the master," considered Avorrita. "And the husband. In any case, I think you'll do well as a mage," she praised. "You're really good at this. As good as Arryn is at math or Leonna is at complaining."

"I'm not certain that's a fair comparison," her friend laughed. "Leonna has studied for years at complaining, I'd guess. What do you think you'll do?"

Avorrita shrugged. "That depends on my parents. Probably a tutor at first, and then perhaps an apprenticeship. We'll just have to see how good I am."

———

GATINA WAS STARTLED AWAKE THAT NIGHT, JUST AFTER SHE'D FALLEN ASLEEP following Vespers, when someone knocked on her box bed. That alone wasn't unusual; like the other Nocturns, she was occasionally summoned in the middle of the night for special devotions, special instruction, or special service. She sleepily slipped her teeth in and then donned her habit and pulled up the cowl over her head before opening the door to her box bed.

What was unusual was the boy who was waiting for her downstairs after Sister Nimandi tiredly escorted her down to the common room. It was her brother—in his Dain alias, of course, but she did not expect that.

"Cousin!" he said, a little too loudly for this hour. "You have been summoned for special instruction. I hope you got a good nap," he added.

"Not nearly long enough." Avorrita shook her head.

"Then best get this done quickly and back to bed before dawn, if you're lucky," Sister Nimandi said with a yawn. "That's what I'm doing."

"Come along, Nocturn," Dain commanded, and began walking before she could say a word. Avorrita sighed and begrudgingly followed. She was tempted to break her alias prematurely as they crossed the darkened abbey grounds. It was an overcast night—the sort the Saganites hated—and there were few enough people around. If it hadn't been for magesight allowing her to see in the dark, she would have tripped and stumbled a dozen times.

"Where are we going?" Gatina finally asked as they passed the last little row of darkened cottages at the edge of the abbey grounds, the humble residences of the many lay retainers needed to keep the busy temple working. They had passed all of the regular halls already, but Atopol kept purposefully striding along.

"You'll see when we get there," he said mysteriously. "Do try to keep up!"

"Do try to slow down!" Gatina replied. "Your legs are twice as long as mine!"

Before she knew it, her brother had silently ducked onto the densely wooded path and followed a winding trail that led up the side of the great cliff. It wasn't until they crossed one of the little streams that tumbled down from above that she realized how high up they were.

"What is this place?" she demanded, as she saw a fairly large building through the trees.

"This used to be the abbey's own grist mill," Atopol explained. "It was built on the side of the mountain about the time Kiera the Great came to Alshar, so I'm told. But a local lord built a bigger and faster one a few miles away, and the abbey grinds wheat there now. Watch your step!" he called as she stumbled.

"I'm fine!" Gatina insisted, exasperated. She hated it when Atopol was smug. And tonight, his smugness seemed in high form. "I'm assuming we won't be watching the stars tonight? So, what will we be doing?"

"Shadow sent for us" was his cryptic reply. Gatina nodded in the darkness. That made sense. For a moment, she was thrilled—this might indicate he was sending them on another mission.

With great ceremony, Atopol opened a small, narrow door in the ancient mill. And Gatina's grand ideas about a mission came crashing to a sudden stop.

The inside was quite dusty, she saw, and the wooden gears and cogs that turned the power of water falling down the cliff into a force strong enough to turn the two great grinding wheels filled the space inside. She actually understood how that worked now, mathematically, she realized. It was a function of gravity, pressure, motion, and work. That surprised her. Of course, the millwork had been silent for years, and the great stones were still.

Atopol led her to the bottom of the mill, down a narrow staircase and into what must have been where the flour was expelled from the millstones above and collected. It was empty now, save for three shadowy shapes.

"Cat and Kitten, as requested, Master!" Atopol announced.

A single flame suddenly ignited, and the wick of a lantern began to burn, illuminating the room. Her father stood in the shadows, in his guise as Dareth. There were two others with him, a man and a woman, both dressed in the gray habits of Duskbrothers, only without any insignia showing.

"Thank you, Cat." Her father nodded. "You've already met Atopol. May I formally present my daughter, Gatina anna Furtius, the Kitten of Night. And allow me to introduce Master Andivor, of Rhemes, whose name-of-art is Lord Steel, and Mistress Silva, also of Rhemes, who is known as Lady Mist of House Furtius, of course," he added.

"Rhemes?" asked Gatina, surprised.

"Not everyone from Rhemes supports Count Vichetral," assured the woman in a rich voice. "Indeed, some of us despise him."

"Andivor and Silva are your cousins—second and third, respectively—and they have been sent for to give you some special lessons," Hance informed them. "Andivor is a master swordsman and trained me, my sister, my cousins, and your mother over the years. His wife, Silva, is a mage—but a very special kind of mage. Shadowmagic," he explained. "She is to begin your tutelage in photomancy."

"I taught your mother that, as well," Mistress Silva nodded with a fond smile. "Your father was taught by one of our uncles . . . Lonreer, I believe?"

"Hastamult, actually," Hance chuckled. "He was my great-uncle. And a great wizard, before he died. But Lonreer is also a good shadowmage. As are you, of course," he added.

"In order to make the best of your time at the abbey, it has been decided to accelerate your training, since both of your *rajira* has emerged."

"Photomancy?" Gatina asked skeptically. "I've been learning basic magic for only two weeks! How am I ready for shadowmagic?"

"I will take your elementary level into account," assured Mistress Silva. "While I work to catch you up on what you need to know, Andivor will work with Atopol. And vice versa.

"And I will work with you both," her father announced. "While we are waiting on . . . well, for what we are waiting on, this is the best use of your time. I think you will be particularly challenged by Master Andivor. Your mother was," he added as Andivor nodded. He was a large man, half a head taller than her father and much broader across the shoulders. He looked more like a woodsman than a swordmaster.

Gatina did remember Mother talking about her time learning from the master swordsman. "Yes, Father, she did mention him when she began instructing me herself. She said he was an unrelenting taskmaster."

Hance laughed—a deep, full-body sound that had always made Gatina happy. Andivor joined in, adding a bass note to the laughter.

"He is that, indeed, Kitten, but you are far more accomplished in swordplay than was your mother when we married. Her family was far more focused on magic."

Gatina looked up at her father, surprised by what he had said. In her mind, her mother was always the best at everything, just like her father. She had never considered that her mother had not always enjoyed mastery at swordplay; she had always assumed so, since the first time they trained that summer.

"Do not worry, I have every confidence you will do fine," her father assured. "You have actually used a sword in a fight, and that is more than your mother and your brother did when they began working with him. And Silva, you will find, is a true adept in photomancy, one of the best shadowmagi in Alshar. She will build on what you have learned so far, with a bit more of the theory to start with, and then you will move into the applications of the spells. An essential skill for your service to the House."

"It will take many lessons for you to understand the complexities of this most subtle of arts," assured Silva. She was a large woman, a good match for Andivor in size, with a pleasant voice. She spoke with confidence. "Photomancy is, of course, only one important aspect of shadowmagic, but without it, the rest of the discipline fails."

"What, exactly, is photomancy?" Gatina asked, hesitantly.

"It is the practice of producing, bending, filtering, and banishing light," explained Silva as she took a seat on the edge of an old crate. "A small thing, it seems, but from such details entire worlds of understanding may manifest."

"I've already learned about reflection and refraction in poetics," Gatina bragged.

"Then you understand some of the essentials—one reason why our family prefers the Saganite temple to other orders for the instruction of the young. The Mysteries of Sagan prepare you for the discipline of photomancy better than any others. When you understand that light is neither particle nor wave, how it reacts in air or in vacuum, and all of its other peculiarities, you can shape and manipulate it as easily as you can arcane energies. But it is a long process. And it begins with . . . the *photon*," she said breathlessly.

For nearly an hour, Gatina listened raptly to the wizard explain the fundamentals of light and how magic affected it and was affected by it. She became fascinated by the discussion, and she enjoyed having a tutor who was so willing to entertain her questions. The sound of clashing blades faded into the background as she was drawn by her imagination into the mysterious realm of photonic thaumaturgy, until she was completely ignoring her brother's struggles against Master Andivor. She was almost startled when her father called her name.

"Kitten! You're next, before your brother falls over with exhaustion," he called. Gatina dutifully thanked Mistress Silva and headed over to the open space where the swordmaster and her sweat-covered brother were waiting.

"Isn't this a bit of a waste of your time, Father?" she asked Hance as she passed him. "With all that is going on in Falas, why are you spending time on . . . this?"

"Because sometimes, circumstances dictate that you wait for other developments to occur before you take action. Your mother is working in Falas. Do not worry about my mission, Kitten; focus instead on your training," he encouraged her strongly. "You have the best tutors in the family here, ready to work with you and Atopol. It is time you learn all you can so that you may be of service, just as your mother and I are, to the duchy and House Furtius. That, too, is part of my mission."

Her father's response caught Gatina off guard. She had not expected him to chide her. She wanted him there, with her, while she learned. She had missed her father so much while she trained in Falas with Mother.

"Yes, Father," she said, "I understand, and I will stay focused on my mission. I was just hoping to hear more about what's going on and what the Council is doing."

"If you needed to hear about anything, I would have told you," Hance said guardedly. "All you need know is that your mother is fine, as are your cousins . . . for the moment. And all you need care about is mastering your studies."

"Which begins with your grip," agreed Andivor, who handed her a practice blade. "And your stance. And your footwork. I've heard you've received introductory instruction. Let us see how much you have absorbed," he boomed, selecting a similar-sized practice blade for himself before leading her to the open space under the mill.

Cousin Andivor had arranged several different styles of practice blades for Gatina and Atopol to work with, all neatly laid out against the wall. There seemed to be everything from a collection of lethal-looking daggers to cavalry longswords, from infantry shortswords to scimitars, and from falchions to a massive two-handed Narasi blade that was taller than Gatina. Andivor wanted her to begin her work with a practice blade similar to the one she was used to, for now.

From the moment she took her stance, she realized that she was facing a much more demanding teacher than either her father or mother. She also began to question her abilities. She had thought herself capable with a sword, but she quickly realized how little she knew.

Andivor immediately began criticizing every aspect of her form, starting with the grip her fingers took on the dull shadowblade. He corrected her relentlessly before he took his own stance. There was no praise or words of encouragement if she managed to get something right. There was only constant assessment of her deficiencies.

It was frustrating, but she would not let herself complain. And from the moment Andivor finally took his own stance, she understood why. As soon as he called for her to begin, the big man moved with a grace and a speed that challenged her imagination.

He was strong. He was fast. The tip of his blade seemed to be everywhere at once and never where she expected it to be. He did not hesitate to beat aside her sword and lightly touch her shoulder, or abdomen, or torso, or arm, or even neck as he lectured her. This was not the fun sparring she'd shared with her father and mother. This was subjecting herself to the critical eye of a true swordmaster, someone for whom a blade was a natural extension of his arm.

"Again!" he commanded, as he returned to his spot and resumed the guard position. "I have precious little time with you, so we must be diligent. Elbow up! Feet angled! *More* angled," he demanded. "Bend your knees. Keep your wrist flexible but strong. This time, you take the initiative and attack me. Now begin!"

By the third pass, Gatina's arms were starting to ache, and her brow was thick with sweat. Even her palm hurt where she gripped the hilt of her blade. By the fifth, she was getting tired. But there were no breaks under Andivor's instruction. Nor was there any let-up on his critique.

By the ninth, her chest heaved like a bellows and her arms and legs were blazing in pain. What was worse was that she had yet to strike Andivor even once. He parried every blow she was certain would land with appalling ease. Nor did he give her credit for her performance. Indeed, every word out of his mouth seemed to find new flaws in her swordsmanship.

It was frustrating, but she bit her lip rather than complain in front of her father. Only after the twelfth bout did Andivor cease his barrage of criticisms. After two hours straight of fighting, there wasn't a trace of sweat anywhere on him. Nor was he even breathing hard.

"That is our time for this evening," the big man pronounced. "I know I took things easy today, but tomorrow we begin training in earnest," he assured her as she gasped for breath and trembled to stay on her feet.

"How did they do?" Hance asked as Gatina returned the small, thin practice shadowblade to the wall. She expected to hear some praise about her performance. She was disappointed.

"The lad has some skill, if he's clumsy and lax in his posture," Andivor murmured. "His stance needs much work, but he has good balance. The lass has adequate reflexes but no control, and while she moves quickly, she thinks too hard before doing so. They will take much work, Hance," he decided. "But I might be able to make them competent swordsmen. The boy, at least. It's too early to tell with your Kitten."

That stunned Gatina—*she had worked so hard!* She thought she had done much better than that, and hearing Andivor's assessment made her cheeks burn in embarrassment.

That wasn't the only thing burning, she realized. Her dominant sword hand looked as though the blade had burned into her skin. A deep red angry welt appeared across her palm, even though the hilt of the sword had been well wrapped in leather. It seared with intense heat, like a burn, but it also tingled, as if it were magical in nature. She touched it and jerked with pain.

The wince caught Master Andivor's attention, and when he examined her hand, he gasped loud enough to get everyone's attention. He motioned for Silva to approach them while he held Gatina's palm in his hand.

"Have you seen anything like this before?" he asked his wife, concerned. Mistress Silva took Gatina's hand in her own, then bent to one knee to get closer and inspect the wound, likely with her magesight.

"Very rarely," Mistress Silva said as she carefully studied the wound.

Hance and Atopol also walked over to see what the fuss was about. Her brother blanched at the sight of his sister's palm. He had never been squeamish, but the sight of the raw, red wound affected him, and he made a face.

"Darkness, Gat, what did you do? Did you cut yourself gardening last night?"

"Despite what it appears, this is not a laceration or even a friction burn," pronounced the shadowmage. "This is a magical allergic reaction to the metal, without a doubt," Mistress Silva said.

"That never happened to me," Atopol said, looking at Gatina sympathetically.

"Such things are rare but not unheard-of, especially with the onset of *rajira*. Her body is still getting used to producing a magical field," Silva explained. "Sometimes, the cells of a new mage's skin can become inflamed as it adapts. Just one of the many challenges *rajira* presents at the beginning of the quickening. You will be fine in a few days," she pronounced, "but you cannot touch metals unless you have the protection of a special salve. It's goose grease with pompiry root extract, mostly, and some powdered willow bark. It's anti-magic in nature and should ease the reaction. If it doesn't clear up, I can compound a stronger dosage," she assured Gatina as she retrieved a brown leather satchel from the corner. She opened a satchel, dug inside, and pulled out a glass jar.

"You spread this thickly over the wound and the rest of your hands and fingers. This should help with any stinging and allow it to heal," she said as she smoothed it over Gatina's palm, which instantly began to feel better. "I recommend gloves until your cycle is over."

Embarrassed by the attention, Gatina took over the application and coated both of her hands with the thick grease. "Do you think . . . *that* caused this?" she asked, confused, as she glanced toward her father and brother.

"I cannot say for certain," sighed Silva in a low voice. "Every mage endures the onset of their *rajira* differently. For women, it often coincides with Trygg's Blessing . . . and is often more erratic than what men suffer through. Among many other injustices in this world for women," she said, pointedly staring at the three men. "But usually these things fade quickly as your body and psyche adjust to the new condition. If they persist beyond your third month, we will have recourse to a psychomancer," she assured.

"Psychomancer?" Gatina asked, confused.

"A Blue Mage," explained Silva. "They specialize in magic of the mind. And since magic is largely a product of your mind, there are some interventions we can take if necessary. Tell me, have you ever demonstrated sensitivity like this before?"

"I've always had an ability to sense metals," Gatina confessed. "I suspected it was magical in nature, of course, but . . . well, nothing like this," she said, holding up her wounded palm.

"Most magi display an affinity for one of the Greater Elements during the emergence of their Talent," Silva nodded. "The sphere of Earth is less common than others, but when it does manifest, it does so as either organic—through living or once-living things like animals, plants, wood, or seashells or even bone—or inorganic, through minerals or crystals or . . . metals. That one is rare." The shadowmage considered. "You know, Kiera the Great is rumored to have had a pull toward metals. Perhaps you are following in her footsteps," she suggested.

"The metal attraction has been strong, very strong, lately," she admitted. "It has honestly made me feel ill today. The more I sparred with Master Andivor, the worse it got."

"I wouldn't worry about it, dear," sighed Silva. "It is likely temporary. But it is interesting," she nodded. "You have Kiera's white hair and lavender eyes. You even look a bit like the images we have of her. And a sensitivity to metals. Perhaps you favor her in other ways, as well," she added, raising an eyebrow. "There are worse things in life than to resemble an important ancestor."

The discussion haunted Gatina for the rest of the night, even after Atopol escorted her back to her residence hall. As she fell asleep only a few hours ahead of morning devotions, she could not help but consider it.

Kiera the Great. The founder of House Furtius. A Talented mage of great power, a thief of uncommon skill. Famed for her boldness, her bravery, her cleverness, and her wisdom. The subject of scores of accounts of her adventures.

Yes, she decided, as Blessed Darkness took her to sleep, there were worse things in life.

CHAPTER FOURTEEN

A STAIN ON THE TABLE

Fortune intervenes when we least expect it, and rarely in ways we can predict. Be prepared for circumstances to change, always.
— *from **The Shield of Darkness**
Commentaries*

THE NEXT MORNING, GATINA FELT DISTINCTLY EXHAUSTED. NOT ONLY WAS her head swimming with the novel concepts about light and shadow Mistress Silva had introduced her to, but her body ached in the wake of the strenuous regimen that Master Andivor had subjected her to. The arches of her feet throbbed, and the pain from the wound in her palm was distracting even after she applied the salve. Worse, she had the beginnings of a headache, something she was unaccustomed to.

But she persevered. She woke, slowly did her ablutions, dressed the wound on her palm with the salve, and donned white kid gloves from her luggage before joining the other girls, belatedly, at breakfast.

Unfortunately, Sister Nimandi was not present, leaving the five of them at the table without supervision. The nun was in some breakfast meeting with the other clergy of the house. The level of noise in the dining chamber was dramatically louder than usual—a fact that made her head ache even more.

Gatina mused that this was what death might feel like as she sat down at the table and slipped on Avorrita's bland, bucktoothed smile.

"It's about time you arrived," growled Leonna in a low voice from across the table. "Sister made us wait until you did to eat. Now we'll have to scarf it down like dogs!"

"Less barking, more scarfing," dismissed Dina as she passed the porridge to Avorrita. "The blessing has been said in your absence," she added kindly. "Go ahead and eat."

"Don't give Avorrita any grief, Leonna," Mathilde chided with uncharacteristic boldness. "She's had to start magical training on top of her devotions and her classes. That wears on a body," she said, sympathetically looking at Avorrita.

"And she's got special assignments," added Arryn as she buttered a toasted butt of bread and handed it to her. "We all do. Try to be understanding," she suggested.

The Coastlord girl was not persuaded. "I'm suspicious of magi," she said slowly as she took a piece of toasted bread from the basket for herself. "How can you really trust them? I'm still concerned about the fact that Avorrita found her spark when she was plotting to kill me in the gardens," she said, with a sniff.

"Plotting to *kill* you?" Avorrita asked, confused.

"Why else would you summon sharp garden shears to your hand while standing behind me?" she demanded, scowling. "One moment, I'm making perfectly reasonable criticisms of the abbey's ideas about improving spirituality through menial work, and the next, there's a rabid witch at my back ready to stab me dead," she said matter-of-factly before she bit viciously into her bread.

Avorrita was stunned at the admission to the point where she gasped. Did Leonna really think . . .

"I never intended to stab you!" she argued, sounding both horrified and hurt at the suggestion.

"Really?" Leonna sneered. "You summoned a blade from across the garden because you suddenly felt the need to *prune* something?"

"Leave her alone, Leonna!" Arryn defended. "You're just angry that someone other than you got all the attention!"

"That is not the kind of attention I desire, Nocturn!" Leonna said hotly. "Really, just because some provincial maid had a fainting fit because she was half-mad with Ishi's Curse and ready to kill does not warrant this kind of indulgence," she lectured, haughtily. "She should be under care somewhere away from civilized folk after an outburst like that."

It was clear to everyone in the room that Leonna was trying to bully her. Avorrita was tempted to shrink in the face of such shaming talk. Gatina badly wanted to reconsider whether she was really trying to stab the girl in the garden.

Avorrita won out.

"I swear by the planets, the moons, and the billions of stars that I wasn't trying to stab you, Leonna!" she insisted lamely as she invoked the Saganites' most powerful oath.

"Then why, Nocturn Avorrita, did you summon sharp shears to your hand while standing behind me?" accused Leonna. She was not inclined to accept Avorrita's story.

That's when Gatina's voice won out.

"Because I wanted to yank you down to your knees by the roots of your hair and then hack it off like weeds because you are such a vicious, ungrateful, and unkind beast!" Avorrita burst out. There were shocked stares from around the table, and a few of the girls giggled at the admission.

"WHAT?" demanded Leonna, rising from her seat. "You wanted . . . you wanted to cut my *hair?*" she asked, shocked, as she cradled her long, dark braids protectively. "What kind of monster *are* you?"

"I just . . . I . . ." Avorrita stumbled, while Gatina delighted in Leonna's reaction.

"Why would you try to cut my hair? My *hair!*" she continued, her eyes wide in outrage.

"You're more upset about that than thinking she was trying to *murder* you?" asked Dina, surprised and amused. The northern girl was enjoying this far too much, in Gatina's opinion, but she couldn't blame her. If she hadn't been the focus of Leonna's ire, Gatina would have been entertained by the Coastlord girl's reaction.

"It's not like the thought hasn't crossed all of our minds, Leonna," Mathilde added, with a shrug. "You can be rather unbearable sometimes. It's not Avorrita's fault that her *rajira* chose that moment to manifest. You can't control that sort of thing."

"She's just jealous!" Leonna accused, viciously, and then began picking out the other girls by sight. "And so are you!" she said to Mathilde, before whirling toward Dina and Arryn. "And you! Just because I'm the prettiest one, and of highest rank," she said, coaxing a snort of disbelief from Dina, "you're all . . . conspiring against me! You hate me and want me dead or worse! I can tell!" she said hotly. *"You want to cut my hair off!"*

"I was thinking about pulling on it hard a little first," Mathilde murmured as she took a spoonful of porridge.

"Ever since I came here, you all have been nothing but evil to me!" Leonna accused. "All I've wanted to do is get through these godsdamned

Mysteries, help you all by exposing you to proper culture, and go home! All you've done is make life miserable for me!"

"You've done quite enough of that yourself," Dina observed coolly. "Honestly, Leonna, there hasn't been a day that's gone by that you didn't find something petty to complain about. Stupid things! And you blame everyone else for your misery without seeing that it's you causing it. You ribbed Mathilde mercilessly when she got her *rajira*, and now you're going after poor Avorrita, who never says an unkind word about anyone!"

"I'm . . . I'm beginning to reconsider that," Avorrita said, quietly, while Gatina gloated a bit at the consensus among her group.

"She . . . wanted . . . to cut . . . my *hair*!" Leonna nearly screamed. All around them, the other tables in the chamber had stopped eating and were staring at their group's outburst.

"She didn't—and she didn't even *try* to kill you," Dina pointed out. "Which makes her a model of self-restraint. Honestly, Leonna, you've been irritating everyone at this table since you arrived. Nothing is good enough for you, nobody is remotely up to your lofty standards, and you disdain just about everything about the abbey. You know, some of us actually *like* it here!"

"It's horrible!" Leonna whispered, barely able to control her rage.

"It is not!" Arryn insisted. "It's not a palace, but it isn't meant to be. It's not a formal ball. It's not a garden party. It's not a tournament. It's a place of wisdom, devotion, and learning," she said, quivering. "The only thing that's really bad about it is . . . is enduring your complaints every day!"

"See? You *do* hate me!" Leonna said with an angry groan. "You all hate me! You want to cut my hair, and stab me in the back, and . . . and . . ."

"Uh, somebody?" Arryn said, suddenly, as she stared at the table. "Is *that* . . . supposed to be happening?"

"Don't change the subject!" insisted Leonna, screeching as she grasped the edge of the table. "Admit it! You all hate me! You're all against me! You're all a bunch of godsdamned Narasi and magi and . . . and . . ."

While she shouted, it became clear what Arryn was staring at. A spot the size of Gatina's hand near the center of the well-polished table was blackening, as if it was being scorched. The stain spread slowly as she and the other girls watched.

"What in the Cosmos is that?" Dina asked, her eyes wide.

"What?" demanded Leonna, who was clearly upset by the interruption to her tirade. "What is it?"

"I think . . ." Mathilde murmured as she stared at the stain. It began smoking. "Oh, yes, I think that's . . . *magic*," she explained, confidently. "Not mine," she hastened to add, then looked to Gatina. "Is it yours?"

"I do metal," Avorrita assured her, shaking her head. "And I haven't raised any power. I've been busy being . . . accused," she said, glancing up at Leonna. "In fact, I think there's only one person here who's likely to be producing enough emotional energy to transform it into arcane power. Leonna."

"Me? What?" demanded the Coastlord girl in disbelief. "What did I do?"

"Leonna, you're doing magic!" gasped Arryn. "You . . . you have *rajira*!"

"I do not!' insisted Leonna skeptically. "What are you talking about?" She glared at the other girls as if they were playing a prank on her.

"The table is starting to smolder, Leonna," Mathilde pointed out, as more smoke appeared. "And you're the one who's doing it. You are displaying symptoms of emergent *rajira*—trust me. You have Talent. You . . . you're going to be a mage," she said, simply.

"That's ridiculous!" snorted Leonna. "I can't possibly be a mage. I'm not like you two . . . you two aberrations," she said, a note of disgust in her voice. "I'm to marry into a wealthy Coastlord family, thank you very much. I do not have *rajira*!"

"It looks like you have *rajira*," Avorrita said with a nod toward the table. "That's a spontaneous indication, as Sister Tavane calls it. Like me summoning the shears, or Mathilde freezing the chamber pots. You're the only one upset enough right now to do this."

"It appears you have an affinity with fire," observed Mathilde, glancing at Avorrita for support. "That often emerges with anger."

"What were you feeling when you froze the chamber pots?" Avorrita suddenly asked her friend.

"Homesickness," admitted Mathilde. "I miss my dog. And you, with the shears?"

"I . . . It wasn't anger; exactly, it was resentment," Avorrita confessed. "I didn't mean to do any harm. Leonna, do you feel sick at all? Ill in your stomach? Dizzy? A headache?" she asked, listing the symptoms she knew sometimes accompanied the emergence of *rajira*. "Are you . . . Do you have your monthlies?" she asked, her voice barely above a whisper.

"What does *that* have to do with anything?" the girl asked angrily.

"I think that means yes," Dina quipped.

"I think we need to get Nightbrother Heziak to examine you," Mathilde suggested. "And quickly . . . before she sets the entire hall on fire."

"I do not have *rajira!*" Leonna said, her eyes growing wider as she realized that they were being serious in their suggestions. "I cannot have *rajira!*"

"You have *rajira*," Arryn said sympathetically. "I'm so sorry, Leonna!"

"Don't be sorry," snorted Dina. "She's lucky. There are plenty who would kill to have Talent."

"There are plenty I'd kill to not have it!" Leonna said bitingly as she stared at the smoldering tabletop. But with each new outburst, the charred stain got perceptibly wider, and more smoke was emitted. "Dear gods, I can't have *rajira!* I'm to be a noblewoman! I'm to marry a knight! What about my *dowry?*" she protested, tears beginning to stream down her face. "I cannot! I . . . just . . . *can't!*"

———

THE NEWS OF LEONNA'S *RAJIRA* SPREAD THROUGH THE HALL LIKE FIRE AFTER supper, and while Brother Heziak was summoned to inspect her, as he did with all new magi, Gatina was forced to trudge halfway across the abbey grounds to her introduction to thaumaturgy. She walked with Mathilde, and the two discussed the unexpected development until they arrived at the hall. She nodded toward her brother—portraying her cousin—before sitting down. Atopol would certainly be intrigued by the news. Gatina got the impression that he was more interested in Dina, for some reason, but he had an eye for Leonna, too.

Gatina was growing more and more frustrated with her magical class—not because the material wasn't interesting, but because it was going so slowly, compared to her nightly sessions with Mistress Silva that she was getting bored. It took a week for Sister Tavane to get around to teaching the Talented students the next staff of runes after painstakingly presenting the theory behind their employ. By that time, Gatina and Atopol had already learned two staffs of the special runes employed in basic photomancy.

Still, Avorrita's demure demeanor demanded that Gatina sit quietly and attentively while the other students fumbled through mastering each new rune. Nor could she, despite the great temptation, show off how quickly she could learn the lessons. Avorrita wasn't a magical prodigy, after all. She was just . . . plain.

So, it was quite the shock when the door of the class chamber opened and a Royal Censor strode in.

Gatina could not stifle her gasp. Thankfully, nearly everyone in the room joined her at the unexpected interruption.

The man was not dressed in armor or geared for war, she could see when he strode in as if he were the abbot himself. He wore a well-cut doublet and hose under his big black-and-white checkered cloak, and a wide-brimmed pointed hat with a checkered band instead of a helmet. But his face certainly looked as if he were going into battle, she noted at once.

"Blessed Darkness!" swore the nun, as she whirled around to see the source of the disruption. "What is the meaning of this?"

"Are we being . . . raided?" someone asked in a fearful whisper. That caused a stir of panic and a swell of whispers amongst the students that Gatina was tempted to join. Instead, Avorrita sank down into her chair, while Gatina prepared to spring into action toward the window—the only other exit from the room.

"No," the Censor answered. He was decidedly Narasi and spoke with a heavy Castali accent. "You are not being . . . 'raided.' You are being *inspected*. I am Censor Lantripol, recently reassigned to the Falas commandery. It is my task to ensure that everyone—everyone!—who falls under my jurisdiction is compliant with the well-established regulation of the magi. That includes each and every one of you," he added, wearing a smug expression.

"Why must you inflict this on these innocent children?" demanded Sister Tavane. "They have just discovered their Talent. They are just learning the very elements of their nature. What purpose does it serve to terrify them so?"

"To instill in them the importance of compliance," answered the Censor as he strode into the room. "Fate or the gods have destined them to this fortune. It comes with power and responsibility. I am here to ensure that they properly understand and appreciate the responsibility."

"And the terror you inspire?" the nun asked, clearly offended at the response.

"Terror is highly motivational," Censor Lantripol replied with a shrug. "The Censorate represents the sovereign authority of the common people over the power of the magi. It is best if they understand that now as a foundational principle. Extraordinary powers do not grant extraordinary privilege," he pronounced. "Quite the contrary. They invoke extraordinary responsibility. You object to that, Sister?" he challenged.

"Of course not, Censor," the nun said. "Reasonable constraints on power are always beneficial. But one considers whether the Censorate's approach is the best application of that power," she proposed diplomatically.

"Four hundred years of successful regulation suggests that," he agreed, fixing the nun with a steely eye. "It has come to the notice of the Censorate that Alshar has been appallingly lax in inspections and enforcement of magi. Due to . . . recent developments," he said, a flash of anguish washing over his face before it vanished, "the Censorate will be increasing our examination of the magi here. Rigorously," he pronounced. "Censor Captain Stefan himself has taken a personal interest in the matter and has pledged to review the activities of all Talented subjects in Alshar. Registered and unregistered."

"Just what does that imply?" the nun asked suspiciously, her eyes narrowed.

"It implies that there will be an increase in scrutiny and an increase in enforcement," Censor Lantripol declared as he removed his gloves. "Too long we have spent our time chasing petty footwizards and hedgewitches in Alshar while magi from the nobility have been able to flagrantly defy the Bans on Magic. It has come to our attention that some violators have been using magic to aid in other illegal activities. In direct violation of the Bans. They will be discovered, examined, and punished." There was malice in his voice, Gatina could tell. A man with a petty nature, she decided, who enjoyed his unchecked authority.

But the nun was skeptical, not cowed. She snorted disdainfully. "What proof do you have for that?" she demanded.

"Why would I need to show that to you?" he sniffed, amused.

"Extraordinary claims require extraordinary evidence," Sister Tavane quoted. "I have not heard of such things. And if there are, indeed, magi committing such crimes, it is doubtful that you will find them in a class of children who have just achieved their *rajira*," she added.

"Perhaps not," admitted the Censor. "But the clandestine nature of Alshar's old Imperial families is well known to the Censorate," he said, looking out at the students. "Secret apprenticeships, forbidden texts hidden away, unregistered magi operating as nobility in defiance of the Bans, proscribed disciplines being taught outside of our regulation . . . Alshar is rife with violators amongst the nobility. Many of these children come from families who may practice such crimes. It is our intention to investigate the matter . . . thoroughly," he promised darkly. Gatina listened intently as Nocturn Avorrita sank down lower into her chair. This Censor was speaking about what her father had warned her of on their journey back from Inmar.

"They . . . are . . . children," the angry nun countered. "My registration and license to practice are in good order. You may inspect my materials—you will find nothing 'clandestine' or 'forbidden' among them. The abbey has submitted every required document to the office of the Ducal Court Wizard. And it is highly unlikely that a group of freshly emerged magi who don't know how to cast the simplest spells are going to be a threat to the rest of humanity."

The Censor was unmoved by her reasonable arguments, Gatina could see. The man was committed to his cause. While Avorrita's face displayed a wide-eyed expression of fear, Gatina's mind was running furiously. She realized that the Censorate was using the heists she and her family had conducted as an excuse to become involved on Count Vichetral's behalf. A pang of guilt settled in her stomach, and she grew fearful for her entire family. It was one thing to be a magical thief when no one suspected you existed. But the Censorate apparently knew about House Furtius and the rest of the Shadow Council's families.

That did not bode well, she knew. Most of the magi in Alshar were descended from the Imperial families, she knew, the magelords of the Later Magocracy. Her own included. She had learned, through formal lessons and informal discussions, how many, if not most, of that old arcane aristocracy had survived intact over four centuries of Narasi rule. Of Censorate domination. They had resorted to bribery, obfuscation, underground schools—like the one she and Atopol were enrolled in—and quietly held records that detailed the old ways, before the knights had stormed the Magocracy and overthrown them.

House Furtius might be an extreme example, thanks to Kiera the Great's strict code, but there were plenty of Coastlord families who had hidden their powers without resorting to such radical practice. Families where the magi hid as eccentric cousins, unacknowledged scions of successful trading houses or hereditary estates. They had mastered the art of the low profile, keeping their arcane business a secret from both the Censorate and the duchy at large.

And now her family's highly successful outing had placed all of that in danger.

"That is what I am here to ensure," Lantripol declared. "Students! You . . . *Nocturns*," he said, pronouncing the word like a curse, "by decree of the Censor Captain, you will be required not just to hear the terms of the Bans on Magic from your teacher; you will hear them from *me*. Each and every one of you is subject to examination by the Censorate. You will tell us everything," he promised. "What the scope and extent of your Talent are, the names and occupations of your family members, the existence of any known Talented relative—everything.

"In return, I will instruct you as to what your duties and obligations are under the Bans. You will learn about the dangers of prophecy, the necessity to submit yourselves entirely to the Censorate's oversight, and the perils of unregulated magic. Prophets get people killed. Unregulated magi can cause great harm to the mundane population. Deceitful wizards who use their spells to cheat and steal have taken advantage of their fellows over and over again across the centuries. Only a few years ago, one mage in Farise used forbidden artifacts to exploit his powers, and as a result caused a war in which tens of thousands died.

"The Censorate intends to ensure that sort of thing doesn't happen in Alshar anymore. All Talented abbey staff shall be investigated, and each of your records will be thoroughly reviewed during this process. If there are any violations or discrepancies, there will . . . be . . . consequences!" he insisted.

Well, Gatina sighed to herself, at least magic class would not be boring anymore.

CHAPTER FIFTEEN

AN UNEXPECTED INVITATION

Aliases are challenging to maintain. While it's true that staying close to the truth makes it easier, it is still a struggle to carry both personal identity and alias identity at the same time. Sometimes, my true self wants to speak her mind, but that would doom my mission.

— from Gatina's Heist Journal

TWO LONG DAYS WENT BY AFTER THE CENSOR HAD SUDDENLY APPEARED in class. For those two days, Gatina did her best to further sink into her Avorrita alias, trying to appear particularly dull and unworthy of note. For he was not alone; there were at least five other Censors strutting around the abbey now, their big, checkered cloaks at visual odds with the gray and black raiment the clergy wore.

There was a decided change in the mood amongst the clergy of the abbey, too, she noted. The monks and nuns whispered to each other now instead of greeting and blessing each other in a jovial fashion. Though there were only a handful of Censors and a score or two of students or staff with *rajira,* the presence of the enforcers of the Bans permeated the abbey grounds.

Gatina dutifully kept to her lessons—not only her regular ones during the day and her evening forays into thaumaturgy, but the late-night sessions with Silva and Andivor where she continued her work on shadow-magic and swordplay. She mastered the eye-coloring illusion quickly, and she eagerly absorbed the other basic principles of photomancy from Silva for an hour before spending a second hour with Andivor and the practice swords.

The lessons were even more intense because Atopol had been called away for some reason. That left both of her cousins ample time to instruct her without distraction. While she feared being stopped by the Censorate either coming to or leaving the old, abandoned mill in the middle of the night, it also gave her the opportunity to practice the lessons of moving stealthily.

Her skin, thankfully, was responding well to the healing salve. The wound in her palm was recovering rapidly, and by the third day, she didn't even really need the gloves. She also began to appreciate Andivor's exacting standards and high expectations. It took effort to overcome the idea that she was not, as she'd suspected, a natural with a sword.

Instead, she tried to take every harsh criticism to heart and understand why the swordmaster found fault in her. She worked additionally hard to fight up to his expectations—even when it meant tedious practice to strengthen her wrists, for example, or mindless exercises to improve her accuracy. Each night, after she crawled into her box bed, she lay on her back with her arms flat on the bed. She drew the tops of her hands up and down thirty times each, twice. She quickly became accustomed to the burn in the tops of her wrists. When those exercises were done, she stretched out her fingers as wide and as long as she could, and she drew the sheet into her palms. Strong fingers would improve her grip, she knew.

But she could see his point in these exercises, as she practiced. The more she sparred with Andivor, the more she realized just how poor she was at the art.

The time was all the more tense because her father, Hance, had left the abbey as well.

"He's had to return to Falas with your brother," counseled Silva when Gatina asked about his absence. "He said something about having a date for the theater—but you know how he is," she soothed. "He's always been the mysterious one, even when he was a boy."

"The theater? In Falas?" Gatina asked, surprised. She knew her mother was still there, and that Cousin Huguenin was involved in the theater somehow. She wondered what was happening in the capital.

"The theater has always been the province of Coastlord society," Silva assured. "Why, there was no decent theater before the Magocracy took Alshar away from the Sea Lords. It is the essence of culture . . . and a convenient excuse to hide all sorts of things away," she added, a knowing look in her eye. "Actors and directors make great psychomancers, honestly. They understand how to manipulate human emotion without magic. When you add a little *rajira*, they can work wonders."

"But why did he have to go, I wonder?" Gatina asked.

"Council business," shrugged her tutor. "And none of ours until they make it so. There is much happening in Alshar beyond the abbey walls, Kitten. We bide our time and do as we must until House and duchy call upon us for service."

That answer did little to satisfy Gatina's curiosity. But she stewed on it while she worked through the second staff of special photomantic runes and demonstrated a few of the first staff to Silva before Andivor called her. Then she worked with the practice sword until she was covered in sweat and her entire body ached. But through the entire lesson, she wondered acutely about where her father and mother were and what clandestine adventures they were having without her.

It just didn't seem fair. To be stuck in the abbey, surrounded by Censors, portraying the most boring girl in the world while her parents were off in the city, chasing the evil Count Vichetral . . . well, that was just insulting. Thankfully, her father had left behind an assignment for her with her secret tutors.

"The Council is concerned that some of the Talented Coastlord families are working with the Five Counts," explained Silva as Gatina prepared to leave after her lessons. "Shadow suspects that some are eager to see a new regime established that will see their Houses dominate. But there is some question about just which ones and how they are using their own family ties to support Vichetral and his cronies—and inform to them," she added darkly.

"Isn't that the same information that the Censorate is hunting?" Gatina asked, surprised.

"In some cases, yes," Silva agreed. "In others, we are unsure where loyalty and obligation lie. It's reminiscent of when the Shadow Council was last invoked, during the reign of Enguin, the Black Duke. That dark regime had many supporters, despite the man's depravity. Indeed, Vichetral traces his lineage directly to Enguin and is likely invoking those old loyalties to support his rise to power. It would be helpful for the Council to know which of them feel any kind of debt or obligation to him on account of that history."

"So, what am I to do?" Gatina asked, surprised. She hoped her task involved breaking into someplace and stealing something, perhaps the very book that the Censor Captain was compiling. She was disappointed.

"Research," Andivor said, handing her a folio of parchment. "Among other treasures, the abbey has extensive records of most of the great Houses of Coastlords. This place has been a quiet repository for such things for centuries," he informed her. "We will arrange for you to get access to those secret libraries where you can search for the connections between those traitorous families and Vichetral's House."

"Research?" Gatina asked skeptically. "Not . . . not swordplay, or magic, or a heist, or . . ."

"It needs to be done, Kitten," assured Silva sympathetically. "At the moment, you are the one best suited to do it. And the one least likely to arouse suspicion from the Censorate. Indeed, Andivor and I will be departing Palomar for a few days while they are here. We are not listed as the abbey's staff, and we are needed for a task elsewhere. But this should give you something to keep you occupied while we're gone. Occupied and out of trouble," she added with a smile. "And beneath suspicion."

"The Censors," Gatina said disdainfully, wrinkling her nose.

"I hate the sight of those bloody checkered cloaks," agreed Andivor, shaking his head ruefully. "Just having them around puts me on edge. That's why we're leaving too. Apparently, I'm too belligerent for my lady wife to trust me not to slaughter one of them."

"It would be uncharacteristic for a monk," offered Gatina.

"Just so," agreed Silva. "Now, let me tell you about your resources, should there be problems while we are gone . . ."

No Atopol. No Father. No secret tutors. For the first time since Gatina came to Paloma Abbey, she felt alone. Especially when she had to make the trip up the cliff to the main temple every night to do her research after Vespers. Silva and Andivor had arranged for her to be admitted to the lower sections of the tower, where the extensive archive was kept, but she saw virtually no one except the attending monk while she was searching the ancient, dusty genealogies of the Coastlord families. That was work that made mathematics seem entertaining. Every night, she hid her folio of work within the library, then quietly walked back to her hall through the Blessed Darkness without escort. There was still no sign of Atopol, Father, or her secret tutors.

She understood the necessity, of course. Palomar was suddenly dangerous for House Furtius. The Censorate was making a big show of its presence, with the lower-level Censors standing prominently around the abbey grounds, quietly intimidating even the non-magi amongst the clergy with their cloaks and their mageblades.

But it was Censor Lantripol who was the worst. He conducted interviews with all of the magically Talented Saganites, she discovered, making surprise visits to their stations or having them summoned to an office he took (without even asking for permission, she discovered) in Nadir Hall. He seemed to delight in disturbing the clergy and keeping them off balance, perhaps in hopes of learning something useful. Brother Heziak, Sister Tavane, and even Brother Henri were visited, she heard. And then he began interviewing the Nocturns.

One by one the students were summoned to Nadir Hall to be interviewed . . . but from what the others in her magical class said, it sounded more like an interrogation. Poor Mathilde was nearly in tears when she came back from hers just before supper. Leonna, still adjusting rather poorly to the news that she was magically Talented, was highly irritated from her own interview. Casual details from both of them gave Gatina some idea of what to expect.

Thankfully, it sounded as if Censor Lantripol was not using truth-tells or other magic during the Nocturn interviews—likely he saw them as wasted on young students. He was also asking detailed questions about the Nocturn's families and histories, so Gatina made certain to review her alias's particulars on that subject. Poring through centuries worth of historical accounts and family trees was helpful for that, at least. She knew precisely where the fictional Maid Avorrita of Dentran fell in relation to her supposed relatives. Gatina felt confident she could answer any question the man asked.

Indeed, she was summoned the next morning, during history class, and escorted by a big, hulking Censor who was clearly trying to intimidate her while they walked. Avorrita grunted barely audible responses to his rude questions until they arrived and she was ushered into Lantripol's stolen office.

"So, you are Maid Avorrita of Dentran," the officious little man began when she sat down in front of his wide table.

"Nocturn Avorrita," Gatina corrected automatically.

"Ah, yes, you have taken holy orders . . . lay orders," he added. "A temporary designation as 'clergy' that will be gone with the waning summer. Then you will be Maid Avorrita of Dentran again."

"I . . . I suppose," agreed Avorrita. Gatina studied the man carefully from behind Avorrita's dull eyes. "Is that important?"

"That depends," shrugged the Censor. "You are the third daughter of Lord Arman of Dentran, it says here," he said, tapping a parchment. "A Coastlord of relatively modest means and moderate aspirations. Your House is a rural cadet branch related to a handful of more powerful families. Yet . . . you are *here,*" he said, gesturing around at the abbey.

"My father thinks I will get a good education here," Avorrita said, confused. "That I'll experience some culture."

"Oh, that you will if you mistake this flat-headed little sect as culturally relevant," mocked Lantripol. "Most girls your age are content to do a few weeks as an acolyte of Trygg, or Ishi, or even Briga. But you chose the Saganites."

"My parents did, actually," Avorrita informed him. "They didn't tell me until a few days before I was to go. Father says knowing the stars is a good way to find your path, like the ships at sea."

"Of course he does," Lantripol said sarcastically as he studied the parchment in front of him. "And now you suddenly have *rajira,*" he observed.

"It was as much of a surprise to me as anyone, Censor," Avorrita agreed.

"Have you a family history of magi?" he asked, as if it was a disease.

"An uncle, I think," Avorrita said. "Maybe some cousins?"

"Yes, your cousins," the Censor nodded. "One of which is here with you. And he also saw his *rajira* emerge. Lord Dain of—"

"Nocturn Dain," corrected Avorrita with a smile. Gatina fought to maintain her composure, to keep meek Avorrita in control.

"Of course. He's a first cousin, then? Do you know him well?" he asked.

"Second cousin. And I'd only met him a few times before we came here. He lives twenty miles away or more," Avorrita answered blandly. "He's nice, I suppose. He's terribly smart. But he likes to hear himself talk," she added.

That produced a chuckle in the Censor, which Gatina counted as a victory.

"Many lads his age do. But you, Avorrita, by all accounts you don't talk much at all. Your friends in your group both said as much. I can respect that in a maiden your age." The tone was almost friendly and clearly meant to put Gatina off her guard. She knew better than to trust him. She knew he was not her friend. "What do you intend to do now that you've received your Talent?"

"I . . . I really don't know." Avorrita shrugged. "I suppose I'll get apprenticed somewhere. I expect my father will arrange that. I'm not good enough at mathematics to consider holy orders here," she added, intentionally sounding dejected by that prospect. "I just don't know."

"Have you considered a career in the Censorate?" Lantripol asked, surprising Gatina.

"What? The *Censorate*? But I'm a *girl!*" she objected.

"Oh, the Royal Censorate of Magic employs all sorts of Censors," Lantripol assured. "Including a small number of female Censors. It's not all warwands and mageblades. Sometimes, we need a more delicate touch. Someone who can go places where a checkered cloak would raise an alarm."

"You mean . . . like a *spy*?" Avorrita blurted out. Gatina was actually intrigued. She had no idea that the Censorate recruited girls. But she had to let Avorrita steer the conversation as best she could.

"We consider it more of a clandestine observer or an informant," Lantripol explained diplomatically. "Indeed, we seek young candidates with a dedication to our charter, high ideals about our mission, and a certain level of intelligence. As well as the ability to keep their eyes and ears open and their mouths shut about what they see. The magi can be crafty in how they skirt the rules and violate the Bans," he reflected. "Countering those violations can require a delicate touch, lest we invite civil unrest."

"Me . . . a Censor," Avorrita said, trying the idea on for size. Behind her plain brown eyes Gatina was laughing uproariously at the idea.

"It is perhaps not as lucrative as some successful Practical Adepts can be in private practice," he admitted, "but there are certain benefits to working for the Censorate. From what I can tell your family has never had a serious violation of the Bans—it's difficult to find much on them at all, actually."

"We tend to be quiet folk," Avorrita assured him. "We keep to ourselves. No need to go looking for trouble when trouble is looking for you, my father says," she said, as if quoting scripture.

"Well, in this case you would be looking for trouble—magical trouble," sighed Lantripol. "Some of our most successful cases have been pursued by young, idealistic magi such as yourself. I— What is it?" he asked, a little irritated, when the door opened and revealed another Censor, this one wearing armor and mageblade.

"Just got word: Captain Stefan will be at Lindule Hall tonight," the man explained, with hardly a glance at Avorrita. "He expects a full report."

"He'll get one, he'll get one," dismissed Lantripol. "I'm just finishing up here, I think. Send word to expect me around the tenth bell." The Censor nodded, gave Avorrita another glance, and shut the door. "So sorry," sighed Lantripol. "The Censorate's business is never done, and there's no end to the meetings. Or the oversight of our superiors—it keeps us honest," he promised. "But you seem like a good, steady young woman with a bright future. Someone from a Coastlord family, but not one with the strongest magical tradition. That might prove helpful to our order."

"You don't come from a Coastlord family, do you?" Avorrita asked, her eyes narrowing.

"Well, no, I hail from the Upper Riverlands in Castal," Lantripol explained. "I've been in service since I was not much older than you. Two years of fieldwork, then promoted to overseeing four other Censors," he bragged proudly.

"So . . . didn't the Duke of Castal throw all the Censors out? Or that's what I've heard," Avorrita pointed out inconveniently. Gatina watched, enjoying seeing the man squirm.

"There have been some . . . political problems of late," agreed Lantripol in a murmur.

"And . . . and Remere, too," Avorrita continued. "Wasn't the Censorate kicked out of that duchy, too?"

"We live in a time where some have forgotten the vital role that our regulation of arcane affairs plays in the successful functioning of society," reasoned the Censor.

"My friend Dina says they were kicked out of Vorone, in the north, too," Avorrita continued, ignoring the man's discomfort. "Just kicked right on out." Her matter-of-fact discussion of the matter clearly made Lantripol uncomfortable.

"There was some interference by some lawless thugs," dismissed Lantripol. "It can happen that a sovereign favors political expediency over their moral duty. Your late Duke was convinced by an unscrupulous spellmonger who was already in violation of the Bans to take some unfortunate action, as was Duke Rard. It was a political maneuver," he added defensively. "Our charter was signed by no less than King Kamaklavan himself, who outranks both Rard and Lenguin as mere Dukes. And it is a temporary measure."

"So, your order is no longer allowed in Castal . . . Remere . . . and half of Alshar," Avorrita said, as if she was just figuring it out.

"Temporarily," reiterated Lantripol.

"Which is . . . Well, I guess that's why you're all here, isn't it?" she asked blandly. "You can't serve in Castal anymore."

"But Alshar is in need of our services," argued Lantripol. "Especially after the unfortunate death of your Duke and Duchess. In a time of chaos like this, it is vitally important that we maintain the institutions that keep our society stable. Count Vichetral and his fellows have asked that we help maintain order and decorum in Alshar while the political situation gets sorted out." The man was speaking very defensively, Gatina noted. "Just . . . just consider my offer," he sighed. "We could use a few quiet girls like you, Avorrita. There's a lot of forbidden arcane activity in Alshar now, and we need good people to help us get to the bottom of it."

"I . . . I'll consider it," she decided, with a sigh of her own. She stood. "It's just that . . . Well, it doesn't seem like you fellows in the checkered cloaks are doing so well right now," she observed. "I am not certain it would be a good career for me. But I'll consider it," she said before she left.

Gatina was both relieved and irritated as she left the hall, and she made certain to use that feeling to shape Avorrita's gait. She kept her shoulders slumped and her movements painfully slow as she shuffled back to her residence hall. The interview with Lantripol had been exhausting, as she tried to present Avorrita without betraying Gatina. But it had also been revealing. She'd learned much more from the arrogant Censor than he had from her, for instance.

She'd had no idea that the Censorate had female Censors. She wasn't aware of any clandestine branch of the order until Lantripol had revealed it. And she hadn't realized that the Censorate knew about the hidden nature of the Coastlord families who had protected the magi in their midst from the checkered cloaks for centuries.

Individually, the revelations were disturbing enough. Taken together, they wove a sinister tapestry that made her feel that the Censorate was a far, far larger threat to the conspiracy than the Brotherhood of the Rat had ever been. These weren't mere dockside thugs and would-be pirates; these were meticulous and fanatical enforcers of an archaic code that saw their struggle against unregulated magic as a nearly sacred vocation, not merely a decent-paying civil service job.

By that light, knowing that the descendants of the nobility of the former Magocracy had gone underground, so to speak, told her that the Censorate played a long and subtle game. They had their own spy network, and it included the occasional girl. It made complete sense, of course; as her understanding of the shadowy game had grown, she'd come to recognize the absolute necessity of gathering information and keeping some things hidden.

Everyone considered the Censors as burly, violence-happy men who had an excuse to use their powers against others under the color of the Censorate's untouchable checkered banner. Few thought of them as capable of cultivating informants and agents who would not be suspected.

But Censor Lantripol's invitation for Avorrita to enlist with the Censorate had shattered the idea that it was the mere bureaucratic organization it was perceived as. They had guile and were willing to recruit unusual sources of information. From what Censor Lantripol had told her, the order not only knew about the clandestine Coastlords who had eluded them for centuries, they were eager to infiltrate them. Likely with the intention of eliminating them.

Eliminating us, Gatina corrected in her mind.

For there was no good reason why, if the Censorate was already aware of the Coastlords and their Shadow Council, they would not move to counter them . . . especially when they had the permission of Count Vichetral.

The Count of Rhemes might be a usurper of sovereign authority in Alshar, but that gave him enough pretext to grant the Censorate exiles all the power they needed to fight the long hidden Coastlord magi. And, in turn, the Censorate's acceptance of that power legitimized Count Vichetral's rule. By destroying the Shadow Council and crushing the hidden power of the Coastlords' magi, the Censorate would gain a victory that would sustain them and their purpose in exile. By supporting the Censorate efforts against his enemies, Vichetral would appear as the legitimate authority in Alshar.

Gatina's head whirled with the implications. She'd read enough history by now to understand just how political alliances formed, sustained themselves, and eventually broke apart. Political power, like magic or the laws that governed the stars, themselves, obeyed certain rules. Studying the often-vicious rise to power of the Archmagi of old and even the Narasi's often-crude application of power after they had taken over the Magocracy demonstrated the potency of Vichetral's alliance with the Censorate.

Gatina realized that from a purely historical perspective, if they could remove the only force defying their mutual goals—the Shadow Council and its agents—both would be victorious. Duke Lenguin's murder would go unavenged. And Alshar would be locked into a despotic dictatorship, perhaps for a generation.

The only way that could happen, she also knew, was if the Censorate, with Vichetral's blessing, slew every member of the Council and every Talented member of their families. Including herself and her entire family. Father, Mother, Atopol, her cousins, aunts, and uncles—every member of both sides of the family was in mortal danger now that the Censorate was involved in Count Vichetral's quest for power.

That was a horrid realization. For the first time, she realized what the struggle of her parents and the rest of the Shadow Council really meant. And she understood what and how serious the stakes were. The Censorate was willing to hang an accused footwizard without so much as a second thought. Traitors to the regime with a centuries-long legacy of violating the Bans? They would be slain outright.

This was no game, she was starting to understand. This wasn't even about justice. This was a struggle for survival. She had seen her friends at the broken fountain in Falas, the orphans, struggle to survive every day during her mission there. That thought dug at Gatina's heart painfully as she lingered outside of her dormitory. The Brotherhood of the Rat had been dangerous, she knew, and would have killed her or her family or her friends without compunction if there had been a reason to. The Censorate, however, didn't need a reason. And they were far more organized than the Brotherhood.

But as painful as that was to learn, that wasn't the only thing that she'd learned from Lantripol. The officious Censor had given her a valuable scrap of information without knowing it. For she knew that the Censor Captain of the region was the one who was compiling the lists of potential enemies of Count Vichetral's regime amongst the Coastlords. That little book she learned about at Lemon's Reach was in his possession, and soon it would be used to round up and arrest anyone who might be opposed to the rule of the Five Counts.

"Captain Stefan will be at Lindule Hall tonight," the other Censor had reported to Lantripol. Lindule Hall was one of the neighboring manors

to the abbey, a mere five miles to the south, more or less, from the temple along the main road. The estate sold produce and meat to the abbey's kitchens, she remembered hearing, and the manor lord was supposedly well disposed to having such a prosperous ecclesiastic client for a neighbor. While Gatina didn't know anything about the man and why he might be hosting the Censor Captain at his home, that really didn't matter to her.

All that mattered was that she knew where and when he'd be there. With his little book.

Gatina struggled with the weight of that information. She couldn't tell Father, or Atopol, or Silva, or Andivor, or anyone connected with the family—they were all gone. She was by herself. She could, she figured, give the information to her great-uncle the abbot, but while he was related to her and pledged to protect her, he was not knowledgeable about the operations of the Shadow Council—by design.

He could not grant her permission to investigate Lindule Hall, nor would he, she estimated. It would be too dangerous, to his mind. Even knowing about the little book would be dangerous for him in his position. Sending a half-trained thief with just the first glimmerings of *rajira* into the unknown with no preparation, no support, and no one to rescue her if she were caught would be an insanely foolish risk to both her and his position, Gatina could see clearly. It would be laughably irresponsible. And she realized that it would be just as irresponsible to put the man in that difficult position.

No, she decided with a sigh, there was no one to tell. There was no one to give her permission to go steal that book.

Of course, she reasoned in the next breath, there was no one to really *forbid* her from going, either.

Certainly, it was impetuous, foolish, and unbelievably laden with risk . . . but then there was also an invaluable *opportunity* to steal something of incredible value. Something vital to the Council's efforts. And she was the only one who could act on that if she chose to take the *initiative*.

Gatina knew of two cards in Mother's deck that would support her decision, OPPORTUNITY and INITIATIVE. She had the chance to make a difference by acting. The dreaded Censor Captain was nearby with his book. The book that would likely place her family and their efforts, the Shadow Council's efforts, in mortal danger. She could take the lead on this effort and embrace the opportunity Fortune had placed in her path.

It was a difficult situation. Gatina knew full well what her father and mother would say about it. She'd already gotten in trouble for a series of unapproved heists in Falas. She'd been lectured endlessly about doing such foolish and dangerous things. Nor was she dealing with the thugs of the Brotherhood but the arcane soldiery of the Royal Censorate of Magic. She should really think long and hard about the consequences of even considering going to Lindule Hall. Which she did . . . as she turned away from her dormitory and began walking through the twilight, toward the stable.

CHAPTER SIXTEEN
CONVERSATION AT LINDULE HALL

Mere opportunity and initiative should not be confused with planning a heist. An incautious approach to stealing oft leads to mistakes and errors that can end in calamity. Success demands decisive action, which requires a strong objective and a stronger plan.

— *from **The Shield of Darkness***
Commentaries

IT HADN'T BEEN AS HARD AS SHE'D ANTICIPATED, OBTAINING A HORSE FROM the stable at this hour, as the stableboys had all retired for the evening. Gatina didn't know much about horses, and it seemed one of the weaker portions of her plan. She chose a small black gelded rouncy who seemed agreeable to a nighttime journey. Finding a suitable saddle in the tack room was more difficult than finding a horse, and Gatina struggled with fastening it onto the beast without help. But she worked with determination and commitment once she made up her mind to do it.

She sneaked back to Moon Hall to retrieve her working blacks from her box bed, slipped them on under her habit, and left a brief note in code tucked away in her hidden heist journal in case the worst happened. Her parents and Atopol at least deserved to know where she'd gone if she disappeared.

Her heart pounded with exhilaration and excitement as she quietly led the rouncy to the edge of the abbey's grounds before mounting him. It pounded even more furiously when the horse lurched forward and began moving quickly down the road to the south. Gatina had only ridden a handful of times, after all, and rarely at night. Or alone. Or toward a place she'd never been before. Only a few minutes into the journey, she began to feel terrified at the stupidity of her actions.

Thankfully, the horse was a gentle mount, and after initially pulling at the reins, the rouncy settled into a practiced gait down the narrow road from the abbey. As the stars shone brightly in the moonless sky, Gatina felt more confident about taking the beast out alone. It was a gloriously clear summer night, the kind the Saganites loved for their observations and devotions.

The summer portion of the Sacred Zodiac was visible overhead, she noted, the eternal pathway of the planets and moons across the sky: Agtron the Angry Octopus on the eastern horizon, followed by the Crab, the Circle, and the little bit of the Hook that was visible in the west this time of year. She was proud she knew their names and stories and their annual progression as the moons and planets followed their sacred course. She was proud that she knew that the light of the planets was reflected from distant worlds, fellow travelers around the sun with Callidore when every peasant thought them just wandering stars.

The smell of the fields and orchards and meadows she passed through filled the air as bats and nightwebs darted across the sky. She chanced to use magesight while she rode, just on the chance of finding a natural arcane channel of energy. There were a few near the abbey, but her recent studies encouraged her to look for them in the wild. Some spellsigns could be seen that way, too, she'd heard, remnants of magical enchantments cast in the past. Her attention was soon turned back to her journey and the urgent matter before her.

Lindule Hall was not that far away, according to the painted map in the stables—she could likely reach it on foot if she wanted to take the time. But she didn't want to spend her energy trudging across the landscape and then be too tired to run away if things went awry. She only wished she'd been able to secure her mageblade before she left. She was forced to rely on the dagger she'd worn in Inmar at Lemon's Reach. Not that she was planning on stabbing anyone, but she liked to have the option.

The manor house of Lindule Hall was not terribly large, from what she understood. The lord's name was Halanric. He was a Coastlord. That was all she knew about him. That was not usually considered enough information on a target to lead to a successful heist.

As she got closer to the road that led to the estate, her insecurity about her plan plagued her mind. A good thief did not go into a heist blind, she knew with certainty. She did not know the layout of the manor, the number of people or where they might be, or where or even who Captain Stefan might be. She would have to improvise, and that was dangerous. What she was doing was incredibly foolhardy.

But she'd come this far, she reasoned, as she passed the boundary stone of the estate. She could not back out now. She was committed.

As soon as she glimpsed lights from the manor house in the distance, she pulled the reins to stop the horse and dismounted near a small grove of sycamore trees near the road. It didn't take long to lead the rouncy to a secluded, hidden portion of the wood and tie his reins. She could easily make a quick escape from there, she reasoned, as the horse was entirely hidden from the road or house. She slipped off the gray Nocturn's habit and secured it to the saddle before pulling the cowl of her black cloak over her head, hiding her hair and face under its soft cloth mask.

Quiet as a shadow, she reminded herself, as she took a breath and started to pad her way toward the manor house. A continuous chorus of crickets and frogs throbbed in the background as she slid stealthily from one shadow to another. At least the weather was good for a heist, she thought, as she came to the edge of the compound.

Lindule Hall was not nearly as elaborate as Cysgodol Hall back home; there were no balconies or porches to speak of, nor much in the way of ornamentation around the doorways. But it was sturdily built, two stories high, with a small refuge tower hardly larger than a grain silo built on one end. It was well kept, she saw, with a smaller range of cottages surrounding it to the north and a host of agricultural outbuildings sweeping around the southern and eastern ends: chicken coops, dovecotes, kennels, a pigsty, storehouses, drying houses, smokehouses, and a small stable. A normal Falas country estate, she decided, as she slipped through the fencing around the gardens and into the compound proper. There were no guards visible—and no reason for them. This was a peaceful country.

Gatina suppressed a thrill of excitement as she moved from one shadow to another across the grounds, avoiding the animal pens. The last thing she needed was to attract the attention of a sleepless hound or a chicken out for a nocturnal stroll. As she went, she frequently paused to study the manor house, where lamplight peeped feebly through the open windows. She climbed to the top of a storehouse fifty feet from the doorway that afforded a good view of the front of the manor, to take her bearings of the place.

There were still some folk awake, of course. Indeed, it seemed as if the main chamber of the hall had a late supper being served, she could see through the open door. It wasn't even the ninth bell, after all. She had more than an hour before Censor Lantripol was scheduled to arrive.

Gatina was about to move closer to get a better view when she stopped herself. She had recourse to magesight, she remembered. She didn't need to expose herself to the risk of being found out when she could magically magnify the doorway. The spell was growing familiar to her now, and when she silently invoked it, the wide doorway suddenly revealed the feast inside as if she were standing there.

That is incredibly handy, she remarked to herself as she peered into the manor. Gatina gained an immediate appreciation for the advantages that shadowthieves had over their mundane fellows. Inside the dimly lit hall were trestle tables where a number of men were sitting and eating through the last portion of their meal. It all looked very normal and congenial . . . until she saw the unmistakable pattern of black and white checks swirl briefly in her vision as a man came outside to relieve himself.

It was a Censor, she was certain. No one else would bear that stark livery. One of the common sorts, she decided as he stumbled over to a convenient bush. He appeared to have been deep in his cups. Likely there were at least two of them accompanying a Censor Captain, she suspected. He bore no blade that she could see, and he had left his helmet inside, but he was definitely a Censor. A moment later, he finished his business with the bush and headed back inside.

While helpful, the information was only the first thing she needed to establish. She knew the Censorate was, indeed, present for the evening. What she didn't know was which part of the manor they would be staying in. It could be anywhere in the main house or amongst the cottages nearby. Without knowing where, she had no real clue where the Censor Captain might have stored his book. Or, she suspected, he would keep such a valuable thing on his person.

This is why you shouldn't conduct a heist without proper planning, she chided herself, imagining her mother lecturing her about the subject.

As much as she resented hearing that from herself—in her mother's voice—she knew the wisdom implicit in the idea. Only amateurs broke into someplace with no idea about how the interior was laid out or what there was of value inside. That sort of foolishness got you caught.

Still, she was there, and she was committed. Gatina took a deep breath and proceeded to study the place more attentively.

The main hall was clearly built on the standard for such buildings in the Coastlands of Falas. She could see that there was one large room in the center that acted as a dining hall and workshop during the day. To one side was a dark area that lacked windows—storerooms, she guessed. On the other side was the kitchen and workshop, where the meats and produce were processed for preparation and storage. It was the side closer to the pigsty, where waste from the kitchen would be turned into scraps for the hogs.

The second story would be where the manor's staff lived, as well as accommodations for any guests. Many of these country estates took in travelers for a fee and provided them a bed and meals for extra coin, she knew. The rooftop—covered in dark red clay tiles—was shaped in a manner that suggested three big bays protruded from the opposite side of the house. Each one could serve as miniature living quarters in its own right, or it might be used for working space. And, of course, the manor lord and his family would dwell within the safety of the refuge tower.

Gatina could see at least four easy means to access the steeply peaked roof if one were so inclined. This far in the countryside, casual theft was rare, and houses were built without much concern for the possibility of housebreakers that the folk of Falas or Inmar might have. The heat of the season saw nearly every paneless window in the place open to the cool night breezes. She could ascend by the open shutters as easily as walking up the stairs.

Still, that did not suggest where the Censors might be staying. If they were mere rent-paying travelers, then they might be put in any of the three bays or simply given space in the main hall to sleep. If they were esteemed guests, then the manor lord himself might vacate his quarters and offer them to his visitors. Or he might turn over one of the tidy cottages for their use. Some manors even had ranges of guest cottages for such occasions.

No, she decided with a silent sigh, she would need more information before she could figure out just where to enter and how. That meant getting closer—close enough to overhear the conversation in the main hall. There were magical spells that could allow a wizard to listen to faraway voices as clearly as if you were standing next to the speaker. With only a few weeks of magical training behind her, Gatina did not know them. She would have to spy on the Censors the old-fashioned way for now.

Slipping silently down the storehouse wall and hugging the shadows brought her closer to the building, and a conveniently bushy honeysuckle shrub under a front window provided a fragrant place of concealment once she navigated quietly across the grounds. The untended honeysuckle was thick enough to hide her from casual inspection even if it was within arm's reach of the door.

It was easy enough to crawl between the shrub and the wall without making too much noise, as it was so cramped that no one would reasonably suspect it concealed a spy. And its proximity to the main entrance also lessened the likelihood that someone would casually spot her, she knew. Gatina had learned much from Mistress Silva about how light worked and how the human eye registered light and shadow. Moving from a place of even dim illumination to darkness would mean that anyone coming out of that door would likely not see until their eyes adjusted, and that would be after they were well beyond the doorway.

As she settled, she took the chance to glance inside the open window from the shadows, relying on her cowl and her slow movements to preserve her from discovery. In her brief glance, she saw only a few left at a table—two Censors playing chess. A third Censor in a much finer quality cloak was speaking with two men sitting closer to the window. They were smoking pipes and drinking wine, their meal clearly finished. Had it been winter, she reasoned, they would have chosen a spot nearer to the fire. That would have made it much harder to overhear their conversation. She also noted a staircase and two large doorways in the background, as well as a number of cupboards, before she quietly slunk down into the flowering shrubbery.

This isn't bad for an improvised plan. It smells better than the sewers, Gatina encouraged herself as she settled in amongst the leaves, sticks, and pretty yellow flowers.

And the bugs. Though it was too late in the evening for the bush to be filled with bees, she discovered that spiders seemed all too happy to ignore the cycle of night and day as they spun their webs and hunted in the underbrush. Gatina was not fond of spiders.

But as she settled in and focused on listening to the conversation inside the hall, all thoughts about inconveniences such as spiders faded. The voices she heard were much clearer now, and the men within were speaking loud enough for their voices to carry through the open window above her head. With a little effort, she managed to determine how many were engaged in conversation and who they might be. She sat absolutely still as she stretched her ears out and tried to figure out who was who.

"... a long journey but largely uneventful after we crossed the frontier with Castal," a man with a deep voice and a Castali accent was saying.

"There were too many of us to tempt the bandits in the Sea of Gravel, and of course, the Alshari guardsmen at the Narrows accepted our credentials without question."

"Well, no one in their right mind wishes to question a Censor," pointed out a male voice with the common Alshari accent. Gatina thought he might be the host, Lord Halanric. "Your order has a harsh reputation that can cause a man to sweat, my lord. None in my family has magical Talent, and you still intimidate us."

The other man chuckled. "The mundane have no cause to fear the Censorate, I assure you, lest you are abetting some violator of the Bans. We might have been given grand discretionary powers by our charter, but they are reserved exclusively for the magi. But our trip down the Mandros was similarly uneventful. It was not until we reached Falas that we encountered any difficulty. Riots," he sighed.

"So we have heard, Captain, so we have heard," agreed the other voice. "Bad business, that. I didn't always hold with Duke Lenguin's policies, but he kept the peace. I've heard things have been terrible in the capital of late."

"Oh, this unpleasantness will pass quickly enough as the council consolidates their power," assured the Censor. "In my experience, most folk want peace, not mischief, in their lives. Would you not agree, Goodman?"

"Oh, aye, aye," a third voice said. It was low and gruff, and not nearly as educated in accent as the Censor's. "A trader like me sees all sorts of folk in our journeys. Only ruffians and troublemakers seek that kind of mischief. Riots? Bad for business!" he said, a scowl in his voice. "But good to know. Mayhap I'll avoid Falas for a while after this trip, until this fire dies down."

Gatina realized that Lord Halanric and his checkered-cloaked guest were not alone. Some merchant had purchased his hospitality for the evening. That, too, was common practice, she knew. There were scarce few inns out in the countryside. Overnighting at a manor could be far cheaper and more comfortable than even an inexpensive inn.

"Oh, it's just a bit of rabble upset over the change in regime," the Censor assured. "It happens when politics turns like this. Count Vichetral is a very capable man and a lord of exceeding wit. His men are loyal and well equipped. Indeed, most are from his personal household. He uses the riots to reveal his enemies. Within another fortnight, I daresay there won't be any more riots in Falas. I took that from the lips of the man himself when I visited him in the palace."

"You? Visited the Count?" asked the trader, surprised.

"Protocol demands it," agreed the Censor. "I must introduce myself to the leading lord in any land before I begin my operations. Which is one reason I came to you tonight, Lord Halanric," he added. "It is far superior to enjoy the support of the local gentry when one is investigating. And you come highly recommended in Falas."

"I do?" the manor lord asked, surprised.

"One of Count Vichetral's men suggested you would be helpful—Baron Regarapol, I believe."

"Ah!" the manor lord exclaimed. "He's my cousin! Well, he married my cousin," he amended. "Regarapol is a true gentleman, too. He has a grand holding over in Rhemes. He is with Vichetral?"

"The Count's cause has attracted many to his banner," the Censor informed. "I believe he placed Regarapol in charge of some aspect of his security. When I told him I would begin my investigations close to Falas, he told me to meet with you should I come near Lindule Hall. He suggested your hospitality was without peer. He was quite impressed by it when he and your cousin lodged here last year. More wine?" the Censor requested.

"Oh, of course, of course, my lord!" the manor lord said, clearly pleased at hearing his reputation spoken of in such high circles. "Where are the servants?" he added a moment later.

"You sent them on to bed," reminded the trader. "I'll get my boy to fetch it; no need to ring the bell."

"What other news do you bear from Falas, if you don't mind me asking, my lord?" Halanric begged. "We haven't heard much since Count Vichetral came to power. Rumors, mostly, and not very many of them. We heard about the bad business with the clergy. The . . . executions," he added in a low voice.

"Yes," murmured the Censor Captain. "His Excellency is not inclined to brook any rebellion in this time of crisis. Perhaps not the route I would have chosen, but power demands extraordinary things from those who pursue it. News? There is less from Falas than beyond the frontier."

"Please tell us," encouraged the trader as Gatina heard the clink of glass and pewter.

"I wish it was better news," sighed the Censor. "Duke Rard will be declaring himself king in a few weeks, king over Castal, Remere, and Alshar. He claims the support of all three duchies in defiance of custom and tradition, citing the goblin incursions in the Wilderlands as pretext. But it is just a naked grab for power. It is well suspected that it was his agents who assassinated Duke Lenguin and Duchess Enora, not the criminals. The man will stop at nothing to claim a crown, not even murder and kidnapping."

"He married that . . . vicious cur," Lord Halanric said distastefully. "Lenguin's sister . . . Grendine? Grendine," he assured himself. "My father disliked her when she was at court. Ambitious one, that."

"She's likely behind all of this chaos," the trader agreed. "Alshar was blessed when she got married off out of the duchy. Have you news of the heirs?" he asked, curious. "Word was that they were taken into custody and shipped off to Castal."

"The Orphan Duke? Yes, that's well known," the Censor reported. "He's a virtual prisoner in some abbey—or some dungeon, if Grendine has her way. She is ruthless, even to her family. She bribed our Grand Master to betray the order and forswear his oaths. She would try to talk a Tryggite nun into infanticide, if she thought it would advance her ambition," he chuckled. "General Hartarian was given a powerful magical device and high position to convince him to change his cloak. And then Duke Rard expelled the Censorate from his lands to quell any protest of his claim on the crown."

"So, that's why there are so many of you fellows around now!" snapped the trader. "Been working Alshar from the Narrows to the Great Bay all my life and never saw more than a handful in all those years. Now I see them everywhere, it seems."

"Well, even the Censorate has to respect political reality, Goodman, even when it defies our charter," admitted the Censor. "Rard may have transgressed the ancient law when he overturned the Bans, but he still holds a great deal of secular power. The Censorate is not a military order; we are regulators. In the face of such enmity, we had no choice but to find refuge with a more traditionally minded lord."

"Count Vichetral," the trader stated, matter-of-factly. "You are in service to him now, then?"

"Oh, no, no, that, too, would be a violation of our charter . . . officially," the Censor added with another chuckle. "We are an independent agency, deriving our power from King Kamaklavan himself. But we do rely upon secular lords to help enforce our rulings, and if the sovereign Duke of a land is against us, prudence suggests we find a friendlier land . . . for now.

Count Vichetral invited us to Enultramar, under his protection. He is a gentleman who understands the value of our order and the great service we provide. He's also had some cause to complain to us about certain magi working against him illegally."

"The magi are against him?" Lord Halanric asked, surprised.

"Not all of them, of course," the Censor quickly corrected. "But there seem to be some wizards who object to his stabilizing influence during the crisis. And who preferred Duke Lenguin's lax policy toward effective enforcement of the Bans to Vichetral's more traditional approach. Only a few families of them, it is suspected. But they have employed magic against him and his fellow counts while they strive to maintain order and recover from Lenguin's untimely death."

"Magic?" the trader asked, his voice filled with curiosity. "Are they cursing him, then?"

"Oh, the magical arts have far more specific uses in the hands of a capable mage than mere curses," Captain Stefan said with an indulgent chuckle. "Spying, communications, coercion, theft, murder—all quite against the Bans, of course. Which is why His Excellency contacted us and asked us to investigate. He desires a return to a far more rigorous enforcement of the Bans and wishes us to track down these scofflaws and bring them to justice before they take advantage of the current emergency and cause real damage to the realm."

"Seems to me like every adept I ever knew was a schemer," agreed the trader. By his voice, Gatina guessed he was getting deep into his cups too; he was starting to slur his words. It must have been good wine. "Always charging more than they say, all for waving their hands and muttering a few bits of nonsense. Better off paying a priest to do it, for all the good it does."

"His Excellency's foes are not mere practical adepts, alas," sighed Captain Stefan. "Those we have records of, and they know that they are not supposed to dabble in politics, lest they incur the harshest penalties. Nor are they common witches. Vichetral finds himself assailed from the shadows by clandestine sorcerers who thumb their noses at the authority of the Censorate and have for years. Unregistered magi who hide their Talent and training behind castle walls."

"Secret wizards," scoffed the trader. "That makes sense. Just the type to stir up trouble when we've already gotten a barrel of it. Sneaky bastards," he said loudly, confirming Gatina's suspicions about his sobriety.

"I've heard of such," Lord Halanric insisted, in a tone of voice that suggested to Gatina's ear that he hadn't but wanted to impress his guests. "You say they're real?"

"They are Coastlords, mostly," the Censor explained with a snort. "Remnants of the Magocracy who yearn again for the rule of the magi over all. Alshar is filled with them. Devious warlocks who hide behind their mundane kin and lie about their true nature. And who resent the legitimate authority of both the Dukes and the Censorate. The very worst kind of traitor," he sneered. "They have vexed Count Vichetral, and he has asked us to find them and bring them to account."

He's talking about us! Gatina realized, feeling insulted and flattered at the same time.

"So, that's why you're here?" asked the trader, surprised. "You suspect old Halanric here to be a secret wizard?"

"No, no, not at all," soothed the Censor. "Indeed, it is Lord Halanric's reputation and lack of a legacy of *rajira* that bring me here. I need a safe and secure installation in which to debrief my agents. I have had Censors investigating all over County Falas for weeks, and they are to report to me here for the next few days. Piece by piece we shall reveal these rebels to authority and bring them into custody. Indeed, one should be arriving at any time from the local abbey to give me his report. I shall see another two in the morning. With your permission, of course, Lord Halanric," he added diplomatically.

"What? Of course!" the manor lord agreed. "Always happy to help. I'm a good and loyal man," he boasted, without mentioning to whom he was loyal, Gatina noted.

"I assure you, your assistance will find favor with the Count," Stefan promised.

"You predict he will maintain power, then?" the trader asked shrewdly.

"Oh, of course," Captain Stefan said confidently. "In the absence of the Duke or the court, he has managed to stitch together quite a coalition of supporters and keep the business of state operating. He has strong allies among the coastal cities and the havens of the Sea Lords. The great merchant houses are amenable to his rule and his policies. His opposition is disorganized and scattered. Unless Duke Rard decides to invade, or the Orphan Duke escapes and returns, or he falls to the assassin's blade himself, he's certain to outlast his domestic foes. No, gentlemen, I would anticipate Count Vichetral will rule for some time to come. I would not chance to prophesize, but perhaps with the Ducal coronet on his brow, if he's ambitious enough to pursue it," the Censor added slyly.

That thought disgusted Gatina. She had never even seen Count Vichetral, but she knew that his ambitions had thrown the entire duchy into chaos after the Duke's death and led to the loss of hundreds if not thousands of lives. His willingness to permit slave-taking once again appalled her. Her parents had told her how he had schemed against Duke Lenguin since before she was born, he coveted the coronet so much, and the idea of him usurping the title and position of Lenguin's captured heir was repugnant.

Indeed, the fact that he was willing to employ such folk as the Brotherhood of the Rat and the Royal Censorate to beat down his adversaries told her everything she needed to know about the man.

But before Captain Stefan could continue, the clatter of a carriage and its team arose on the road. In moments, it appeared from between the trees lining the lane and brought all three men to the window.

"Ah! That must be my man Lantripol," Stefan observed. "Just at the tenth bell, as he proposed. I do appreciate promptness. Goodman, could I get your boy to run upstairs and retrieve my satchel from the tower? I'll need to take notes as he briefs me. And Lord Halanric, could I trouble you for another bottle of this most excellent wine? It's going to be a long evening, I'm afraid, and it will go better if Lantripol and I are both sufficiently relaxed."

That's it! Gatina thought excitedly. *His quarters are in the refuge tower.* She now knew where she had to go to steal the book. The only question now was whether she could get there before the servant did . . . and get out again without being discovered.

Slowly, she extracted herself from the honeysuckle bush without attracting notice, then crawled across the foundation of the manor house to the corner, concealed by her black cloak. Once she rounded the corner, she stood, glanced around to ensure she wasn't being seen, and then stretched her aching muscles.

It was time for her heist. And it would be best to be limber.

CHAPTER SEVENTEEN
THE CENSOR'S LITTLE BOOK

There are many ways to enter a place by stealth. A concealed entrance is best, followed by a disguise permitting entrance without note of the occupants and raising their alarm. The traditional method of entering through an unguarded window is, of course, one of the easiest methods. But be certain you know what and who lie beyond the shutters before you go through.

*— from **The Shield of Darkness***
Commentaries

GATINA'S LEGS WERE CRAMPED FROM SITTING IN A SINGLE POSITION UNDER the window for so long, so it took her a moment to shake them out. But all pain was forgotten when she began scaling the exterior of the refuge tower. She delighted in climbing, and the old fortification provided an ideal exercise in the art. Had it been well maintained and protected against such assaults, it might have been difficult, but the stones and bricks of the walls didn't seem as if they'd been properly kept in a generation. There were only scant signs of faded whitewash on them, and there were plenty of spots where the mortar was cracked and broken.

That was as good as a ladder to the Kitten of Night. Gatina's heart surged with elation as she stretched her arms up to find fingerholds in the gently crumbling masonry. Her tired legs extended at her command to put her toes on protrusions that allowed her to ascend the face of the tower quickly and easily. The ivy vines that had been allowed to grow on the backside of the fortification gave her plenty of indications of where it would be safe to pull herself up. Within moments, she was two stories above the ground, and to her delight, the climb got even easier.

The third floor proved to be the lord's chamber, given over to the Censor Captain in the name of hospitality. Thankfully, the windows there, while narrow, had been left open to let in the cool night breezes. Gatina squeezed herself through the largest, a double-arched opening with weather-worn shutters barely larger than an arrow slit . . . but just big enough to admit a determined kitten.

She didn't have much time, she knew, as her feet silently touched the wooden floor. The wine merchant's servant would be up there soon, she knew, and that gave her only a few moments to locate the satchel and the book she suspected was within. She surveyed the room with mages-ight, allowing what tiny bit of light was available to better illuminate her search.

There was but one bed in the round chamber, set between the tiny fireplace and the window and made up with a rich-looking summer quilt and a down pillow. There were wardrobe presses and cabinets lining the other walls, save for a narrow door that led downstairs, she assumed.

But she was spared searching the cabinets, because Captain Stefan had dumped his luggage on the press at the foot of his bed. There were two well-made traveling bags there, and between them she found the well-worn leather satchel she assumed contained the prize she was looking for.

Gatina made a point of not disturbing anything else in the room as she pulled the satchel on the bed and tried to open it . . . only to find the flap that closed it secured with a small brass lock. She sighed. Of course it wouldn't be that easy.

Using two tiny steel lockpicks from her pouch, she only took a few moments to spring open the simple mechanism. She'd practiced that essential skill for hours, during various coach rides and journeys by barge. There was a satisfying *click* when her nimble fingers finally encouraged the two tumblers within to part ways. With a feeling of triumph, she put away the picks and opened the flap.

She was not disappointed. Within the Censor Captain's satchel, there was a thick sheaf of parchment, much of it blank, a tiny inkpot, a pouch of sand, well-trimmed goose quills, a pen knife, and not one but three books.

The largest was professionally copied, she could see: the title was embossed in faded gilt on the cover: *Manual for Arcane Interrogations*, it read, with the sinister device of the Royal Censorate of Magic stamped below the title. A brief glance confirmed her suspicion, as the entire book was copied in the same neat hand—the work of a professional scribe like her cousin Onnelik. As fascinating as it appeared, Gatina reluctantly put it back in the satchel.

The second book seemed to be Captain Stefan's personal journal and notebook—which was fascinating enough in its own right. There were directions for spells copied there, notes on places he'd been and people he'd met with over the years. It was thicker than the manual but smaller in length and width, and filled with the captain's neat, flowing handwriting. There were diagrams and pictures sketched in charcoal pencil as well as his notes, she saw. Fascinating but not what she was there for.

The final book was tiny, compared to the two others, a volume of but a hundred or so pages bound in plain undyed leather and tied with a thong. The kind of book that traveled well, she reasoned, without a title on its face or anything that might suggest it was important.

Eagerly she untied the thong, committing to memory the knot the Censor had used as she opened it. She was about to confirm that it was, indeed, the notebook she was after when she heard the creak of wooden stairs from the door. It was just one creak, but she assumed that the servant had finally made it up the tower to fetch the book.

Darkness! she swore to herself as her heart raced.

Gatina looked around in a panic as she anticipated the interruption of her heist. She could dive out the window, of course, but the pile of parchment and books on the bed would immediately reveal the theft to the servant. If she took the time to return the contents to the satchel and lock it again, she risked being discovered too. Once again, she reflected on the foolishness of inadequate planning for a heist. She could not help feeling her mother's disapproving frown in her mind. It was almost as great as the panic that she could feel rising up her spine.

She tried her best to shove the sheaf of parchment back into the bag, but only succeeded in scattering half of them across the bed and onto the floor. The sealed inkpot skittered across the floorboards as she pushed the two other books inside—only to discover that they were at the wrong angle to fit properly. Before she could correct them, the door to the chamber opened unexpectedly.

Darkness! her mind screamed again as she whirled to face the intruder, her hand on the hilt of the dagger behind her back.

It proved to be a young man only a little older than she, with a shock of long black hair over one eye and a scraggly swatch of beard on his chin. He bore a lantern in his hand which cast wild shadows about the room. He looked at her, startled, as she looked back at him in surprise.

There was a moment's pause as the two of them regarded each other. Then the servant's shoulders sagged, and he looked down at the ground with a heavy sigh before he looked up again with a familiar expression.

"Kitten," her brother's voice said softly, "you have simply *got* to stop doing this sort of thing."

Gatina was so shocked, she almost dropped the book she was holding.

"*Cat?* Cat, is that *you?*" she asked in a harsh whisper.

"Of course it's me!" he answered with a toss of his head. The shock of hair flipped up, revealing a face that was at least somewhat familiar to her eye.

"What are you *doing* here?" she demanded.

"I'm on a mission! What are *you* doing here?" he asked, his tone accusing.

"I'm on a heist!" she replied defensively.

"You're messing up our mission!" he warned her as he crossed the room.

"And you're messing up my heist!" she snapped.

"We're not supposed to steal the book!" he explained. "Not yet! It's incomplete!"

"Then what are you doing here?" she asked.

"Never you mind!" he said, shaking his head angrily. "Do you realize how badly you just complicated our mission? No, of course not!"

"I . . . I was going to take it before anyone noticed," she defended, knowing that it sounded like a hollow excuse the moment the words left her mouth. "Why aren't you trying to steal it?"

"Because the Council wants it complete before we do, for one thing," he said, his voice intense as he took the book from her hand and tossed it on the bed. "For another . . . look at it with magesight," he instructed. "In the thaumaturgical mode," he added.

There were several ways one could use magesight, she'd learned: for seeing in the dark, for seeing minute details, or for seeing far away. By magically altering an arcane field in front of the pupil, you could do all sorts of things with the spell.

One of which, she had learned just a few days before, was to reveal the invisible vibrations of directed thaumaturgical energies. That was how she had searched for naturally occurring channels of power on her journey to the estate. They rarely showed themselves to the naked eye, but if you tuned the refraction of the magesight spell to just the right way . . .

The little book on the bed suddenly sprang to life as her eyes adjusted to the spell. The unassuming volume suddenly grew a thick cocoon of arcane power surrounding it. Gatina gasped involuntarily.

"What is that?" she asked, her mouth agape. She didn't recognize that pattern of energies at all.

"A location spell," Atopol explained, frustrated. "Shadow detected it when we first made contact with the captain. It's powerful. Powerful enough to let him track it anyplace in the duchy. Censors are wizards, you recall. They use spells," he informed her sarcastically.

"Of course they do!" Gatina admitted, annoyed. "Can't you dispel it?"

"Can you? No? I've had only one year more of magic training than you have, and I haven't remotely gotten to the point where I could do that sort of thing," he said, anger tinging his voice. "Shadow says it would take him at least a week to undo it. We'd get nicked long before then."

"Then . . . then why are you here?" Gatina pleaded, suddenly feeling guilty and foolish about her adventure.

"We're here to put our own tracking spell on it," Atopol reasoned as he gingerly picked up the book. "Just be glad it isn't spellbound—that's a kind of magical lock that is insanely difficult to dispel. Even the attempt can raise an alarm. Thankfully, Captain Stefan didn't see the need for that . . . yet." He opened the book and began scanning the pages. Gatina peered over his shoulder. Unlike the larger notebook, this one was written in many different hands. There were pages and pages of lists—mostly names, she could see—and locations.

"Well, at least he didn't use a code," she offered lamely.

"We were afraid he might," her brother nodded. "But this is definitely the book: the first page is headed *Adversaries*. This one," he said, turning several fully-filled pages, "is listed *Potential Adversaries*. There are a lot of names on this list," he added worriedly. "There are at least thirty pages filled in here. The Censors have been busy."

"Well, if we're not going to steal it, what are we going to do with it?" she asked, scowling.

Atopol was silent for a moment. He closed the book and stared at the bed in the gloom of the lantern, the scattered blank leaves of parchment and the bundle of quills scattered across the quilt. "We might be able to salvage something from all of this and not get caught," he sighed. "It means a change in plans, and a bit more risk, but . . . well, I think I have a plan."

Quickly, he sketched out to his sister an idea that did, indeed, involve much more risk than she'd anticipated.

"Can you do that?" he asked, fixing her with a stare. "It means writing faster than you've ever written before. And riding faster, too."

Gatina nodded. "I can do it," she agreed reluctantly. "I think I can do it," she corrected. Atopol was asking a lot of her, and she suddenly felt far more tired than when she'd entered the tower room.

"The important thing is not to get caught. Just leave it where I told you, at the bridge. That way, it will just look like it fell off your horse. It's . . . it's not an ideal solution, but maybe we get something out of this tipped-over chamber pot. You really shouldn't have come," he said, shaking his head.

"I didn't have anyone around to tell me not to," she defended as she helped him gather up all of the contents of the satchel. "Everyone else left the abbey. What was I supposed to do?"

"What you were instructed to, perhaps? Not plan and execute another unauthorized heist that cocks things up for everyone else?" he proposed, raising an eyebrow.

"Kittens are impetuous," she said as she secured the satchel and pulled the strap over her shoulder. "I saw an opportunity and took some initiative."

"We'll see if Shadow agrees," he said, doubtfully. "There's one last thing you need to do. They're going to come looking for me before long. And when they find me, it's going to be seven hells of uproar."

"What?" Gatina asked, confused.

"Hit me," her brother said with a resigned sigh. "In the face. On the chin. Really, *really* hard."

The rest of the night was a whirlwind in Gatina's memory. She climbed down the tower so quickly that she almost fell, much to her dismay, as the satchel banging against her hip unbalanced her. By the time her feet touched the ground, she was already winded with the effort.

But it had been just in time, she realized. A moment after she landed, she heard a loud exclamation coming from the tower above, and lights began to flicker from the window. She quickly hid herself in the shadows of the yard and watched for a moment. She was perfectly still, understanding that anyone who cared to glance outside would see movement far easier than her still form.

It was just in time, too. She did, indeed, see a man stick his head out and scan the yard before reluctantly pulling back inside. A moment later, a second head emerged. She waited for thirty heartbeats after the second head vanished before she began her journey through the grounds and back toward her horse.

She made all the speed she could without sacrificing stealth. Nimbly dodging around the outbuildings, skirting the edge of the pigsty, and vaulting over the split-rail fence at the edge of the grounds all seemed to fly by her as she focused her attention on getting as far away from the manor house as quickly as she could. She avoided the roadway, of course, threading her way between the trees of the wood surrounding the estate instead. If it hadn't been for magesight, she would have tripped and stumbled a dozen times on inconvenient roots and fallen branches.

But she finally made it back to where her horse was impatiently waiting. Unfortunately, she had made it wait for so long that a pile of dung had accumulated behind it. Despite her better judgment, she took the time to obscure the manure with leaves and sticks before mounting the rouncy and urging it away from the manor. Only then did she make her way back to the road, where she encouraged the horse into a gallop.

That was more frightening than descending the tower by far. Gatina had ridden a few times, it was true, but always at a staid and steady pace—and always in daylight. But the speed at which the horse thundered away was breathtaking, and she felt like she was being pounded to death in the saddle as she jostled around.

Atopol had given her clear instructions about what to do next. Going directly back to the abbey would be insane, they had decided. The book had a location spell upon it, so that would ensure that the place would be full of Censors by morning. Even moving in that direction was problematic.

Instead, she turned south, not north, and rode relentlessly for half an hour. At the next crossroads, she turned right and made her way down the road at a more leisurely pace until she came to a covered bridge spanning a stream of some size.

There she halted. This was the road that led to Falas Town, Atopol had informed her, in the opposite direction of Palomar Abbey. The bridge was just large enough to permit a single cart to cross, but its walls would provide cover for what she needed to do.

After securing the reins to the wall of the bridge, Gatina quickly unslung the satchel and crouched on the thick wooden planks of the bridge. She searched the pouches at her belt until she found a stub of tallow candle and carefully set it on a stone before she removed the flint, tinder, and striker from another pocket. She devoutly wished she knew the spell to make a flame by magic. She knew it was possible, if difficult. It required a lot of thaumaturgical power, for one thing, and the way she felt after her adventure, she didn't think she could manage more than simple magesight.

Adeptly she sparked the tinder until it caught, then blew it into a flame and lit the candle. Quite enough light to read by, she decided, as she extinguished the tinder and put it away. Then she got to the serious work: copying as much of the book as possible onto the blank parchment that Censor Captain Stefan had so conveniently provided.

Taking a breath, she plunged into the work with dedication, beginning with the first page and scribbling as fast as she possibly could. She had decided to write down the names and places in the code known as the Ivy, as it allowed her to relate entire words with just a few strokes of the pen. It was just faster than writing in Narasi or, Darkness forbid, the complicated Old High Perwynese so many of the old texts from the Magocracy used. Cousin Onnelik had taught it to her during her mission in Falas. It was the first code she had learned, and so far, it was her favorite code because it was more akin to painting than writing. One by one, the names she wrote flowed across the page until she required another.

She sped along without too much consideration of the names themselves, until she began coming across some she recognized. Families, mostly, whom the regime had determined were set against it, and the prominent members whom the Censorate thought might be involved in seditious acts and activities against Count Vichetral. Her long hours in the temple's archives, and the extensive lists of Coastlords she'd compiled, suggested that the Censorate was, indeed, aware of those plotting against the new ruler of Alshar.

Her heart nearly stopped when, toward the end of the list, she came upon a name she was very familiar with: *Huguenin of Falas, House Sardanz.*

Her cousin Huguenin was a master of disguise and had tutored her on the art of appearing as someone other than herself. He lived in Falas, where he was associated with the grand theaters of the capital somehow. Cousin Huguenin was adept at costumes, hair coloring, and cosmetics, as well as the finer points of accent and mannerisms. He'd helped her become Lissa the Mouse, a street orphan in Falas. But he was also, she suspected, a Talented Blue Mage, a master of the arcane art of psychomancy. Her mother had said as much back in Falas.

But in Stefan's deadly little book, he was listed as a *Probable Leader and Suspected Clandestine Mage* at the top of a long list of fellows collectively called *Theater Gang*.

She didn't know why the Censorate was so eager to harass a bunch of actors and singers, but it was disturbing that someone so close to her was involved in this. It brought home just how important this book was.

Gatina raced through the next few sections, abbreviating liberally when it seemed wise to do so. She constantly kept her ear on the road to listen for the sound of hoofbeats, footsteps, or carriage wheels, but only the chirping of crickets and the occasional hoot of an owl answered her. When she came to the next section, entitled *Speculations*, she copied a list of questions that Captain Stefan had formulated in pursuit of his investigation.

Underground gang of magi coordinating opposition: who leads? was the first. *How funded?* the second line read, followed by *Robberies & Smuggling; investigate.* That's where the name of the Inmar fence, along with Lemon's Reach, was listed, along with half a dozen other names and places.

One question after another in the captain's terse hand explained his reasoning, and she had to admit it was quite insightful. She dutifully copied every word, every line connecting two names or places in association, and moved as fast as possible. She had been at it for more than an hour, and the candle was nearly spent.

Finally, she finished with the last few notes, something about a goldsmith getting robbed in upper Falas, and the notes ended. That was as far as Captain Stefan had gotten, she reasoned, although there were plenty of blank leaves left in the book. No doubt it would be filled with more after Stefan interviewed Lantripol and his other agents.

She blew out the candle, replaced it in her pouch, and carefully threw the tallow-covered rock into the river. There were no stains or soot left behind to alert anyone to what she had done, she hoped. Gatina rolled up her own messy notes and tucked them away in her harness before carefully retying the knot of the thong that bound the book and replaced it in the satchel with its fellows. She ensured she used the exact knot she'd untied.

But to make the recovery believable, she had to make a convincing scene. It would be foolish to assume that a thief breaking into a remote, rural manor house would choose to steal a specific satchel and then just leave it behind . . . unless it was clearly an accident. Such things happened all the time, in the middle of a heist, she'd seen herself. No matter how well you planned and how much you were informed, something could—and almost always did—go wrong. Sometimes, things went so wrong that you abandoned the loot in order to escape.

In this case, she ensured to tell a story to the canny investigator that suggested his theoretical thief did, indeed, have a bad heist and that in running away from the scene, he had inadvertently let the prize drop as he galloped over the bridge.

To that end, Gatina carefully pulled out the seams binding the leather strap to the satchel, on one side, and then just as carefully smashed the brass lock with a rock. It was, after all, merely to ensure secure privacy, not designed to withstand a concerted attack. The hasp of the lock snapped quickly enough, as if it had fallen from the back of a horse and broken.

She scattered Captain Stefan's papers, both blank and composed, across the decking of the bridge, along with the quills and sand. Then she took what little remained of the ink and splashed it, dashing the tiny glass bottle in the process. When she was done, she surveyed her work: the bag seemed cast away, not carefully prepared, the victim of unfortunate circumstances and rough handling.

But was it convincing? There was no sign of her presence or copying that she could see by magesight, and she checked carefully. Perhaps the Censorate's spells might detect something if they used them, but she hoped that they would accept the premise of the unlucky thief and enjoy the close call of recovering a valuable record instead of looking too closely at where and why it was found.

It would have to do, she decided. If Stefan had used his location spell, he'd soon know where the book was—he might be headed there already, Gatina reasoned. She finally pulled herself into the saddle and urged her sleepy horse back down the road whence she came, pulling her Nocturn's habit over her head as she rode. Before she came to the main road, she headed cross-country in a direction she was fairly certain would circumvent encountering Captain Stefan's men on the road.

It was late, after all. The people in the countryside were still sleeping, most of them, and while nighttime travelers weren't unheard-of, neither were they common. She wanted to avoid any notice she might attract on her way back to the abbey.

Of course, the gods could not let her have that, she found. Her shortcut over the fields brought her to a tiny hamlet in short order, and while it was handy for having a lane that likely reconnected with the main road to Palomar, it also had the very first stirrings of the day in the neat little huts of the settlement. Gatina tried to ride through quickly and quietly, without attracting attention, but was startled when she finally got to the road . . . and ran into a peasant trudging his way back from the fields.

"Sister!" he exclaimed in surprise as she nearly rode over him.

Jarred by the sudden voice after a night filled with silence, Gatina squeaked involuntarily. She quickly pulled on the persona of Nocturn Avorrita, though she wished she'd brought her dental prosthetic.

"Goodman!" she finally managed, as she pulled her horse to a halt. "You scared me near to death in the Blessed Darkness!"

"Sorry, Sister, I'm so sorry," the man said, apologetically. "Wasn't expectin' a nun to ride through, myself," he pointed out. "I was out with a cow, birthing a calf. Came in the middle of the night, of course, because Bova hates to see a farmer sleep."

"Oh," Avorrita said. "I was taking measurements of the stars tonight and had to wait until some of them made an appearance. It is for the abbey," she added.

"Oh, of course, of course, I've seen you all scuttling in the fields at all hours, over the years," the older man chuckled. "Craning your necks to look at the pretty things in the sky. Get bored of that sort of thing myself. But Sister . . . could I impose on you for . . . for a blessing? I know you're not a priestess of Bova, nor even Trygg, but the calf had a hard time, as did his dam. I'm . . . I'm worried," he said, swallowing. "I know it's not your pasture, so to speak, but could you . . . could you say a few words on their behalf?" he pleaded. "Maybe get them stars to intervene and see them well?"

Gatina was doubly surprised. She'd never been asked for such a thing outside of regular devotions. Certainly, the Saganites were clergy, in all senses of the word, but they were a scholarly order, not one that ministered to the people as such. Still, the man seemed genuinely concerned and in need of some spiritual comfort.

"I . . . I suppose I could," she admitted, shyly. "I'm only a Nocturn, but if I can . . . Well, what's the cow's name?" she asked. In truth, she had no idea how to craft a blessing for a cow. The Liturgy of the Cosmos was light on blessings.

"Her name is Rose," he said with a sigh. "Sturdy old bugger. Great milker. Gave us a fine heifer calf tonight, if she lives. But she's not suckling proper, and she shakes. Makes me nervous. Don't even want to name her, 'till I see she's going to survive. Rose looks right staggered, too, after a hard labor."

"Rose," Avorrita repeated. She could work with that, she decided. She looked up beseechingly at the sky, already lightening in the east. "Sacred stars of the Blessed Darkness, we beseech you to stream out your benevolence to touch the eye of Rose and her new calf. May your eternal light shine over them, may your . . . generosity extend to see them both fit, healthy, and well to serve this loyal man's need. A billion blessings upon them," she finished, bowing her head.

"Ah," the farmer sighed. "That's mighty gracious of you, Sister. Thank you," he said with sincerity. "I'm certain they will make it now. Why else would I meet with a nun unexpectedly on my way back from the field?"

"A billion blessings upon you, Goodman," Gatina said just as sincerely. "Go home and get some rest. On the morrow, mayhap cow and calf will be strong and fit."

"Good night, Sister!" he called after her as she nudged her horse forward toward the road to Palomar. "Get some rest yourself! You've had a busy night!"

CHAPTER EIGHTEEN

EXCUSES

Finding balance in one's alias is essential to success. The best alias is based in truth. How you depict the alias is born from the mind, the body, and the emotions. Be careful to maintain that balance, lest you confuse your true self with your alias. That can lead a thief into folly and discovery. There is no excuse for that.

*— from **The Shield of Darkness**
Commentaries*

GATINA WAS ON EDGE AFTER HER ABORTED HEIST.

She managed to return the horse to the stable and replace the saddle in the tack room without the notice of the sleepy stableboys, just before dawn, but not before she'd ridden it to the old mill. There, she stowed her working blacks and the thick sheaf of notes. She wanted neither in her quarters, as she expected—or at least anticipated—the Censorate returning to Palomar in search of the unlucky thief. By the time she had finished at the stable, she was able to stumble to the morning Lauds service at dawn, quietly yawning her way through the ritual as the Nocturns of her hall greeted the rising sun and the conclusion of the Blessed Darkness.

But while she attracted little attention from her peers in the hall, she could not help but feel a sense of foreboding. The extensive lists of names she'd copied kept swirling around her mind as she collected eggs from the chicken coop, then did her best to stay awake in history and mathematics. It had been a very long night, after all, and her body and mind were both exhausted. She finally succumbed to sleep in the middle of poetics class, and she was even called out for her nodding off by the irritated Nightbrother who was passionately lecturing about the spiritual importance of cometary orbits.

But there were no checkered cloaks bursting into the chamber, wands drawn, ready to question everyone. At least not yet.

She knew that she was indulging in paranoia—never a good thing for a thief. It would take hours for the Censors to locate the stolen satchel, she reasoned, and perhaps days before they were able to figure out any details from the theft. And the longer it took, she understood, the safer she was from detection. Her focus should be on blending back in with the rest of the Nocturns as if nothing happened. After all, for Avorrita, nothing *had*—beyond an unexpected blessing of a newborn calf.

Still, she suffered from anxiety over the episode, anxiety and embarrassment. Once again, she had violated the instructions given to her by her father and the other agents of the Shadow Council. She could claim she was just exercising opportunity and initiative to her brother, perhaps, but she knew she had been wrong to indulge in such an impetuous and dangerous adventure when the stakes were so high. Indeed, she chided herself continuously as she reflected on her actions. Gatina replayed the conversation with Atopol over and over in her head. She acknowledged that she had known better than to leave the abbey. But she did leave. She felt nervous. She was not used to that, though it fit Avorrita's personality, of course. Each time a door opened, her heart raced.

When Atopol—Nocturn Dain, she corrected herself—did not appear for the evening's magical class, her anxiety rose. But the lack of the presence of the Censorate also quelled it a little. As far as anyone was concerned, Censor Lantripol's interrogations of the magi in the abbey were concluded. There shouldn't be any further reason for the Censorate to linger in Palomar Abbey.

But things weren't quite normal in class. Not only was Nocturn Dain absent, but Nocturn Leonna was finally present—reluctantly and resentfully.

Avorrita did feel bad for the Coastlord girl sometimes. In one instant, the carefully constructed dreams of her young life—a good marriage, children, being part of a distinguished noble family—had been dashed by the emergence of her *rajira*. Avorrita could tell that she had yet to fully adjust to the idea, based on the haughty way she took her lessons. It was frustrating to even watch Sister Tavane patiently try to teach her to engage her magesight while the other students worked on the difficult third staff of thaumaturgical runes. Leonna seemed determined to fail, arguing with the nun about how she was trying to manifest the simple power. She complained that it was too complicated, that it was pointless and useless, and that it made her eyes hurt.

Avorrita might have been sympathetic, but Gatina was both amused and appalled by the excuses the girl gave for not being able to accomplish such a simple exercise. Thankfully, Sister Tavane was adept at explaining the process in such a simple way that, eventually, Leonna grudgingly admitted that she could suddenly see the testing glyph the nun conjured for her.

By the end of the class, she had managed both microscopic and telescopic vision, if only for a few moments. But Leonna still loudly claimed that the entire thing was useless, that her more advanced classmates were stupid, and that she never wanted *rajira* in the first place.

Things almost seemed normal the second day after the heist. But that normalcy also preyed on her mind, as none of her family had yet to return from their own missions. It wasn't until magic class that she finally spotted Atopol in his disguise stride into the chamber that she felt even the smallest relief. He was wearing a scraggly beard on his chin now, a few miserable hairs that resembled a patchy meadow more than anything. Completely fake, she knew, but convincing.

She did not speak to him until after class when he used his alias's relationship as her cousin to pull her aside for a few moments and spoke with her just outside of the building.

"Is everything—everyone—well?" she asked hesitantly as Nocturn Dain led her to a quiet corner of the grounds.

"As well as can be expected, under the circumstances," he answered, quietly. "Shadow is unhappy with the experience," he added, referencing their father's code name. "He's not the only one. You nearly compromised the entire mission," he said accusingly.

"I did manage to copy the records," she said, uncomfortably. "Did they recover the book?"

"They did," he sighed. "It was fascinating watching them use a location spell to find it, too. They were convinced that the thief dropped it as he galloped over the bridge. I was there," he added. "Shadow continued to Falas after that, but he gave a convincing-enough performance to suggest that was where the thief was headed. I got thoroughly questioned about the intruder, by the way."

"They didn't use truthtell spells, did they?" she asked, as she inhaled sharply.

"No, I was fairly convincing myself: I said I saw a figure clad in black taking the satchel and retreating through the window, and that's what I saw. The bruise on my chin was pretty convincing too. Thanks for that."

"Sorry!" Gatina said, biting her lip. "Is that why you're wearing that . . . that fungus on your chin?"

"It was decided that it would distract anyone from looking too closely at my face," he grinned. "And I wasn't being sarcastic. The bruise convinced Captain Stefan that I was, in fact, just a dumb servant who interrupted a robbery and got clobbered for his trouble. He was quite sympathetic, actually."

"And they didn't suspect anything?" she prodded.

"Oh, they suspected plenty . . . but all the wrong things, thank the stars," he sighed. "Misdirection is a wonderful thing. Captain Stefan lit into Censor Lantripol about security. He reasoned that Lantripol must have let something slip that allowed the thief to know where and when he would be at Lindule Hall. No one else knew about it, apparently. Stefan has a low opinion of Lantripol, anyway."

"Well, we agree on something, then," Gatina snorted. "I find I loathe that man."

"Apparently, he's not much of a mage. More of a bureaucrat than a wizard. It was suggested that he joined the Censorate because he wasn't good enough to survive in private practice," he chuckled. "That was entertaining, watching that smug little slug get berated by his Captain. But in the end, they concluded that they had narrowly avoided having their precious information stolen by the enemy. They'll increase security now, but we have the hook for the location spell on the book, so that shouldn't be too much of a problem.

"But that brings me to my next mission," he continued as they slowly walked toward Gatina's residence. "I'm to fetch the copy you made and have it sent to Shadow for review. There is a messenger waiting to deliver it. Where is it?"

"Where we practice swordplay, behind the largest old cog on the western end," she revealed. "As are my working clothes. They need to be laundered," she added.

"I have no doubt," nodded Atopol. "Did you get all of it?"

"Every word," she promised. "I wrote it in the Ivy, so you'll have to translate, but it's all there. Some of it was . . . concerning," she added.

"Every word was concerning, I'm guessing. I'll fetch it directly and have it sent to Shadow as quickly as possible. Don't worry; it will be in the proper hands soon enough. And now we can track Captain Stefan by tracking the book, using his own spell. Things went poorly, but I suppose they could have gone worse," he reflected philosophically.

"Is that . . . is that what Shadow thinks?" she asked, hesitantly.

"Oh, no, he thinks you endangered dozens and kicked over the chamber pot," Atopol said, shaking his head.

"But things turned out all right!" Gatina defended. She was more worried about her father's opinion than her brother's. She wanted him to be proud of her.

"But things didn't go according to plan, and that upset other plans and caused a lot of bother for a lot of people you've never even met," he countered. "The kitten got into the milk again, and now the cheese is spoiled. Don't worry; just give it a few days to blow over," he suggested. "But your orders are to stay here—and that means to *stay here*—and avoid suspicion. Now that the Censors are gone, you shouldn't have any trouble with that."

"I will," she promised. "But at least we got the lists."

"Yes, we got the lists," her brother admitted. "Once they're in the right hands, we can take steps to protect our people. And figure out who is informing on us."

"Someone is informing on us?" she asked, surprised.

"Of course," he shrugged. "That was expected. Shadow is no fool. We've known that we have a traitor or two in our midst for a while now, from what I understand. Some of our operations have been compromised in ways that could only be the result of the Count receiving information from within the Council. It's just a matter of identifying who they are and . . . taking action," he said softly.

Gatina nodded. While she didn't know a lot about the inner workings of the Shadow Council opposing Count Vichetral, she did know what penalties the Council imposed for treachery. They were lethal. They had to be.

"So, when is Shadow returning?" she asked eagerly.

"When his business in Falas is done. No extra classes tonight, either. Steel and Mist are still in hiding for the moment. They'll probably return soon, though, now that the checkered cloaks are gone. I don't expect that they will be particularly happy with you, either," he warned. "Steel, especially. He's not the sort to appreciate an undisciplined approach to such matters."

"I took initiative," Gatina argued. "He tells me to do that constantly!"

"In a fight, yes," Atopol reasoned. "This isn't mere swordplay, Kitten. A lot of lives are at stake. And the future of our efforts. One wayward kitten can mess all of that up. Keep that in mind."

Gatina stared at her brother for a moment, then looked away. "Are you mad at me too?" she asked.

Atopol chuckled. "For hitting me so damned hard? A little. You've got quite a punch for a kitten. For ignoring your orders and doing something rash and stupid? Part of me is disappointed. Part of me is impressed. I'm not really mad," her brother decided. "But I am concerned."

Gatina sighed. "I was just trying to help," she said glumly.

Atopol gave her a look, his expression quizzical and amused. "I wonder how often that's been used as an excuse after some disaster. I understand," he stressed. "It's tempting to see what we've seen and feel like you have to do something. I've messed some things up myself, because of that," he added, guiltily. "But if I've learned anything in the last year it's that there is far more in motion than I'm aware of. I might think I can change things if I just . . . if I took some initiative," he said, with a grin. "But we're not given all the information for a reason. It's dangerous to know too much. But it's also dangerous to act without knowing enough. So, our best course is usually to do what we're told to do until we're old enough to understand more."

"That's not a very satisfying conclusion," Gatina said, biting her lip.

"Get used to it," he shrugged. "If Shadow doesn't know everything and is cautious in how he acts, what makes you think you know better?"

"I . . . I suppose you're right," she said, heaving a heavy sigh. She realized just how serious her indiscretion had been, and that realization sent a surge of emotions through her body. Fortunately, those emotions could be used in her guise as Avorrita, who was accustomed to awkwardness. Gatina, however, was resolved to maintain stronger composure when faced with future such opportunities.

"Of course I'm right." He nodded, pleased. "Now go back to being dull little Avorrita for a while until this blows over. Go back to the archives and keep researching who our adversaries might be. Hopefully, the Censors will all be chasing their tails down in Falas and leave us alone."

———————

GATINA TRUDGED UP THE CLIFF TO THE MAIN TEMPLE AFTER CLASS, PREPARED to spend the evening in the bowels of the great tower seeking out yet more genealogies from dusty archives by candlelight. She had gotten to know a few of the Nightbrothers and Nightsisters by sight now as they tended to their own research and devotions. She bowed shyly to the familiar faces as she made her way up the broad stone steps to the door of the temple.

But the prospect of scribbling the names and positions of long-dead Coastlords just did not have much appeal after what she had been through. Indeed, she considered just finding a quiet corner of the archives and taking a quick kitten nap.

When she entered the great round chamber at the base of the tower, however, instead of seeking the narrow door that led down to the library and archives, she was drawn toward the staircase that led up to the gallery on the second floor. That put her at eye level with the great orrery that was suspended by wires over the main chamber.

She'd been startled and impressed with the magnificent device when she'd first seen it. The orrery was a kind of map, a moveable sculpture that depicted the sun and all of the planets as they actually were, not as they appeared to men standing on Callidore's soil. The gilded sphere in the center of the sculpture did not move, of course, but the rest of the spheres that orbited the sun were on thin brass tracks that allowed them to move with precision.

It was fascinating to watch sometimes, especially after a few hours of researching and copying, when her mind was tired and bursting with names and titles. The spheres that represented the planets were so simple, compared to the other things in her life.

At the center, there was the unmovable sun, constantly shedding its light across the Sacred Cosmos. Six orbs flew eternally around it. The tiny red world of Randor was closest to the star, portrayed in the orrery by a brilliant vermillion globe that made its way around the sun every one hundred and twenty-two days, she recalled from memory.

Then there were Callidore itself and its two moons. Three hundred and forty-four days it took to make a complete circuit around the star, one Callidoran year. The moons were also on tracks marking their own orbits around the world: The larger white satellite, Caluna, took just under twenty-eight days to complete its course, while the smaller green moon, Berdea, took almost seven—the basis for the Callidoran week. The two moons had a dramatic effect on the tides, she knew. When they were both on the same side of the world, the seas surged powerfully, while when they were on the opposite sides, they were tame. That was the entire useful purpose of the abbey, she suspected: predicting when the tides came and how high they were to be.

Third was Simorda, an arid world of sand and heat, its own two satellites flinging themselves around their primary far faster than Callidore's moons. Then there was the Inner Belt, a floating mountain range of tiny worldlets that ranged around the sun in a pack. Only a few of them were large enough to be seen with the naked eye from Callidore, but dozens could be seen if you used magesight or a telescope.

Great Ishune dominated the orrery. It was more than a hundred times larger than Callidore and depicted by a shiny ochre globe larger than her head. Around it flew three great moons. It wasn't like Callidore or Simorda, she had been taught; it was a giant ball of gasses surrounding a rocky surface that was unimaginably dense. Ishune was an easy planet to spot in the sky. It appeared as a large orange star in the Blessed Darkness, and even its moons could be glimpsed with aid.

Beyond that was the Outer Belt, another band of worldlets and rocks that could only barely be glimpsed in the sky even with magic. But the orrery portrayed its two largest nodes—the Greater Band and the Lesser Band—eternally leading and chasing the orbit of Ishune, respectively. It was five times larger than the Inner Belt, according to the Nightbrothers, and was likely the remnant of a long-destroyed world far larger than Callidore.

The very idea that a world larger than her home could be dashed apart like that sent shivers up Gatina's spine. The world was supposed to last forever, in her mind. Even though the calamity that had shattered that long-forgotten planet had happened in eons past, it gave her a sense of finality about the universe that challenged her optimism. Perhaps the events of the previous days were weighing on her, she decided. The fear of Captain Stefan and his Censors turning up at Palomar Abbey to hunt for a thief danced in the back of her mind despite what Atopol had said about Falas. Instead of thinking about Lindule Hall, she turned her focus back to the orrery for distraction.

Beyond the Outer Belt was another great planet of gasses, half the size of Ishune but with thrice its moons: pale green Minmasir. And beyond that, so far away it could not even be seen with magic's aid, was lonely Ardagon and its three moons. It was absent from the night's sky. It was so far away it could not be seen, but it could not be ignored. Even at that unimaginable distance, it affected the other worlds of Callidore's star. The

Nightbrothers dutifully tracked its location as meticulously as they did the others.

"Beautiful, isn't it?" a deep male voice asked from behind her. Gatina was so involved in studying the sculpture that she had not noticed someone approaching. She whirled, startled, only to see the imposing figure of Abbot Handrig standing behind her, his deep black robes and mantle making him seem indistinct in the gloom of the chamber. "When I was a novice, one of my tasks was to keep the orrery accurate every night. I still come here often to look upon the wonder of the Sacred Cosmos," he said as he joined her at the railing. "It reminds me that there are far, far greater things in the universe than one man and his problems. It gives me perspective," he reflected.

"It just makes me feel small," Avorrita admitted with a squeak. "Small and insignificant."

"Oh, you are, Nocturn," the abbot chuckled. "But don't let it concern you: in the billions of eyes of the Sacred Cosmos, we are all small and insignificant. Even this world," he said, gesturing around him. "Eons passed before Callidore was wrought by the Cosmos. In eons ahead, it will be swept away and forgotten, mere dust and starstuff. Only the light of our star will be eternal, though it, too, will fade with time and distance."

The abbot's assurance about her world's destruction sent an involuntary shiver down Gatina's spine. He seemed so calm and matter-of-fact about it.

"So . . . it doesn't really matter what we do," she proposed as she turned back to the orrery.

"What? No, no!" the abbot said, shaking his head. "That is not the wise conclusion to draw from the Mysteries, Nocturn. Quite the contrary. Do we matter to the Sacred Cosmos? Perhaps . . . perhaps not," he suggested with a shrug. "We might be small, insignificant, and temporary to the holy forces that keep the stars and worlds in their courses, but such things are always relative. We may only exist for an instant, but within that instant, our lives manifest glory and greatness," he explained.

"What do you mean?" Gatina asked, genuinely confused.

"The Sacred Cosmos may take little heed of us and our actions, but *we* do," he said, still staring at the orrery. "And that gives us strength. For the Cosmos may not be able to regard us with any seriousness, but the fact that we, as short-lived and ignorant as we are, can discern the Sacred Cosmos indicates that we have the potential for glory. We may glimpse and even understand part of the unfathomable Cosmos. We can conceive of powers and forces and places that are billions of miles away, or billions of years in the past. That is a power greater than the gods and the magi can appreciate."

"But . . . but what use is it, if it makes us feel this way?" Gatina asked, frowning. "Yes, it's pretty. It's even interesting," she decided. "But besides predicting the tides and keeping the ships on course, what use is understanding the Mysteries of Sagan if they just make us feel so unimportant?"

"It is the fact that we *can* understand the Mysteries of Sagan that demonstrates that we are important," countered the abbot. "Without them, our ancestors never would have crossed the Void and come to this beautiful world."

Gatina looked over at the ever-present purple cloud painted on one side of the chamber that represented the Void. This time of year, along the Great Bay, it was said, you could glimpse the pointed tip of it on the southern horizon. "I don't see why we did that in the first place," she said, honestly.

"We had our reasons, I imagine," the abbot said, kindly. "I wonder myself sometimes. But it wasn't that nebula that we crossed to come here," he corrected. "It was the vastness of the Sacred Cosmos itself. We built a mighty ship of steel and secured all living things from our old home inside before we launched ourselves into the unforgiving Void. They could easily have perished in doing that," he told her. "Yet it was our understanding of the Mysteries and our ambition toward glory that compelled us to take that risk, I believe. And in doing so, we reflected a little of the glory of the Cosmos. We are the only race to come to this world without magic," he reminded her. "That is no small feat."

"But . . . but why, if everything is just going to get ground to dust someday?" she asked.

The abbot smiled indulgently. "You are not the first Nocturn to consider that . . . Avora?" he asked suddenly.

"Avorrita," Gatina corrected. "Nocturn Avorrita of Dentran."

That name made the abbot's eyes widen with recognition. "I remember now," he nodded. "You were introduced to me on your first day. You and your . . . cousin."

"Yes, that was me," Gatina nodded. "One of the 'special' students."

"And I recall you've had your *rajira* emerge recently, too, as expected. That should prove helpful to these contemplations, as well as maddening.

Well, Nocturn Avorrita, as a special student, you are asking a special question," he considered. "Why make the effort to learn the Mysteries? Why learn anything at all, if we are just going to die, and our children's children's children are just going to die, and all we know and love will fade with the passage of time?" he asked, amused. "Beyond glory and greatness, I think we do it because we have no choice," he answered.

"No . . . choice?" she asked. "We are compelled by fate, then?"

"The Sacred Cosmos has determined that we are to do so, just as it has for the Sea Folk, the Tree Folk, and all the life on Callidore. As small and insignificant as we are, it has seen fit to grant us the minds and the eyes necessary to figure for ourselves what lies in the firmament beyond our sight. Dogs do not enjoy this gift, nor do cows, cats, or cantaloupes—at least, as far as we know. Only to man and our fellows did it grant that potential. And only man used it to escape from one world to thrive on another."

"So, we should strive for knowledge just because we have the potential to have it?" she asked dubiously. "That sounds like an excuse. Something we made up just to make ourselves feel better. I don't mean to doubt the wisdom of the Mysteries, but . . ."

Her tone made the abbot laugh. "Yes, you are your father's daughter," he chuckled. "Don't apologize for doubting; even Sagan himself demanded proof of each and every factor in his sacred calculations. It is the mark of a good scholar and something shared by all great minds. And I cannot in good conscience say that you are wrong—no man is so wise or powerful to understand the inner clockwork of the Sacred Cosmos and its designs, no matter what he might claim. It's a matter beyond the understanding of the gods themselves, if we are to trust our histories.

"But while it might be an excuse," he conceded, "it is a far better answer than the alternative. Even when they learn that all you see and hear and know in this world originated as gas in the belly of a long-dead star, they fail to grasp the glory of it all. Some contemplate the same question you pose and lapse into base despair over their conclusions: that life doesn't matter. That our efforts don't matter. That nothing we could possibly do will change the courses of the stars and planets, nor our eventual doom as individuals or as a species."

"But some don't," she countered. "Why?"

"Because they gain perspective," the abbot answered thoughtfully. "Of all of the great forces that shape the Sacred Cosmos—gravity, energy, mass, distance—none is more potent than *time*."

"Time?" Gatina asked, confused.

"Time can be stacked in layers to make eons . . . or it can be bisected infinitely. What is a 'long time' from one perspective is but an instant from another. How we view a particular event revolves around where we are and what we are regarding. It's a matter of relativity. Considering only the entropy of the universe ignores its complexities and denies its cyclical nature. Time gives us perspective: over the courses of stars, the limits of the Sacred Cosmos, or the importance of our own lives. We are born, grow, mate, breed, age, and die, all in the proper time. Whether or not the Cosmos takes notice of it, the fact is that we take notice of it."

"I . . . I don't really understand," Gatina confessed.

"You probably won't, for years yet . . . and then, when you think you do, you'll have gotten it all wrong. The Cosmos is a gift to us, an eternal puzzle provided for us to figure out. It doesn't matter if we do so—it's admittedly impossible for us to, actually. But it is how we approach solving that unsolvable puzzle that defines us," he explained. "When a Nocturn gains perspective, the ability to use perspective, then they also gain an appreciation of the precious gift of time."

"It doesn't seem like much of a gift," Gatina said, wrinkling up her nose in confusion.

"It is amongst our most precious," the abbot said, shaking his head. "We are all allotted only a certain, finite amount of it. And while the Cosmos may not give two damns and a goat fart for us as individuals, it does make a record of how we spend that time. Make every bit of it count, Nocturn Avorrita," he counseled. "In study, in contemplation, in devotion, and in merely living. The gift of life was made unto you by the Sacred Cosmos. Do not waste it with idle things and trivial matters. Your attention to the universe and how you act within it *do* matter; you just do not have the perspective as yet to understand *how*. In truth, you may never understand that . . . but it is how you try that is important. It may just be an elaborate excuse," he sighed, patting his tummy, "but it is the best answer we have.

"Now, I've seen the look of exhaustion on a thousand Nocturns' faces, and you wear it as plainly as any. You are relieved of your duties for the evening and will return to your quarters and *sleep*. Abbot's orders," he added with a grin. "You've done your devotions with these contemplations, and I think your tired mind must rest before it can truly appreciate the wisdom you might gain from this discussion. Sleep!" he ordered.

"Sleep while you can. And live while you can. And when all is over and done with, leave a brilliant streak across the sky of the Cosmos to be seen by its billions of eyes. That, Nocturn Avorrita, is the answer you seek for your questions. Indeed, it is all the answer you are ever likely to get."

CHAPTER NINETEEN
CONSEQUENCES

*There are consequences for what we do, I'm learning. Both good
ones and bad ones. Magic and swordplay both instruct us on this
point, but those are straightforward applications of the idea that one
action can have many consequences. In life, I'm learning, the repercussions of our actions, regardless of how well intended, are rarely
predictable. Or if they are, I have little talent in that prediction.*
— from Gatina's Heist Journal

"IN MOST BASIC CHORDIC SPELLS, THE PRIME RUNE ACTS ON THE SECONDARY
rune using the active component of the tertiary rune," Sister Tavane
lectured. "For example, the energetic rune *Tardeth* acts on the passive
component of the Marlareth rune, which is frequently used to represent
oxygenation. Tardeth is not fire, it's *energy*, but with energy and oxygen,
all you need is a spark. In this case, it is the tertiary rune Siseth, whose
active component is *ignition*. When you energize them sufficiently in
turn, they act together to produce a flame—however brief. Indeed, without additional support from other runes or a ready source of fuel, such an
arcane effect will last but a few seconds," she concluded, scanning their
faces to see if they'd been paying attention.

"That would have come in handy," Avorrita murmured to herself.

"How much power does it take to make a flame?" Mathilde asked Sister
Tavane, curious.

"It varies from mage to mage," answered the nun thoughtfully, "and it
can depend on other circumstances. Some, with an affinity for the greater
element of fire, could manage it with much less power than others. For
some magi, they can raise the power in a few moments; others might take
half an hour or more to gather that much thaumaturgical energy. Usually, the more time it takes to build that kind of power for a mage, the

more draining the experience is, especially when you are first learning the process. I can do it in a few moments, of course," she said, and then demonstrated.

A quick, brief flare appeared before her, unsupported by candle or taper. It illuminated her face and crackled for but an instant before it faded into nothingness. A few eyes grew big at the sight. For some of the students, Gatina guessed, it was the first time they had seen tangible, flammable results of magic.

"The flame cantrip is simple and is often used by practicing adepts to judge the abilities of a potential apprentice," Sister Tavane continued. "It's useful, too. As such, it is one of the chordic cantrips that you should know before you leave Palomar. If nothing else, you can get employment as magical lamplighters," she said, producing a chorus of giggles.

"Now everyone select a partner and practice. Take turns and monitor each other using the thaumaturgic mode of magesight. You'll quickly discover just how much power you need to raise and maintain to ignite the cantrip," she instructed.

Avorrita quickly found Mathilde to practice with. The two had become closer friends since gaining their *rajira*, and Avorrita found the girl to be friendly, witty, and good-hearted. Gatina found her a little bland and boring, but in comparison to Leonna—who was struggling to find a partner to practice with—she was decidedly a superior companion.

She was also a very good mage, as she proved when she managed to create a flame six inches in front of her nose in mere seconds. She grinned broadly at the accomplishment, and Avorrita giggled in delight. When it was her turn, she found it a little difficult to hold the three runes in her mind all at once, but she was able to quickly raise the arcane power required to ignite the spell. A flare of flame appeared like a butterfly in front of her.

"That . . . is fun!" Avorrita laughed. "Your turn!" Gatina also found it to be enjoyable, she realized, surprised.

"Let's see if I can make it larger this time," Mathilde said as she settled into a determined stare.

Before Mathilde could manifest the arcane flame, however, a much larger fire had emerged over Avorrita's shoulder. It was nearly the breadth of her hand, and it took her very much by surprise.

"Leonna!" Sister Tavane reproved. "Do be careful!"

"Did . . . did I do that?" the Coastlord girl asked, her eyes wide with shock and wonder.

"Yes! And you nearly caught poor Avorrita's hair on fire!" chided the nun. "Use your sense of focus to locate the proper spot to manifest the spell, else you'll have flames bursting out just anywhere!"

"Hmmpf," Leonna snorted. "It would serve her right for trying to cut my hair."

"Avorrita did not try to cut your hair!" objected Mathilde, irritated. "And you could have burned her face off with that! Do try to control your spells," Mathilde said, annoyed. "No one wants to employ a sloppy wizard."

"I do not want employment as a wizard!" Leonna insisted. "I can think of nothing more tedious and unrewarding than that."

"She can always be a magical lamplighter, then," snickered Avorrita to her friend. Gatina was gratified to know that her alias could manage to be a little catty sometimes.

"Control of your spells is essential," lectured Sister Tavane as she moved next to Leonna. "If you cannot manage it at this stage, it will be difficult to progress to more complicated cantrips. You must focus your attention and choose the point of manifestation with genuine intent," she emphasized. "Losing control of your spell could be disastrous . . . and invite an unexpected and uncomfortable visit from the Censorate," she warned.

As if summoned, the door chose that moment to open, revealing the checkered cloak and stern expression of Censor Lantripol. Once again, a chorus of gasps filled the room.

"Not all visits from the Censorate are ill fated," the Censor responded congenially . . . but his expression was anything but friendly. Indeed, Gatina thought he looked haggard, compared to the last time she'd met with him. He looked like he hadn't slept much. Or as if he had spent a few days being berated by his superior.

But it was not his condition that concerned her—it was his very presence. The Censors had supposedly concluded their investigations at Palomar, she'd been informed. Indeed, the atmosphere at the abbey had been decidedly relaxed, compared to the cloud of anxiety that seemed to hang over Ejecta when the Censors had been conducting their reviews. As he strode into the room, she noticed something else that heightened the tension: he wore a mageblade on his hip. When he had first arrived for his inspection, Censor Lantripol had been unarmed, though his men had borne blades. The addition of a sword was foreboding.

Sister Tavane also took note of the sword, glancing at it briefly before affixing the Censor with a glare that could have melted steel.

"You again?" she asked, her voice trembling with disgust and outrage. "I thought you people were finished with your . . . inspection. How do you expect these children to learn any kind of magic with all of these interruptions?"

"It's an elementary class," dismissed Lantripol as he moved to the front of the chamber. "They will recover. I've returned to clear up a few details . . . answer a few questions, clarify some possible misunderstandings, is all," he said, turning to face the class. "It's a normal part of the process. Just to ensure that our records are accurate," he said, enunciating the word. "I need to meet with a few of the Nocturns, if you don't mind."

"And if I do?" Sister Tavane challenged.

"Then I will meet with them anyway," shrugged the Censor.

Sister Tavane uttered a frustrated sigh that expressed her contempt for the man. "As you wish," she finally said, throwing up her hands. "We were nearly done for the evening, anyway. Although I can't imagine what you could possibly need to learn that you haven't already heard."

"As I said, just some bureaucratic details," he murmured as he scanned the faces of the anxious Nocturns. "Let's begin with . . . *her*," he said, pointing directly at Avorrita.

There was a collective gasp in the room as his gauntleted finger stabbed the air. Avorrita shrank in her chair.

"*Me?*" she squeaked. "What did I do?"

"I think that's best discussed in private," Lantripol said menacingly. "The rest of you are dismissed. If I need you, I will summon you. Please make yourselves available."

"You may question her," Sister Tavane said evenly, "but not here. There is a class for Initiates about to use this chamber for advanced lessons. Please take your interrogation elsewhere," she said, waving dismissively.

"Very well," Lantripol agreed unexpectedly. "You, girl, come with me," he ordered.

The rest of the Nocturns stared anxiously at Avorrita as she reluctantly rose from her seat. She felt Mathilde's hand on her arm, and she glanced at the girl with a worried expression. There was nothing she could do, of course; the Censorate had every right to question any mage—or anyone else—under the law.

"I knew there was something about her!" Leonna muttered accusingly, a triumphant smile on her face.

"Oh, shut up, Leonna!" Mathilde snapped at the Coastlord girl. "Can't you see she's frightened enough?" Avorrita gave her friend a grateful smile and realized that she did, indeed, have a friend in Mathilde.

But while she turned to glare at Leonna, she caught sight of her brother standing behind her shoulder. He quickly mouthed something to her: *the mill.*

Of course, Gatina could not acknowledge his message, even in a small way. But she did not need to. She understood at once what he was suggesting.

"Not everyone who gets called to the Censorate's attention is a criminal, Leonna!" Avorrita defended. "He said so himself!"

"No one is accusing anyone of violating the Bans," agreed Lantripol, who seemed surprised at her response. "I'm just asking a few questions. You're Nocturn Leonna?" he asked sharply. That caught the girl by surprise, and after her mouth gaped, she slammed it shut and gave a terse nod. "I might be questioning you next," he suggested. "Don't wander too far from your residence, please. The rest of you, have a pleasant evening in the Blessed Darkness, squinting at stars," he added mockingly.

As the room quickly emptied, Lantripol placed a controlling hand on Avorrita's shoulder. "There's nothing to be frightened of, Nocturn. Not yet, at least. Come with me; we can speak in the courtyard."

Gatina's mind worked furiously as they slowly walked out of the hall. This had to be about the heist, she knew, it *had* to be. She must have done something or left something undone that had convinced the Censorate that she was involved. But how? She could not think of a single mistake that she'd made in her flight. She had been so careful, after all. Head hung low and eyes downcast, Avorrita allowed herself to be led outside by the imposing Censor. She considered all of the routes to the mill from the courtyard.

"Let me know if you're planning on hanging her," Leonna said as they were leaving, one final snipe being too tempting for her. "I may want to attend."

"You shouldn't jest about such matters, Leonna!" Mathilde nearly shouted.

"No, you shouldn't," Lantripol agreed grimly. "Now leave us alone. This should not take long, but I've ridden a very long way today to be here, and my patience is thin. Don't you have some sort of devotions to attend to? Then attend to them and leave me to mine," he said to them both sternly. With one final sympathetic glance at Avorrita, Mathilde grabbed Leonna's hand and dragged her off toward the residence hall. Nocturn Dain—her brother—was nowhere to be seen. He had dispersed with the rest of the students.

That actually made Gatina feel better. Atopol knew how bad this was, and he also knew what to do. Of course, Gatina didn't have any idea what to do. Her only plan was to immerse herself in her role as Avorrita and let the dull girl answer for her. She had to bide her time and wait for the proper moment, just as in swordplay.

"What is this all about?" she asked, feigning confusion. "What did I do?"

"We shall get to that shortly," Lantripol said in a businesslike manner as he faced her in the empty courtyard. His expression was somber. "You see, there was a crime committed a few nights ago," he revealed. "The details do not matter. But the only way the crime could have been committed is if someone knew when and where I was to meet Censor Captain Stefan. That meeting was secret, for reasons of security. No one outside of the Order could have possibly known. Now, I questioned my men most carefully, and they have assured me that the details of our meeting remained secure. I trust their word."

"Where are they?" she asked, cocking her head before looking around for them.

"They are otherwise deployed," Lantripol dismissed. "I do not need assistance to ask one girl a few questions. The point is the message that was sent to me by the captain was sealed. Only they had read it, and they told no one else. The captain certainly did not share the details casually.

"So, I had to think back to who else could have possibly overheard us," Lantripol continued, softly. "And the more I thought about it, the only answer that came to mind was . . . *you.*"

"Me?" Avorrita asked, surprised.

"You. The girl I was interviewing when my man carelessly revealed sensitive information about the meeting. You were the only other person in the room, after all."

"I didn't . . . I don't know what you're talking about!" Avorrita said, shaking her head in frustration. "I didn't hear *anything!*"

"You did!" accused Lantripol. "You overheard that I was to meet Captain Stefan at Lindule Hall!"

"Who? Where?" Avorrita sputtered in confusion. "I don't remember that at all! I just remember you asking me a bunch of stupid questions and then trying to recruit me for the Censorate!"

"You were the only one outside of the Censorate who overheard," Lantripol insisted, repeating the accusation. "It *had* to be you who gave away the location and the time of our meeting. It *has* to be you!"

"I have no idea what you're talking about!" Avorrita claimed, getting upset. "I don't think *you* know what you're talking about, either! If something happened, it sounds like you got in trouble and are looking for someone to blame!"

"That's *not* what I'm doing!" Lantripol said, a hint of desperation in his voice. Gatina figured that the man was, indeed, afraid of being seen as doing just that. "I was ordered to track down any way that the message could have gotten intercepted, and that's what I'm doing. Someone found out the details and gave that information to . . . some very bad people. Criminals," he pronounced. "Perhaps assassins. We don't know. But we will find out. The Censorate is very thorough," he said menacingly.

"And you think *I* did it? I barely talk at all! I don't know any criminals!" Avorrita proclaimed, allowing her anxiety to paint her voice. "I barely have any friends at all, and you're saying I told something I don't remember to people I don't know?" she asked, incredulously.

"It *had* to be you!" Lantripol said, anger coming into his eyes. "You're the only one! No one else overheard the news!"

"I don't know what you think you know about me, but you're completely mad if you think I told anything to anyone," Avorrita said with a shaking voice, as Gatina forced a tear from her eyes. It wasn't hard. She was genuinely frightened. "All I've done is go to chapel, go to class, and do my chores. It's not fair to blame . . . whatever it is you're in trouble for on me!"

"Nocturn Avorrita," Lantripol pronounced patiently, "did you speak of our conversation to anyone? Anyone at all? Your teachers? Your fellow Nocturns? Anyone?"

"I don't know! Maybe I said something to someone, but we were all talking about your . . . your interrogations! I didn't say anything about Censor Captain Stuffy meeting with you at Lardypool Hall, or whatever it is you think I heard!" she said adamantly.

Lantripol studied her carefully. "I almost believe you," he said, softly. "And I might, if it wasn't for one thing. In my investigations, I chanced to question a peasant about the night the crime happened, near the scene. And he told me that he encountered a Nocturn that evening, near dawn, riding a sable horse. He said she blessed his newborn cow," he added.

"That?" Avorrita asked in disbelief. "I did bless a cow! It was my very first blessing! Is that against the Bans on Magic?" she asked skeptically.

"What were you doing at that hour, in that place?" Lantripol demanded.

"I was observing and recording the rising of Randor, the Morning Star!" snorted Avorrita. "It's a common Saganite devotion. We *do* study the stars here, you know," she chided. "As it only rises before dawn, that was the best time to view it!"

"Why there?" Lantripol asked, sharply. "Why not here, at the abbey?"

"Because you can't get a good view of it this close to the escarpment," she said with a snort of disgust. "You have to go south from here, or north, to see it emerge on the horizon. I suppose they don't teach you that sort of thing at Censorate school," she added derisively.

"Mayhap," Lantripol conceded. "But it is just too much of a coincidence that the very girl who overheard my message was also in the vicinity of Lindule Hall the very night the crime occurred," he suggested, fixing her with a steely stare. "Far too much of a coincidence. Which makes me think that you, Nocturn Avorrita, had something to do with it. I don't know what, precisely, your role is, but I will find out. There will be consequences," he said sternly.

"You're mad," she said, shaking her head. "Do you think I told the *cow* about your meeting? The peasant? I was barely awake!"

"We shall see," Lantripol said, straightening his shoulders. "But I think you do have something to do with it. It *has* to be you. So, we shall get to the truth of the matter. No matter how long it takes."

"I have devotions and classes and—"

"You will make time for this," Lantripol said darkly. "Your superiors will be happy to cooperate, else they will have consequences themselves."

"I've told you the truth!" Avorrita insisted, tears pooling up in her eyes. "Blessed Darkness, I've told you nothing but the truth, and you won't believe me!"

"We shall see," repeated the Censor. "The Royal Censorate has means to compel truthfulness," he informed her as he flipped open his cloak, revealing the hilt of his mageblade. "Some are magical . . . some are less . . . delicate," he threatened as he put his hand on the sword.

Avorrita's eyes opened wide in fear . . . and Gatina was secretly elated. That was what she was looking for. An excuse. A good reason for Avorrita to do what Gatina had desired from the beginning of the interrogation. Threatening her—poor little dull Nocturn Avorrita—with violence was sufficient for her purposes.

Avorrita squealed at the implication of his threat. Then she gave over control of her legs to Gatina.

And Gatina ran.

"Girl! *Nocturn!*" shouted the Censor at her back. "Get back here *now!*" he bellowed.

But Gatina was not about to return to face the man who had come so dangerously close to discovering her secrets. She fled as fast as her feet could carry her, diving around the corner of the hall and continuing toward the east. Toward the mill. She knew the path and all of the buildings between her and her destination. She had walked it often enough.

It was growing dark, and she did not have the presence of mind or the time to conjure magesight. But Gatina was at home in the Blessed Darkness. Her feet found the path she needed to get away from the Censor. She could hear his heavy boots thudding behind her as he shouted for her to halt. She took another turn in an effort to lose his pursuit or at least look like it. She was near the back of Planetary Hall, she saw, where a large outdoor kitchen was used to provide food for large events. There were few people there now, of course—supper was long over, and the few drudges who lingered were dutifully scrubbing pots or hauling garbage to the pigsties. Gatina threaded her way past the trestle tables, pausing only to turn and see how far behind her Lantripol was.

The little man was surprisingly quick, but he was already huffing his breath with the exertion of an unexpected run. He angrily shouted at her when she stopped, but he had a hard time getting the words out.

"Get . . . back here . . . this . . . *instant!*" he commanded through gritted teeth.

Avorrita shook her head tearfully, putting a trestle table full of drying pots and kitchen implements between her and the Censor. Lantripol gave her a baleful look, then snarled and drew his blade. "I *mean* it! None of this foolishness, girl!"

"I won't let you hurt me!" she shouted shrilly. Then she glanced around and saw the implement on the table that would serve her purpose. She grabbed the end of a long iron spit, used for roasting, and held it up defensively.

"I'm not going to hurt you if you tell me the truth!" Lantripol admitted, looking at her makeshift weapon disdainfully.

"You're not going to hurt me at all!" Avorrita insisted, lifting the iron bar threateningly. Of course, she must have looked silly to the drudges watching the spectacle. But that's what Avorrita would have done.

Gatina, on the other hand, was busy judging the distance between her and the Censor, and mentally mapping out her course of retreat in her mind. When Lantripol started to come around the table, she went in the other direction, careful to stay out of his blade's reach. Then he shifted direction and tried to come around the other way. Gatina did likewise.

Then, in frustration, Lantripol kicked the trestle table over with his boot and lunged at her. Gatina was grateful. It was an excellent reason to retreat without giving herself away. Issuing a frightened squeak, she hiked up her habit with one hand and ran, carefully balancing the iron spit in the other as she fled.

"Get back here!" Lantripol demanded with an exasperated groan as he chased her.

Avorrita didn't reply. Gatina was in charge now, and she stopped trying to pretend to be meek and afraid. She was close enough to the mill now, so it would not be unusual for her to flee for her life in that particular direction. The fact that Lantripol was clearly out of breath already was helpful too: it was a steep pathway up to the old mill, and that would take a toll on the man.

He should have brought his men, probably, Gatina thought to herself as she cleared the row of huts where the lesser servants lived and darted through the gates of the village. Three of them might have been a challenge for her.

But Gatina had played elaborate games of hide-and-seek and tag for years as her parents had groomed her for the family business. She and Atopol had spent countless hours attempting to evade each other's grasp, and Lantripol was nowhere near as quick as her brother. Indeed, she had to be careful not to go too quickly, lest Lantripol give up the chase altogether and summon help. The key was to be just far enough away from him to be out of reach, yet close enough to promise the possibility of capture. Gatina excelled at that sort of kittenish game.

Lantripol, on the other hand, was getting exhausted. Despite the sword, he was no real warmage—he was a bureaucrat with a blade. He specialized in interrogation and intimidation, record-keeping and writing correspondence. And he did indeed look like he was considering giving up the chase, she saw as she glanced over her shoulder.

That would not do, she knew. Should he give up pursuit, he would simply return to the abbey and organize a search party or send for more Censors to assist him—Censors who were real warmagi. Gatina wanted to avoid that.

So, she slowed, as she made the first leg of the switchback path, feigning being exhausted herself. The little footbridge that spanned the stream was only a hundred yards ahead of her. But they were out of view of most of the abbey now, so she felt confident that she could bait him the rest of the way.

"Don't come any closer!" she demanded, as she turned to face him, her iron spit in hand. The metal burned in her palm and fingers, but she ignored it.

"You aren't going to keep me away with *that*," Lantripol said, breath heaving, as he gestured contemptuously at the spit.

"We shall see," Gatina replied coolly, as she took a more professional stance. The spit was heavier than her shadowblade by half, but it was sturdy. And pointed. "If you think you can capture me, go ahead and try!"

"I have no intention of killing a foolish little girl," he snarled. "Just come back to the abbey and answer my questions truthfully, and we can put this episode behind us both," he pleaded.

"You'll have to drag me back bleeding at the point of a sword," she said with a toss of her head.

"Very well, then." Lantripol shrugged in return and lunged at Gatina. He was using the flat of the blade, she saw in the gloom. Much to his surprise, her makeshift weapon parried the strike efficiently.

And then she riposted, nearly striking him in the face. He was barely able to parry.

His expression changed as the realization that Avorrita was no mere flower of femininity. He threw another blow at her, aimed at her midsection. She flicked her wrist and sent the point of his mageblade safely out of line. A second blow came to a similar end when he reversed the direction of his attack.

"Someone has practiced swordplay, I see," he said, cocking his head and narrowing his eyes at her.

"Not you, apparently," Gatina said arrogantly as she took a more practiced swordsman's stance. He regarded her in a new light as the spit came up to point at his face. "You strike like a girl. A very young girl," she added.

"And you fight like . . . like someone who has been taught to fight," he answered as he approached her more cautiously.

"Brothers," she shrugged. "A girl needs to know how to protect herself."

"So, you *were* involved in the theft!" he accused triumphantly as he swung again. Instead of parrying, Gatina retreated, her feet shuffling quickly to put a few more yards of distance between them. When he made up the distance, she lunged again, threatening his face once more.

"I'll tell you after a very long and pointless interrogation," she promised.

"You know I have leave to use torture, if I must," he warned her as he made a rapid advance. She parried three blows in quick succession with the spit, and she retreated up the path some more. "Don't make me do that," he pleaded unconvincingly.

"I didn't say I was the one to be interrogated," she said, and gave him another blow to parry before retreating more.

"You're far bolder than you let on," he admitted as he continued his assault. "And quite a good liar, for one so young. But you've as much as admitted that you were involved now," he pointed out. He attacked more confidently now. He was also trying to use the edge of his blade, not the flat.

"And you've demonstrated that you're a crappy swordsman," she taunted. "And even your fellows consider you an inferior mage. I'm guessing that Captain Stefan raked you over the coals. And then sent you back here to clean up the chamber pot you tipped over. Am I right?"

"I will show you what kind of swordsman I am, you brat!" he snarled, the speculation affecting him far more than it should. He angrily attacked in the darkness, likely using his own magesight to direct his blade. Gatina continued to block or dodge his blows. They were predictable and growing weaker, she noted critically. His arm must be getting tired, she reasoned. It was unused to holding a sword in combat for so long.

Then she was gratified to see his eyes get wide in the gloom. She thought that he was ready to concede that she was the superior swordsman, but his stare was not directed at her—he was looking over her shoulder.

"Why don't you show *me* what kind of swordsman you are?" the deep voice of Master Andivor came from behind her. Sparing a glance, Gatina saw the swordmaster emerge from the darkness as if a cloak had lifted. He held a sturdy-looking cavalry blade in hand, and he quickly moved into guard position. In a moment, Silva's form seemed to shimmer into existence beside him. There was a wand in her hand. Neither of them looked pleased.

"So, it *was* you!" Lantripol snarled at Gatina as she fell back to where her cousins were standing. Andivor advanced, his form perfect against the night sky.

"That depends on exactly what you mean," Gatina shrugged, finally letting her guard down as her swordmaster faced the Censor. "Was it me that did what? And which me are you referring to?" she asked.

"You won't get away with this," Lantripol swore, and rushed to attack Andivor. He realized his mistake at once. Even in his monk's habit, Andivor looked like a seasoned warrior. His feet were placed in a precise fighting stance, Gatina saw. With three expertly placed strikes in short order, he had countered the Censor's attack, knocked his blade wildly out of position, and used the guard of his sword to smash across the man's face. Lantripol dropped like a stone.

"Good work, Kitten!" Atopol's voice called from the darkness. "I knew if you could get him up here, we could contend with this!"

"Your form was decent," conceded Andivor as he glanced in her direction. "But you need to keep your wrist supple, not rigid. And your footwork still needs practice," he said as he kicked the mageblade away from the unconscious Censor.

"Hush, Andivor, she did perfectly!" chided his wife.

Gatina looked down at Lantripol's sprawled form and then back up to her swordmaster. "You know, I did warm him up for you," she pointed out.

"Of course you did, Kitten," soothed Atopol as he emerged from the darkness. "Now let's get him into the mill. Lady Silva wants to have a word with the man . . . in private."

CHAPTER TWENTY

INTERROGATION

*Understanding one's duty varies greatly, depending on the source
and the level of your loyalty, I've found. It is a matter of relativity,
as the abbot said. My duty to my House should never be confused
with a duty to the duchy or crown. Great lords die and empires fall.
Family is eternal. My House shall always come first.*
— *from Gatina's Heist Journal*

MASTER ANDIVOR MANAGED TO RELOCATE THE UNCONSCIOUS FORM OF
Censor Lantripol by the simple expedient of slinging him over his shoulder and carrying him into the bottom of the old mill like a sack of turnips.
But instead of the central warehouse area under the mill, Silva opened a
nondescript door that led to a much smaller room—once used to store
spare parts and supplies for the millworks, Gatina guessed, as she looked
around at the remains of cogs and gears on the shelves and old tools
stacked against the wall.

There, Andivor flopped the Censor to the floor unceremoniously and
then carefully searched his person. He found a number of items in the
pouches of the Censor's belt, which he piled up out of reach of the man,
and even removed his boots. Then he bound his hands behind his back and
tied his feet together with a length of rope before straightening and sighing.

"I knew that he was coming after us the moment he walked into the
room," Atopol explained as the swordmaster worked. "You could tell by
the expression on his face."

"It's my fault," Gatina confessed guiltily. "I didn't think that he'd track
Avorrita back here. I didn't think I'd left any clues about that. I guess I was
wrong."

"It was a calculated risk, Kitten," her brother soothed.

"Fortune is always a fickle mistress," agreed Silva. "Don't let it worry you. He just as easily could have forgotten about you. But since he didn't," she said, taking a deep breath, "I think we would be remiss if we did not take advantage of Fortune for a change."

"What do you mean?" Gatina asked curiously.

"Since he has come to us—alone—then we should seize the opportunity to learn what he knows," she said, folding her arms in front of her.

"We will wring him of his information like he was a wet dishrag," agreed Andivor.

"Do you mean . . . *torture?*" Gatina asked, whispering the word. She knew circumstances were dire. The Censorate seemed determined to root out the Shadow Council, even if they didn't know the name.

Yet she could not stomach the idea of torture. As loathsome as Censor Lantripol was, deliberately inflicting pain on him to coerce him to speak seemed . . . *unseemly.* It was decidedly something she did not want to witness.

"Torture?" chuckled Lady Silva. "My dear, I am a *mage.* We needn't resort to such brutal methods unless absolutely necessary. A simple truthtell spell will suffice," she answered. "I do not know a lot of Blue Magic, but that spell is standard amongst the clandestine magi. As are others of greater power, should I need them," she said, staring at the unconscious Censor. "I will learn what we need to know; rest assured of that."

"Doesn't the Censorate have means of evading such spells?" Atopol asked.

"Perhaps the stronger ones," conceded Silva. "But somehow, I don't think this minor functionary has the resources to resist. Especially while he's unconscious," she said, her eyes narrowing. "Pray give me a moment to cast it, and by the time he awakens, it will be in full effect."

The children were quiet while Lady Silva began her spell, and they watched, enrapt, as she drew power from the Magosphere and shaped it to her whim. Gatina felt compelled to use her magesight to witness the casting; she was fascinated by the arcane energies her cousin was summoning to compel the Censor's testimony.

"She's really very good at this," murmured Master Andivor. "I've seen her do it before. She can tell if a man is lying as easily as she could see him breathing. A very disconcerting power in a wife," he added with a smirk.

"I shall keep that in mind," Atopol said solemnly.

"As shall I," Gatina said with a snort. "Thank you for coming to my rescue, by the by. It is greatly appreciated."

"We cannot hazard the enemy learning of our plans, nor our composition," Andivor agreed. "Every effort must be brought to bear to avoid that. And every advantage against Vichetral must be taken," he added. "He must be denied the coronet. The man is evil," he said solemnly. "I've known him for years. He is someone who craves power so badly that he is willing to do anything to achieve it. Such men must be countered by those who wish for peace and prosperity in their lives. Those who want power so badly are inevitably those least desirable to wield it."

There was more to the big man's condemnation than he was letting on, Gatina realized. There was some specific reason Andivor despised Vichetral and his cronies. A reason he did not care to discuss. Of course, that only piqued Gatina's curiosity.

But now was not the time to probe the man's past, she understood. There was business to be done in the millhouse. Gatina knew that her cousins were correct in their assessment, and appreciated their willingness to do what needed to be done. She doubted if she and Atopol together could have made that judgment.

"It is done," whispered Silva finally. "When he awakens, I will be able to know the instant he departs the path of truth."

"What if he doesn't say anything?" Atopol asked.

"I can get him to say . . . *something*," assured Andivor with menace in his voice. "We can learn as much by what he doesn't say as by what comes out of his mouth. Trust Silva," he encouraged. "She is quite good at this sort of thing."

"We come from a Talented family," said Atopol to his sister, shrugging.

"So it seems." She nodded. Then something caught her notice: the space behind the Censor's sprawled form.

The mill was built directly against the side of the cliff, Gatina realized, with the foundations in which they stood constructed to take advantage of the natural wall of the earth. The far wall was, indeed, mere rock . . . except in one specific place. There, behind the unconscious man's slumped body, was an expanse almost a yard long that lacked the irregularity of the rest of the wall. It was smooth, she realized, as smooth as a windowpane. And remarkably similar to a door.

Moreover, she suddenly realized that it was throbbing. Her sensitivity to metals let her know that the expanse was made of the stuff—steel, most likely, according to her senses. She was surprised she hadn't noticed it when she'd first entered the room.

"Is that . . . is that a door?" she asked, wrinkling her brow.

"What? That?" Andivor asked, pointing to the spot on the wall. "Mayhap," he admitted. "It has been here since I was a boy. I've always been curious about it. But if it is a door, it won't open. Not by magic or force."

"That is . . . unusual," Atopol said, chewing his lip as he studied the spot.

"Not at Palomar Abbey," Silva countered, shaking her head. "The abbey has been here for nearly seven hundred years. It abounds in such mysteries. There is writing on it, if you look closely enough," she revealed. "In Old High Perwynese. A riddle, perhaps. But there is no keyhole, no knob, no latch. It's as smooth as a piece of parchment."

"A magical door?" asked Gatina, mystified.

"Not that I can tell," shrugged Silva. "And I am a passing good mage. Indeed, it belies all arcane efforts to get it to open—if it is a door at all. But it is unimportant," she pronounced. "It has stood unyielding for centuries. It will likely remain unopened for centuries more. The Ancients delighted in such mysteries, I have come to know. Alshar is filled with them."

"As is Farise," Andivor added. "I was there during the invasion. A fascinating land. There are mysteries in Farise that not even the Archmagi understood. Our ancestors were inscrutable when it came to their secrets," he said, a note of admiration in his voice.

"I just thought it was . . . interesting," Gatina said, realizing that she was looking for a distraction. Avorrita was uncomfortable with the idea of a rigorous interrogation, no matter how necessary. Gatina knew better. She resolved to steel her heart for the moment. This needed to be done, and she was the one responsible for it needing to be done.

"I think he's coming around," Silva said, amused, as Lantripol's head jerked. "Do not be afraid to be candid. He will not be repeating anything he hears tonight."

Lantripol's nose was bloody and bruised from the heavy brass guard of Andivor's sword smashing into it, but it didn't look like he had lost any teeth from the blow. It took only a few more moments for the Censor to finally waken from his unconscious state. His eyes were unfocused, and he was clearly confused.

"Good evening, Censor Lantripol," Silva began when it was clear he had come around.

"Where . . . where am I?" he asked, as he realized that his hands and feet were bound. "Who are you people?" he demanded.

"We are the ones you were seeking, Censor Lantripol," answered Silva calmly. "We were the ones who stole Captain Stefan's little book."

"Actually, I did it," Gatina confessed. "Impetuous of me, I know."

"I helped," Atopol added a little defensively.

"I *knew* it!" he said, staring at Gatina accusingly. "I *knew* you had to be involved! And you . . . you were the . . . the wine merchant's servant!" Lantripol said as he recognized Atopol's face.

"Indeed." Atopol bowed. "The one you were quite rude to. Now you are at our mercy. You should hope we display better manners than you did."

Lantripol looked around at the faces that peered at him from the shadows of the small room. "You're all a bunch of unregistered magi!" he accused.

"Don't be foolish, Censor," sneered Silva. "We all have our registration documents . . . in one name or another. But that's another matter. We are here tonight to learn what you know," she said, her voice turning menacing.

"Why would I tell you that?" he asked. "You're just going to kill me afterwards. You will learn nothing from me!"

"We have already learned a great deal from you and your brethren," Silva countered. "That little book holds a lot of secrets."

"Ah! But the book wasn't stolen!" he said triumphantly. "Your thief failed! He—she—dropped it while making her escape. You learned nothing!" he scoffed.

"Actually, I only made it look like I dropped it," Gatina continued. "And only after I copied each and every word in it. No need for you to track the book back to our lair by magic. It was the information we needed, not the actual book." She watched the vile man, and she was happy to see some of that smugness he bore fade. She remembered how much he had frightened her and Avorrita as well as Mathilde. Now, she felt, the power had shifted. Avorrita's voice urged caution. *What if he escapes? He'll know who we are!* But Gatina knew that her cousins would not allow that to happen.

"We needed to know what the Censorate had found out about us," Silva agreed. "In that, we succeeded. But the Censorate doesn't know that we know. In that, we have an advantage."

"You should have never allied yourself with that bastard Vichetral," Andivor said, his deep voice filling the chamber. "We will not permit him to steal the coronet."

"Count Vichetral is a true gentleman who understands his duty!" Lantripol snarled. "He was justly concerned about the opposition to him from the clandestine magi in Alshar. He will uphold the Bans on Magic. And we *will* help him!"

"Then you will suffer the same misfortunes as he," Andivor said condemningly, shaking his head.

"Just what are the Censorate's directions from the Council of Counts?" Silva asked. "The true directions, not the cloak of regulatory enforcement you proclaim."

"I will tell you nothing!" Lantripol said, defiantly. "You will have to kill me first!"

"There is no need to kill you. You *will* begin talking," Andivor warned, producing a short, heavy-bladed curved knife, "or I *will* begin cutting off your fingers, knuckle by knuckle starting with your left pinkie, until you find your tongue. Feel free to scream, as we are well isolated, and there is no one nearby to hear you. And it would make me feel gratified by the work," he added, menacingly.

The swordmaster delivered the threat in such a calm and matter-of-fact way that there was no doubting his sincerity. Though her cousins had promised no torture, they had not promised not to *threaten* torture, Gatina realized. As the blade caught the tiny bit of light in the room, it reflected in Lantripol's suddenly fearful eyes.

It was a moment where she saw a man confront the idea of pain and dismemberment by the hand of people who truly had motive to indulge in such brutality. Lantripol might have been a bully with his authority, but he was not brave. His shoulders sagged.

"We . . . were instructed to discover opposition to Count Vichetral's rule and arrest them," he finally spat out, defeated. "If our efforts are successful, we will be put in charge of all magic in Alshar. The Censorate will take over the duties of the Court Wizard. And take possession of the Tower Arcane as our headquarters, as well as the revenues due to the Court Wizard for fees and such."

"We have a court wizard already: Master Thinradel," Silva reminded him.

"That traitor?" scoffed Lantripol. "He is under a warrant of death from the Censorate now. He betrayed his oaths and violated the Bans by accepting irionite from that damned spellmonger in Vorone."

"He may be in exile, but until the Duke replaces him, he is still

Court Wizard," insisted Silva. "Irionite, you say? And Thinradel has a shard?"

"What's irionite?" Atopol asked.

"A very, *very* powerful kind of magical amber," Silva answered softly. "It dramatically increases the amount of thaumaturgic power that a mage can draw into himself. Once, it allowed the Archmagi and the magelords of the Imperial Magocracy to work mighty wonders and hold dominion over all the land. After the Narasi Conquest, it was proscribed by the Censorate. Possession usually carries a death sentence," she said thoughtfully. "That would explain Duke Rard's sudden antipathy for the Censorate . . . and why he will make himself a king next week. His warmagi have irionite. That will make him a formidable power."

"That will make him a criminal in the eyes of the Bans!" insisted Lantripol. "Our charter was given to us by King Kamaklavan himself!"

"And it was taken from you by King Rard, it appears," Andivor chuckled. "Think what you will of him, you have to admire the man's audacity."

"What was your purpose in coming to Palomar Abbey? Your *true* purpose," Silva added with emphasis.

"I was tasked with interviewing anyone whose families might consider rebelling or opposing Count Vichetral," answered the Censor reluctantly. "And to intimidate the parents of the students here. It was suspected that there was a cell of criminals hiding under the hem of the abbot's habit. I can see now that we were correct," he added smugly.

"Yes, how lucky you are. Now," Silva continued, "just when were you planning on arresting those you suspect of conspiring against Vichetral?"

"Not until Luin's Day," Lantripol offered.

"Lie," Silva observed. "Try again, Censor. You are under a truthtell. I will know when you purposefully tell a falsehood."

Lantripol scowled. He looked around sulkily but kept his mouth shut.

"You know, most of your position involves writing," observed Andivor sharply. "A man can still write without a pinkie. Lie again and I will take my first prize." The Censor's face turned pale in the gloom at the suggestion.

"Fine! We move at Midsummer's Eve, the day before Huin's feast day! But there's nothing you can do about that. We have scores of Censors preparing to descend on Falas and the other large cities. One sudden strike and all opposition to Vichetral will be dashed!"

"Huin's Day?" asked Silva, surprised. "The summer solstice? That's in just a few days!" The summer festival in honor of the Sacred Tiller of Soil was celebrated across the land and marked an important point in the agricultural calendar, Gatina knew. While most popular amongst the peasantry, particularly the Narasi peasants, the break from planting and mowing in devotion to the Grain God was celebrated by all classes. At Palomar Abbey, it was especially sacred, as it was an important astronomical event as well. Indeed, that was when the Nocturn Initiates would receive their honors and undergo their final initiation into the lay order.

But in Falas, Gatina guessed, the celebration would be far more raucous . . . and therefore a perfect time to strike an unprepared foe.

"And everyone will be preparing for the festival," agreed Lantripol. "They won't expect any action the night before a holy day. I'm to lead a party against the criminals in Falas," he added proudly.

"The 'theater gang'?" Gatina asked, suddenly curious.

"It appears you really did read that book." He scowled. "Yes, I will be going after the actors and performers. It is widely suspected that they have been involved in all manner of espionage and sabotage in the palace, and Count Vichetral is sick of it. And it is undoubted that they are employing clandestine magi to do their work. We found traces in the palace," he claimed. "Listening spells, detection spells, glyphs of all manners and kinds, all designed against Count Vichetral's government. We cannot—yet—trace just which magi cast them, but we have a good idea . . . and that theater is clearly involved!"

"My cousin was on that list," Gatina said with a frown.

"Four of my cousins were on it," agreed Silva. "I read it while we were waiting. The theater has been highly valuable in learning what is going on inside Vichetral's inner chambers, apparently. Even despots enjoy a good night out and the company of a pretty face."

"They're all going to hang on Midsummer's Day," boasted Lantripol. "Count Vichetral has already approved it. They employed illegal magic against a sitting lord of the realm. That is a violation of the Bans on Magic," he reminded them.

"He's telling the truth, alas," sighed Silva. "Which other groups will you pursue on Huin's Day?"

"The cell in the Oxbow viscounties, the cell in the southern Falas baronies, and two others in Falas Town," reported the Censor, who looked pained to speak. "After interrogation, they, too, will be imprisoned or executed on suspicion of violating the Bans."

"Suspicion?" Andivor asked sharply. "The lawbrothers require proof, not mere suspicion!"

"This is outside of their jurisdiction." Lantripol chuckled wickedly. "Civil authority has no control over the verdict of the Censorate. We need only procure the permission of the sovereign—or acting sovereign—to fulfill our judgements. And if a few nonmagical families get caught up in the arrests . . . well, the fortunes of war." He shrugged. "I'm certain they are guilty of something."

"You would see innocent people imprisoned or slain?" Atopol asked, appalled. Both Avorrita and Gatina agreed with his tone. Enough lives had been lost already at Vichetral's hands, she knew.

"As he says, the fortunes of war." Andivor nodded grimly. "The Censorate acts with the pretense of respectability, but they are as desperate and opportunistic as a band of Calrom right now. Their leaders have left them, they have lost their power in three duchies, and they fight for their very survival. They are at *war*. As are we," he added. "It might be a shadow war, fought in darkness with daggers and spells, but it is no less a war. It is best if you consider it that way."

"You think it is a war now?" taunted Lantripol. "Three of the top Censors in the western lands have met in emergency session, after the expulsion from Castal and Remere. They have agreed to arm themselves with irionite for the duration of the emergency. The Censorate has confiscated quite a few pieces of it over the years. Thus armed, they will make short work of you villainous Coastlords. There won't be an unregulated mage left in Alshar!"

Gatina watched as Silva's face grew pale now. Despite what the shadowmage had said, Gatina wasn't certain what irionite was or what powers it had, but clearly it was a threat.

"He does not lie. You would violate the Bans yourself to keep the Censorate in power?" she demanded judgmentally.

"The Bans restrict such devices to those *authorized* to use them," Lantripol reminded her with a wicked chuckle. "Authorized by the Censorate. We have every right to use them against you in the name of protecting the public. And now that we know where you all are . . ."

"I read your little list, and let me assure you that you only know a tithe of our agents," dismissed Silva. "And mostly the few in Falas Town. There are hundreds of us. Thousands. How many Censors are there in Alshar?"

"Sixty or seventy at the moment," conceded Lantripol after some thought. "But there are many more on the way. We have authority on our side," he gloated.

"Illegitimate authority," growled Andivor. "I would not depend on that to spare you from what is coming. If the Censorate is foolish enough to draw their wands against the Shadow Council, then they will learn what consequences mean."

"So they will," came a new voice from behind them. The four conspirators whirled around, and a blade appeared in Andivor's hand as if it had been conjured. "Put away the sword, Steel; it is only me," the man said, and entered the small room.

It was Abbot Handrig. Gatina was surprised, nearly shocked, at the appearance of the senior clergyman of the temple at a clandestine interrogation in the old mill.

"Nightfather," Silva said, bowing respectfully to the old man. "I wasn't expecting you."

"When I heard that a Censor was chasing a Nocturn through the abbey grounds with a drawn blade, I figured that our 'special students' were involved," revealed the abbot. "It did not take long to conclude where he was being led and to what purpose. Well done," he told them all. "And thank the Blessed Darkness he came alone. The last thing this temple needs is an invasion of checkered cloaks."

"That is the first thing you will receive when I am free," taunted Lantripol. "This place is a haven for clandestine magi, and I will reveal that to my entire order! Palomar will be razed to the ground and its clergy banished," he promised. "Those who are not hanged as complicit!"

"Then who will give Count Vichetral and his Sea Lords the star charts they need to navigate?" the old monk said calmly as he regarded the captive. "You? Your magical thugs? Can you compute when the high and low tides will come? Taking the gravity of both moons into account? We are in no danger from the likes of you," he said confidently. "We have existed here before the Magocracy and long before the Narasi Conquest. When the Five Duchies are no more, Palomar Abbey will still be here. Now, what has he told you?"

"Many things, Nightfather, but the most pressing is the Censorate's intention on attacking our cells in Falas Town—and other places—on Midsummer's Eve."

"They would defile a holy feast day?" he asked contemptuously. "The depravity of the Censorate knows no frontier."

"Technically, it is the day before," Lantripol pointed out. "There is no violation of religious ceremony involved. Just rounding up a bunch of miscreant magi and their lackeys to face justice for their crimes."

"We must warn them," Gatina insisted suddenly, though she was the youngest in the room. "If they don't know . . ."

"You are, of course, correct, Nocturn," agreed the abbot with a sigh. "We cannot let our family suffer at the hands of such brutes."

"So, you are a hidden mage, Abbot?" Lantripol asked, sharply. "You would defile your own holy orders by abetting criminals?"

"My charter is significantly older than yours, Censor, and does not even mention magi," Abbot Handrig reminded him. "But, no, I never had *rajira* rise, thank the Darkness. There are quite enough interesting things in the Sacred Cosmos without complicating things with magic. But there is no prohibition against ministering to family, and I am related to many of those you would imprison. I resent that you brought your thugs here to menace our peaceful abbey. And I find you personally distasteful. So, I have no compunctions about assisting in this action. Indeed, I think I will quite enjoy it."

"When my fellows hear of what you have done to me—" Lantripol began to stutter.

"They will not," the abbot said soothingly. "Indeed, they will only find your cloak and your personal belongings at the top of this cliff, above the water. It will appear that you threw yourself off in shame and despair at your failure. Tragic," he said, shaking his head in mock sympathy.

"You aren't really going to . . . to throw him off, are you?" Atopol asked, his face concerned.

"No, no, my boy, we are not nearly as bloodthirsty as our opponents," assured the old monk. "The Cosmos has means of seeing justice be done without us getting bloody hands."

"Then what will come of him?" Gatina asked, concerned as well.

"He will go to sleep," Silva informed them. "When he awakens, he will have no memory of his service to the Censorate. Nor even of his name or past. Within my family's secret libraries are certain spells that date back to the Magocracy that can darken a man's mind: Blue Magic. I will place a powerful psychomantic charm on him so that he forgets every personal detail about himself. He will spend the next several years, I predict, as a barely conscious peasant for one of the Hill Lords," she promised.

Gatina snorted in appreciation. The "Hill Lords" were hardly a sophisticated or powerful group of nobles. They subsisted on what little they could grow in the high mountains of the Farisian or Minden ranges. They were universally poor, compared to the Coastlords or Sea Lords or Vale Lords. Their lives were tough, as they had to wrest their living from rocky, unforgiving soil far away from the nearest village. Consigning Lantripol to become one of their hardworking peasants had an appeal to her . . . and would assure that the man was never discovered by his fellow Censors.

"A live Censor with no memory can have his memory restored at need," agreed the abbot. "A dead Censor is quite a bit more difficult to work with."

"I grow weary of this," Andivor sighed. "Have we learned enough from him yet?"

"A few more questions, darling," Silva assured her husband, placing a hand on his thick arm. "But you needn't stay. I think we know enough now to take some action: namely, warning our people in Falas Town of the coming strike against us." She looked up at Atopol and Gatina. "I lay that charge on you two. Go to Falas Town and warn . . . Well, you know who to warn," she said, casting a sideways glance at their captive. "I'm certain they can be spared from their duties, Nightfather?"

"Oh, of course," agreed Abbot Handrig. "Not only that, but I shall also issue a proper permission for them to draw a carriage and team from the stables this time," he said, giving Gatina a meaningful look. "No need to steal them."

"I merely borrowed the horse, and he was eager for the exercise," Gatina defended.

"In any case, it would be too dangerous for Nocturn Avorrita to linger in Ejecta for the next few days, anyway. That would inspire too many questions. I'm afraid your studies at Palomar have come to an end temporarily," he said apologetically. "Now is the time for the Cat and the Kitten to chase a few checkered mice."

"You . . . you know our names-of-art?" Gatina asked, surprised.

"I know far more than you suspect, Kitten." The abbot smiled. "And far, far more than the Censorate suspects. Now let me write out the requisition, and you can be on your way by midnight," he said as he fumbled in his pouch. "Does anyone have a scrap of parchment?"

CHAPTER TWENTY-ONE

ON TO FALAS TOWN

A good thief might work alone, but he does not work well without the support of others. Beyond the family and its retainers and allies, House Furtius shall quietly cultivate relationships between the House with the clergy and their temples, for piety's sake and for the usefulness of the temples in our Craft. For while we may violate certain finer points of law with our work, good relations with the clergy help keep our House from corruption and immorality, and ensure that we have secret allies who owe us their assistance in difficult times.

*— from **The Shield of Darkness**,*
written by Kiera the Great

THE CARRIAGE ROARED ACROSS THE PLAINS OF FALAS AS ATOPOL DROVE THE team through the night. The roads were good this close to the capital, Gatina reflected as she was continuously jostled in the carriage. Not good enough to read or write, perhaps, but almost good enough to afford a nap. With the blinds drawn up to let the night breeze into the cabin, Gatina tried repeatedly to fall asleep, if only for a few moments. But if it wasn't the bumpy roads that kept her from slumber, it was her own excitement at the events of the last few days . . . and the dangers promised in the days to come.

She had managed to sneak back to Moon Hall with her shadowblade to retrieve her few vital belongings while Atopol secured the team and carriage. Silently, she packed up her heist journal, sketchbook, and some clothes without discovery . . . until she heard one of the box-bed doors open.

Thank the Shadows it wasn't Leonna! she'd thought at the time, when Mathilde emerged from her coffin-like bed. The girl looked both concerned and relieved at seeing Avorrita and motioned her into the stairwell to speak without alerting the other girls.

"Thank the sacred stars! We were so *worried!*" Mathilde said, embracing Avorrita when they were alone. "We knew that Censor took you away, and then at Vespers all anyone could talk about was the fight that broke out behind Planetary Hall. I was certain he'd . . . he'd . . ."

"I got away!" Avorrita assured the anxious girl. "I'm quite fast, actually, and somewhat small. I ran away and hid until he gave up looking for me. I'm sorry that I worried you!"

"*You're* sorry? Don't you dare! It was that awful Censor who's entirely to blame, and everyone knows it! What did he want with you?" Mathilde demanded.

"I'm not certain," Avorrita sighed. "From what I understand, he got into trouble with his superiors, and he was seeking someone to blame. Why he chose me, I haven't the slightest idea. He kept asking me questions that I didn't know the answer to, then insisted I was lying. He was very upset," Avorrita said, biting her lip. "He said he would make me confess or throw himself off the cliffs—he was in that much trouble."

"They say he drew his sword!" Mathilde gasped.

"He wasn't particularly good with it." Avorrita said, shrugging. "Really, he was clumsy. And half-mad with rage. He must have really kicked over the chamber pot," she suggested.

Mathilde shuddered. "I hope they never come back here!"

"I can't be here if they do," Avorrita said sorrowfully. "It's too dangerous. Whatever they're after, they could do me harm."

"We can hide you!" Mathilde suggested. "In the temple! In the stables!"

"They have magic," she reminded her friend. "And unlike us, they know how to use it. No, I need to get far away from here. My cousin Dain is going to take me someplace safe. We have relatives in the Great Vale who can hide us until it's safe to come back. He's worried that if they don't find me here, they'll . . . they'll threaten him until they find me. He wants no part in that! So, he's going to see me to safety."

"Your cousin is quite brave," Mathilde said unexpectedly. "There's more to him than meets the eye. Quite handsome, too," she added appraisingly. She paused. "There's more to you than meets the eye as well," she observed.

"Me? I'm just Avorrita," she said in response, shrugging. "Plain, dull, boring Avorrita."

"Who isn't really plain, dull, or boring," Mathilde countered. "Indeed, I think you just pretend to be. You're really quite brave yourself. And far smarter than you let on. And there is that other thing . . ."

"What other thing?" Avorrita asked, taken aback at the girl's shrewd praise of her and wondering how and when her alias had slipped.

"Your . . . your teeth seem to have magically fixed themselves," Mathilde pointed out quietly. "You haven't lisped once yet."

Gatina was floored and brought her hand to her mouth in realization. *She had forgotten to replace her prosthetic after the interrogation!*

"Oh . . . *that* other thing." Avorrita nodded. "Well, it's difficult to explain . . ."

"Don't bother," Mathilde said, shaking her head. "I mean, it's undoubtedly a fascinating story, but if I don't know, I cannot tell. I'm going to credit it to you being a far better mage than you let on, too. And I won't tell anyone I saw you tonight," she promised. "Or where you are going. It is our secret. You can trust me!" she said sincerely.

Avorrita gave her another embrace, more heartfelt this time. "Thank you! I don't know what's going on, but it's nothing good."

"Darkness protect you!" Mathilde said, and helped her sling her satchel over her shoulder. "And *do* be careful!"

———

THAT WAS HOURS AGO AND MILES AWAY. THE REST OF THE NIGHT WAS spent in a relentless drive across the countryside toward the capital—and danger. If the roads were getting better under the wheels of the carriage, Gatina also knew that the risk of getting caught by the Count's guardsmen increased with every turn of the wheel. That alone made it impossible to sleep.

But it was nice to know she could trust Mathilde, she reflected as she tried to get comfortable enough on the thinly padded bench to at least rest, if not slumber. She was quiet, like Avorrita, and clever. Gatina only hoped she could indeed keep a secret. If the Censors somehow got her to confess to meeting her after Censor Lantripol had chased her, the poor girl would be subject to the same kind of questioning that Lantripol had wanted to use on Avorrita. She could not bear to think of her new friend suffering through that.

But that only added fuel to her anxiousness as they approached the capital. What Lantripol had wanted to do to Avorrita was nothing compared to the methods the Censorate would use on the magi and other members of the conspiracy they planned to arrest. She could not imagine poor, sensitive Cousin Huguenin responding well to such duress. Clandestine mage or not, he didn't seem like the kind of man who would bear up much under torture. And if they made him speak . . . they would learn enough to find Cousin Onnelik. And Mother. And Father. And everyone else on the Shadow Council.

Including her—not dull Avorrita, but Gatina anna Furtius, Kitten of Night and apprentice shadowthief. And her brother. And everyone else they knew. That thought overlay her excitement with a thick sense of dread. If they did not warn them in time . . .

"Falas ahead!" Atopol called from atop the carriage. "I can see the walls! We're only a few miles away!"

Gatina sat up and stretched—hard to do while the carriage started rumbling across dressed cobbles near the city gate. But as they got closer, she could hear an additional noise above the din of the wheels and the hoofbeats of the team: a low, growling vibration that was ceaseless. It hadn't been there a few miles back, she noted. Gatina was apprehensive for a few moments before she realized what it was and grinned.

"The falls!" she said to herself. "The twin falls of Falas Town! We're back!"

Even though they had only lived there only a few weeks, there was something about the Ducal capital that made it feel like home to Gatina. She had gotten to know entire neighborhoods when she was Lissa the Mouse, a lowly nit—the street orphans that filled the city, unseen and disregarded by nearly all. The western precincts, in particular, had become a kind of home for her as she made friends with the other nits. The tall buildings, the stately temples and abbeys, the wineshops and tea shops, and street after street of artisans and merchants had taught her the rhythms of urban life.

But behind all the noise and clutter of the city, there was a genuine hum to Falas Town: the great twin falls of the Mandros River, at whose base the city was built. The great river split above the escarpment, she knew, and fell hundreds of feet down to the big lake at the bottom. Falas represented the last navigable point in the Mandros from the south. If you wanted your barge to proceed north of there, it had to be loaded on the giant wooden crane at the top of the falls and painstakingly hauled up the cliffside.

The hum of the falls never ceased, day and night. Gatina hadn't really paid it much attention before, but now as she returned to the city from quiet Ejecta Village, it was one of the first things she noticed. It was still on her mind as Atopol was stopped by the first military checkpoint. She could feel the carriage slow to a stop, and hear the bootsteps of men surrounding it.

"Halt in the name of the Council!" demanded a stern voice. "What business do you have in the city this morning?"

"Ecclesiastical mission," answered Atopol confidently. "Special guests for the Midsummer festival," he added.

"Who?" barked the guard.

"Some nun or other," Atopol answered. "I don't know. You want to read our papers?" he offered.

"Do I look like a fellow who can read?" snorted the reply. "Let me take a look at her . . ."

"Nay, Captain!" Atopol insisted. Gatina could hear him jumping out of the seat of the carriage. "None may disturb the clergy within this carriage; do you not understand the warning? Or recognize the sign?" he asked scornfully. She fumbled to put her false buck teeth into place in case the man insisted on seeing her. Mathilde's comment had reminded her that she was still Avorrita and, as such, she must maintain that persona.

"What is this? We can't look at a nun?" came the incredulous reply.

"You fellows must be new to Falas," sighed her brother. Gatina found the hilt of her mageblade, under the cushion, and made certain it was accessible. "The Saganite Order forbids its clergy be disturbed by anyone—that means *anyone*—in transit. To protect the Nightbrothers' sleep, between their sacred observations. Only a direct command of the Duke can override that," he added.

"I'm from Rhemes," the man replied defiantly. "My Count says that I can!"

"If you want to bear the penalties, that is your business," Atopol said loudly. "I care not—I'm just the teamster. But the law is written and established. The customary punishment is . . . Well, it's rather dire. Disturbing any of the Saganites in their carriages demands a stiff fine, possible imprisonment, and potential assignment of your liberty to the temple for five . . . *long* . . . years," Atopol announced. "There is no appeal of that, by Ducal decree. Any magistrate will impose the penalty once suit is brought before the bench. And Palomar Abbey is quite adamant about protecting its hard-won rights in these matters. The abbot is not a forgiving man, for a clergyman," he added apologetically.

"Godsdamned clergy," the man grunted. "All right, all right, pass along."

"Thank you, Ancient," Atopol said as she heard him climb back up to the bench. "I'm certain the gods will reward your attention to custom."

"Move along!" the man barked, and the carriage lurched forward.

"That was . . . entertaining," Atopol said from his coachman's seat as they pulled through the checkpoint. "All of them were Rhemesmen. Count Vichetral's handpicked troops. What does that tell you, Kitten?"

"That Vichetral has control of the city," Gatina replied, her heart sinking.

"At least the main routes in and out," conceded Atopol. "He's moving to consolidate power. And he's expecting trouble at Midsummer. We'll be coming to the main gate shortly. Where to after that?"

Gatina considered. "Let's go to the orphanage," she decided, knowing that it would be a perfect place to hide. "It's not unusual for clergy to visit other clergy. Then we can go to Onnelik's house. We can make contact with the others from there."

The main gate into the city had twice as many guards, Gatina could see when she peeked through the blinds, but they were less intrusive and more willing to let the carriage pass without inspection—they were local men, City Watch, as opposed to soldiers from Rhemes. As dawn broke over the city Atopol drove the carriage through the awakening streets toward the southwestern section of Falas Town. Daylight had banished the Blessed Darkness by the time they pulled up in front of the orphanage—an orphanage that Gatina was entirely responsible for. Indeed, she had paid to have it built.

After her mission to infiltrate the Brotherhood of the Rat was successfully complete, Gatina had used the funds she stole from the criminal syndicate to fund a small orphanage for the nits she had befriended. Her old tutor, Sister Karia, had agreed to take charge of the building and the half dozen orphans it housed under the auspices of the Tryggite Order. As Atopol ceremoniously opened the carriage door for her, Gatina blinked in the morning sun and saw that the quaint little two-story shrine was the only new construction in the older, largely crumbling neighborhood.

She assessed the building and noticed no signs of fire damage. The charred timbers and bricks had been long cleared away. During her time in Falas, this had been the burned-out building haunted by the Rat Orphans, the Brotherhood's street gang. Now it was a modest but growing structure that promised to spread out over the lot eventually. A home for dozens of orphans someday. Something she could be proud of.

"Just in time for breakfast," her brother murmured as they approached the simple door to the place. The smell of bacon and porridge was already heavy in the air. "I'm starving!"

"I wouldn't say no," agreed Gatina, who realized that she hadn't eaten since . . . She could not remember the last time. The aroma of food cooking was enticing. "Is there a bell, or . . ."

"We'll just knock," Atopol said, and banged on the door. A moment later they heard footsteps, and then the door opened to reveal a young woman about Gatina's age dressed in the reddish-brown habit of a Tryggite novice. A very familiar young woman: Marga.

Gatina was thrilled at seeing her young friend again, and she nearly blurted out her name. But it was clear that the novitiate did not recognize her in her Avorrita alias.

"Trygg's blessings upon you, brother, sister," Marga began, a curious expression on her face as she glanced at their robes. "Can I help you?"

"I'd like to speak to the house sister, if I may," Gatina said, keeping up her role.

"Sister Karia? She's cooking right now, but . . . Who may I say is calling?" she asked politely.

"You can call me Sister . . . *Kitten*," Gatina revealed, quietly.

It took a moment for Marga to realize the implications of that name. She had given it to her friend as a kind of password if she returned. Gatina watched as Marga's eyes bulged and her mouth opened. "And this is Brother Cat," she continued smoothly, gesturing to Atopol. "Recently of Palomar Abbey. May we wait inside? I don't want to attract too much attention out here."

Marga was nearly speechless, and she stammered a moment before she opened the door widely. "Of course, come in, come in! Lissa? Is it really you? Really?" she asked in a whisper. "You look so different!" She embraced Gatina in a sudden, fierce hug that seemed designed to establish that she was real to her friend.

"More or less," said Gatina, grinning. "I may have changed my hair." She shrugged.

"You look like an entirely different person! Those teeth! The eyes . . . It's amazing," Marga said, shaking her head in wonder. "What are you doing here?"

"It's a long story." Atopol sighed. "And it's been a long night in a coach. If you could tell Sister Karia we're here, we'll be glad to explain . . . well, as much as we can."

That caught Marga's attention. "Is there trouble?" she asked anxiously.

"When Kitten is involved, there is always trouble," chuckled Atopol. "But yes, there is. No one will be busting down the door or anything, but we wouldn't mind a safe place for a meal and a nap."

"And some advice," Gatina added. "We've just gotten to town, and we need a little assistance."

"What kind of assistance?" Marga asked as she led them down the corridor into the orphanage.

"Some of whatever I'm smelling, for one thing," Atopol said hungrily. "And a nap." Gatina rolled her eyes at her brother.

"And . . . I was wondering if you had a spare habit I could borrow?" Gatina asked. "This one is stylish, but it might stand out more than I prefer."

———

SISTER KARIA WAS JUST AS PLEASED TO SEE THEM BOTH, IF NOT QUITE AS surprised as Marga. The young nun came out from the kitchen, wiping her hands on her apron, and took only a moment to recognize them both. That irked Gatina somewhat: she'd thought she'd done an excellent job with her Avorrita disguise, but Sister Karia saw through it almost at once. Probably because she had known them both since they were small children, she reasoned.

She welcomed both of them to the orphanage's hospitality and ordered two more places be set at the long trestle table in the middle of the common room. A crowd of orphans descended from the upstairs as soon as the nun called that the meal was ready.

"No business talk during breakfast," the nun reminded them unnecessarily. "We can speak afterward, in private. What are your names?" she prompted.

"I'm Avorrita, currently, and this is my cousin Dain. Both Nocturns of Palomar Abbey, visiting the city for Midsummer."

"Palomar Abbey. Of course." Sister Karia nodded and introduced them as such to the unruly mob of children who eagerly took their places around the table, cramming themselves onto the long benches on either side.

It was fascinating to Gatina to watch how the meal proceeded. She didn't know most of the children, of course, but she did see her old friends Toscar and Gan, who looked significantly taller and better fed than the last time she'd seen them. They didn't recognize her, of course—she was just another visiting nun, something to which they'd grown accustomed.

After Sister Karia led the devotion before the meal, she sat at one end of the table with Marga and the siblings. The orphans, Gatina was pleased to see, accorded them privacy by largely ignoring the clergy at the end of the table. She also saw that the inside was a work in progress. The walls were built, yes, but there were crates stacked just inside the hallway. The downstairs furnishings were designed for practicality, not comfort. She imagined that the trestle table was also used for lessons. She spied a basket of slates in a corner, along with chalk.

"So, how have things been here at the orphanage?" Gatina wondered aloud, as a girl no older than seven brought her a bowl of porridge and treated her like she was a duchess.

"Better than expected, under the circumstances," Sister Karia related. "We got the place built fairly quickly, as there was a halt on a number of civic projects after the riots and there were carpenters and masons who lacked for work. The boys helped, of course," she said, nodding toward the far end of the table where Gan and Toscar seemed to dominate the conversation. "In fact, Twopenny was so good at carpentry, he's taken an apprenticeship," she said proudly. "So has Liddy, with a seamstress a few blocks over. Good masters, both of them—I checked thoroughly and still look in on them from time to time. Marga has been instrumental in helping me with lessons, both academic and needlework. She has proven to be a quick study herself."

"And your funds?" Gatina asked, curious.

"Our . . . wealthy patron has given us enough for at least a year, but . . . well, we're housing fourteen right now, eight girls and six boys, and we get asked for shelter every day, it seems. We take in a few to sleep in the common room at night if they're well-behaved. I'd like to expand to another floor and bring in another seven or eight. But that will take more money . . ."

"I'm certain something can be worked out." Gatina nodded. "The food is good," she added as she spooned another mouthful of oat porridge.

There was just a hint of spice and honey in it. The bacon that had been cooking was rationed, and it was clear that Sister Karia was very careful with her budget. Still, Gatina knew full well that this was a feast compared to what nits on the street usually survived on.

"We're getting better deliveries now that it's summer," the nun agreed. "This spring was a little rough. More riots," she said sadly. "There's another one at the palace every other day, it seems. Demonstrations, angry mobs, and anyone who takes issue with the Council of Counts has been screaming in front of the gates. Honestly, I thought that most of the city would relax and accept the new regime, but they keep doing things to upset someone every week. The public executions don't help," she added quietly.

"More executions?" Atopol asked, surprised.

"Too many more," agreed the nun. "Traitors, accused of conspiring with Duke Rard of Castal, or with Remere, or with anyone else Vichetral feels like blaming. Entirely without the sanction of the Lawfathers, of course. And there's a list now of prominent nobles 'wanted for questioning.' Of course, anyone who shows up who's on that list usually finds themselves in a prison cell or a noose before long," she added distastefully. "The old Warden of the Palace made that mistake. He was a good friend to the Duke and proclaimed his support for his heir in public. That got him on that list. He showed up at the palace with a lawbrother and three friends to witness to his good character. Vichetral let the lawbrother go free. The rest . . . executed."

Gatina winced. "That's appalling! No wonder there are riots!"

"Vichetral has not had an easy time pacifying the city," Sister Karia informed them. "His men are everywhere, it seems, but they only foster resentment in the townsfolk. The edicts coming from the Council are irritating the artisans and the petty nobility something fierce. And those who spy on behalf of the Council are now coming to light. A few have shown up in alleys with their throats slit after they've been discovered. More than a few," she corrected. "Someone is making war on the Council of Counts and Vichetral in particular. It's turning Falas Town's streets red as a result."

"But you're safe here," Gatina reminded her.

"Mostly safe," sighed the nun. "We do seem to have some protection, but I keep the children from going out at night. So far, we haven't been affected much. Oh, save that we had to register with the palace as a charity, and I had to answer a thousand questions to some suspicious functionary who clearly thought an orphanage was a cover for a place to plot rebellion," she answered, shaking her head.

"They're right to be suspicious." Atopol nodded sagely as he glanced at the far end of the table. Gan, the ginger-haired boy whose face was a constellation of freckles, was balancing a biscuit on his nose. "That's a rough-looking crew down there."

After the meal, the clergy retired to the tiny one-room chapel that abutted the main body of the orphanage. The scenes crudely but reverently painted on the plastered walls weren't the usual bloody depiction of maidenhood and motherhood she was used to seeing in the temples to Trygg but emphasized the mother goddess' role as a caregiver. That was refreshing, to Gatina's estimation.

"So, what are the Cat of Enultramar and the Kitten of Night doing back in Falas?" Sister Karia asked carefully when she closed the door to the chapel.

"It's a mission" Atopol shrugged. "We just need a safe place where we can change into something less noticeable. Then we'll be on our way again."

"Your father is involved, then?" Sister Karia asked, arching an eyebrow.

"And Mother," Gatina agreed. "It's business. But a lot is at stake. Unless you enjoy public executions."

"Ah. One of *those* situations." The nun nodded thoughtfully. "Of course, as our patron, you are entitled to whatever meager hospitality we can provide. But I do caution you against dragging trouble back to the orphanage."

"That's the farthest thing from our minds," Gatina agreed. "It's not much of a safe house if it isn't safe. Or secret. If we can stash our carriage and team here for a few days, that would be helpful. We'll gladly pay for the upkeep, of course."

"Luckily, we had a two-stall stable built, behind the main hall, just in case we needed it." Karia nodded. "We let the nits sleep there in safety during the summer. I'm sure they won't mind sharing it."

"And, of course, we'd like to keep our presence quiet," Atopol continued. "There might be people looking for us."

"What kind of people?" Karia asked suspiciously.

"The kind who wear checkered cloaks," Atopol said quietly.

"Oh. *Oh!* That makes sense," sighed the nun. "We've seen quite a few of that sort over in the palace quarter. They tend to stand out."

"The Censorate was expelled from Castal and Remere by order of Duke Rard," Gatina reported. "And the Wilderlands. Many of them are seeking refuge in Alshar. With Count Vichetral. That has presented some problems."

"Yes, yes, of course it would," agreed Sister Karia with a sigh. "Detestable people, the Censorate. As bad as the Brotherhood of the Rat," she pronounced.

"Speaking of whom, have you had any trouble with the local butcher shop?" Gatina asked curiously.

"Not since I confronted the butchers and told them to quit harassing my children," Sister Karia said proudly. "I cannot save every nit in Falas Town, but I can protect my own. I threatened to make trouble for them if they didn't do as I requested. I may have suggested that I had powerful friends and patrons," she confessed with a tiny giggle. "But I made it clear that it would be easier to leave us alone than to contend with the consequences of harassing us. Goddess, they even give us alms upon occasion.

"But let's quit exchanging pleasantries and get down to business," the nun decided. "Just what are your plans? And what do you need from us besides shelter and Trygg's holy blessing?"

"Nothing, really," admitted Atopol. "Breakfast, a stable, and a nap."

"And then we're going to visit a scribe over by the Tower Arcane," Gatina decided. "That's where we'll begin." Sister Karia nodded knowingly.

"You know," Marga said for the first time as she regarded the three of them, "I'm a clever girl . . . but I have absolutely *no idea* what you are all talking about."

CHAPTER TWENTY-TWO

REUNION IN A WINESHOP

Our House, whether magical or mundane, must always be aware of whispers that haunt the shadows and the dangers they can imply. For we are especially sensitive to the dreaded Game of Whispers and must remember that it is a game that is always playing. Whilst it might seem natural for us to play, it is wiser to avoid the betrayal, blackmail, bribery, and assassination that lurk in Darkness and content ourselves with honest theft. It is our duty to observe and stay aware. The knowledge of who is ascendant and who is not, who is ambitious and who is cautious, keeps our House strong and secure.
*— from **The Shield of Darkness***
Commentaries

THE SURPRISING THING TO GATINA ABOUT SUDDENLY APPEARING OUT OF THIN air on their Cousin Onnelik's doorstep was that the man was not in the least bit surprised.

"I've grown used to the unexpected when dealing with House Furtius over the years," he explained with a smile as he ushered them into the kitchen at the back of the house. "One never knows who will show up at what hour of the day or night needing what."

"Don't the neighbors gossip?" asked Gatina curiously. She'd lived in Onnelik's house for weeks but had spent most of her waking hours during that time in other parts of the city. She realized she didn't know that much about his quiet neighborhood. It suited her quiet cousin. He was one of the tidiest gentlemen she knew, and he did not seem inclined to a life of excitement. But, then, he dealt regularly with people deceitful by nature—her own family included. It made her wonder what other secrets might lie in the stately confines of the affluent neighborhood.

"I have a lot of perfectly legitimate clients as a scribe and translator, some of them quite exotic." He shrugged. "My neighbors are used to the occasional strange visitor by now. And I keep extremely good relations with them. So, what do a Cat and a Kitten need from a scribe?" he asked, almost jovially.

"We need to meet with Shadow and Night," Atopol answered. "We've just come fresh from an interrogation, and we have important intelligence."

"It involves the Censorate," Gatina agreed, "and is of the utmost urgency. We thought you would be the most direct way to contact them, wherever they are."

The old man pursed his lips. "I can," he agreed. "But it might take them some time to respond. They are quite occupied at the moment. But there are some means of communication for emergencies. Is this a family matter?" he asked politely. "Or business?"

"Both, alas, but more business than family," Atopol said after a moment's consideration. "That is, a lot of people are involved, and some of them are family."

"I see," sighed the scribe. "This wouldn't happen to involve a certain list, would it?" he asked curiously. "One perhaps scrawled by the light of a tallow candle using the Ivy code? And who was using a quill a little too long for her hand?" He gave Gatina a meaningful look.

"How did you know?" Gatina asked with a small gasp, intrigued and surprised.

"I'm very good at what I do," Onnelik chuckled. "I taught you the Ivy code myself. And you have a very distinctive hand for your age. I knew it was your work at once. And you dripped a bit of tallow on one of the leaves, which suggested you copied by candlelight. In any case, I was tasked to translate the work for the Council, so I'm assuming this has something to do with that," he observed, scanning their faces for agreement. Gatina was surprised that Onnelik had already deciphered her notes. "Once your father got it to me, I began to work on it immediately," he explained.

"If you translated it, then you know what that list means. We have it under excellent authority that the Censorate is planning a raid on much of that list," she predicted. "On Midsummer's Eve."

"Huin's Day?" asked the old man, mildly surprised. "That is interesting. And soon."

"Which explains our haste." Atopol nodded. "We believe that Cousin Huguenin and dozens of others are targeted—a great deal of that list."

"Huguenin?" he asked, startled. "And you got this information from . . ." Onnelik asked.

"A very cooperative Censor," Gatina reported. "Lady Mist and Lord Steel were involved. They're dealing with the results now and sent us to warn the Council. And there's more," she said, remembering the irionite. "But I should save that for a full report."

"Yes, yes, you probably should," sighed Onnelik. "Well, it seems I need to go arrange for some messages," he said, standing. "You two have a pot of tea and leave plenty for me. I anticipate a long evening ahead, and it's not even noon."

The siblings took the opportunity to rest, finally. Onnelik had ample space for unexpected guests in his townhouse, which looked smaller from the outside than it seemed on the inside. They both threw themselves into bed, forgoing tea altogether, and slept blissfully for several hours.

Indeed, it was evening before they awoke to the sounds of Onnelik's cook making supper. The scribe was in his professional study, sipping tea, while he read a series of parchments. Gatina yawned and stretched as she approached his wide work desk. It was already dark enough to require a triple-wicked oil lamp to provide enough illumination for him to read.

"Sleep well?" he asked without looking up from his work.

"Yes, thank you," she said, sitting down in a small leather-covered chair she'd grown accustomed to during her earlier stay in Falas. It didn't quite fit the way it used to, she noted to herself. "We needed that badly. It has been a busy few days."

"'Sleep restoreth the humor of all men,'" Onnelik quoted, although she did not know his reference. "But it's time you were awake. I received word back from Shadow," he said, picking up a sealed envelope of well-cut parchment. The wax was black and did not bear a stamp, but there was a simple sketch of a large cat and a small cat on the opposite side. "I believe this is for you," he said, and handed it to her.

Gatina did not wait for Atopol to break the seal and devour the message. Unfortunately, it was a short meal. Only a few sparse lines, and not even in code.

Will set meeting. Busy now. Tell all to O. Will contact him. Shadow.

In fact, it was extraordinarily terse, even for a secret message, in Gatina's estimation. This was her father, after all. Could he not spare a word of endearment? Encouragement? Or praise for their quick thinking and decisive action?

Stop being such a little girl, Gatina, Avorrita's personality seemed to assert in her mind. *This is a matter of professionalism, not an exercise or a game. Lives are at stake!*

Gatina felt a brief flush of embarrassment that her alias was, seemingly, more mature than she was. *You know your duty,* Avorrita affirmed in her mind.

"It . . . it says we should give our full report to you," she revealed to Onnelik.

"I thought it might," the scribe said, clearing his throat. "I did read that list, and I noted who was on it. In most cases, I can guess why. I may not be privy to the inner workings of the Shadow Council, but I'm clever enough to know what I'm copying.

"In this case, not only was it a startlingly complete list of the conspiracy's agents and principals, but there was another list toward the end of the work that seemed . . . *off* to me. They were important names, but they were separated out oddly. There were odd notations after them, too. So, I concluded—and spoke with Shadow about it—that this was not merely a list of our people but one of especial importance. And when I looked through the entire work, some patterns began to emerge. I would learn more if I had access to the original text, of course, but I'm confident about that particular list, based on the notations alone. And certain corroborating factors," he added.

"I don't understand," Gatina said, shaking her head.

"That list wasn't merely our agents but a list of our agents who were collaborating and informing the Censorate, Kitten," he explained, his voice hoarse. "Traitors to the Council and the effort against Vichetral."

"Traitors?" she asked, her voice a whisper. She knew the penalty for treachery within the Council. She'd been there when it had been established a few months before.

"I'm as surprised as you," Onnelik admitted. "You would think it would take more than a few months after you've committed to a conspiracy to decide to betray it. It usually takes years."

"Most conspiracies don't involve the Censorate," Gatina reminded him.

"That may well be playing a role in this," the scribe agreed. "But I'm certain that the people on that list are somehow providing information to the Censorate, according to that book. It is just a theory, but when I revealed it to Shadow and Night, they went to investigate. But now that we know that there is a raid planned on our best operatives, they may well have to shift their focus," he reflected.

"I'd hate to see anything happen to Cousin Huguenin," Gatina said quietly.

"Me as well, Kitten," Onnelik said in a surprisingly thoughtful tone. "We were close once when we were young. He's a delightful fellow and as loyal as they come. And I do enjoy his theater," he added with a sigh.

"That's the 'theater gang' the Censors were talking about." Gatina nodded.

"That's right—one of the conspiracy's most effective cells here in Falas," Onnelik agreed. "They've managed to infiltrate the palace, spy on the Council of Counts, and—most importantly—kept up the string of protests around town. They even managed to rescue three prisoners scheduled for execution," he added in an admiring tone. "It is that cell that we believe was betrayed by someone. Almost the entire theater troupe is involved, so there are a number of possible suspects. Huguenin is the leader of the cell," he added.

"Really?" Gatina asked, surprised. Cousin Huguenin was entertaining and very knowledgeable about the craft of disguise, but he didn't seem the type to lead an underground revolutionary movement. She wondered just how effective he could be.

"He's incredibly effective. Don't let his mild appearance or his flamboyant ways fool you: Huguenin is a master at convincing other people to do what he wants. He's also a very intelligent leader. His performers are extremely loyal to him, and as most of them come from good Coastlord families, they have been eager to undermine Count Vichetral's regime. That's why I'm concerned," he said, frowning. "If they've discovered the theater cell, then that puts many of our operations in danger."

"So, what are we going to do?" Gatina prompted. Onnelik gave her a thoughtful look in response.

"We are going to sit here and wait for Shadow to contact us," he said firmly. "No doubt he will want to confirm the information before we act on it. But while we are waiting," he said, pulling a fresh leaf of blank parchment in front of him, "why don't you tell me about this interrogation?

Every detail, please," he said as he pulled a quill from a cup full of them at the edge of the table. "And do be thorough. You never know when some minor bit of information is going to be important."

———

Despite the score of lamps that lit the interior of the wineshop, the place still seemed gloomy to Gatina as she and Atopol entered. There was a subdued air about the shop; it was half-empty, with only a half dozen well-to-do patrons sitting and sipping while the wine man polished glasses in front of a shelf full of bottles. Pipe smoke filled the air above the tables and chairs where the patrons drank and nibbled on cakes and other morsels. The perfect sort of place for a clandestine meeting in disguise with your parents, Gatina reflected.

The message they'd received at Onnelik's that afternoon had been just as terse as the first one, containing the name of the shop—the Golden Hare—a time, and an order to wear noble attire. Fortunately, Onnelik had clothing on hand from House Furtius's wardrobe room. The Golden Hare was small but popular, as it was only four blocks west of the palace and many lower-level palace officials had to pass it on their way home. The children made a point of being punctual and had dressed accordingly, Gatina in a modest velvet gown of dark blue and Atopol in a handsome doublet in green. Her brother had added a short sword he'd borrowed from Onnelik to complete his look as a dashing young nobleman.

"There they are," Gatina whispered when she spotted a middle-aged couple sitting at a table along the back wall. The two of them looked little like their parents, but they recognized them immediately for who they were. Gatina suppressed the urge to run to her mother for an embrace like a little girl. This was a mission, after all, albeit a small one. She stifled the urge.

"You're on time," her mother remarked with a hint of surprise in her voice as she and their father rose to greet them. Both sported the dark hair of the Coastlord nobility, and Hance was wearing a thin mustache while their mother had developed a dark beauty mark on her cheek. There was a glass bottle of wine already in front of them, and both were drinking a glass. "You weren't followed?"

"Of course not," Atopol said, chancing to kiss his mother's cheek as they sat down. "We were careful." Both of their parents seemed agitated, on edge about something, Gatina could tell. As if they were expecting the door to burst open and a party of guardsmen to arrest them at any moment.

"Of course you were!" Their mother smiled. She gave them an appraising look. "I can't believe how much you've grown in so short a time!"

"The food at Palomar is good." Atopol shrugged.

"And we've gotten plenty of exercise," Gatina added. "Especially swordplay."

"I heard about both your courses arriving and your *rajira*—congratulations, Kitten! Country living agrees with you." Minnureal nodded approvingly. "I miss it myself. We've had a busy time in Falas since you left."

"Things are just . . . tense right now," Hance agreed, his voice low. "But we should be safe to talk here. I've cast a spell for privacy. The shopkeeper is one of our fellows. Your intelligence was correct: the arrests have already begun."

"But they weren't supposed to start until the day after tomorrow!" Gatina reminded them.

"Their plans have changed, apparently, at least for some of their less important targets," their mother suggested, as their father motioned for the wine seller to bring more glasses. "Three of our street operatives have been taken in already. Completely by surprise."

"It's caused a crimp in our plans, too," Hance agreed. "But Captain Stefan has not yet returned from the countryside with the book with the complete list, according to our sources. We expect him tomorrow sometime. His timing is atrocious: we had a major street protest planned. Just a cover for another prisoner rescue, but we'll have to scramble to find another distraction."

"It's getting harder and harder to get people into and out of the city without notice." Their mother sighed. "Vichetral's troops are on the eastern side of the city and the riverport. Every coach and cart gets searched, into or out of the town. And every barge. The Midsummer festival would have made it easier. Thousands descend on Falas Town for Huin's Day and then leave. He could not possibly question them all."

"That's probably why they chose the day before to strike." Her brother nodded. "Wait until the city was full, then weed out our people. How many people do we have now?" he asked, curiously.

"You don't need to know," their father said flatly. "But our recruitment efforts have been highly successful. Every time Vichetral and his council issue a new edict, dissatisfaction with his rule increases. We've dramatically expanded our operations as a result. We've made alliances with other . . . factions," he explained carefully. "And we've identified a few that are firmly on the Council of Counts' side. And some who are wavering and might go either way."

"That's why your little unexpected heist was so rewarding, Kitten," Minnureal added. "As improper as it was, it netted us some terribly useful information."

"That doesn't excuse it, however," Hance said sternly. "You nearly ruined everything."

"I know, and I'm sorry," Gatina said, casting her eyes to the tabletop. "I'll try not to let it happen again."

"Twice is a pattern," her father reminded her. "Thrice could see someone killed. Would you want that on your conscience?"

Gatina shifted in her chair and looked at her cup, wishing the wine were stronger or that she could vanish. She felt everyone's eyes on her for a brief moment, then Avorrita's voice loudly said, in her mind, *Of course you don't want that! Not even Leonna should have to face such a thing as the Censors. You must be smarter.* Gatina knew that was right. She did not want anyone to face such a fate.

"Here is our report," Atopol said, abruptly changing the subject by presenting Hance with a scroll of parchment. "The scribe made a copy. It's accurate. But the part we didn't want to commit to writing is the important part. The Censorate is resorting to using irionite," he revealed.

That took both of their parents by surprise, and Hance and Minnureal gave each other a meaningful glance. "You're serious?" she asked.

"Mist put him under a truthtell, so we believe him," Gatina affirmed. "He chased me through half of the abbey with a sword," she added, hoping to regain a measure of respect after her father's rebuke of her behavior.

"Irionite? That . . . is extraordinarily bad news," said Hance, who did not mention the chase. "It will make them far more powerful, for one thing. The Mad Mage of Farise sank dozens of ships with his shard of the stuff, and it took three duchies to take it away from him."

"It indicates an escalation against us, for another," their mother agreed. "They don't need irionite to go after footwizards and fortune-tellers. They would only employ such forbidden things to counter our efforts. I suppose that they are tired of being made fools of by the shadows."

"We've enjoyed some great successes in infiltrating the palace," Hance reported as he tucked the scroll away under the table. "Not only rescuing prisoners but listening in on the most secret councils of the Five Counts. Discovering which among them is the most eager to name Vichetral as Duke, and those who appear far more reluctant. That has allowed us to sow discord amongst them."

"We've also learned that they will, indeed, approve a 'temporary' measure to allow slave-taking by the fleets once again." Minnureal sighed. "The first slaves will start arriving in port this autumn when the trading fleet returns," she said mournfully. "Supposedly to provide labor during the crisis with Castal, but that is just a pretense. They plan on opening a regular market. We were close to establishing which Sea Lords were opposed to the policy when your news arrived."

"And since our best spy within their councils happens to be on that list, we may soon lose that avenue of intelligence," Hance said, shaking his head.

"Have you sent warnings to everyone?" Gatina asked as the wine man poured her half a glass of dark red wine . . . then irritated her by adding a third as much water from a pitcher to it. He did the same for Atopol, which made her feel a little better.

"We're starting to, but that isn't easy in some cases," Hance revealed. "In others, the agents in question are too highly placed just to disappear suddenly. And there are traitors in our midst," he added warningly. "We want to avoid letting them know, as it will give away our ability to surprise. And, of course, we don't have the complete list that they will be working from. We have no idea who else was added to that book after you stole it," he reminded them. "Thankfully, neither do the Censorate goons at the palace. Not until Captain Stefan returns, that is. He's the one leading this operation against us. He's a canny investigator and quite thorough. But there are thirty or forty Censorate warmagi lurking at the palace, ready to execute his orders as soon as he gives them."

"Then why can't we steal it again before he delivers it?" Gatina asked.

Minnureal stifled a laugh. "You are your father's daughter! That is just what he suggested not an hour ago, in council. If that book can be stolen and destroyed before it's acted upon, it would give us some room and set back the Censorate's efforts significantly."

"Unfortunately, since your last heist, they have improved security around the Censor Captain," Hance revealed. "We don't even know where the captain will be staying once he returns to Falas. He has taken residence in three different places since he first came to Falas, and it is likely he will find a fourth just to confuse such efforts."

"And we're going to let that stop us?" prodded Gatina.

Hance gave her a tiny smile. "Of course not, Kitten. It just complicates things if we don't know where he's going to be. We have to properly position what forces we have. And the timing would have to be perfect. We would have to strike as soon as he arrives, before he can write out warrants and issue orders from the book."

"And there's that location spell," Atopol reminded them.

"That's why it needs to be *destroyed*, not just stolen," Minnureal agreed. "We have our sources looking for information on where he will be lodging. As soon as we know, we can plan the heist."

"Can we . . . participate?" Gatina asked, choosing her words carefully.

"I don't know yet," Hance admitted. "There may be a role for you. In the meantime, I feel obligated to use you while you are here. I want you both to go visit Cousin Huguenin at his theater tomorrow and make him aware of all of this. He is not himself on the Shadow Council, but he is highly placed in our confidence. His Talents make him one of our better agents."

"He's that good at disguise?" Atopol asked, amused.

Minnureal stared at him. "My cousin is one of the most accomplished Blue Adepts in Alshar, if not the world," she informed him. "He is a master psychomancer, among his other abilities. His magic works on the human mind."

"It's also why he's such a successful theater owner," Hance added. "He uses subtle magic to make his plays and shows more entertaining for his customers. He can persuade anyone of anything if given proper motivation. No one knows human emotion like Huguenin," he admitted. "His troupe is likewise talented at infiltration and spying, and he runs them like an army general at war."

"This is a war," her mother insisted. "A shadow war. The Game of Whispers."

Gatina had seen that term over and over in her research. *The Game of Whispers* was the common term for the clandestine sniping various old houses of the Imperial Magocracy did against each other. She had learned that it employed courtiers, gossip, intimidation, extortion, bribery, and occasionally assassination in the noble halls of Alshar and beyond. The Game of Whispers was a complicated way in which noble Houses used subtle manipulation to play a long strategic game designed to advance their own ambitions and fortunes. It was, she understood, a form of subtle art and dark wisdom combined with cunning minds to yield cutthroat results.

"This time, most of the Houses are united against Vichetral," Hance agreed. "Most, but not all. But that's why Huguenin's cell has been so valuable: they are welcome in nearly all the social circles where our friends and enemies like to conspire against each other. So, if you go to him and explain what is happening in person, he will likely know what to do better than I could tell him," he admitted.

"We can do that," Gatina assured. She had always liked Cousin Huguenin. "I'd like to see his theater, anyway. I've never been. It's not exactly welcoming for a street orphan," she reminded them.

"You won't be a nit this time," her mother agreed. "Pull on your noble aliases, both of you. Besides, if the Censorate is looking for you, they'll be looking for a couple of Nocturns, not a pair of high-born urban dandies visiting the theater district. We should know more about Captain Stefan's plans by tomorrow night . . . if our sources are still active. We should have a plan by then."

"In the meantime, we can warn those we know are in danger," Hance said, finishing his cup. "And I can figure out some alternative to a protest to help rescue those poor souls Vichetral has in the palace dungeon. I hope," he added ruefully.

"You'll figure it out, Father," Atopol said encouragingly.

"Of course he will; he always does." Minnureal nodded, glancing at her husband. "He has worked miracles in the last few weeks. You have no idea. You two have quite the legacy to live up to. Speaking of legacies," she said, removing a small pouch from her belt and opening it, "I have one here for you, Kitten."

She drew forth a silver coin—a very familiar silver coin: one of the four Vorean pieces that had been in the family since Kiera the Great stole them. She slid it across the table.

"It is a tradition in your father's House for the mothers to give one of these to their daughters when they are given Trygg's Blessing. You should carry it in your hoard and protect it. It is a token reminder of the duty you owe to your House," she said meaningfully. "When you have birthed your first child, you will return it to me, indicating that you have attended to that duty."

Gatina stared at the coin in front of her, the implications of it suddenly staggering. Her . . . *having a baby.* That seemed as foreign an idea as her growing wings or fins.

"I . . . I don't know . . . I don't even know whom I will marry yet!" was all she could think to say as her head whirled.

"Of course you don't." Her mother chuckled. "Indeed, I did not think I would ever marry, before I met your father. But when you meet the man, you will know. You will know in your heart, your head, and in every part of your being. The choice is yours, but your legacy demands that he be a mage of great power. Knowing my daughter, I'm predicting that he will also have to have uncommon wit, valor, and charm."

"That rules out any of our fellows at Palomar Abbey, then." Atopol snorted. "None of them is worthy of Kitten. Do I get a coin?"

"Your legacy is different, Cat," Hance assured him. "You must marry a thief of surpassing skill: one worthy of our House. That is a much higher tower to climb, believe me!" he said, looking at their mother affectionately. "There are far fewer female thieves than there are male wizards. But Kiera designed those rules on purpose, to strengthen the House. Not that I expect either of you will discover your mates anytime soon, but it is best you know what is expected of you now before your young hearts lead you astray."

"This seems like an odd discussion to have on the eve of a major operation," Atopol said skeptically.

"Even in times of chaos and strife, the business of our House continues . . . as do our lives," their mother reminded them. "Our lives do not cease just because we are committed to a cause. Or a heist. It is all part of the same legacy. It is what keeps our family growing over the years, and is as important as any other lesson. Just be prepared for it when it happens."

"Until then, go see Cousin Huguenin tomorrow and inform him of all we've discussed," reminded their father. "You'll find him at his theater, most likely: at the sign of the Gentle Wave."

CHAPTER TWENTY-THREE

THE GENTLE WAVE

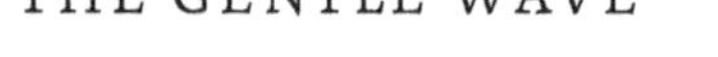

The easy path and the righteous path are rarely the same. Choose wisely.

— *from **The Shield of Darkness***
Commentaries

GATINA HADN'T REALIZED JUST HOW LARGE A THEATER WAS UNTIL SHE STOOD outside of the Gentle Wave, gawking up at the big three-story building that seemed to take up a quarter of the block. Indeed, she quickly realized that there were actually two theaters within the timber-framed structure, as was confirmed by the hand-printed parchment bill tacked to the ornate double doors.

GENTLE WAVE DAY THEATER PERFORMANCES CLOSED UNTIL FURTHER NOTICE, it read, in large, blocky red letters across the top. Below, printed in black ink, a more flowery hand declared, *Night Theater Open for Special Performances of Drama, Music, and Dance; Please Consult the Staff for Specific Times and Performers. Private Performances Always Available!*

The sign had been posted for a while; she could tell by the way the parchment was growing yellow in the sunlight. Indeed, she saw, as ornate as the exterior of the building was, with brightly painted columns and rows of lanterns across the front of the façade, the Gentle Wave theater looked as if it had seen far better times in the past.

The whitewash over the wattle-and-daub walls was fading and cracking, there were weeds growing from between the cobbles on the street in front of it, and the windows on the second floor had several broken shutters. The great double doors were elaborately carved and gilded, but the gilt was well worn and there were plenty of places where the carvings had been chipped away. Even the signpost with the stylized blue wave was showing its age, as the bright blue paint of the cresting wave was peeling and cracked.

"So, this is a theater." Gatina nodded as she took in the sight. "It's big," she added unnecessarily.

"It's the third largest in Falas Town," Atopol agreed as he joined her in gawking. "And the second oldest, from what Onnelik told me. 'A refined staple of the entertainment quarter for over a century.' He also said that it constantly loses money and changes hands frequently," he added with a smirk. "But he says the company of actors, singers, and dancers was one of the better troupes in the capital."

"It . . . smells funny," Gatina realized, as Atopol opened the smaller door next to the ornate entrance. It was painted with a smaller blue wave and a floral script that declared THEATER BUSINESS ONLY! But the air from within was musty, and it had a peculiar scent to it.

"That's just all the entertainment they keep in there," Atopol jested as he ushered her inside. "It gets stale if it isn't allowed to come out every now and again."

Beyond the brightly painted exterior, Gatina got the sense that the structure of the place was no better constructed than a cheap warehouse. The stairs they immediately ascended were creaky and rickety but stable enough to climb. At the top, they were met by a dull-looking lad with a wide face and a suspicious demeanor.

"If you cannot read, this is for theater business only," he recited in grunting tones. "The Day Theater is closed. Night Theater won't be held until Midsummer's Eve. If then," he said with a snort.

"We're here to see Master Huguenin," Atopol assured him, putting his arm protectively around Gatina. "On theater business," he added.

The man looked them both up and down, a critical look in his eye. "You want to audition?" he asked finally. "We aren't taking new players right now. Trygg's Grace, we've got more mouths to feed than we need right now!"

"Theater business," Atopol repeated firmly. "We'll discuss it with Master Huguenin. Please inform him."

Gatina was impressed with her brother's insistence—he sounded for all the world like a snobbish Coastlord, confident in his position and status. The kind of man who was used to dealing with servants and petty functionaries.

The man sighed and shrugged. "Wait here. Who shall I say is calling?"

"Lord Astin and Lady Murel," Atopol supplied. "It's about the cat and its kitten," he added. "Master Huguenin will know the reference."

As the man shuffled off through a thoroughly decrepit door, Gatina glanced around the gloomy landing. It was cluttered with bits of scenery left over, she presumed, from performances past: canvas trees, wooden waves, a rickety white trellis with faded silk roses and parchment leaves, and stacks of brightly colored costumes. It all had a shabby air about it, a mix of must and mildew, cheap wine, lamp oil, and nervous sweat.

"Master Huguenin will see you," the man said when he returned a moment later. He seemed a little friendlier now in Gatina's estimation. Perhaps Huguenin had informed him of their special nature. "Through there," he added, nodding toward the door he'd come from, "up the stairs and first door on the left."

"Thank you, Stage Warden," Atopol said with a gracious nod of his head as he led Gatina through the door.

"Stage Warden?" Gatina asked, surprised.

"He's the fellow that keeps the unwashed from mobbing the good performers after the show and making certain that the patrons only throw rotten vegetables at the poor ones and not rocks or bricks," Atopol explained. "He provides security. There are all sorts of staff that run a theater. Only some of them actually perform."

"How did you learn all of that?" she asked, surprised.

He shrugged. "I read. I listen. I pick up things."

Huguenin's office was tiny but ornate in a shabby sort of way. It, too, was filled with costumes and scenery from old performances, but Gatina could tell that he'd selected only the grandest of the pieces to decorate his office. In addition, there were shelves piled high with parchment manuscripts and books, adding the aroma of old archives to the mix. There were playbills from past performances touting names of singers and dancers she'd never heard of. There was even some faded art on the walls between cases and cabinets, though she guessed that they were props as well. It was incredibly dusty, she noted as they entered the room.

Huguenin himself was seated in front of a block of three tables, one on each side of him, where numerous parchment leaves, ink pots, and discarded quills were scattered. He looked older and more worn than Gatina remembered; his clean-shaven cheeks were drawn and his eyes tired. Instead of the dapper-looking doublet she was used to seeing him in, he wore a simple linen shirt with the laces open. His close-cropped hair looked grayer than before, too, she noted, and there were a lot more lines on his troubled face.

But his expression changed as soon as he saw them. He grinned and stood, giving them each a ceremonial embrace before closing the narrow door behind them.

"Lord Cat and Lady Kitten!" he gushed as he returned to his seat. "My dear cousins . . . you've grown so big since I last saw you! And that was but a few months ago! How are you? Your parents?" he prodded. "Are they well?" Everything Huguenin said seemed to be expressive, Gatina noticed, as if he were constantly performing for an audience. He had a tendency to speak in long, meandering explanations that captivated your attention, and used the tone of his voice to great effect. His mannerisms had always been flamboyant, Gatina recalled, but here in the theater, he acted without restraint. It was hard to ignore Huguenin.

"They sent us, actually," Gatina began as she took a seat on a low stool, one of several scattered about the cluttered room.

"Ah, so you are emissaries from the shadows today, then," he sighed. "And I had such high hopes for this season! We were going to do two of Hallmaker's Sea Lord operettas on the Day Stage, if the city permitted it. I've got a new girl with a voice like a nightingale," he mused. "A face like a cow, but a voice like a nightingale. Pity. She'll probably be married by next year, if she finds a nearsighted fellow."

"What's the difference between the Day Theater and the Night Theater?" Gatina asked, self-consciously. "I've never been to the theater," she explained.

"In Falas, my kitten, there are plenty of patrons hungry for entertainment—but not all of them can afford the best," Huguenin explained. "The truly magnificent spectacles oft require dozens of players and staff to create the illusions needed to sweep a patron out of their appallingly boring lives and into a story of love, adventure, tragedy, or romance. For those, a theater needs a great stage, open to the sky—and subject to its whims," he admitted. "A theater large enough to pack in as many patrons as you can, for as much as you can, purchasing as many cups of ale or watered-down wine as they can afford. That's why we have the very expensive large stage.

"For more intimate performances, and those attracting a more rarified crowd, we rely on an enclosed, indoor stage that can be lit by lots of expensive lanterns but secluded against the common artisans in search of a good time. For those patrons willing to pay the fare, we offer the Night Theater, where smaller performances allow a more private and exclusive experience, as well as significantly more expensive wine of slightly greater quality." Then he frowned. "Since the Duke died, the Day Theater has been closed by order of the Town. The Night Theater still enjoys a lucrative-enough existence to allow me to keep my very best performers from begging in the streets. At least, that's what my former partner told me before he sold me his interest in the Gentle Wave.

"Of course, this isn't a social call, is it, my kitties? You may speak freely here; there is no one to overhear us in this dusty old tomb. Well, I hate to inform your esteemed parents, but I'm having difficulty getting my troupe all together, the lazy scoundrels. A good many of them are sick, a few are drunk, and all of them will be looking for additional pay for the service. If they're expecting a large turnout for the protest, they might be disappointed."

"Actually," Atopol began, "there has been a change in plans. We're here to warn you of some danger. The Censorate is planning a raid on some of our friends. The theater included."

The mention of the Censorate immediately turned Huguenin's demeanor serious. Indeed, he looked deeply troubled to Gatina's eye.

"The Censorate, you say? That's not bloody good news," he murmured as he rubbed his tired-looking eyes. "I warned your father about that possibility when he brought me on, but he said it couldn't be helped. My company was needed, he said, to help with the resistance effort. And, of course, I cannot defy the Shadow Council—that wouldn't be proper. I know my duty. Oh, I had such high hopes for this season. Tell me everything," he insisted, tapping his fingers on one of the ink-stained tables.

Between the two of them, they managed a reasonably complete summary of the recent events, from arriving at Palomar Abbey to the arrival of Gatina's *rajira* to the unexpected intrusion of the Censorate. From there they related the aborted theft of the little book, the list they'd taken from it, and the interrogation of Censor Lantripol and its results.

". . . so, we know they're planning a raid on Midsummer's Eve, they know you are a member of the conspiracy and the head of a cell, and they suspect that you are a clandestine mage," Atopol concluded. "Shadow wanted us to warn you. He doesn't think that the protest you planned will be allowed now. It might just be an excuse to gather up your people."

"That is precisely what it would be," agreed Huguenin, his expression troubled. "Damn Vichetral! An entirely despicable man. It was bad enough he hired those thugs from the Brotherhood to keep the streets in line, but allying with the Censorate? Is he *mad?*" demanded their cousin, his voice tinged with outrage and disgust. "The Coastlords will never stand for it! We have not been practicing discretion in our arts for four hundred years merely to be at the mercy of those checkered-cloaked brutes at Vichetral's whim!"

"What are you going to do?" prompted Gatina.

"Well, the original plan was to get my company to lead a protest in front of the palace gates—nothing riotous, of course, just some angry shouting, perhaps a bottle or two thrown at the guards. We've been doing that sort of thing for weeks now," he revealed. "When Shadow needs a good distraction, there's always some pretense I can use to get my fellows to raise a crowd. And we've been passably good about slipping into and out of the palace, which is no small feat these days."

"You're using shadowmagic?" Atopol asked, clearly interested.

"Shadowmagic? No, my boy, we're using plain old-fashioned greed and lust for power and status." Huguenin chuckled. "That's far better than mere magic for our purposes.

"When Vichetral's little army showed up and took over the palace, most of our friends in court were dismissed from their positions . . . those that didn't end up in the noose or on the headsman's block," he added, making a distasteful face. "But Vichetral still had to govern once he claimed to rule. As one would expect, he imported an entirely new crowd of officials to help him govern. Men newly made important by their association with the Count and his peers on the council. Oh, there were a few old faces—Baron Jenerard, Captain Silogas, Viscountess Berendine, no one I'd be nice to at a party—but most of the governing officials are entirely new to palace life. As such, they were subject to the usual temptations involved in such a rise in their fortunes."

"What temptations?" Gatina asked, knowing that it sounded naïve the moment she said it.

"What temptations?" Huguenin repeated. "Why, everyone who finds themselves in power is tempted to do all sorts of things—as well as fear all sorts of things. Some have dreamt of power all their lives, and once their ambitions are fulfilled, they are eager to enjoy the perceived benefits of their position. Others come to it unexpectedly and quickly become drunk on the novelty of the experience. Both are usually subject to flattery, bribery, extortion, and corruption as they seek to appease their greed or indulge in their secret passions at public expense. Corruption," he pronounced decisively, "it's inevitable. It's part of our fundamental human nature.

"That, you will find, is true in any institution that truly wields power. There are always those who seek to flatter, to influence you to their whim through bribery or merely a good meal and fine wine. There is always a swarm of such people infesting the corridors of power, trying to gain some for themselves or at the behest of their employers to influence policy—or avoid it altogether. But the old court understood that and kept it in its proper place.

"That was before Vichetral took power. The Council of Counts? Their lackeys are new to the game, and like your first sip of good wine, it quickly goes to their heads."

"So, how do you use that?" Atopol asked, curious. Gatina had to agree; it sounded fascinating.

"Oh, in the simplest of ways! Attend, children, for I lay upon you great wisdom." He chuckled mirthlessly. "Consider that I am a young Coastlord from Rhemes whose uncle is Vichetral's favorite bootblack and for whose favor I find myself in grand Falas Town, at the very Ducal Palace, suddenly in charge of . . . well, just about any office. What is my first impulse? Why, to protect my new and reasonably lucrative position from those below me who seek to take my place and those above me who fear I covet theirs."

"I can see how that would be a difficult position," Gatina agreed, imagining what someone like Leonna would do in that place.

"That's the fear: accountability to your superiors and vulnerability to your inferiors, no matter the job." Huguenin nodded. "What is more, you are expected to represent your superiors and their glorious exercise of power to the rest of the world. You begin indulging in casual displays of your own importance: parties, feasts, tournaments, balls—and, we hope, the occasional night at the theater for a festive indulgence in sophisticated entertainment," Huguenin said dreamily. Gatina was captivated. Huguenin had always seemed a funny sort of fellow before, but there, in the theater, he seemed in his element.

"So, you get them to come to the theater," Atopol nodded.

"Oh, it is far more subtle than that—we allure them here, and then enchant them with mysteries and intrigues, evoking their desires and their finer sensibilities, seducing them with good company, amusing performances, enticing companionship, and slightly watered wine of decent—but not expensive—quality. They are flattered here by both player and fellow patron: their mere presence amongst such high-born sophisticates tells their tiny little minds just how important they are. How much people like them. How rare their certain personality is to attract such an intriguing cluster of fellow aficionados of sophisticated culture, and how that assures their insecure souls that they are, indeed, amongst the rich and powerful.

"And if they cannot, alas, spare the time to attend regularly, why, the stalwart company of the Gentle Wave Players is all too happy to come to the palace or their residence and entertain them in private, away from the swell of the stinking masses."

"*That's* how you get into the palace?" Gatina asked, smiling at the idea.

"Aye, with a simple message—and a token of our quite reasonable commission—they can summon from our company singers of exquisite quality, comic players whose impure jests will relieve the ponderous burdens of power, nimble-footed dancers who will tantalize them with graceful gyrations and the exotic dances of a score of cultures, perfect to distract them from their cares. I can provide jugglers, acrobats, and clowns to the wealthy to flatter their sense of importance. I can bring them drama, comedy, music, art, romance, passion, distraction, and delight—all for a reasonable fee," he explained. "My good fellows can come to their office in the palace or even their private residences to entertain.

"And once there? My lads and lasses know their business," he assured them adamantly. "Good players all: a lonely old man gets a shy smile from a comely maiden, a decrepit old bag gets flattery and attention from a handsome young fellow, whilst my senior performers grace their patrons with powerful—and entirely distracting—performances that challenge their imaginations. Then my ushers and stewards are ever at their elbows, pouring wine like an endless fountain and burying them in fawning assurances that, yes, they are indeed as special and important as they think they are. For reinforcing the mind's own flattering lies about ourselves is the surest way to exert influence on it," he informed them. "And the more novel the feeling of power is for them, the easier it is to play upon their insecurities about it."

"And then they just tell you all their secrets," Atopol proposed.

"Or they're so distracted, they don't notice you picking their pockets," Gatina added.

"Either, both, and much, much more, my kitties," Huguenin sighed. "Everyone wants to be liked. To be trusted. To be included in a society that is exclusive and ostensibly based on their unique personality. Every man imagines himself as a capable and commanding leader, and every woman mistakes herself for a clever and beautiful influence on all who cross her path. The sad truth is neither is true. But that belief, aye, that can be used against them to get them to do nearly anything."

"That's psychomancy," Gatina observed. Huguenin's eyes shot to her instantly.

"Exactly so! And it doesn't take a spot of *rajira* to perform. Indeed, much of psychomancy is based on such understandings of the human mind. Once you know how the various pieces fit, you can use that knowledge to influence and manipulate it. A good psychomancer will meet you and be your best friend in five minutes," he reflected. "You will trust them, like them, even love them a little . . . all while they are pawing through the hidden pockets of your personality with every word you speak and glance you deliver.

"That's why the Shadow Council recruited me—and my troupe—in the first place," he explained. "We know human nature and the arts of deception. Indeed, all theater is deception at the root of it—entertaining deception, if we're any good at it, but deception nonetheless. You have to know how a patron's mind works and what he wants and desires before you can cater to his need for entertainment. Showmanship provides that in droves," he assured them. "Add in a little arcane power here and there? You can get quite a bit accomplished if you are skillful, thoughtful, and lucky."

"Why don't they teach these things at temple schools?" Atopol said with a grin, clearly impressed by Huguenin's explanation. "I can think of all sorts of things that this would be useful for!"

"Of course you do—but if it was commonly known, it would become less effective," Huguenin pointed out. "Psychomancy is the province of memory, of perception, of sensation, of suggestion, of self-image, of truth and lies, self-deception, and wild imagination. It is Blue Magic, the color of feeling and emotion, as much as logic and reason. It is a powerful discipline that can be used to improve someone's life immensely or make it a hellish existence bereft of peace of mind. That's why psychomancy is best taught in secret, by a master you can trust, and preferably far from the ignorant eyes of the public.

"Most practical adepts only know a sample of it, for use in other spells. Or they stumble on some old grimoire with a few old spells which employ it. They do not understand the theory of it, though they may guess at it. A very few can practice hypnosis and mentalism and appreciate its use and potency. But most avoid the subject in favor of more lucrative and flashy magic."

"Isn't it illegal to teach it?" Gatina asked, recalling she had heard that somewhere in the past—likely in the gossip that followed a magic class by the Censorate.

"Blue Magic is perhaps the most powerful of the arcane disciplines, which is why it is frowned upon by the Censorate. While not precisely proscribed by the Bans on Magic, it is rigorously policed by those scoundrels. They decidedly don't want it taught, master to apprentice, as a formal discipline—though there are stacks of books on the subject, if you know where to look. They understand how dangerous it can be in the wrong hands. And to the Censorate, all hands but their own are the wrong ones."

"Which brings us back to our message," Atopol said diplomatically. "Will you cancel the protest? It seems dangerous in light of this news."

Huguenin sighed. "I suppose I must, which is a pity. I was going to have a little party here afterwards with a few select friends. We'd talk business, of course, but it's traditional to throw a party after a performance. Some of my company will resent the cancellation, of course—times are getting hard, and they need the money. But none of them like the Council of Counts that rules us, and they have consented to my direction on how it is resisted. They will stay home or find different employ that day."

Huguenin suddenly looked thoughtful, was silent for a moment, and finally sighed. "I knew this would not be productive in the long term," he said, shaking his head. "I told your parents as much when we agreed to work with them. As committed as the fellows in my company are to the cause, and as grateful as they are for the work, they are not necessarily the most reliable off the stage. And they are just as subject to flattery, bribery, and coercion as anyone. I trust them . . . mostly."

"But can you get them to flee? Or hide?" Gatina asked anxiously. Part of her was enchanted with the idea of the theater now. She had an earnest desire to see a play or a song performance in the Night Theater.

"Some of them," Huguenin conceded. "If I can get word out quickly enough. As I said, I've had difficulty getting them organized if there isn't a party or a performance involved. But that doesn't remove the danger from them," he reminded them. "If the Censorate has their names, they will be hunted."

"The Council is working on that," assured Atopol, with far more confidence than Gatina felt was appropriate.

"They can, of course, flee the city, change their names and appearances, and eke out a meager existence as tavern performers," he said, making a sour face. "But they would mislike it. As would I. I've invested quite a lot in this sinking ship of a theater," he said, looking around at the shabby décor.

"Sinking ship?" Gatina asked, surprised. "It's a little dusty, perhaps, and could use some paint, but it seems like a splendid theater to me. It must be an exciting life, to be a player in a company," she surmised.

Huguenin did not take the suggestion as she thought he might—but then, he was used to flattery, empty and sincere, she reasoned. Instead, he made an even more disgusted face and launched into a passionate critique of the entire idea.

"Exciting?" he began, his eyes wide. "If dodging creditors and contending with impossible players is excitement, you can get your fill at the Gentle Wave!" he warned her. "When my partner wisely sold his share to me, he treated lightly with the matters of upkeep on this ancient relic: the stages in need of repair, the stands falling apart, the roof leaking in inconvenient places, the sheer amount of cleaning required after every performance—and don't even mention the problems with the privies!" he said, shaking his head with disgust. "The neighbors are a constant irritant; they complain of the noise when we are busiest, dislike the traffic we draw, and bemoan the garbage and filth our patrons leave behind. Oh, and the beggars—when you attract a man with a full purse to your show, you also attract the thieves and beggars who prey upon him!

"And the players—only half have the talent they think they have, and the ones who possess it in good measure lack the wit to employ it without strong direction, to which they take the greatest of exception. Ego is the staple of Blue Magic, and by the gods, I have to contend with egos the size of leviathans every day!" he complained. "Either they aren't getting enough lines or too many, or they want to play another character, or reinterpret their interpretation, or change lines in the script, or demand a private dressing room, or more money, or more wine! Most of them are drunks to one degree or another, and plenty of them have no sense of time or schedule! And those are the *normal* ones!" he insisted. "Those with real talent who have the poor grace to know it are the worst: raging narcissistic egotists who have no greater desire than to be the center of the universe's attention at every moment, reassuring them of their own perceived greatness!

"They cannot contend with a universe that does not see them as the most prominent of players, regardless of if the role calls for their talents or not. They storm and rant and start petty feuds within the company based around gossip, lies, and slander! The musicians think that they are actors, the actors think they are writers, and the ushers think that they can do any of the tasks better than the professionals because they believe in their own deluded ideas about their ambitions for fame and success. Success! To a player in a company, it is measured in paying the rent on time and having a morsel for supper, yet these ingrates complain if they have to wait a day for their payment, and lament its size the moment they get it! They should all be as rich as dukes, they insist, and whine at their share of every show!

"And the vendors—wine sellers, seamstresses, carpenters, drapiers, glaziers, butchers—all of them think that our grand building means a grand purse, and charge us extra for our supplies and repairs. The barkers I hire to prowl the streets and tout our performances are lazy scoundrels, inept in their coverage and volume, and seem to think their employment entitles them to the privileges of players. If I can manage to scrape together an audience, they are either nearly paupers or so stingy that they will have the one cup of wine required and no more! My debts are increasing like a rushing river, while my building is falling apart and I am surrounded by drunks and reprobates! It's enough to make me pack it up and retire to my country house!" Huguenin said, clearly exasperated.

"You . . . you have a country house?" Gatina asked, confused.

"Yes, it's a lovely estate about thirty miles south of Falas Town." Huguenin sighed. "Quaint little manor house, jolly peasants, abundant fields, the very picture of rural prosperity. My beloved grandmother left it to me when she died, may Trygg ward her soul."

"So . . . you don't have to do all of this," Atopol said, gesturing around at the theater. "Not to mention the spying and protests and the Counts and the Censors and such . . . You could just escape to the countryside and live a life of comfort?"

"Oh, I could," Huguenin said as if the very idea was tortuous. "Some days I get very, very tempted!" he promised, sagging back in his chair. "The exasperations, the poverty, the aggravation, and now the mortal danger . . . it makes me tempted," he admitted.

Gatina looked at Atopol, who shared her confused expression.

"So . . . why don't you?" she suggested hesitantly.

Huguenin looked aghast at the idea and sat up straight in his chair. "What? And give up *the theater?*" he asked, sincerely appalled.

CHAPTER TWENTY-FOUR

MURMURS OF DISCORD

A good thief questions everything about a heist, lest he stumble into mayhem and discovery. Questions of "What is beyond that door?" and "Is there a guard dog?" are the easiest to answer. The more important questions are "What are my reasons for stealing this?" and "Why am I taking this risk?" and they should be treated with concern. Skepticism is the thief's friend as much as the cover of darkness.

*— from **The Shield of Darkness***
Commentaries

IT HAD BEGUN TO RAIN BY THE TIME GATINA AND ATOPOL LEFT THE GENTLE Wave Theater, a sudden shower in the afternoon that seemed determined to soak every inch of the town. Water started to pool quickly on the streets as they walked back to Onnelik's house. Wisps of steam rose from the cobbles as the rain cooled the summer's heat stored in the rounded rocks. People pulled the hoods of their light summer mantles over their heads if they had them. Gatina recalled the times that Lissa the Mouse had to contend with the rain without the benefit of a mantle. It usually meant finding a bridge to hide under or a scrap of roof next to a building to escape the wet. But as they walked, the pace of the downpour picked up, dousing everything and everyone in a stiff rain.

"Let's stop and have a cup," Atopol suggested as they passed by a familiar-looking tea shop. "I feel the need to collect my thoughts after talking to Huguenin."

"He is an interesting fellow," Gatina observed. "And I could stand a good cup of tea right now. Kittens don't like getting wet," she reminded him.

"Neither do cats," he agreed.

Onnelik had originally introduced her to the small, friendly little shop months before, when she was beginning her Lissa the Mouse alias. At the time, she had felt very grown up about visiting it. It had seemed like a special privilege. Such places were the province of adults, after all, where business was done and gossip exchanged around a variety of aromatic teas and tisanes served in delicate earthenware cups. Now, she reflected, she just wanted a cup of tea and a chance to get out of the rain that threatened to spoil her carefully applied cosmetics.

"So," Atopol began after they were seated and had given their order to the busy tea matron, "what do you make of our cousin?"

"He's fearful," she proposed, recalling Huguenin's reactions to the news of the Censorate. "He has a right to be, if he's been that active. If he's unregistered, then they have every legal right to take him into custody on that charge alone."

"He has every right to be," agreed Atopol as he hung his dripping mantle over the back of his chair, along with his sword belt. "But he's also committed. Maybe more so than before, now that the Censorate is involved. What I'm wondering is how many others are in such danger now. I'm guessing that the Council has expanded their reach dramatically, since we went to the abbey."

"Isn't that a good thing?" Gatina asked, careful to keep her tone and her words nondescript. Not attracting attention was the cornerstone of shadowmagic, from what Lady Silva had taught her. She didn't yet know the spells that would keep her and her brother's conversation from being overheard, but she was starting to understand the art of subtle conversation. A good thief should be able to speak about the most sensitive things in public, if they knew what not to say that would attract attention.

"I suppose," answered Atopol with a sigh. "Clearly, they are having an effect on the palace, else Stefan and his fellows wouldn't be involved as they are. But I have to wonder to what end this will come. I mean, I understand the objective we're trying to reach. I just don't understand how we're to get there this way."

That admission surprised Gatina. Usually, her brother was as enthusiastically loyal to their parents, their House, and the work that they did as she was. But Atopol looked troubled somehow. As if he was starting to doubt the purpose of the Shadow Council and their family's involvement in it.

"We're not supposed to understand, remember?" Gatina pointed out. "We're just supposed to follow orders and do what we're told, like good apprentices."

"I don't mind that part so much," Atopol admitted. "I still don't really know what I'm doing yet. What concerns me is just how long this is going to go on. That talk we had in the wineshop, last night, it got me thinking," he said thoughtfully. "We're supposed to find adequate mates and marry, according to tradition. That's going to take a while. How are we supposed to do that when all of this is going on?" he asked as the tea matron approached with a tray bearing an ornately painted teapot and two cups. There was a small tray of sweet biscuits and a dainty honey pot next to it.

"Just as you ordered, just as you ordered," the woman said as she set the tea down on the table between them. As she did so, she chanced to glance at Atopol's chair, his dripping cloak, and the hilt of his sword. She halted, for a moment, then continued more slowly. "You wouldn't happen to be in one of those 'debating societies,' would you, m'lord?" she asked suspiciously.

"Debating societies?" Atopol asked, confused. "No, my sister and I are here from the provinces, attending the Huin's Day festival. It's our first time. Our father insisted I carry a sword due to the crime in the city. He says Falas Town is simply filled with thieves," he explained.

"Oh, that it is, that it is, m'lord," she assured him, frowning. "It's proper that a young man be able to protect himself and his kin on the streets," she agreed.

"What debating society is this?" Gatina asked, interested.

"Oh, just something the nobility in Falas get up to, m'lady," she said, looking visibly relieved. "The younger ones, mostly. Dueling clubs," she explained as she tucked her tray under her arm. "A bunch of younger sons and arrogant bravos who 'debate' each other with steel. As if they've nothing better to do than to slaughter each other in the street. As if Falas Town doesn't have enough blood flowing right now."

"I've never heard of them," Atopol said as he drizzled honey into his tea.

"Oh, it's a tale, it's a tale," she said, shaking her head. "They used to terrify the whole town, back when I were a girl. Whole troops of them would wander around, getting into brawls, after a few cups at the wine shop. It got bad enough the Duke took note. They were forbidden by the Duke's edict . . . until yesterday," she revealed. "Heard about it at the fountain. That new rascal of a Rhemesman count restored them!" she said, scandalized. "'In an effort to secure the safety of the public,' it says! As if a bunch of bravos with naked steel are going to keep the footpads down. Just terrify common folk, more likely," she warned. "Bloody count!" she said, shaking her head as another patron was calling for service.

"Dueling societies," Gatina said.

"Debating societies," corrected Atopol with a sigh. "That's ominous news. You realize what Vichetral is doing, don't you?" he asked her.

She shook her head. "I don't see how a bunch of duels is going to help him stay in power," she admitted.

"It's not just a bunch of duels, I imagine," Atopol explained. "You just have to understand who benefits. Our hostess is not wrong: by permitting those societies, Vichetral is filling the streets with men he can recruit to his cause and tamp down the opposition. He did it in response to the riots. Who is going to start throwing bricks and cobbles when a gang of young toughs could appear and stab you 'in the name of public safety'?" he proposed. "That's going to be more effective than regular guardsmen or even soldiers."

"Why would anyone want to do that?" Gatina asked, confused.

"There are plenty of young Coastlords and Sea Lords who fancy themselves great warriors and seek to prove it," her brother answered. "Believe me, that's half of the topic of discussion back in the boys' dormitories at the abbey. Most of the Nocturns in my group can't wait for their term of service to end so that they can find good swordplay tutors or start jousting. Not Lord Dain, of course—he's a scholar with no time for such pastimes," he said.

"What's the other half?" Gatina asked, sipping her tea gratefully. The rain had been jarringly cold, and the tea was warming her.

Atopol shrugged. "Girls, of course. Both in general and specific examples. Believe me, you don't want to know what they say," he assured her.

Gatina grinned, happy to not share in *that* particular knowledge. "It's just as bad in my group. Most of them are obsessed with whom they'll marry, and some are actively seeking husbands. Your name has arisen occasionally—Lord Dain, that is," she corrected herself, crinkling her nose at the idea. "Most of them think you are adorable."

"I am adorable," Atopol admitted solemnly. "It's a curse."

"But that brings us back to the subject of . . . well, our legacy." Gatina sighed. "Of course, it's going to be a struggle, but it's our duty," she reminded him. "Just as our work is. It sounds like you're having . . . doubts."

"I don't doubt the noble goals of the enterprise," he said as he stared at his reflection in his teacup. "Horrid people should be fought by good people. Justice should win out over tyranny. Duty to our House is its own reward, of course. But I wonder if we'll ever accomplish those noble goals. Before we're old and decrepit. What if we spend the rest of our lives at this? It's hard to meet an attractive female thief if I'm busy fighting tyranny."

"That's . . . an interesting perspective." Gatina nodded. "I'm certain that Father has a plan."

"I'm not," Atopol said quietly. "Don't mistake me—he seems to know what he's doing. But will it be enough? Enough to take back the throne? The Counts have control of the Narrows, the Straits of Sinjar, and the entire river," he pointed out. "They've sealed off southern Alshar from the rest of the world. Castal won't come to our aid, lest it's in conquest, and the other duchies are too far away to help. He's using the Rats to control the common folk and the docks, threats of execution to control the clergy, his armies to keep the petty nobility and disloyal barons under his thumb, the Censorate to keep the Coastlords at bay, and the promise of piracy and slave-taking to win over the Sea Lords. I just don't see how we fight against all of that without help," he said, discouraged.

"We . . . we do the best we can," Gatina proposed. She was troubled that Atopol was having such doubts, especially when they were about to execute an important heist. Usually, he seemed optimistic about such things, she reflected. "This might take years. This might kill us," she admitted. "We might end up in a dungeon and never see the sunshine again, or we might end up under the headman's blade. But it won't be boring," she reminded him. "We have some things to do. And some things to learn while we do them. We have our duty to our House and our country. Think of the lives the others in our groups have ahead of them: dull, boring, and lacking adventure."

"That . . . that is a good point." Atopol sighed. He ventured a small grin. "It's not that I'm not having fun, and I don't mind the danger; I just don't want to spend my entire life worrying about who's going to come in the door looking for me when I sit down for a quiet cup of tea. It would be nice to wear my own hair. Have my own friends who know my real name. Talk to a pretty girl without worrying that I'll mess up my alias. Like the girls in your group—they're pretty, most of them," he observed.

"Except for plain little Avorrita," Gatina said, making a face.

"Oh, she has her own sort of homely charm; some of the fellows have noticed," he teased. "I wouldn't mind chatting up just about any of them—"

"*Not* Leonna," Gatina interrupted sharply. "She's horrid."

"She's still pretty. But what would I say to them?" he continued. "'Oh, I just happen to have a dozen different names and a profession I can never talk about and I'm constantly running from Censors and gangsters, but would you like to take a walk somewhere private?" he said sarcastically.

"Now you know why you have to marry a thief," Gatina realized. "No one else would understand what we do."

"Maybe," Atopol said, folding his arms. "And I'm not opposed to the idea; it's just . . . it's a lot to contend with on top of everything else. And it's making me think. You know," he said, after a moment's pause, "when we return to the abbey? Try to convince one of your friends to start stealing things. Just to give me hope," he proposed.

That made Gatina burst out in giggles. She finished her tea and just stared at her brother for a moment. "I might," she decided. "But that won't be until after we're finished here, if ever. Which is a pity. I was actually looking forward to the initiation the day after Midsummer. It's supposed to be nice. And I wouldn't have to study mathematics anymore."

"Father and Mother will still make you study," he warned her. "Believe me, you've got an awful lot of scholarship ahead of you before you finish your apprenticeship. So do I." He sighed.

"I suppose we can discuss it when we meet with them tonight," she agreed. "Let's go. It stopped raining."

THE MEETING WAS HELD IN THE HIDDEN FORTRESS THE FAMILY OWNED IN THE center of Falas, a mansion obscured by buildings on all sides. It had been carefully cultivated for centuries into the perfect secret retreat. There was no front door—the only way it could be reached was by a secret passage from one of the several shops around it that House Furtius had a quiet interest in. From the street, you could not tell there was a building there at all.

But inside the house was filled with the working gear of a family of shadowthieves. Costumes, weapons, supplies, and a certain amount of loot were stashed within its hidden walls. It was not a residence, save at great need, but a hidden refuge that allowed House Furtius a secure base of operations in the center of Falas Town.

Gatina had first come to the place several months before, when the Shadow Council was first convened. A portion of the maze of rooms and passageways was used for the conspiracy to meet in and prepare their operations. It was within one of those chambers that Gatina and Atopol met with their parents—and several other cell leaders.

Everyone wore masks, of course. That was for security. The participants were not entirely anonymous, but the custom was rigorously adhered to when anyone visited the secret fortress. There were seven members holding council tonight, and others came and went with messages and news while they were meeting. While some of their identities were known to the others, their father had insisted that tight protocols be observed to preserve the safety of everyone. Code names were part of that defense, but so were the masks.

Gatina's was fashioned as a kitten's face, while Atopol had a larger and more masculine version to represent him. All of those in charge of the operations in Falas Town were present, sitting around a long trestle table. And all present were wrapped in a cloak of tension that told her that there were serious things afoot. More than she could fathom, she guessed by looking at the participants through the eyeholes in her mask.

She had seen most of them before, when the Shadow Council had first been convened. Lord Hound, Lady Gull, and a few others. Some were new to her: a tall, thin man in a mask rendered to look like a black crow, a woman with a mask in the shape of a dark cloud, and a bearded man whose wolf mask blended in with the whiskers on his face. New recruits, she realized as she and Atopol took their places behind their parents.

But there was a profound strain on all of them, a sense of alarm that seemed to hang in the air as they discussed the approaching danger.

"Captain Stefan should be arriving within the next few hours," her father reported to the others around the table. "He has six Censors accompanying him. On the last three occasions he visited Falas, he lodged at the palace, at the home of an acquaintance, and at an inn near the northern docks. We have no information on which of those he might return to, or if he's planning to stay somewhere else. Regardless, we will prepare to strike tonight, if necessary, and secure that book before he has a chance to employ it. Wherever it might be.

"To that end, I can tell you that we managed to get a location spell of our own on it while it was in our possession," he said, nodding toward his children. "That means we can track it magically, and thus the captain's location, once he's within the city."

"Why not take him in the street?" one of the other masked participants asked—a woman in a fish mask that was the oddest-looking one at the table. She spoke with a distinct Sea Lord lilt in her voice.

"Because of the six Censors he's with," Hance answered. "They are all expert warmagi and fanatically devoted to the Censorate. They'd enjoy nothing better than a fight with us, out in the open, where they can use warmagic without regard to hurting bystanders. And they're expecting that sort of trouble," he reminded them. "They could call upon the City Watch, the palace guards, and Vichetral's entire army, at need. That is a fight we could not win. No, we must take the book by stealth."

"I will begin tracking it," the lady in a bird mask said, rising from the table. "Your workshop is available?"

"Of course, Lady Gull," Minnureal assured her, nodding toward the far door. "You have what you need?"

"Of course," the mage agreed, smiling under her plaster beak. "This should be simple."

"The question is, what do we do when we do locate this Censor Captain?" a stout man in a bulldog mask asked. "I have men waiting for orders, but it is difficult to prepare them if we don't know where they're going!"

"Your patience is appreciated, Lord Hound," Minnureal—known as Lady Night in these chambers—said in a businesslike manner. "As are your forces. We shall know shortly, I believe. It all depends upon what Captain Stefan considers his highest priority. We are assuming that he will travel to the Censorate's headquarters at the palace to issue his warrants and orders. We are hoping that he is confident enough to take his lodgings first. If so, then we will strike while he is there."

Gatina was impressed at how well her mother handled the gruff man, who was clearly anxious about the outcome of the operation. There was no trace of stress in her voice, and she spoke confidently about things that were unknown. It seemed very professional.

Another man, the one bearing a mask in the shape of a crow, looked at their father skeptically. He had the accent of a Sea Lord, Gatina noted.

"Lord Shadow, I was persuaded to join this endeavor because you promised thoughtful, competent leadership," he said, shaking his masked head. "Yet here we are, the very core of our effort threatened from an unanticipated source. I brought my House's magi into this fray, and thus far, they have seen little more than unimportant actions that have done nothing—nothing!—to drive the usurper from his course."

"We strive against potent opponents, Lord Crow," Gatina's father said after a moment's consideration. "Thus did I invite your aid. If the situation was not dire, then why involve you and your House? By tradition, you remain aloof from the affairs of the duchy. Yet the danger is clear enough for you to consider our proposals. Pray have the patience to see our plans through, in good faith, and judge them accordingly.

"We knew this would be no easy struggle," he continued, almost to himself. "We face a foe who places no value on human life, or liberty, or long-established rights. Vichetral seeks only to use his power to muscle his way into the void left when Duke Lenguin died. The man is determined," pronounced Shadow. "We must be doubly so, or all is lost. Yes, he has recruited the Censorate in no small way. Your House has five hundred years of experience in countering magic arrayed against it; your arcane prowess has no peer in Alshar. Are you concerned that a few Narasi and Wenshari warmagi will overcome the defenses your family has spent centuries cultivating?" Shadow asked pointedly.

"I . . . I understand," Lord Crow agreed reluctantly. "My House has given you the intelligence it has been able to gather by arcane means. Yet . . . *irionite*," Lord Crow pronounced, with awe in his voice. "If the Censorate has access to such potent arguments—"

"Then I trust your House will live up to its reputation and counter it!" Hance said in a low tone. "Either you are the embodiment of the thaumaturgic arts . . . or you are not. Now is the time in which such things are proven, before the eyes of men and the gods. If you do, indeed, conserve the power and traditions of the Magocracy, then prove it! Cowering in fear of a checkered cloak belies the repute your House claims!"

Gatina was surprised. She'd never heard her father speak so adamantly, especially in a time of crisis. There was much she did not understand about the situation, but she could see it was serious.

"I . . . We . . . That is . . ." stammered Lord Crow.

"Yes, Lord Crow, the Censorate is upon us," her father said in calm and reasonable tones. "Yes, we have no allies that we don't conjure ourselves. Yes, they are vicious and brutal. But if we do not halt their aggression here and now, we have no hope of overthrowing Vichetral."

"But . . . irionite!" whispered the man, still shaking his head. "Do you understand how powerful those fabled stones are? What chance do we have against that?"

"I wonder at the leadership that has led this conspiracy into such danger," Lord Wolf—Gatina assumed from his mask that was the bearded man's code name—said arrogantly. "My House has been involved for only a month, and we've gone from relative stability to being chased with Censors with witchstones!"

"Had it not been for this council, you would not even be aware of the danger," Lord Hound assured the man. "We invited you as much to protect you by sharing such warnings as to utilize the skills of your House against the Council of Counts. Lord Shadow has done an impressive job leading us in a short period of time. I credit his leadership for sustaining us and building our strength in the most trying of circumstances."

"Master Thinradel himself invited me to participate," Lord Wolf growled. "He would not have done so if he did not value the power of my House. I anticipated striking against the usurper, not cowering in the shadows, sniping at his knees." There was an undisguised critical tone to his voice. "When the Court Wizard summons, we come. But I see little that has been accomplished since I came. Surely, this is not the purpose in mind when Thinradel gave us this direction."

"Master Thinradel initiated this council, but he does not lead it—*I* do," her father said forcefully. "In just a few weeks, we have gone from an idea to a body with more than a dozen cells. How many have we rescued from Vichetral's grasp?"

"How many have you failed to rescue?" Lord Wolf asked sharply. "How many have been executed in front of the palace now? Falas is filled with Rhemesmen, collaborators, thugs, and now Censors. Count Vichetral still looks comfortable as he sits on Lenguin's throne!"

"And he will sit there until he wears the coronet if we do nothing!" reminded her mother pointedly. "I have every respect for Master Thinradel, but he is not here. We are. Now is not the time to discuss grand strategy; now is the time we act to preserve what strength we have gathered. What would you have done, Lord Wolf?" she taunted.

"Taken action!" the man said. "True action, not skulking in the shadows. Not planning riots and protests. Assault the palace," he suggested. "That's what we did in Farise," he recalled proudly. "And against irionite, no less. Sweep these Censors away. Put the usurper to death. Lay claim to the coronet in the name of the heir. I would have done . . . *something!*"

"But would you have succeeded?" her father countered. "Or would you have ended up under the headsman's axe yourself because Vichetral had strength you did not know about? Patience and persistence are more productive than pointless heroics, Lord Wolf. And if you fear to cross wands with the Censorate, Lord Crow, know that the Censorate has no such fear of you and your House . . . as of yet," he added. "We are being tested right now. We can only pass through this by working together and working wisely. The Council is always open to suggestions, but in the end the goal is to win, not to die trying."

"Lord Shadow has forged our entire company in just a few months," reminded the lady in the disturbing fish mask. "He has done so carefully and with great deliberation. We now know more of what happens inside the palace than Vichetral does," she pointed out. "We know which nobles lead their Houses in support of the Council of Counts, which are against it, and which will sit neutral. And we know about this record the Censors have compiled against us only because of his attentiveness. Had it not been for his foresight, we would have been awakened in the night by banging on our doors, unprepared."

While she was speaking, one of the doors around the room opened a crack. She and Atopol could see it, but most of the others did not. Atopol went to investigate and whispered to the person on the other side before returning to his place and whispering to their father.

"Word has just come that the first cell leader has been arrested," Hance sighed. "I was not anticipating this until tomorrow, but someone gave the order. He and a goodly number of his group. They are being taken north of the city," he related, "away from the palace and the docks."

"Who arrested them?" demanded Lord Wolf.

"Censors, with Vichetral's Rhemesmen guards supporting them," Atopol said, speaking for the first time. "He's a theater owner. And a clandestine mage." *Huguenin,* Gatina realized at once. *They had arrested Huguenin.* A mixture of fear and sadness washed over her, but she forced herself to remain calm and focused.

"Why north of the city?" questioned the lady with the fish mask.

"To keep them from getting rescued, perhaps," suggested Lord Hound. "It's hard to arrange a protest when no one knows where the prisoners are being kept."

"They don't want such a ruckus when the city is about to be flooded with pilgrims and celebrants of the Midsummer festival," agreed her mother. "A protest could turn into a riot if they are not careful."

"Where would they take them?" asked Lord Crow.

"There is a small watchtower complex at the top of the escarpment," Lord Hound reported. "Relian Tower, it's called. It's designed to hold the crane in defense against invaders, at need, and keep them from taking such a strategically important location. Usually, it sits empty with but a small garrison. That's where I would take them."

"That's a long way from the city proper." The crow frowned.

"It's also far less secure than the palace dungeons," her mother pointed out. As she spoke, Lady Gull returned from the workshop, a smile under her beak.

"I've located the book!" she said excitedly. "Captain Stefan is on the eastern side of the city—and heading north up the main road to the falls."

"So, it seems we know where our foe and his book might be headed." Hance nodded. "To interrogate the prisoners and add to the Censorate's store of information. That makes sense. Let us all prepare, then, to intercede and strike at our foes while we rescue our friends. Arm yourselves," he instructed. "Tonight, the Shadow Council goes to battle."

CHAPTER TWENTY-FIVE

A PUNGENT ASCENT

Ships mean hope or the hope that each of us carries. Kiera the Great took a ship from Vore to Falas, where she established our House. Her hope for a better future led her here as much as her fear of retribution for her many heists in Vore. Maintaining that hope also is a familial duty. We will build a stronger House and restore the throne to its rightful ruler.

— from Gatina's Heist Journal

"The book had already passed Northmarket Street when I began the spell," Lady Gull told them, as they studied a map of the city. Gatina tried to keep out of the way of the adults moving around the table. "Moving fast, too—likely a carriage and a team of four. At this pace, they will gain the road up the escarpment within an hour or so."

"That doesn't leave us much time," murmured Lord Hound. "I can pursue with a few men on horses for support, but no more than a half dozen."

"I can add five," Lord Crow said unexpectedly. "Two are trained warmagi."

"Give me an hour, and I'll get you four more," Lord Wolf agreed. "Perhaps more."

"I'm certain that they will not begin aggressive interrogation immediately," their mother offered. "We should have a short time before they are ready for that. But we must make all haste."

"We shall make two sorties," decided Hance. "The first will locate and raid the prisoners. The second will attack the Censor Captain with the object of stealing and destroying his book. Lord Hound, I name you captain of the first sortie. I will command the second."

Gatina's head whirled as the tension in the room increased but the acrimony decreased. Now that there was an objective, the Shadow

Council had come together and was moving. While their father discussed the details of the prisoner raid with the others, their mother took the two of them aside.

"We cannot wait for everyone to arrive before we take action," she said quietly in the far corner of the room. "I want you two to go now and go quickly. Find out where the Censor Captain is lodging and watch the place until we arrive. *Just* watch!" she ordered sternly. "Cat, you remember the inn we went through on the road north a few months ago? That's where we'll be coming to. The innkeeper is a friend of ours. We will meet you there. You can also leave word there where you discover he's staying. We will make further plans then.

"Now assemble your gear for a heist," she directed. "Working blacks. Including shadowblades. I don't expect you will use them, but I want you to have some protection. Don't worry about the prisoners—others will see to them. Your assignment is locating and stealing and destroying that book once your father and I arrive. Do not concern yourself with anything else. Are there questions?"

"That's . . . that's a lot of responsibility on us," Atopol said doubtfully.

"If I didn't think you could do it, I wouldn't send you," their mother said patiently but firmly. "Stealing that book is going to require stealth. We could send warmagi against Captain Stefan for days, and he would protect it fiercely. It needs to be stolen while he is distracted. This raid will provide that distraction. He will not be expecting an attack on the book while he contends with the raid. And don't worry: your father and I will be along shortly to lead the raid and direct you further. For now, you two merely *observe*," she stressed. "I trust you to do that. I would appreciate knowing what we're walking into when we get there."

They both nodded and embraced their mother before Atopol took one last glance at the map, then led Gatina into the recesses of the hidden mansion, to the storehouses and armories contained within. Both had worn their working blacks to the Shadow Council meeting. They hurriedly added items to their kits, calling out suggestions to each other as they prepared.

"How are we getting there?" Gatina asked as they began down the long passageway that led into the city.

"Across the lake," Atopol decided. "We need either horses or a boat to make it to the escarpment. It's easier to steal a boat," he reasoned.

As it happened, it was easy to steal a boat, much to Gatina's amusement. And far easier than when she'd stolen a horse. While the long wharves that jutted into the lake did employ Watchmen, the tired old man who was in charge of keeping the bobbing boats of fishermen and bargemen safe was sleeping peacefully as the two sneaked through the wooden gate to the docks. Atopol chose a small, narrow punt and borrowed a couple of oars from a nearby rowboat before they cast off into the misty gloom of the lake.

The recent rains had kept the air humid, and tendrils of fog laced the surface of the dark water as her brother began rowing. The distant falls roared in the background, adding a constant flow of moisture in the air that seemed to spawn the clouds of fog. The skies to the west were overcast, as another line of storms was approaching, but the eastern side of the lake was clear, revealing a field of stars across the night sky. The waxing crescent moons were darting in and out of the clouds in the west, occasionally brightening the surface of the lake with an eerie reflection that picked out the fog and transformed it. She preferred the stars to the mists, however, and kept watching the west.

Gatina realized that she knew all of their names now and took pleasure at picking them out in her head. She began to appreciate just how much she had learned in such a short period of time at Palomar—astronomy, mathematics, history, the liturgy—and that didn't even count the magic, shadowmagic, and swordplay. At the time, she reflected, it had seemed boring . . . as boring as her alias, Avorrita.

But now she had a new appreciation of the classes, the books, the observations, and the trials she and her fellow Nocturns had completed. She was even a little saddened that it was unlikely she would return to the abbey for the Nocturn initiation at Midsummer. Her exciting life and flirtation with danger took precedence. But there was no denying that she had improved herself through her experience at the abbey. She understood the stars above her in the Blessed Darkness for what they were, not mere lights in the sky. Her perspective on the universe had grown dramatically, and she looked at them with new wonder and appreciation.

As if to acknowledge her realization, a shooting star flashed overhead for one splendid moment. Gatina was so pleased by it that she didn't even call it to Atopol's attention. She indulgently kept the experience for herself.

Atopol bent his back to the oars, steering toward the wide peninsula that jutted out between the two giant falls. With every stroke of the oars, the sound got a little louder and the mists became thicker. It was a little scary, she realized as they made their way across the gloomy surface, to be steering so close to the unfathomable amount of river water that spilled over the escarpment and into the lake. When the moonlight returned for a few moments, she could see them clearly: two massive pillars of falling water quite sufficient to dash the tiny boat to bits if they were to venture under them.

Atopol stopped after about a mile of rowing, his chest heaving with exertion.

"I can help row, you know," Gatina informed him, as he lay back in the boat to catch his breath.

"No . . . you can't," Atopol gasped. "You just don't have the strength and mass. It's more difficult than it looks. Trust me!" he moaned.

She knew he was right, but she resented it. Atopol was strong, and he had taken much practice in rowing when he was using his bargeman alias. While she had spent her time learning to survive on the streets of Falas Town, he had paddled and poled his way across the lake and up and down the river. He knew what he was doing when it came to rowing, and she did not. While that was a tough admission to make to herself, she had to accept her limitations.

Atopol stopped twice more on their journey, his shoulders heaving as he tried to recover from the exertion. But they were making good progress. The roar of the falls was loud enough at that point that they had to raise their voices to be heard at the other end of the boat.

"Why are we going this way?" Gatina asked during the third pause. Atopol tiredly gestured to the northwest, where Falas Town sprawled to the edge of the water.

"If we try to land over there," he explained, "we still have to travel up the switchback, and that will take more than an hour. I'm going to dock at the station between the falls, where the barges come in."

"There's a path that goes up from there?" Gatina asked, surprised.

"No"—he grinned—"but there is a crane that runs day and night, hauling cargo and the occasional small boat from the bottom to the top. We'll go up that way and be there more directly."

Gatina's jaw dropped. "We're going to *ride up on the crane?*" she asked in disbelief.

"That's the plan," he nodded. "I've been to the place twice as a bargeman. I've seen how they operate the thing, and I think we can hitch a ride pretty easily. No one is guarding it, really, because the only people there are the stevedores and the bargemen who use it. We'll just sneak aboard one of the cargoes and be at the top of the falls in no time!"

Gatina stared at the dark cliffside between the two columns of white. She couldn't even see the crane's massive cables in the gloom or the structure itself overhead. But she could imagine it. And she could imagine dangling from it. It was not a soothing vision.

"If you say so," she sighed reluctantly. "Are you certain it's safe?"

"Hundreds of tons of cargo go up that thing every day," he assured her. "The chains that hold it are as thick as my arm. We'll be fine. All right, I think I'm rested enough to get us there now," he said as he grasped the handles of the oars once again. "Besides, if we took the long way around, you'd have to carry me after this. I'm beat!"

Nonetheless, he put his back into the motion and propelled the little punt forward once again. The dark mass of the rocky peninsula loomed in the mists, only a few lights from the cargo station glowing in the night. Gatina could start to hear the rhythmic splash of waves against the rocks, in addition to the loud, sustained roar of the falls

Finally, after steering to avoid the main passage to the docks that barges took to load and unload their cargoes, Atopol found a relatively gentle portion of the peninsula on the western side where he could bring the boat in safely. Gatina nimbly sprang out of the punt as it scraped the bottom and tied the rope to a nearby boulder before helping her exhausted brother get to shore. He spent several moments sprawled across one of the rocks, recovering from the exertion of the crossing, before he was ready to proceed.

"They say that the original lords of Falas used to bring their prisoners up to the top of the falls to execute them by tossing them over the side to land on these rocks," he informed her while he was resting. "That's about how I feel right now."

"That seems an awfully long way to go just for an execution," Gatina observed as she stared up at the stark cliffside of the escarpment. "But it would be effective."

"It's probably just a bargeman's tale—believe me, they tell some whoppers," he assured her as he struggled to his feet. "Let's go. The loading platform isn't far."

At this hour, the platform was nearly deserted, with only a few stevedores present to load and unload the great nets that descended and ascended the cliff. There were two sides to the crane operation, Gatina saw as they crept closer to the important complex. They both operated at the same time, using each side's cargoes as counterweights to help raise the other.

"There's a kind of horse mill at the top," Atopol explained as they surveyed the site. Six men were waiting around, smoking pipes as they waited for the next arrival in the fog. "It powers the crane. These are used to add weight to balance the thing so it doesn't wear out the horses too quickly," he said, patting a boulder.

Not a boulder, exactly, Gatina realized. She and her brother were hiding behind big round stone weights, like millstones, that were lined up and waiting for use.

"So, we're going to ride the next one up?" she asked, anxiety over the idea starting to creep into her mind. "Won't they notice us?"

"No, if we can get close to the back side of the complex." He nodded. "They don't pay much attention to it once it's loaded. Besides, who would be foolish enough to try to take a ride on that thing?" He grinned.

"Just . . . us," Gatina admitted.

"Exactly. Come on; we can get closer if we move around to the other side of these weights."

Gatina didn't see the huge net descend through the mists until it was only a hundred feet above them, appearing as a dark blot against the night sky. It lowered slowly as the crane hoisted the other cable into the air. She watched, fascinated, as the great net dropped, foot by foot, until it came to rest on the great wooden platform.

The moment it touched, the crew went to action: one man climbed aboard the cargo and unfastened the great net from a hook the size of his entire body, while others pulled the net open. Then all of them hurried to remove the cargo—great bundles of cotton, she guessed—out of the net and onto a loading platform where it could be loaded onto a barge in the morning.

As soon as the last bale was removed, the stevedores began loading the net with barrels from another platform. Gatina watched with interest as they rolled the casks down a ramp and into the center, where they were carefully stacked three high in a circle.

"What is that?" she asked. "Wine? Olive oil? Glue?" Gatina recalled the casks of glue and tar in the warehouse that was the scene of her first heist. The barrels were about that size.

"Maybe vinegar? I don't know. Let's go," Atopol urged in her ear, patting her shoulder. "They're almost ready to clear the platform and hoist the cargo. We'll only have a few moments."

Gatina nodded and followed her brother into the night. They threaded their way around the stacks of crates and bales awaiting shipment until they were on the cliff side of the compound. The foreman called for the platform to be cleared and then fastened the net back on the hook. He called for it to be pulled taut, and someone rang a bell loudly enough to be heard far above, over the roar of the falls. The great chain inched upward a few feet until all the slack from the net was taken up, and the barrels were jammed together within.

"Now!" Atopol said, and began running toward the cargo. Gatina followed, appreciating that the great dangling pendulum obscured their approach from the notice of the stevedores. She began climbing up the net as soon as she reached it, Atopol scaling it halfway before stopping.

The thick ropes were easy enough to provide purchase and holding still on the gently swaying load was simple . . . until the smell hit her.

She had never smelled anything like it. As her face was pressed against the net, a foul odor emanated from the cargo, so sickeningly putrid she had to steel herself against retching. As bad as it was, she managed to keep her composure and keep silent while the workmen prepared for the crane to lift up the cargo. When she felt the massive load shift and the ground began falling away under her, she and her brother scrambled to the top of the load and secured themselves just under the giant iron hook.

"What . . . what is that *smell?*" she demanded as soon as she could breathe again.

"This must be garum," Atopol said with a mirthless chuckle as he patted one of the barrels.

"Garum? What's garum?" she asked, feeling ill.

"A fish sauce made by the Sea Lords and prized for its flavor," Atopol informed her as he made himself more comfortable. "It's mostly sea brine, coriander, a bit of garlic . . . and putrefying fish. Sardines, usually, but different recipes add oysters, shrimp, or other fish. Even a couple of squid."

"And people *eat* that?" Gatina said, appalled.

"People pay good coin to import it," Atopol assured her. "It's used sparingly, of course, but a few drops does add dimension to a cook's preparation. But when you have this much of it together in one place, it's . . ."

"Revolting?" Gatina offered. "Disgusting? Smelly? Darkness, Cat, the sewers of Falas didn't smell this bad!" she declared, stifling the urge to cough. "Every breath I take is . . . foul!"

"It won't last long," he promised. "It's going to be a short ride. But it saves us walking uphill for a few hours. These boots weren't made for walking," he reminded her, patting his foot.

"I'm not certain that it was worth the trade," she said, shaking her head. "This is worse than putting slugs in my hair. Rotting fish sauce? *Really?*" she complained.

"It's highly prized up in the Great Vale and beyond," he counseled her. "In fact, the bargemen say a barrel of it doubles in price after it makes the trip up the cliffs. We're probably sitting on fifty ounces of gold right now. I doubt you've had a richer means of transport."

"It smells disgusting!" she complained. "It's in my nose . . . my clothes. . . my *hair!*"

"You'll get used to it shortly," he promised. "Just one more romantic adventure in the life of an apprentice shadowthief."

"How can you sneak up on someone when you smell like rotting fish? I'm starting to reconsider taking holy orders," she joked. Then she sighed and settled in, taking the chance to view the great lake from her increasing vantage.

The view really was magnificent, particularly when the clouds allowed the crescent moon to illuminate the great lake below. The dark, misty expanse of water stretched out below her like a carpet, while the opposite shore shone with a few timid lights. There were few folk awake at this time of night in Falas Town, but a city that size always had men working through the night, in need of light.

With the great falls on either side of them like two watery columns, it was actually very pretty, she decided. She could pick out the dockyards, the spires of temples in the center of the city, and the sprawling Ducal Palace on the southern shore, where their enemy, Count Vichetral, currently resided. She gained a new appreciation of just how large the city was from there. The lights seemed to stretch in all directions, giving her an idea of the size of the capital. Soon, she realized that she barely smelled the pungent sauce anymore; her nose had become almost blind to the odor.

"When we get to the top, we're going to have to move quickly," Atopol counseled as they were nearing the top of the lift. "We'll only have a few seconds before the foreman swings the cargo around for off-loading. The moment he does, we have to jump and run and hide, and hope we aren't noticed."

"Won't we be kind of obvious?" she asked skeptically.

"Who in their right mind would ever consider riding up the cliffs like this?" he countered. "One little slip and you'd plummet to your death. Those workmen aren't paying attention to that sort of thing. They're too busy avoiding getting crushed by the loads they move to keep watch for stowaways . . . especially on a shipment of pungent fish sauce. Trust me," he assured, "as long as we don't make any noise when we dismount, we should be fine."

"What about . . . the unnoticeability spell Lady Silva taught us?" Gatina asked hesitantly.

Atopol snorted. "Do you really think you can raise sufficient power for that? Have you ever tried it in the field?" he asked. "No, I think plain, ordinary stealth is the answer. We just need to be sneaky."

Gatina sighed. "I can do that," she decided. "Just tell me when."

They were silent as the great, creaking crane above them swung the net and its barrels back from the cliffside and toward another wooden platform, surrounded by yet more cargo. The two of them saw which side the stevedores were waiting on and made their way to the opposite. When the swaying load swung into position, they both leaped off the net and rolled their way into the maze of barrels, crates, sacks, and bales.

When they had dived behind the merchandise, Gatina instantly turned and checked to see if they'd been spotted. There was no cry, however, and the stevedores proceeded to unload the garum sauce with the same steady pace their fellows had taken below.

"That was . . . fun, if smelly," Atopol said as they started to creep around the piles of cargo. Both had their sable cloaks assisting in concealing them in the darkness, and both had pulled their hoods up to obscure their faces.

"It was . . . educational," Gatina grumbled. "Where to now?"

"According to that map, we should be within the confines of Relian Tower," Atopol informed her. "There's a great wall that blocks off this portion of the island we're on. It's to keep out any possible invaders who want to take this place. The crane is a strategically important asset. The Duke gets a small cut of the fees from every load that goes up or down."

Gatina surveyed the large stockpiles of goods and saw that there were warehouses for temporary storage as well as a short road that led to the docks on the upper river. There was a circular area for the horse mill, boasting a huge wooden capstan and four teams of working horses whose effort helped drag the cargo up and down the cliffs. There was, indeed, a tall stone wall, complete with crenelations, that spanned the breadth of the island. Behind it was a range of halls that took up most of the length of the wall. And in the middle was one squat four-story stone tower that looked functional, not ornamental. It also looked nearly deserted.

But there was activity around the gatehouse next to it, she could see: four wagons and carriages were parked on the roadway where tomorrow, she assumed, teamsters and carters would line up to receive their shipments. And in the distance she could see long stone bridges spanning the river—the rivers, actually, she decided, as the mighty Mandros River forked itself on the rocky promontory before it tumbled over the cliffs. One went east and one led west, she saw. Beyond, on the far banks, were small villages that served the busy trade provided by the crane and the barges headed north.

"Those don't look like regular carts for cargo," Atopol observed from their hidden vantage point. "They're enclosed, for one thing."

A moment later, a man walked between the wagons—wearing a checkered cloak. Behind him, two guardsmen were leading a prisoner, hands bound behind him and a bag over his head, out of the back of one of the carts.

"Yes, this is where they're bringing them," Gatina decided. "I can see why, too. No one would ever know they were here if they came in the night. The noise of the falls is too loud to hear any shouting or screaming, I'm guessing."

"And if they need to dispose of the bodies, they can just chuck them over the falls." Atopol nodded. "As long as they don't get caught on the chain," he added.

"What chain?" Gatina asked, confused.

"There are two great chains that stretch across the rivers to catch any wayward barges that pass under the bridges, to keep them from plummeting over the falls," he explained. "I heard about that as a bargeman, too. They're made of old crane cables that are too worn out to lift anymore. They've kept a few horrific accidents from happening over the years. Look, they're bringing out more of them," he said as another carriage pulled up. "They must have been arresting people since sundown."

One by one, the prisoners were taken from the wagons and huddled into a group, under the watchful eye of the guardsmen. All had their faces obscured by bags, and no one was allowed to talk—they watched as one of the guardsmen beat a helpless prisoner who ignored that command. Gatina winced as the soldier used a truncheon to strike the wiggling captive in the shoulder and shout at him to be silent.

"There must be a dozen of them so far," she counted. "Probably some of the theater troupe."

"Hard to tell unless they burst out singing," Atopol noted. "But they are our people for certain. Anyone the Censorate is taking captive is our people," he reminded her.

Then Gatina's eye noticed something in the gloom. She wasn't certain at first, but at least one of the prisoners appeared to be familiar to her. She quickly employed magesight to take a closer look, and grew more confident. The size was right, for one thing, and the man's build. While she could not see his face, she did note a ring on his hand that she'd seen before.

"Cat, I think that one is Huguenin!" she declared in a loud whisper. "Look at his hands! His shoulders!"

"I think you're right." Atopol nodded. "I recognize those shoes from yesterday. Nice ones, too," he added.

"Where do you think they'll take them?" she asked.

"There's likely a dungeon in the tower," he answered after considering for a few moments. "They usually have underground storerooms and such. That would be a good place to keep them until they're ready to be questioned."

"That's . . . that's not good," Gatina decided.

"Since when is a dungeon ever good?" Atopol asked rhetorically.

"I mean that once they are in the dungeon, we're going to have a time getting them back out," she reasoned.

"Well, yes, that's why we have an armed sortie coming to break them out," he pointed out patiently.

"Yes, but it would be far easier to free some of them—all right, maybe just Huguenin—before they get locked up. He's our cousin," she reminded him. "If we can get him free, then he might be able to help with the rest."

"That's . . . that's going to be hard, Kitten," Atopol said, frowning in the darkness.

"So was riding up the cliffs with barrels of rotten fish sauce, but we did it," she pointed out. "If we distracted the guards, one of us could get him through the piles of crates and . . . and . . ." she said, at a loss for what to do next.

"What, throw him over the wall of the castle?" snorted Atopol. "We're inside a fortress of sorts, Kitten. That wall stretches from river to river. The bridges are on the other side of the gate," he pointed out. "We could try to send him down the crane, I suppose, but a couple of rings of that bell and they'd grab him as soon as he landed."

"There has to be a way," she said, shaking her head as she stared at her poor cousin. There were more prisoners being unloaded now, under the eye of the Censor standing guard and the other Watchmen. She racked her brain, trying to think of the situation as a problem to be solved, not a dire matter that raised her anxiety at the expense of her intellect.

Then it came to her. It was a dangerous idea . . . but no more dangerous than ascending the cliffs by crane.

"I know what to do," she said with false certainty. "Hear me out . . ." she began, and then described the plan her imagination had conjured.

"That's crazy, Kitten," Atopol said, shaking his head.

"Do you have a better plan?" she asked. "We have to get out of here anyway, to report to Shadow. This way, we're just taking someone with us."

"Someone whose profession involves attracting attention, not avoiding it," her brother reminded her. "He's a Blue Mage, not a shadowmage."

"It really only matters if he's brave enough," she said firmly. "And considering the alternatives . . ." she said, nodding toward the prisoners, where another captive was getting the attention of the Watchman's truncheon.

Atopol sighed. "All right. I just hope Huguenin can swim. Because if this goes wrong, he's going to have to."

"Can it work?" she prodded. "Realistically?"

"Yes, I think it can," he admitted. "But it's a crazy plan. I just want to establish that before we go and do it. And this is *not* what Mother told us to do."

"Understood," she acknowledged. "Now let's go save our poor cousin!"

CHAPTER TWENTY-SIX

DANCING ON A CHAIN

*Daring and boldness are the servants of the thief and the mage.
When the time comes to act, do so fiercely.*
— *from **The Shield of Darkness**,*
written by Kiera the Great

IT DIDN'T TAKE LONG FOR THE SIBLINGS TO ENACT THEIR PLAN. WHILE ATOPOL sneaked closer to the prisoners through the maze of crates and bulging sacks, Gatina stealthily moved to the other side of the prisoners, beyond the wagons that were now departing—likely to go collect more prisoners. It was her task to provide a distraction.

She found what she was looking for in the very barrels of garum that she and Atopol had ridden to the top of the cliff. They had been stacked near the end of the raised loading platform by the stevedores—as far away from the workmen's noses as possible, she noted. Each cask was only two feet tall, and they'd made a neat row of them across the boards before chalking a number on the side of one of the front-facing ones. She had no doubt that they would be among the first loads picked up in the morning. No one wanted the stench of fermenting fish around longer than necessary.

But that odor was the very thing that made them ideal as a distraction.

Quietly, she mounted the platform behind the barrels, trying not to retch as she became reacquainted with the smell. She tried to ignore her discomfort as she considered the possibilities of a distraction. The Watchmen were mostly congregated in front of the gatehouse as they received the prisoners, standing around talking and casually leaning on their spears. The Censor looked bored, while the prisoners struggled in their bonds behind him.

Time to liven up the party, Gatina told herself as she silently tipped one of the garum barrels over on its side and lined it up with the gatehouse.

From this vantage, she reasoned, she should be able to get enough speed on the thing to accomplish her purpose.

It took a healthy shove to get the barrel moving, and as she heard the liquid within sloshing around, she put her feet against the others to grant her the leverage she needed to speed it across the platform . . . and then down on the ground . . . and then across the cobbled yard. By the time it had rolled over to the carriages, it had picked up more speed than she'd anticipated. It was also leaking badly from the impact and making a racket.

But when it careened off a post set near the roadway, things got really interesting: it glanced to the side, the lid becoming badly unsealed, and it began spinning as it continued its roll, splashing the dark liquid every-where—on the horses, on the guards, and across the paving stones.

Cries of surprise and dismay filled the air as Gatina retreated from her position, confident that she had not been spotted. She moved quickly through the stacks of goods, ensuring that she still enjoyed cover from the men, and waited for the inevitable investigation into what had caused the barrel to spill to begin. The sudden motion and the loud noise were too much for the team of horses closest to the rapidly approaching cask; when it came too close, one of the horses reared in a panic. Its hoof came down squarely on the barrel, shattering it into pieces. Sticky, stinky, wet pieces.

She had to stifle a giggle as she heard the groans of dismay and disgust as the entire compound was filled with the scent of fermenting fish and coriander. A few of the guards even vomited. And no one at all was paying attention to the prisoners.

She watched from her new vantage point with magesight as the figure they'd identified as Huguenin was suddenly dragged back into the stacks and bales without so much as disturbing the prisoners on either side of him. Nodding to herself in satisfaction, Gatina cautiously moved back around to where she had started, near the river wall of the fortress. It was, as Atopol pointed out, relatively unguarded, as it was built as close to the bank as possible to prevent a boat from landing there without the permission of the theoretical defenders of the place. There was one empty turret along the entire crenelated stretch of wall, and the interior side had not been properly finished. There were plenty of handholds that allowed a thief to climb, he'd pointed out.

But not necessarily an aging Blue Mage, she knew. Huguenin might be fit for a middle-aged man, but climbing that wall was a feat that required practice, strength, and experience. She doubted the theater owner had a sufficiency of any of those to escape. Instead, she quietly stole a length of strong rope as she slid through the aisles of the stockpile. By the time she arrived back where Atopol was hiding with their recaptured prisoner, she had uncoiled it and prepared it for use.

Huguenin did not look well when she arrived. Atopol had cut his bonds and removed the flour bag that had been put over his head, but apparently, the man had received a beating or two on his way to this remote place. His face was bruised and bloody, she saw, and his face wore an expression that mixed anger with confusion.

"What's going on?" he asked, looking around wildly.

"Be quiet," Atopol urged in a harsh whisper. "You're being rescued!"

"I am?" he asked, surprised.

"We were sent by the Shadow Council," agreed Gatina. "We need to get you out of here, though. Before they discover you are missing."

"I see," Huguenin said simply as he rubbed his wrists. Then he seemed to recognize them for the first time. "Cat? Kitten? They sent *you* to rescue me?"

"Not . . . precisely. We'll explain when we're safe," Atopol insisted as he took the rope from Gatina with a grateful nod and then began to scale the nearby wall. "Right now, be quiet and still!"

Huguenin nodded and began to look more animated. While her brother climbed the wall, Gatina continued to watch the commotion near the gatehouse. More guards were vomiting now, she saw, and the horses were highly agitated. One of the guardsmen was already moving cautiously over to where the barrels of garum were, his spear ready. By the time Atopol had reached the top of the wall, the man shrugged and called out that there was no one there.

"Time to go, Cousin!" Gatina said as she saw the end of the rope descend from the wall. "Can you climb a rope? Or do we need to haul you up?"

The mage glanced at the swinging rope. "Of course I can climb." He nodded. "But I haven't in years. Still, the alternative motivates me. Dear gods, what is that smell?" he asked suddenly as a breeze wafted the stench of the spilled fish sauce over to them.

"About twenty silver coins' worth of garum," Gatina muttered. "Let's go!"

"Wait!" the mage said suddenly. He then closed his eyes, waved his hands . . . and cast a spell. There was a flash of energy she could only see with magesight.

"What was that?" Gatina asked, confused.

"A simple psychomantic glyph that will convince anyone who encounters it that there is no way we left by this route," he explained. "Now we can go!"

Gatina helped him begin his climb and waited anxiously as the man pulled himself up, hand over hand while steadying his feet on the wall. He eagerly held up his hand when he reached the top, and Atopol pulled him to the walkway behind the crenels.

It was time to go, Gatina knew, and she followed Huguenin's path. Using a rope to climb almost seemed like cheating to her, but she knew it was best to be expedient in escaping. She joined her brother and their freed captive in moments.

"I cannot believe you two children managed to do that so quickly," Huguenin said admiringly.

"We're not ordinary children," Gatina pointed out.

"And we do this sort of thing all the time," agreed Atopol. "The last time we were here in Falas, we rescued about a hundred people from a gang of criminals, if you recall. One actor? That's nothing."

Huguenin nodded and managed a small grin. "Well, I thank you for the consideration! Where to now?"

"Over the wall," Atopol directed as he coiled up the rope and then tossed it down the other side of the wall. "Thence to the river's edge."

"You have a boat waiting?" the mage asked, surprised.

"Sadly, no," Atopol admitted. "But Kitten had a plan. A stupidly dangerous, crazy plan. So, we're going to do that," he said reluctantly.

"What kind of plan?" he asked suspiciously. "Does it involve . . . going over the falls?" Even in the darkness, it was clear that Huguenin was not eager for that plan.

"Only if we mess up," Gatina assured him. "You can swim?"

"As well as I can climb a rope," he agreed.

"Both skills might be useful in the rest of our escape," Gatina informed him as Atopol disappeared over the wall. "Just try to hang on and keep up."

By the time the guards were picking up the shards of the ruined cask, Gatina had untied the rope and joined the other two on the other side of the wall, where they were both staring at the wide expanse of swiftly moving water.

"You know, the western fork is smaller," Huguenin pointed out unhelpfully.

"Shall we go back through the castle, then?" Atopol mocked. "There it is!" he said suddenly as he pointed in the misty gloom.

"What?" demanded the mage.

"Our means of escape," her brother revealed. "See that heavy stone there? There is a chain attached to it. It runs across the entire river. We're going to cross it," he proposed.

"We are going to die, then," Huguenin said, shaking his head.

"Not tonight, we won't," Gatina assured him as she began tying one end of the rope around her waist. "We're going to cling very carefully to that chain and walk across it. Atopol thinks it's not very deep under the water."

"It couldn't be, if it's designed to catch a runaway barge," he reasoned as Gatina handed him the rest of the rope. He quickly tied the middle portion around Huguenin's waist and then the farther end to his own. "We should be able to essentially walk over it . . . sort of."

"You're right." Huguenin nodded thoughtfully as he peered at the end of the chain in the gloom. "This really is a crazy plan."

"This? You should see how we got here. Would you prefer to try your chances with the Censorate?" Gatina proposed.

Huguenin looked back at the wall of the fortress and then at the stone that anchored the chain. He shook his head. "No. Drowning has got to be a more peaceful death than torture and imprisonment. Besides, I hear the food is terrible in dungeons."

"Let's go, then." Atopol nodded. If he was scared of the crossing, he didn't show it. Gatina tried not to show it either, even as she questioned her own plan.

Atopol went first, wading into the cool river water up to his knees while he clutched the great links of the chain. "Hang on for your lives," he directed as the force of the current started to push against his knees. "If one of us gets loose, the other two hang on until we can pull them back and they can grab the chain. Keep the rope as taut as possible between us so no one gets too far. It's only about a hundred feet or so," he reasoned as he stared into the darkness. "I think we can make it."

With a groan, Huguenin plunged into the water after him, clinging to the chain as he went.

Gatina followed, her small hands barely able to grasp the huge iron links. The water was cold, compared to the humid summer air, and at first, it felt refreshing. Then the current took hold. The great Mandros

River was notoriously placid in most places it flowed through, allowing ample barge traffic to ply its length for hundreds of miles. But as it came to the great escarpment, it narrowed, split, and increased its flow appreciably. Gatina was only twenty feet out when the bottom dropped away, and the full force of the mighty river pushed against her.

She felt like a feather in a windstorm as she desperately clung to the chain below her. It was a testament to how powerful the river was that the massive iron chain began to move under her as the ebb and flow of the water pushed against it. On shore, at its anchor point, it had seemed as immovable as if it had been welded there.

Fear rose in her throat as she fought against the current, struggled to keep hold of the chain, and labored to keep her head above water. It was clear that if she let go even for an instant, the current would sweep her away. She was a strong swimmer, but this close to the falls, she knew it would only take an instant to see her flung over the cliff like a floating stick.

So, she kept moving forward. She barely felt the pull of the rope that tied her to Huguenin, the current was so strong. But there were times when that tightness pulled her forward just enough for her cold hands to grasp the next link of the chain.

Near the center of the river, a new problem emerged: though the current was not quite as strong there, the chain dipped much lower in the water. There was no way she could grasp it with her hands and keep her head above the surface. For a few horrific moments, she had to hold her breath and swim, using her hands to pull her forward. But the chain quickly descended to the point where that was impractical. She had to use her feet to navigate the swaying chain, each step bringing her to a new link.

It was terrifying. Her chin was barely above the water, and every step she took threatened to pinch her feet between the great lengths of the chain. Only the constant tugging of the rope compelled her to move forward.

And then the worst happened. She felt the rope pull her more than the current and heard a wail of dismay from her brother in the gloom as Huguenin lost his grip and began to drift away. All Gatina could do was plant her feet within the great links and grasp the rope, desperately trying to pull her cousin back. For several harrowing moments, she struggled, every muscle in her legs and arms straining to hold the position. She could feel the powerful force of the current as it tried to whisk Huguenin away into the night.

But slowly, bit by bit, Atopol moved forward and pulled on the rope behind him. Huguenin was swimming desperately back to the safety of the chain. It seemed to take hours as he struggled . . . but at last he managed to grab the chain again. Gatina relaxed the tiniest bit.

"Sorry!" the mage called in the night. Gatina didn't respond. She was exhausted, and they were only halfway across. But she pressed forward, moving her aching foot to the next length of chain.

It was like dancing in molasses on the back of a great, indifferent serpent, sometimes. There were areas where, inexplicably, it was easier to move against the current, and she could make quicker progress. There were other parts where just forcing her foot forward to the next link seemed impossible . . . until she did it. It was an effort in willpower, harder than anything she'd ever done in magic or thievery or swordplay.

But eventually, the chain started to rise again, after they crossed the middle of the river. For a brief while, progress was slightly easier. The pull of the rope helped guide her from one link to the next and to the next until it became easier to reach down and grasp the chain again than it was to use her feet. The idea that the trial was nearly over helped propel her forward, and a burst of energy allowed her to fight the increasingly strong current as they got closer to the eastern bank.

The riverside on the opposite shore was not nearly as rocky as the promontory they had departed from. It was steeper, however, and the anchor stone for the chain was higher up. Atopol managed to stumble to the shallows but was forced to climb up the chain to reach the bank. From there he was able to pull Huguenin up with the rope, and the two of them managed to tug Gatina up the steep bank to the shore.

For ten minutes, the three of them just lay in the grass and rocks of the shoreline, gasping for breath as they recovered from their ordeal. Gatina stared blankly at the sky, the stars swimming above her like old friends. No one spoke. No one had the energy to speak after the exertions of crossing the Mandros. They just lay still, breath heaving, letting their abused muscles take some rest.

Finally, Huguenin managed to comment.

"That was the stupidest, most dangerous thing I've ever done in a long life filled with danger and stupidity," he remarked, raising his head slightly.

"You're welcome," Atopol gasped.

"I feel ten days dead," he continued, as he pulled himself up to a sitting position. "Really, I don't know how we survived. I didn't expect to."

"Cats are survivors," Gatina offered as she painfully pushed herself to her knees. She was completely soaked in river water, but she didn't care. Just being alive seemed a victory after the chain.

"So you are," Huguenin agreed. "And don't mistake me: I'm incredibly grateful for the rescue. But next time, could we just flee on horseback and get shot at by archers? It seems that would be less effort than . . . this."

"I'll make a note of it," Atopol groaned as he, too, pulled himself up.

"Was there a plan for after the rescue?" Huguenin asked. "Or should we just wait for a tea shop to open up somewhere and get some breakfast?"

"We're to go to an inn at the village, the sign of the Wayward Turtle," Atopol reported. "We're to keep watch on the fortress and wait for the rescue sortie to arrive. And see when Captain Stefan arrives," he added.

"He should be here by dawn," Huguenin said, finishing his sentence with an unexpected yawn. "I overheard the guards speaking with the Censor who arrested me. Indeed, I overheard a great many things during my arrest, though they tried to obscure what they were saying.

"But we're hardly dressed appropriately to pass as simple travelers," Huguenin pointed out. "You two look like . . . well, thieves, and I appear to be a barfly who narrowly survived drowning. We need new clothes. Dry ones, preferably."

"I'll handle that," Atopol volunteered.

"How?" asked Huguenin, surprised. "You know of a good tailor in town? Open at this hour?"

"I'll steal them." Atopol shrugged.

"Ah. Of course, you will. Well, we're in . . . Eastbridge?" he asked, naming the village at the top of the falls. "Eastbridge . . . Well, my kitties, one advantage of having lived in the same place for most of your life is that you eventually get to know everyone in town. On the scenic western side of this hamlet, just south of the Market Square, you will find a row of handsome homes of the gentry who find Eastbridge rural enough to please their sensibilities and close enough to Falas Town to indulge their cultural desires. There, if you make a search, you will find the third house down from the market, the residence of Lady Paladine, of House Merester, who fancies herself a patroness of the performing arts.

"If memory serves, she and her family spend their summers on holiday at the seaside with her sister," Huguenin recalled. "She's absolutely insufferable as a critic of drama, but she does have impeccable taste. Please rob her," he instructed Atopol. "Rob the daylights out of her. She should have in her wardrobe something sufficient for each of us, I believe. And if you see any knickknacks you fancy, by all means, steal those as well."

Atopol blinked. "Really?"

"I must be polite to the woman for social reasons, but she's a horrible person who deserves a bit of misfortune. Nor will she miss it—she and her brood own a number of enterprises around Falas. But she once said I wasn't manly enough to portray the Black Duke in Giero's magnificent play *The Matadine Rose*, and I've never forgiven her for that," he said defiantly.

"Very well." Atopol nodded. "Kitten, watch the bridge and road while I'm gone to see if the Censorate finally shows up. I'll be back shortly."

"And take nothing plum-colored!" Huguenin insisted as her brother slunk away through the shadows. "It's unflattering to my complexion!"

Gatina stifled a giggle. They had just won a struggle for their lives, and her cousin Huguenin was concerned about his wardrobe.

"You children are amazing," he sighed as he settled back into the grass. "Far better than my own children."

Gatina was surprised. "You have children?"

"My kitten, I may be an Andrusine, but I know my duty to my House; I not only have children—three spiteful little brats—but I have a wife whom I married and promised to make happy. As she is happiest when I am far, far away from her, I have done my best to satisfy her requirements."

"Three children." Gatina nodded as she pulled herself into a position to watch the road in the misty gloom. She tried to ignore her wet clothes as she settled in.

"Yes, three spiteful daughters who are determined to spend every bit of my inheritance. There isn't a lick of talent between them—either magical or theatrical. Nor are they particularly bright, sadly—they take after their mother. Arranged marriages frequently produce . . . lackluster results." He sighed sadly. "They aren't at all like you," he added admiringly. "I've never met a girl so brave."

"I'm just doing my duty to my House," she answered, not taking her eyes off the roadway. "And I enjoy the excitement."

"Far too exciting for me," Huguenin admitted. "I prefer tales of adventure acted out on stage, not on me personally. But I do despise Count

Vichetral," he said adamantly. "The man is a conceited brute who has no vision save for his own power and authority. And he does not enjoy the theater," he added, a note of condemnation in his voice. "We cannot allow a man like that to rule us."

Atopol returned within the hour with several sets of clothes he had easily taken from Lady Paladine's estate. If he had taken anything else, he didn't mention it, Gatina noted as she changed into the slightly too-long gown and cotton slippers he'd acquired for her. He and Huguenin changed into doublets and hose of good quality, and by the time the sky was lightening in the east, they appeared as three reasonably affluent travelers, not an escaped prisoner and skulking shadowthieves.

"No sign of Captain Stefan yet," Gatina reported when they had dressed and bundled up their wet clothes. Her hair was nearly dry as she resumed her position to watch the road. "Two more enclosed carriages are bringing more prisoners up, I presume. Other than that, only a few farmers getting an early start and a carter going down to Falas."

"He should be here by now," complained Atopol. "Unless he tarried in northern Falas, he should be here. As should the other sortie."

"It takes time to put such things together," Huguenin counseled. "There are all sorts of things you must take into consideration. But I do hope they get here soon—from what I overheard, that fortress will be stuffed full of dissidents by nightfall. They wanted to avoid the festival crowds in town," he explained. "They intend on using truthtells with everyone to get them to reveal their contacts. That will be disastrous."

"What else did you learn?" Gatina asked, curious.

"That the Censorate is eager to prove their worth to Vichetral, that they are feeling quite demoralized about being booted out of Castal and Remere, that they are drifting and without purpose, and that they are as opportunistic as a hungry monk right now," Huguenin related. "They see Alshar in a sorry state, according to their ideals. And they see this as an opportunity to remake magical practice in the duchy according to their sadly repressive standards. Beastly people," he said, shaking his head.

"Most of that we knew already." Atopol nodded. "Did you learn anything new?"

"Nothing helpful," conceded the mage. "I was too busy being beaten, bound, and having my head stuffed in a bag. Once their precious Captain arrives, they will get their orders."

"Let us just hope that Shadow arrives first," Atopol said. Gatina could tell that her brother was anxious, despite his calm demeanor. "There are an awful lot of us captured already. We cannot let that stand."

"Ah, your handsome father," sighed Huguenin. "You know, when I discovered that my dear cousin had agreed to marry him, I had reservations. Most of us didn't even know your House existed or believed it to be a fable. I was as shocked as anyone when the announcement was made . . . quietly. Minnie has always been a bit of an eccentric, though, so I shouldn't have been surprised. Bit of a wild one, your mother," he said approvingly. "I think it was a natural match, though. Good for both family lines. And just scandalous enough to be delightful to whisper about at the right parties."

"We try not to be whispered about at all," Gatina pointed out. "It's bad for business."

"Oh, I understand," Huguenin assured. "Privacy is dear to me. And essential to you. I think—"

Huguenin was interrupted by the approaching clatter of a carriage on the road and the pounding of hoofbeats. All three of them slunk behind the bank so that they couldn't be seen from the road and watched as it rode by . . . followed by six checker-cloaked warmagi riding horses behind it. It took a few moments for them to pass, and they quickly turned left onto the long expanse of the bridge.

"Well, it seems as if Captain Stefan has arrived," Atopol said, a note of regret in his voice. "I suppose we should go to the Wayward Turtle and take a room and wait for support. I doubt we can handle this on our own."

"Of course not," Huguenin agreed. "You've done quite enough for one night. A very long night. Now let's take a room so that I can change my appearance a bit. And perhaps take a nap," he proposed. "Then we can get down to the serious business of utterly wrecking the Censorate's holiday." He touched the bruises on his face and winced. "I don't fancy myself a spiteful man in most respects, but now that the relief of being rescued has faded, I quite find myself eager to dole out a little painful revenge for this indignity."

Despite Huguenin's flamboyant nature, there was a look in his eye that told Gatina the mage was quite serious about the matter. And that gave her some hope. She was starting to get the idea that the psychomancer was far more powerful than he looked . . . and quite a bit more devious.

CHAPTER TWENTY-SEVEN

ANOTHER ALIAS AND A DISTRACTION

Sometimes, one must rest. No matter the mission, if you're tired, you're careless.

— from Gatina's Heist Journal

THE WAYWARD TURTLE WAS A TRAVELERS' INN, GATINA COULD SEE: NOT the sort of place someone wanted to linger, but a relatively comfortable stay on your way from one place to another. It was much different from the Duke's Dalliance in Inmar, she noted.

It lay at the crossroads between the busy road that led north from Falas Town's switchback and the slightly less busy road that stretched into the estate lands east and west of the Mandros. It was also proximate to the wharves and piers that serviced barges that plied the upper Mandros from Falas all the way past Inmar, to the north. As such, it was a convenient stop for anyone on their way anywhere, and it had prospered accordingly.

It was a mere two stories but stretched back far from the street to accommodate many guests. The sign in front of the establishment featured a cartoonish turtle on its back, clearly drunk, and even had the name of the inn printed in Narasi above the turtle. Its high-peaked roof was more than a story high itself, a testament to the rains that frequently beat down on this section of Alshar.

Gatina, Atopol, and Huguenin strode purposefully to the place just as the early-rising lodgers were preparing to leave—most seemed destined for Falas Town for the Midsummer celebration, Gatina guessed. Pack-traders and pilgrims, Huinite monks, and holiday travelers were busily preparing for the journey down the switchback trail as they arrived in the common room, many stuffing biscuits into their mouths to break their fast before they began their descent to Falas Town.

It only took a few moments to locate the innkeeper, an older, wizened man who seemed to be everywhere at once during the busy period. Huguenin spoke with him and procured a room high up in the rafters on the second floor, and paid extra for a view of the river . . . and the bridge.

Atopol and Gatina played their roles as his nephew and niece, visiting the city for the festival. Gatina guessed that some passwords were exchanged between the two men during their discussions, for there were no questions asked as the old man led them up the narrow stairs to their hired chamber. Atopol snagged a half dozen biscuits from the tray provided for guests on his way up and distributed them to his companions. Gatina ate them greedily and gratefully. She could not remember the last time she'd eaten.

"How delightfully . . . rustic," Huguenin sneered good-naturedly at the three simple beds in the room after the innkeeper left.

"It has a window; that's all I care about," Gatina said as she took up a position near it. From her vantage, she could see the entrance of the bridge, the fortress of Relian Tower, and the river that stretched between them. The same river that had almost killed them the night before. It looked so placid and peaceful in the daylight, she noted. She found herself resenting it because of that.

"It has a bed," Atopol pointed out. "That's all I care about at the moment." He stretched his aching muscles and then threw himself on the quilt-covered straw tick. "A comfortable bed," he amended. "Let me know when you see our people arrive," he added before he closed his eyes. He was asleep in an instant.

"If you can spare me for an hour, I'd like to join him," Huguenin said apologetically. "I find myself entirely depleted after last night, and for entirely different reasons than usual."

"I'll wake you in an hour," Gatina promised. "I can't sleep yet, anyway."

"Ah, the vigor of youth," sighed Huguenin as he sprawled on the other bed. "How I miss it!" Then he, too, was asleep.

Gatina really couldn't sleep, even though she was as tired as her companions. Her mind was too busy buzzing with the excitement of the previous night. She felt compelled to keep a careful watch with magesight so that she could note every detail about Relian Tower. As happy as she was that they had rescued Huguenin, she knew very well that their mission was far from over.

They still had a book to steal and destroy, once their parents arrived. And she wondered what her parents would think of the unauthorized rescue.

She watched the comings and goings of the crossroads with great attention, noting how many more carriages and carts arrived from Falas Town, and how many Censors and City Watch accompanied them. Her head buzzed with the tally she took, and her eyes darted around as she used magesight to get an idea of the morning routine across the river. Much of it was dedicated to carts hauling cargo back and forth from the stronghold guarding the crane and the docks on the other end of the long, narrow peninsula.

But she quickly got a feel for the aberration in the routine: the Censorate's operation at Relian Tower. Though they were trying to be discreet about their actions, Gatina could tell that the porters and stevedores who moved cargo up and down the roads were somehow disturbed by the activity. From what she could see, the presence of a squadron of guardsmen at the castle gatehouse was unusual and disruptive to commerce.

More importantly, she could peer within the windows of the tower itself from her position. Using magesight, she was able to peek into the narrow arrow slits that lined the squat, round little tower. Rarely did she see anything worthy of note, but she did catch the occasional flash of checkered cloak through the slits. So, the Censors were using the tower, she confirmed. If that was the case, she guessed that the highest—and presumably best-appointed—chamber would be given over to the Censor Captain.

That was where, she assumed, he would keep his little book. The one that needed to be stolen and destroyed. She could be wrong, she reasoned, but her experience at Lindule Hall suggested that Captain Stefan was the kind of self-important man who preferred to be in the tallest, most ornate chamber. The one that gave him the best view of what was going on.

"Take a nap," Huguenin ordered unexpectedly from behind her. "You've been awake for hours and hours, and you must be tired. I can watch from here," he promised.

"Has it been an hour already? I'm really—" Gatina began, and then yawned. She realized she really *was* tired. More tired than she'd ever been in her short life. The trip over the river chain had exhausted her, and her body needed sleep as much as it needed breath, she decided. "I'm really appreciative," she said instead of arguing. "I suppose I could use a few hours' sleep."

"Besides, perhaps this old wizard can use a bit of magic to give us some intelligence," he suggested as he replaced her at the window. "The Censorate are adept at magic, but they are used to being on the offense. I doubt they've deployed many defensive spells. I'll wake you if and when the others arrive."

Without another word, Gatina crawled into the warm spot Huguenin had vacated. She slept the moment her eyes were closed.

Gatina's dreams were chaotic—filled with constellations of stars, menacing Censors, helpless friends, swaying cranes, and the terrifying river chain, as well as stranger visions. None of it made much sense, and when someone nudged her foot, she lurched awake with a start.

"Mother and Father have arrived," Atopol said in a low voice from the foot of the bed. "You should be awake now."

"I'm coming." Gatina nodded, rubbing her eyes. "What time is it?"

"Noon, and time for luncheon," Huguenin said from the window without taking his eyes away.

"Time for kittens to be eating," her mother's voice said from the other bed. Gatina rolled over and saw that she'd spread out a meal on the quilt. Bread, cheese, sausage, and strawberries—strawberries! Gatina reached over and grabbed a handful, and her mother smiled indulgently. "After what I hear you did last night, I imagine you're quite hungry."

"You . . . heard?" she asked, realizing that her mother might just be furious at them attempting such a dangerous feat. And that her father would consider her off-plan mission a pattern in such behavior.

"It was a bold move, Kitten," her father said from the other side of the room. "From what Cat and Huguenin said, it almost got you killed. But it worked, and you got the work done.

"Now let's chat about what you saw while you were there. Our men are getting into their places and will need orders soon. There has been a steady stream of closed carriages going to the castle, so I'm assuming that they're beginning their raids. That's not good." He sighed. "I was hoping we'd arrive here more quickly."

"Thankfully, it seems that the Censorate isn't as spry as we feared," Huguenin pointed out. "The Censor I overheard during my captivity said that they'd begin at dawn. In fact, they did not begin to ride out until the third bell, and only a few of them. It's taking them time to write out all the orders and such."

"So, we're too late!" Gatina said, sagging back on the bed in despair.

"No, no, they're starting with the street operatives," her mother consoled her. "Some of them don't even know who they're working for. We got the word out to most of the cell leaders in Falas. They're hiding or fleeing now. If we can destroy that book and disrupt their plans, then we can adjust our plans and keep working. It will take them months to assemble that information again, and this time, we'll be ready for it."

"And they'll lack a few informants, too," Shadow said menacingly. "Those who turned their cloak on the Shadow Council will no longer be informing. Lord Hound's men were given the list that Onnelik deciphered. As soon as the rescue is done and our people get away, then they will face the consequences of their betrayal.

"But our first mission is to steal that book," he continued. "Huguenin thinks it's in the top chamber of the tower. But Captain Stefan is apparently using that chamber to conduct interrogations, too."

"He's using truthtell spells and wringing out their contacts," affirmed the mage. "There are almost a hundred prisoners in there now. Thankfully, not many of them knew much about the leadership of the Shadow Council. That's why the cell system works so well," he added. "It's as if every portion of the conspiracy is in its own little cupboard, with only the leaders knowing who is directly above and below them in the organization. Even if they get interrogated with magic, they can only betray a few others. It limits the damage the Censors can do."

"How can you tell?" Gatina asked, curious.

"A spell known as the Long Ears," Huguenin said. "I can hear all sorts of things being said in that fortress as well as if I was still there. Most of the prisoners are being held in the basements for now. They're being brought up, one by one, to face the questions of the Captain in the tower. Terrible thing to listen to," he added, shaking his head.

"This will be as much prison break as a heist," her father began as he took a seat on the one battered stool the inn provided. "We do not have overwhelming forces at our disposal, but we have enough to conduct a swift operation, if we take them by surprise. One team of men will perform an attack by stealth, designed to get into the dungeons and release the prisoners—while keeping the Censorate and the Watchmen at bay. The other squadron will take control of the western bridge to secure their escape."

"Won't Vichetral's men just be able to hunt them down on horseback, then?" Atopol asked between bites.

"After they cross the bridge, we have wagons waiting to take them up the northern road to the next village. There, we have a barge waiting to take them upriver to . . . Well, the details are not important," he said with a small, tight smile. "We have secured their escape; that is what is important. We should be able to delay the Censors and their men long enough to see them on board the barge.

"During the attack, I want you two," he said, indicating Gatina and her brother, "to execute the heist. You'll need to find some way to make your way to the top floor of the tower, steal the book, and destroy it. Then leave. Do not linger. Do not engage the Censors. Do not rescue anyone else. If the Censorate's records are destroyed, then this is all worthwhile, even if some of the prisoners aren't rescued. But that book *must* be destroyed."

"We will begin at the fifth bell after noon, just before evening—the hottest part of the day. But there won't be many shadows to hide in. Your father and I will be coordinating both portions of the mission," her mother continued, as she handed some buttered bread to Gatina along with a leather mug of weak ale. "We'll be acting as reserves for any of the sorties that need them. But if Lord Hound's men can take the dungeon and Lord Wolf's men can take the bridge and hold it for a sufficiently long time, then that should give you ample time to destroy the book. Are there any questions?"

Gatina considered. "Is there any honey for the bread?" she asked.

"So, how are we going to get into that tower in broad daylight?" Atopol asked Gatina as their parents and Huguenin went over other portions of the plan. "I mislike our chances if there isn't darkness to protect us. And those arrow slits are too narrow for you to slip into, much less me. This is not a country manor house," he reminded her. "This is a real defensive fortress. A kind of crappy one, but it's built to keep people out."

"If we can't rely on the night and shadow, then we will have to rely on distraction and misdirection," suggested Gatina thoughtfully. "If going in a window is impossible, then we'll have to go in through the door."

"Which one of us? Or both?" he asked, a pensive look on his face. "And how?" Atopol asked with a shrug. "Tell them we're part of the shadow conspiracy and we want to turn ourselves in?"

"An interesting idea, but . . . no." Gatina smiled. She considered the matter carefully in her mind. She remembered the crane and wondered if that could be a means to get in—but immediately rejected the idea. It was at the other end of the compound from the tower, and it was only helpful going up or down, not in.

But that did suggest another idea.

"Cat, apart from interrogating prisoners, what do they do in that little castle?"

"The crane," he said automatically. "The stockpiles. Cargo."

"Right," Gatina nodded. "And they let porters and carters in all the time," she pointed out.

"You want us to disguise as porters?" he asked, surprised. "Or maybe cling to the bottom of a cart?"

"I'm thinking of something altogether different, actually," Gatina said, her eyes narrowing. "Who, besides porters and carters, has cause to visit the tower?"

"The cleaning staff? Tax officials? Merchants?" he suggested, confused.

"Or people expecting shipments but who have complaints," Gatina offered. "In fact, they would have to have someone important to deal with anyone important who had anything important to complain about, won't they?"

"I . . . Well, certainly," Atopol conceded. "And that wouldn't be in the stockyard, if it was important enough. All the records would be kept in the castle. In the tower," he corrected.

"So, we just need to have someone who has a complaint that has nothing to do with the hundred or so prisoners the Censorate has taken. Once they're in the castle, then it's just a matter of sneaking upstairs and stealing the book."

"And then getting out again," Atopol pointed out. "That might be difficult."

"Not in the middle of a raid," she countered. "If someone was complaining about something, they'd have a low priority during an emergency. And that's just the time when we'd have a chance to strike. Especially if they were annoying enough about it. Darkness, they might just throw you to the raiders if you were ugly enough."

"Maybe an irate bargeman?" he suggested. "I could play that role."

"Not quite . . ." she said, her mind whizzing with ideas. Which alias did she have that could compel a response from the petty official in charge of complaints? Not Lissa the Mouse, certainly, and definitely not Nocturn Avorrita. Neither one complained much.

But she knew someone who did. An idea began to form in her mind.

"Cat, do you mind breaking into that old woman's house again? I think I need a change of wardrobe. And some cosmetics," she added. "And some shoes. Better shoes. And while you're doing that, I'm going to talk to Huguenin."

***

SEVERAL HOURS LATER, GATINA EMERGED FROM THE WAYWARD TURTLE, transformed.

She didn't know whose dress she was wearing, but she did know from the fabric and stitching that it was created by one of the finer seamstresses in Falas Town. It was cut in the classic Coastlord style, of expensive Gilmoran cotton dyed a deep cornflower blue. The skirts were wide enough to conceal portions of her working blacks and helpful gear, including her slim shadowblade strapped to her left hip. Her stolen wimple was bleached a painfully bright white, the broad belt that cinched her waist was chased with gilt, and her shoes were expensive leather expertly crafted into a stylish form that allowed no doubts about her class and status. If they were just a bit too big for her feet, that wasn't obviously apparent.

She felt like she was wearing a mask, her face had so many cosmetics on it. Huguenin had proven adept at applying it to achieve just the right look for what she intended and had enchanted her eyes to match her dress in a striking way. The entire time he was painting the tinted cosmetics on her eyelids and cheeks and nose, he lectured her about her mannerisms, forms of address, and general attitude. If she was going to pull off this plan, they both knew, she would have to be utterly convincing in her quickly put-together alias.

"You are the entitled scion of an ancient House, used to lackeys and servants jumping at the sound of your voice," he instructed her as he worked. Huguenin's tone was soothing, relaxing, but his instructions were pointed. "You see yourself above everyone but your powerful parents, your ancestors, the upper nobility, and the Duchess of Alshar. Arrogance is part of your nature," he insisted. "There is no doubt in your mind that your very word commands action from all who hear it. Your influence is absolute; your anger compels action. You have no compunctions about destroying every obstacle to your goals, and you do not hesitate to invoke every power at your disposal to get your way."

"Won't they be willing to ignore me because of my age and my sex?" Gatina asked as she kept her eyes closed. The brushes that Huguenin was using tickled her face, but she kept absolutely still.

"You see those as weapons, not weaknesses," the mage said as he worked. "Your age means that your power in Alshar's society is rising; your sex gives you privilege and protection from repercussion. These are not well-born men you will be speaking to. They are workers, easily replaced and fearful for their livelihood. The last thing that they want to contend with is a high-born brat with connections to power. They will do everything possible to appease you, just to get you to leave. They have little experience dealing with the gentry and will feel vastly out of their element by your very presence. None of them will know what influence you truly have, but every one of them will fear the repercussions of displeasing you."

"I sound like a horrible person," Gatina admitted.

"That's it exactly!" Huguenin breathed as he finally put the brushes away. "You are a horrible person. But one who believes that she is the very best of society who truly deserves—demands!—every consideration, no matter how outrageous. Your whim is the only measure of your satisfaction . . . and you are never satisfied. Your ire is all-powerful and shall not be denied. You exist to make life uncomfortable for those who do not bend to your will. Your demands are immovable pillars of the universe to which everyone and everything around you must make accommodation."

"What if they do not listen to me?" Gatina asked anxiously.

"Then you insist, you threaten, you demean and degrade those who think that you are inconsequential until they do listen to you. You speak quickly and precisely and do not stop until you have thoroughly expressed yourself. You punish interruption by redoubling your determination and escalating your anger and derision. You keep your threats vague in nature but devastating in consequence. Everyone you meet is lazy, stupid, and incompetent. You have an entire powerful, wealthy House that will support you in any manner you desire, and have no fear of personal consequences for your actions. You are a young, rich noblewoman who has no possibility of accountability," he stressed. "That is something that any grown man fears."

"So, you do think this will work?" she asked with a wince as Huguenin picked up a stiff brass brush and began attacking her hair.

"I would wager a great deal that it will," he agreed. "Every man in every position fears its loss, and every petty official seeks to get through the end of his day with as little turmoil as possible. If you are that turmoil, then they will do nearly anything to avoid it. Government inspectors?

Angry merchants? Lazy employees? These he can contend with, as they are expected as part of his trade. An irate, high-born brat demanding satisfaction? That is something for which they will be entirely unprepared."

By the time the mage was done with her, she looked nothing like Gatina—or Avorrita. When he held up the looking glass for her to see the result, she gasped. She didn't recognize herself.

"This, my kitten, is the face of an irresistible force of nature that has never known defeat," he pronounced. "She has never faced consequences for her petty tyrannies. She has never felt an ounce of humility, or sorrow, or self-reflection that wasn't shallow self-aggrandizement. Her very word is law. Her every whim is a commandment. Her chamber pot doesn't stink."

"I . . . I'm not certain I can live with myself if this works," Gatina sighed as Huguenin tugged and brushed with efficient speed.

"We can contend with that afterwards—I am an accomplished mentalist," he said smugly as he put down the brush. "Now, let's go over your name, lineage, and personal narrative one last time before you begin . . ."

Gatina was gratified that she was not going to the tower alone; standing deferentially behind her was her brother, a nobleman no longer. Atopol had managed to procure well-made working clothes from Lady Paladine's home, a woolen smock over a sturdy linen shirt. He was to portray her servant, and Huguenin had spent some time preparing him for the subtleties of the role. He bore both her purse and a small satchel for his mistress. His demeanor was entirely deferential . . . and altogether miserable in his position.

"That will be the most convincing portion of your alias of all," Huguenin assured. "A simple young noblewoman might be dismissed if she is alone; if she has a servant who treats her with deference and fear, that will become contagious. Practice your wince, boy, for you will use it like a cloak. You find the entire experience humiliating, but you will endure because that is what you do. You are there to do whatever it is she needs done, no matter how degrading. Yet you despise her for who she is, and you despise yourself for what she has made you into."

"Oh, this will be fun," he said, heaving a deep sigh as he regarded his transformed sister.

"That's it! That's the expression exactly!" Huguenin agreed enthusiastically. "Every moment you spend in her company, at her command, is a punishing exercise in emotional endurance," he directed. "You exist to do her bidding; you lament the day you took the position and routinely consider throwing yourself off the nearest cliff to escape her hellish wrath. Every word from her is an insult challenging your manhood, intelligence, and dedication."

"You're right"—Gatina grinned at her brother—"this *will* be fun!"

"You have the right look, the right dress, the right demeanor . . . all you lack is a name," Huguenin said thoughtfully as he regarded her brother. "Something short and easily twisted into an insult by mere inflection of voice. Gurdi? Rudi? Roop? Roop! Yes, you are Roop—not from anywhere, not of anything, just lowly Roop who is low born and ill-fated and deeply, deeply regretting the choices he has made that landed him in such an unenviable position as her manservant."

"Roop." Atopol nodded.

"Roop!" Gatina tried out the name in her mouth, enunciating the single syllable repeatedly until it became automatic. "Roop. *Roop!* ROOOOOP!" she said, using a number of angry, shrill inflections. Atopol visibly winced at the last one.

"That's it!" Huguenin said, delighted. "Poor, honest, miserable Roop lives a life of apologetic misery in service to his mistress. If you can portray that convincingly, Cat, no one will doubt her sincerity. Sometimes, it takes a supporting character to persuade the mind of the truth of something—one person might be a liar, but two people, playing complementary roles? Utterly convincing," he said with satisfaction. "Now, do you have your documents?" he asked. "Not nearly as good as Onnelik's work, perhaps, but they should be convincing enough. I hope," he added. "Use them as we discussed, and they should provide you sufficient support to get you in to see whatever poor soul is in charge of that operation. A little misdirection, a little sleight-of-hand, and a convincing amount of outrage, and you should be able to gain access to the chambers you need."

Atopol patted the small satchel he'd stolen to conceal the cosmetics in. "Right here," he assured.

"Excellent. Well, my kitties, I have nothing further to tell you. It is in your paws," he sighed. "It is nearly the fourth bell now, and the attack begins at the fifth. Go forth and make a nuisance of yourself. Good luck and try not to get yourselves killed."

With those words echoing in her mind, Gatina led Atopol resolutely out of the inn, across the crossroad, and through the wide stone bridge that spanned the Mandros. They did not speak along the way, as they were both mastering their new aliases. They passed dozens of common folk and travelers arriving for the Midsummer festival on the morrow, but they did not acknowledge them.

Gatina slowed briefly when they made the other side of the bridge and the squat tower of Relian was looming overhead. She took one last deep breath, glanced behind her to assure herself that Atopol was still there, and then strode forward with determination in her step. She paused again before the gatehouse, where carts still emerged from the stockyard within. There was a postern door just inside, and she waited for Atopol to open it for her.

Inside was a harried-looking clerk of middle age clutching a sheaf of parchment, muttering to himself. The man looked up at the unexpected interruption, his eyes blank.

Gatina strode through the door with every confidence, Huguenin's advice infesting every pore of her being now. She looked around the small chamber in thinly disguised disgust and then picked out the clerk with a steely, unforgiving stare.

"My . . . my lady?" the man asked, confused.

"Lady Leonna anna Baskley, to be precise," Gatina said, her voice a high-toned growl. "Who are you?"

"I am Halipol, my lady, assistant clerk," the man said, no less confused.

"Then kindly direct me to a senior clerk, or a foreman, or anyone else who can explain to me why the shipment I ordered from my estate in Ganith a month ago has not arrived at my uncle's manor in time for Mid-summer—and I warn you," she said, her tone dark and foreboding, "if I am not satisfied with his answer . . . there will be *blood!*"

CHAPTER TWENTY-EIGHT

CAPTAIN STEFAN

Our Art mandates that we make quick studies of situations and of people. Other people are excellent sources for aliases. Observe and learn from their behaviors and mannerisms. How do they treat others or react in challenging situations? What are their secret desires? Their fears? Their motivations? Knowing these is more important than a wig or a disguise for passing as someone you are not.

*— from **The Shield of Darkness***

Commentaries

HALIPOL WAS COMPLETELY CONVINCED BY HER ACT, GATINA REALIZED WITH a thrill. The poor clerk was soon stuttering and stammering under her relentless questioning, and within the first five minutes, she had insulted his ancestry, his intelligence, and his ability to utter a complete sentence. True to Huguenin's prediction, he scurried away as quickly as possible to summon reinforcements for her unreasonable and largely incomprehensible demands, leaving her and Atopol—Roop, she reminded herself— alone in his tiny office for a moment.

Her brother wasted no time in inserting a freshly forged bill of lading into the neat stack of parchment on the small table the clerk worked from. Gatina practiced her fuming for a few moments, even as she grew fearful that they would somehow be discovered. But, so far, she felt this heist was going extremely well.

Halipol scurried back a few moments later, looking embarrassed and apologetic.

"My lady, my superiors are occupied at the moment," he said quietly, "and they bid me assist you in finding—"

"You?" Leonna asked sharply. "They want *you* to handle this? Do they have any idea how important this shipment is? It contains my wardrobe, my personal effects, my jewelry, two cases of good Bikavar red wine, a cask of lemons, and a gold-and-silver chessboard that is to be a gift to my uncle, the Count!" she declared hotly. "*You* are not capable of locating it, clearly. Find someone who can!"

"My lady!" the clerk protested weakly, wincing at the mention of a senior noble. "We handle commercial cargoes, not—"

"You clearly cannot handle *breathing* without sufficient instruction," she sneered. "I have been waiting—languishing!—for this shipment for more than a week now, when it was promised to be delivered long before the appointed day! I have suffered wearing borrowed gowns and cheap jewelry while making excuses to my mother's kin for my poor appearance. My uncle, the Count, arranged for this delivery personally and assured me that it would be here *three bloody days ago*!" she nearly shouted. Halipol cowed in the face of her verbal assault and began to paw the parchments on his table.

"If you will—my lady—just give me a moment . . . to find your bill . . . I'm certain . . . we can . . . figure out this inconvenience . . ."

"*Inconvenience?*" shrieked Gatina. "This is no less than disaster, you incompetent fool! There is to be a ball tomorrow, and I will not be tortured by wearing my cousin's third-best gown and her cast-off jewelry when every young knight in the Great Vale is to be in attendance! What kind of woman do you think I am?" she demanded as he pushed leaf after leaf of parchment around his desk, frantically searching for some clue to rescue him. "If you had any idea of what you have done . . ." she said, trailing off angrily.

"It wasn't me, m'lady, it was . . . Wait! Wait! Here it is," he said triumphantly, as he held up the bill of lading Atopol had just planted on his desk. "You said . . . Lady Leonna anna Baskley?" he asked excitedly. "Yes, I have something . . . don't recall it coming in, but—here it is!" he said, shoving the parchment under her nose.

"Yes, I see it," Gatina said coolly. "It's a piece of parchment. It has my name on it. It has the date of departure and expected delivery—*three days ago!* Yet it is not my shipment; it is just the record of my shipment. I do not *need* a godsdamned piece of parchment, Halipol, I need my *godsdamned luggage!*" she spat. "If you cannot produce it, I demand to speak with your superior. *Now.*"

"Master Teressan is . . . he is occupied at the moment, m'lady," Halipol assured. "There have been some disruptions in service, you see, due to the troubles in Falas Town and the . . . Well, there have been some authorities who arrived who are making it difficult for normal business—"

"I do not care one sorry breath for your . . . *difficulties!*" Gatina said, her painted eyes narrowed and her voice hoarse with disgust. "Summon this Master Teressan to me and have him explain why my shipment hasn't bloody arrived!" she said, her voice rising with every word.

"My lady, I cannot!" Halipol pleaded.

"Roop! Beat this man!" Gatina ordered without looking back at her brother. The order made Halipol's eyes open wide with shock and fear. Gatina did not know what expression Atopol was making behind her back, but it was effective. Halipol held up both hands to stay a potential beating.

"My lady! *Please* . . . calm down," he begged. "I'm certain we can discover what the delay is about . . . Let me escort you to Master Teressan's office, and he will come to attend to your complaints the moment he is free of his other responsibilities," he assured in a whine.

"He has no greater responsibilities at this moment than to contend with this shipment!" Gatina hissed. Then she gave a ladylike grunt of resignation. "Very well. Take me to his office. But while I am known for my great patience, Halipol, rest assured that it is running *dangerously* short over this!"

With a nervous bow and an obsequious manner, the poor clerk opened the narrow door that led up to the gatehouse's second floor, where the senior clerk's office was. Halipol escorted them in and gestured apologetically at the simple wooden bench that was available for visitors. Gatina stared balefully at the bench and then turned her gaze on the nervous clerk, clearly indicating that it was entirely inadequate for her privileged bottom. Yes, this heist was going well.

"Master Teressan will be with you presently," the clerk assured as he sidled toward the door. "He is a very busy man, but once I impress upon him the importance of your complaint," he said, ". . . he will . . . attend to you personally as soon as he is able."

"Fetch wine, then, while I wait," Gatina commanded with a wave of her hand.

"Ah, m'lady, we . . . we have no wine," he said, swallowing hard.

Gatina whirled, her eyes narrow. "Of *course* you don't," she sneered.

Halipol could not retreat from the office quickly enough.

"That . . . was surprisingly fun," Gatina said quietly once the door was firmly shut and she could hear the footsteps of the clerk descending the stairs. "Does that make me a horrible person?"

"You are playing a role." Atopol shrugged, relaxing for a moment as he opened the satchel. "The fact that you enjoy it is perhaps a sign that you should consider the state of your soul."

"Oh, I couldn't do that normally and enjoy it," she cautioned. "Part of me is disgusted with myself. But this must be how the real Leonna feels," she reflected as she cracked the door and checked down the stairs to see if anyone was coming. "How terrible, to take such enjoyment in being terrible!"

"There are all sorts of people under the stars," Atopol muttered absently as he removed another parchment and surveyed the desk. "Three weights," he pointed out, at the three great stacks of parchment already there. Each one had a miniature on top of it, like three little toys to hold the stack in place. "A pewter barge, a copper crane, and a . . . waterfall?" he questioned as he looked at the odd hunk of glass on a brass base. "This must be the cargo arriving from downstream, the cargo on-site, and the cargo departing upstream," he reasoned. He tucked the forged documents into the middle stack.

"The door to the tower is across the way," Gatina reported as she peered through the cracked door. "It's only to the second floor, but I'm certain we will find it leads to the third, where the captain is staying."

As if to confirm her suggestion, the opposite door opened, revealing two guardsmen with short swords escorting a bound and blindfolded prisoner down from the upper chamber. The man sagged between the two guards. Gatina quickly and quietly shut the door as soon as she saw.

"Definitely upstairs," she said, turning her attention back to her brother, who had resumed the vacant stare and slumped shoulders of Roop the Miserable. "He must be doing the interrogations up there. As soon as we get the chance, one of us needs to bolt up there and grab the book!"

"Back in character," he warned, muttering. "Master Teressan will be here any time."

Gatina nodded and returned to her rendition of Lady Leonna. It was a little difficult to conjure her again so abruptly, a bit like putting on a pair of shoes much too small for your feet. But by the time the senior clerk stomped up the stairs, there was an authentic scowl on Gatina's painted face.

"There you are!" she said before the man got the door even halfway open. "I cannot believe you made me wait so long! What is so important that you cannot attend to one little matter?" she demanded of the man, who looked at her with dismay.

"So sorry, m'lady," he said with a disheartened scowl. He was older than Halipol by a decade, and he had a balding head with a moat of gray hair fringing his pate. His jowls were large and slack, and he squinted constantly. "You are Lady . . ."

"Lady Leonna anna Baskley! *Surely*, you've heard of my House! I've come because I've been awaiting a shipment of utmost importance, and your incompetent staff can barely assure me that it has arrived, much less that it has been sent for delivery! I was expecting it *days* ago, and now it is almost too late, and if I do not have that chessboard to present to my uncle on time, I will see every fool in this miserable place begging for alms outside Huin's shrines because they lack employment!"

"Now, now, Lady Leonna," Master Teressan said, attempting to calm the irate noblewoman, "I'm certain we can straighten out whatever the problem might be. My man Halipol showed me your bill, but I do not recall such a shipment arriving. Perhaps I can check my records—"

"Of course you should check your records!" she exploded. "That's what they're for!"

"All right, all right, no need to . . . panic," Teressan said, clearly flustered by the situation. He went over to his neatly arrayed desk and began leafing through the parchments under the barge. "I don't see anything . . ."

"Dear goddess, if I do not get what I sent for, I will be completely humiliated—and I am not one to suffer such slights lightly!" she insisted, really working up a Leonna-class fit. "I will see everyone involved personally flayed alive and fed to whatever foul creatures dwell in the Mandros," she promised.

"I think we can find . . . Ah! *Here* it is!" Teressan said, pulling the parchment Atopol had slipped into the stack to the fore. "Lady Leonna . . . shipment of four parcels . . . but there is no arrival date, nor a delivery request," he said apologetically.

"But it *did* arrive!" Gatina said, more of demand than a question.

"Well, it's in the stack of arrivals," conceded Teressan, "but usually when we receive something from down the falls, it gets annotated by the supervising stevedore. I do not see a note about it here," he said, peering at the parchment. "Nor do I see the arrival date . . ."

"Yet it is in the proper stack," she reminded him. She looked over at Atopol. "It's no wonder the duchy is halfway to ruin, with incompetents like this in charge!" While she spoke, the belltower in the temple across the street—a well-patronized shrine to the goddess of commerce—tolled five times. The signal for the attack.

"I think if we go out to the yard, we might be able to find where this shipment was misplaced," offered the clerk hopefully. "If you care to join me—"

"I will *not*," Gatina said, flatly. "It's much too hot, and I am not accustomed to doing the work others should have done. *Roop!* Go with this man and search for my things!" she commanded.

"But, m'lady—" Atopol mumbled.

"Roop! *Now!*" Gatina insisted, doing her best to sound like the real Leonna. Atopol sighed, hung his head, and nodded. Gatina wondered if her actions might cause her brother to reconsider his misplaced interest in the real Leonna. That might be a fortunate side effect of this alias, she realized.

"If you will wait here, then, my lady, I'm certain we can discover just what happened and have you and your shipment on your way as soon as possible," Master Teressan assured her as he led Atopol to the door, parchment bill in hand. He seemed all too eager to retreat. "I'm sure it will only take a few short moments . . ."

They were gone from the chamber for only a few moments when Gatina started to hear the sounds of commotion from the yard outside of the window. There was shouting. There was the sound of angry thumping. It was sporadic at first, but it grew in volume and frequency until she could hear the unmistakable sound of steel on steel.

The attack had begun.

Nervously she glanced outside the window into the yard below. The workmen who were usually so diligent about moving their cargoes around the platforms were fleeing their stations. Guardsmen were running in several directions at once. There was no sign of her brother or Master Teressan. Soon, a bell started ringing wildly—not the deep tone of the temple bell but a tinny clatter from some station that was clearly announcing an emergency.

It didn't take long for her to hear the door opposite the clerk's office open. She risked cracking the door a bit to see who was leaving the tower and was gratified to watch a tall man in a checkered cloak on the landing. Unfortunately, he chanced to look up and see her peeking. Gatina realized she had to say something.

"What's happening?" she demanded, letting a note of fear into her voice.

The Censor turned to regard her with surprise. He wore a confused and troubled expression on his clean-shaven face, clearly not expecting a well-dressed woman in the grimy confines of a cargo depot. He gave her a moment's consideration. This was obviously Censor Captain Stefan, she knew by the cut of his doublet and his commanding bearing. He confirmed it a moment later by the voice she had overheard in Lindule Hall.

"I do not know, but I will find out," he assured her. "Stay in there, and bar the door if you can," he commanded, and descended the stairs.

Gatina knew it was time to strike—the moment she heard the downstairs door shut, she peered down the stairs to ensure there was no one else there, and then she headed through the opposite door to the tower.

She moved as quickly and quietly as she could, considering the old, worn staircase. At the top, she found the door to the suite ajar and quickly slipped in and shut it behind her. She didn't have much time to search, she knew. There was no telling how long the attack would take, nor what the outcome would be. That was not her concern. The book was.

Thankfully, when she came to the captain's borrowed room, she found it—opened on a small table next to an inkpot, more parchment, and an unlit lamp along with other belongings of the captain. Including his mageblade, she noted. An empty, sturdy chair stood on the other side of the table, with ropes already tied to its arms and legs, and she realized that it had been used to secure prisoners for questioning.

Quickly, she scanned the most recent entries . . . and to her horror, she realized that Captain Stefan had made the most of his short time at the tower. His interrogations of the prisoners had yielded quite a few new notes in the book. They detailed several new names and notations about their whereabouts and possible connections to "the opposition," as the Censor had termed it. Next to the book was a stack of warrants for arrest and questioning the Censor captain was preparing. She didn't bother to read them thoroughly, but they indicated that she was just in time.

She had just closed the book when the door burst open, and the Censor Captain looked up at her, startled.

"What are you doing in here?" he demanded sternly, glancing from her to the book in her hand.

"What are *you* doing in here?" she repeated accusingly. Gatina was horrified that she hadn't heard the man climb the stairs, assuming that he had joined the defense of the tower. "I am searching for my lost shipment," she offered . . . but it was clear from the look on his face that Captain Stefan did not believe her.

"I came back for my sword because the tower is apparently under attack. Now I see why. There is no shipment here," he said slowly and calmly as he stepped toward her. "This is my private chamber, which I use for Censorate business . . . and you are not looking for any fictitious shipment, are you?" he asked as Gatina backed up, still holding the book. Gatina trembled. She had been caught.

But she was not defenseless. Though he blocked her only way out of the tower chamber, she felt confident she could dodge him and evade capture. She began picking out likely routes through the room and around the Censor in her mind. She considered tossing the book through the narrow arrow slit in the wall as she did so, but that would not destroy it.

Before she could take action, however, Captain Stefan snatched the hilt of his mageblade and drew it from its scabbard in one fluid motion. The sight of the bare blade, with its odd bulge toward the point, compelled Gatina to take action of her own: she drew her own shadowblade from where it hid under her skirts. It was considerably shorter than the Censor's mageblade, but it was the best defense she had. It also put to rest any possible excuse about bratty noblewomen and lost shipments of luggage.

"You . . . *you* were the thief," he realized. "The one at Lindule Hall!"

"I had that pleasure," she said defiantly as she held her blade in guard while protecting the book in her left arm.

"You gave us quite a chase, but you failed," he said as he approached. "Lay down your arms now and I will be gentle with your interrogation," he commanded, the tip of his blade only inches from Gatina's own.

"I sincerely doubt that," she said, and beat his sword point away from her. "The Censorate has a reputation for brutality."

"It's true, I've burned girls younger than you are alive," he warned, his expression growing firm as he struck at her own blade. It was a strong, calculated strike designed to disarm her quickly. Gatina shifted position and struck back. Stefan parried, struck again, and then parried Gatina's response. He raised his eyebrows. "But I need to know what you know about all of this. You've been well trained, for your age," he suggested. But he pressed his attack.

Gatina realized quickly that this was no mere sparring match, nor was Stefan as inept at swordplay as Censor Lantripol had been. Though Captain Stefan was not trying to kill her, he was trying to disarm her and trap her from escaping through the door. That did not bode well, she saw. She no longer had the element of surprise over the suspicious Censor, and he was determined to capture her.

Gatina was just as determined to avoid capture, and in the process, she tried to make as much of a mess of things as possible. She tried leaping over the table when Stefan approached her from one side of it, and scattered the parchment, inkwell, and lamp as she did so. At the same time, she struck at his face with her blade to keep him at bay.

Stefan caught the blow easily on the guard of his sword and kicked the table aside. Then he advanced again. Blood pounded in her ears as she realized that she was, indeed, fighting for her life against a grown man who was also a trained warrior. Suddenly, the heist was not going well.

That did not deter her, however, and though she was blocked from the door, she wasn't about to lay down her sword and surrender. She attacked, viciously and without concern for her own safety as she tried to get him out of the way. She gave him a flurry of blows that he was pressed to defend against, and for one brief moment, she thought she'd have the better of him.

Then things went horribly wrong. Instead of continuing to fence with her in the cramped space, Censor Stefan dodged her last blow, dropped to one knee, and grabbed her shoulder with his left hand. In a split second, she was thrown across the room until she crashed into the hard stone wall of the tower. Her blade and the book both went flying from her hands. She couldn't help it—the impact had knocked the breath out of her.

Before she could scramble to her feet, Stefan dropped his sword and captured both of her wrists in one of his large hands. He pushed her against the wall again and struck her, a measured blow with the palm of his hand that nonetheless sent her head spinning. She saw stars and nearly lost consciousness, so powerful was the blow. Before she could recover, he had flung her into the wooden chair and began tying her wrists with a bit of cord.

"There is an attack underway downstairs," he said as he tightly bound her wrists together and then to the chair. "Once I have dealt with that, I will be back to finish our discussion. And no, I will *not* be gentle," he promised. "But I *will* wring every bit of information out of your head. I will introduce you to the efficiencies of a truthtell spell. We will discover who sent you. And they will pay." With that, he snatched up his blade, gave her one last look of smug satisfaction, and left—locking the door behind him.

This heist is not going particularly well, Gatina reflected.

Captain Stefan knew his business, Gatina realized after a few moments of frustrated struggling against the ropes that bound her. There was no play in the knots, no easy way to slip through them, despite how thin her wrists were. The chair was heavy, solidly built, and showed no signs of weakness as she tried to wiggle free.

Longingly, she looked at her shadowblade where it lay on the other side of the room. She considered tipping the chair over and trying to drag it over there, where she might somehow use it to cut the ropes but with the tipped-over table in the way—not to mention the mess of ink, lamp oil, and parchment that littered the floor—that seemed to be a futile pursuit. Besides, the chair seemed far too heavy for her to tip over, given her size.

Near the shadowblade, however, she spotted the little book that was the goal of the heist. It was lying open a few feet away from her darkened sword, seeming to mock her ineffectiveness. While it, too, was splattered with ink and lamp oil, it seemed intact and, sadly, completely legible after the struggle. Soon, she feared, her own coerced testimony would join the other notes in the book. That is, if the battle below did not go well.

All she could do was hope for rescue. That was galling—Gatina the Kitten of Night should not need a rescue, she reasoned. She should never have been caught in the first place. That, more than failing in her mission, was humiliating. She should have waited until Captain Stefan had come back upstairs and retrieved his sword before she tried to take the book. That would have given her plenty of time to complete the heist.

She tried to calm herself and listen to the battle raging outside. Though the arrow slits all faced the front of the fortress, she could hear the echoes of a pitched battle below. The sound of swords clashing, the twang of bowstrings and crossbows, and the occasional loud bang that she assumed was some sort of warmagic being employed all told her that the surprise attack had met some resistance. There were screams of the wounded and shouts of defiance, and she could hear muffled orders being given. But there was no way for her to tell by the noise just how well the battle was going, and for whom.

Gatina had been in riots before, but she'd never seen pitched battle—much less been dependent on the outcome of the battle for her survival. For if the Censorate was victorious, there would be nothing to stop Captain Stefan from interrogating her at his leisure. With magic. And once he was done with her, she could only imagine what would happen next: imprisonment in the dungeon, a quick judgment, and then perhaps an execution. She could imagine the Censors simply hurling her over the side of the cliff or shoving her in the waters of the Mandros until she tumbled over the falls. Neither prospect was in any way soothing. But unless her family won the battle and sent someone to find her, that would be her fate, she feared.

Discovery, capture, torture, and death. That she might be able to face, but she had failed her mission as well. She could not imagine what her parents would think about that. Perhaps if she was very lucky, she mused, the Censorate would merely burn the capacity for doing magic out of her brain. They were known to do that when implored for mercy. Of course, they did not yet know that she was a mage—a barely trained, brand-new mage who knew only a handful of spells, none of which were particularly useful in this situation.

Or were they?

Gatina realized, to her surprise, that just because she was immobile, bound, and destined for a nasty end, there might yet be a means to complete her mission. She stared at the book across the room. She could see its open pages almost clearly enough to read them without magesight. The ink and lamp oil were already drying on the parchment leaves. But there was lamp oil there. Indeed, the floor was covered with the stuff now, as the broken lamp oozed its fuel.

She took a deep breath and closed her eyes for a moment. Raising power was difficult in this situation because she was not terribly comfortable nor terribly calm. But she was determined. Reaching out with her *rajira*, she began building up arcane energy . . . and continued to accumulate it as quickly as possible.

When she opened her eyes, she stared at the book and began defining the limits of her spell. Then she invoked the runes, one after the other, in the chordic cantrip she had only recently learned. Pouring energy into the runes activated them, she was delighted to see, and it did not take long for the power to manifest as she willed and intended.

A brief, bright flash of flame appeared on the pages of the book. It only lasted an instant, but that spark was sufficient enough to ignite the lamp oil that spattered the book. As she let the spell play out, the orange flame licked the side of the pages, charring them black. Silently she encouraged the fire as it ravaged the painstakingly taken notes. Page after page caught fire, sending a flickering gout of flame and a thin plume of smoke into the air. Gatina smiled in triumphant delight as she watched the book be consumed.

Her mission was complete.

Then her smile froze as the flames escaped their bounds and ignited the puddle of lamp oil on the floor. It quickly spread to the scattered parchments, and the air began filling with smoke. In horror, she realized that the overturned table could easily catch fire as well and from there the tapestries on the walls, the timber supports, and everything else. Suddenly, the din outside ceased to matter as much as she realized the danger she was in, tied to a chair in a burning room in the middle of a battle.

No, this heist isn't going well at all, she reflected.

CHAPTER TWENTY-NINE
AN UNEXPECTED RESCUER

Blue Magi are not the only people who can take the measure of a crowd or a situation. It is a skill that is essential to the master thief. Observe first, before plunging into a throng of people. Match their pace and model their behavior to avoid drawing attention to yourself. That way, a crowd can be as useful to a thief as the cloak of darkness.
*— from **The Shield of Darkness***
Commentaries

THE SOUNDS OF FIGHTING AROUND THE FORTRESS WERE GROWING LOUDER through the window as Gatina stared with horror at the increasingly large fire that she had started. The indistinct shouting and screams, the pounding, and the clash of steel on steel indicated that the Shadow Council's raid was well underway. She could only imagine the scene below—warmagi and armed guards fighting fiercely against an unanticipated attack. There was enough noise for her to conclude that the raiders had not been quickly and easily been driven off—on the contrary, from what she could tell many of the workmen out in the stockpiles had been pressed into service against the attackers.

But most of her attention was on the fire that was quickly filling the room with smoke. As she feared, the wooden floor below the blaze was starting to smolder. Though the wood was hardened with use, the spilled lamp oil fueled the flames until they were hot enough to start to burn it. The overturned table had already started to burn, encouraged by the loose parchments that had scattered in the fight. It was still several feet away from her, but she could already feel the heat of the fire on her bound legs and the smoke was starting to make her cough.

Gatina continued to struggle against her bonds, to try to tip the chair, to at least pivot it away from the growing blaze. But it was fruitless, she could tell. With each wrist tied to the arms of the chair, she had no means of using one hand to free the other. There was a small blade behind her back, under her skirts, designed for just such a purpose . . . but that was useless, with the way she had been tied up while still wearing a gown. She hadn't slipped out of her dress, in her haste to steal the book. With each ankle tied, she had no leverage to make any movement. The chair had been used to hold fully grown men far stronger than her while they endured interrogation. She had no real chance against its sturdy construction.

But she didn't start to panic until the first of the ratty tapestries began to smolder and then catch fire. The old, dry wool of the hangings caught quickly, and then she felt the radiant heat of the flames on her face. They also produced a lot of smoke, far more than the parchment of the book or the wood of the floor. The narrow slits in the walls were little help in ventilating the noxious smoke. Gatina coughed with the assault on her lungs and started to despair. With a battle raging in the fortress, a little thing like a fire was hardly worth bothering with.

Then she heard a roar as dozens of voices started yelling below. Far more than the defenders of the keep could account for. There were some victorious shouts as well, and some cries of pain and despair.

It sounds as if the prisoners have been freed, she concluded to herself. While that gave her some small satisfaction, knowing that both missions were now successful was becoming less important to her than the choking smoke and the heat of the flames. She considered screaming for help, but with all the noise of the battle and the escape, she doubted that anyone would hear her through thick castle walls. Besides, screaming would waste oxygen, she knew, and for the moment every breath she could manage was vital.

So, this is how the Kitten of Night will die, she concluded as her eyes began to water. *Why did they not teach us magic to snuff a flame as well as ignite it?* she wondered. It seemed a simple matter, after all.

She tried to conjure some arcane power to improvise a spell, some spell, any spell that could douse the flames, but every new coughing fit affected her concentration and made her lose control of the subtle energies. Besides, she concluded, she did not know which runes would be most appropriate for the action. She could guess . . . but not if she could not control the flow of magical power. She could not even use magesight anymore, the smoke stung her eyes so badly.

So, she closed them and thought of the Blessed Darkness and the thousands of pretty stars in the night sky. She thought of her father and mother and her brother and devoutly wished they would come to her rescue. She even wished that Captain Stefan would return if only to free her from the flames before his ruthless questioning. Anyone, really, would be welcome.

Gatina was close to losing consciousness altogether when the door to the chamber finally banged open. She couldn't see who it was at first, due to the smoky haze in the air. But a gloomy figure quickly stepped through the cloud of smoke and began to flog the flames with a cloak, and she recognized it as her disguised brother.

The relief she felt was palpable. Her shoulders sagged as she realized she was being rescued.

"Kitten!" he called to her in an anxious panic as he tore down the burning tapestry and stomped on it. "Are you all right?"

"Roop! Free me *at once!*" Gatina commanded in a high-handed tone as she bitterly coughed. The open door had allowed some of the smoke to leave the room, but it had also added fresh oxygen to the blaze. After a few moments of trying to beat it back, her brother gave up. The floor was burning in earnest now. He shifted his priorities.

Atopol shook his head as he snatched up her discarded shadowblade and went to work hacking through the rope.

"They fought their way to the dungeon," he related to her as the first of her bonds parted. "It was terrible—a bloodbath. Arrows flying everywhere, warmagi using wands, swords, spears . . . but they got them out," he informed her as he started working on the second knot.

"Hurrah," she said weakly as she flexed her aching wrist. "We won. I was discovered and captured, but he didn't know I was a mage," she reported, her eyes pouring with tears against the smoke. "I burned the book. We won."

Atopol looked around at the burning chamber. "We won. Hurrah," he repeated, and freed her other hand. "You couldn't have found a less destructive means of destroying it?"

"I was improvising," she confessed. "I didn't have a lot of options, tied to a chair."

"I can't believe you got caught and tied up," he said, shaking his head as he moved to free her left ankle. "Mother will be vexed!"

"It put me in the right place," she defended weakly. "Captain Stefan left me alone here with the book to go fight off the attack. He's a nasty bit of work," she added.

"They don't prioritize charm when they're recruiting for the Censorate," Atopol pointed out as her ankle came free. "He was leading the defense. He tried to compel the dockworkers to fight, but they weren't having it. When I saw the guards were overwhelmed and the prisoners were escaping, I came looking for you."

"What happened to the clerk?" she asked curiously. Her head was swimming now. It was terribly hard to breathe.

"He's hiding in a pile of cotton bales," Atopol reported. "He said he didn't get paid enough to fight for other people's cargoes. He told me what he makes. He really doesn't get paid enough."

"Did you see any of our people?" she asked as her right ankle came free. Atopol pulled her upright.

"No, just their arrows and their spells," he said as he gave her the shadowblade. "You need to sharpen that," he advised, and then rose. "But it was a swift and decisive attack. The Censors were completely caught by surprise. The prisoners all got out to safety. Now it's our turn!" He pushed her toward the door.

Gatina stumbled ahead of him, gripping the hilt of her sword loosely. Her wrists ached from being tied, and while she appreciated the ability to defend herself, she was in poor condition to do so even with the blade. But Atopol ensured that she got to the stairs, where much-purer air allowed her to take several coughing breaths and clear her lungs of most of the smoke. She coughed so hard that she saw stars again and had a hard time keeping her feet. Atopol lingered anxiously over her until she could finally draw breath—cool, clean, clear air that her lungs desperately needed.

"I'm fine!" she insisted as he hovered over her. "Really!"

Her brother nodded and drew his own short shadowblade from where it had lain concealed under his cloak. This time, he went first. With a final glance behind her—which saw the landing above filling with thick smoke—Gatina plunged down the stairs after Atopol. Escape was only a few steps away, she knew. The stairs led to the gatehouse and thence out to safety. She would be free from the smoke, the fire, and the chaos of the battle, and be able to rest once more. The promise of that compelled her feet, which complained bitterly after being so tightly tied, to propel her forward.

Alas, her hopes were dashed moments after emerging from the gate-house into the stockyard. She had but an instant to glance around the place and saw it was transformed: arrow-pierced bodies slumped against the walls, while others lay bleeding on the cobbles. Guardsmen, mostly, though she saw a few checkered cloaks. Merchandise had fallen or had been pushed around to form barricades before being abandoned. There was smoke in the air, too—not just from the tower overhead, which now blazed like a torch, but from other places. There were even a few steve-dores beginning to crawl out from under platforms where they were hid-ing. The gigantic crane overhead was still and lifeless.

But she got no more than an instant to assess her surroundings when she collided with Atopol—or, more precisely, he collided with her. Just as she was turning to face the tantalizing gates of the gatehouse, her brother had been knocked back into her by a sudden assault that sent him flying and saw both of them sprawled on the cobbles.

The unexpected blow seemed to pull away her resolve. After the pain-ful exertions of crossing the river and then hurriedly learning a new alias, then getting tied to a chair and starting a fire in the middle of a pitched battle . . . her reserves were spent. It was difficult to push herself to even rise, let alone do so to effect.

But she was determined. She was weak, she was tired, she was hurt, but she was determined. Her task was not done until she was safe some-where or dead.

She shook her head to clear it, but she learned the source of the attack quickly enough. A figure loomed in the smoke and shadows of the gate-house, barring their escape. A figure in a black-and-white checkered cloak.

Captain Stefan looked far less professional now than when he had fought her. Indeed, he seemed to have endured several fights, by the state of his clothing and the broad smear of blood across his face, which bore a ferocious expression. His cloak was in tatters, and he held his left arm protectively by his side. But his right arm worked fine, she could see . . . as did the blood-stained mageblade he held in hand.

It was not a comforting image.

"So, you escaped, little thief!" he gasped, his eyes drawn to slits. "And you've brought your accomplice with you."

"Not before burning your notes," Gatina said, heaving for breath. Atopol moaned and tried to stand. "They're all gone now!"

"You little fool!" Captain Stefan sneered as he slowly approached. "Did you think that I haven't memorized every name, every page?" he taunted. "I've been collecting this information for months now. The Order has ways of remembering such things. As long as I'm alive, that book is redundant. In an hour, this village will have three hundred of Vichetral's troops in it, and there will be no place for you to flee to or hide in. What you tell me will add to that collection," he warned.

Gatina flinched at his words. She had been confident that the book was the only real record of the Censorate's investigations. But she was also aware that the Censorate did indeed have a very specialized arsenal of magic at their disposal, spells honed over centuries to aid them in their work.

That meant that Captain Stefan's mind held the keys to the conspiracy. With him pursuing that information on Vichetral's behalf, there was no end to the trouble he could cause. The man was dedicated; that much she was certain. He was the kind of enemy you did not want to contend with.

And he was kicking her brother in the gut.

That enraged Gatina. As depleted as she felt, she could not stand to see her brother abused when he could not defend himself. Cat was tough for certain, but he had not earned that blow.

"I guess I know what I have to do, then," she said, struggling to her feet. Her back hurt and her legs felt like jelly, but she came into a guard position, just as Master Steel had taught her. Her wrists ached, but they obeyed her commands. Her shadowblade was perfectly in line with her elbow and hip, ready to strike.

Whether or not she could effectively deliver a blow was up to the gods, Gatina decided. She'd fought him earlier, however briefly. Even after a pitched battle and with a wounded arm, he would be a formidable opponent, one that would likely prevail in a duel. Her arms felt like runny porridge. But Gatina was not going to allow anyone to harm her helpless brother.

Stefan's eyes widened at her reaction. His grim smile quickly shifted to a flash of surprised concern, as if he had not anticipated such resolve in a thief.

"You could at least tell me who you are before you kill me," he said, his uncomfortable smile returning. "If you're honorable."

"I'm not stupid enough to reveal myself, Captain," Gatina said, her shadowblade quivering as she struggled to hold it. She was trying to give Atopol adequate time to recover. He was twitching, curled into a ball after the vicious kick. But his blade was only inches from his fingertips. "If you need a name, I'm the Kitten of Night," she said.

It wasn't meant to be a brag—it was an attempt to stall him with questions. Nor did Stefan take it as a brag. He burst out laughing.

"A kitten?" he asked derisively. "Hardly an intimidating name. Kittens are weak, stupid, and foolish," he said with a sneer as he drew nearer. "You might be a good thief, but your reputation suffers from your name," he said with mock sadness.

"I'll make my own reputation, thank you, and under the name that I choose. And if I must slay you to keep our secrets . . ." she said with far more conviction and bravery than she felt. She didn't know which of her aliases was supplying it, but she was glad to have it.

Before Captain Stefan could answer, he tripped forward, his expression shifting yet again—this time to stunned surprise. Something had hit him from behind, knocking him off balance.

To his credit, the Censor Captain rolled when he hit the pavement and came up to his feet again in impressive time, in Gatina's estimation. A moment later, his mageblade was back in his hand, and he whirled to face his attacker. Gatina was fairly curious about that herself. She hadn't expected help, under the circumstances. Her mother and father were both occupied with assisting the prisoners to escape.

But the figure who uncurled from behind the captain surprised Gatina. It was Huguenin, and he had a sword in his hand.

She expected some cry of rage or pithy comment from the Blue Mage. He had plenty of cause to take issue with the Censorate. What she didn't expect was the spout of poetic speech that issued from his throat. In a deep, booming voice he began reciting lines.

"*Molest not that which a man holds dear, nor torment his soul unjustly; for you tempt the wrath of the righteous man, who will contend with you robustly!*" he declared as he advanced, sword in hand . . . and in a strong guard position, Gatina noted. He'd had formal training; it was clear from his posture and position.

What was most surprising about the wizard's advance, however, was not his diction, his command of language as he approached, nor even his accomplished style; it was the expression on his face. Gatina had gotten used to the kind and soothing Huguenin when she'd first met him, and then learned about his flamboyant side when she'd visited him at the Gentle Wave.

But the face he wore now was neither. He was aggressive and determined. Not enraged but *committed*—completely—to the fight. He might have been using verse to distract, but there was no doubt in Gatina's mind that he was both capable and willing to engage the Censor Captain.

Captain Stefan did not hesitate. He lunged at the mage with a series of strikes that Gatina knew were strong from personal experience. Huguenin's more-slender blade parried each of them decisively and struck back an instant later. More, Huguenin confidently advanced, a bit of swagger to his stance as he closed in on Stefan.

"'*Hear the roar of the sovereign's call, attend to his command, and harken! Defy his will and invoke his ire, and skies o'erhead shall darken!*'" Huguenin's sword flashed again, keeping Stefan on the defensive, much to the surprise of the Censor and Gatina. Huguenin's strokes were quick, clean, and purposeful as he maneuvered Stefan around the yard . . . and away from Gatina. Indeed, Stefan risked tripping over Atopol's supine body, the way Huguenin steered him. He was having a hard time keeping up with his opponent's pace, Gatina saw. She searched for a way she could intervene to help her cousin, but he had tried to lure the Censor away from her. She had to respect his plan. This was his duel now.

Captain Stefan tried for a sudden attack on the mage's left side. Huguenin grinned, parried, and then switched hands and slid into a left-handed guard. He had a verse for that, too.

"'*A man risen to pow'r by his own hand expects treachery and defiance; oft prepared he is for rebellion, betrayal instead of compliance!*'" As he spoke, he struck, the rhythm of his sword ringing on Stefan's mageblade filling the courtyard.

There were even a few stevedores watching, from behind bales and bundles, their eyes wide at the spectacle. Huguenin strutted strongly into his attack, his footwork pristine, as he continued to savagely quote poetry. "'*Yield yourself and bend your will to your master as your oath commands, fulfill his bloody direction as justice and honor commands!*'" he finished . . . just as Atopol's leg suddenly kicked out, catching Captain Stefan squarely in the ankle. The unexpected blow sent the Censor off-balance.

Cousin Huguenin did not hesitate, even as Gatina was preparing to spring. He parried Stefan's blade completely out of line and grasped his opponent's wrist with his right hand. Then he spun—not away from the captain but inside his guard, until they were face to face. Then the Blue Mage reached up and tapped the surprised Censor once on the temple.

Captain Stefan crumbled to the cobbles, unconscious.

"And she called me *too unmanly* to play Black Duke Enguin," he said with a sigh as he regarded his fallen foe. "I was *brilliant!*"

"What was that?" Atopol asked as he uncurled from the ground and effortlessly bounced to his feet.

"Act two, scene two of *The Matadine Rose*," Huguenin supplied as he knelt to examine the unconscious Censor. "The scene where Duke Enguin rages against his rebellious counts and threatens capital punishment if they don't obey his orders and invade Gilmora with an army of Wilderlords. It's incredibly compelling," he assured Atopol, "if you understand the subtleties involved in the Black Duke's character. I've always loved that play."

"I meant the . . . the *spell* you used," Atopol said as he joined the mage hovering over the checkered cloaked man.

"That? Oh, I've had this spell hung for days now, ever since you warned me of potential arrest; I do detest a jailor's idea of a banquet. But I didn't have an opportune moment to use it, until now. It only works on one person at a time. He's just unconscious for now," he explained. "But that does give me an opportunity for more elaborate magic. Here, Cat, help me drag him into the gatehouse," Huguenin commanded.

The two men dragged the Censor by the shoulders while Gatina looked around at the anxious faces of the stevedores and workmen who had taken refuge in the yard. She brandished her shadowblade threateningly, then followed her brother and cousin inside. She hoped that she was threatening enough to keep them from being disturbed. She was acutely aware of Captain Stefan's promise of reinforcements, and she wanted to leave the tower as soon as possible.

"Here, put him in that chair," Huguenin directed.

"You're going to have to kill him," Gatina admitted guiltily. "He has the book memorized. I destroyed it, but he says he knows everything within."

"Kill him?" Huguenin asked, surprised. "No need to proceed in such bloody-handed fashion, Kitten," he assured. "Keep me from being interrupted for a while, and we can repair that potential problem. Can you manage that?" he asked, one eyebrow raised.

"I . . . can," she agreed, and took a post near the door. No one was willing to venture toward her yet. Not that she could have done much against them. She was exhausted, body and mind. Atopol stood near, his sword still drawn, guarding the opposite door in the chamber.

"Now appreciate for a moment that a man's life is divided into two parts: his ambitions and his memory," Huguenin lectured as he settled down opposite the unconscious Censor. "Psychomancy can prey on both if the wizard is adept enough. In this case, I will ravage his past, not his future—for by doing one, I manage both. Give me peace," he instructed. "This won't take long . . ."

It took nearly ten minutes, to Gatina's estimation. Huguenin settled into a trance, calling forth arcane energy and shaping it into a complex number of thaumaturgic runes. Even with magesight, Gatina had no idea what they meant or what they did. All she could tell was that they surrounded the Censor's head like a circlet before some flash of activation happened. There was no visible change on Stefan's unconscious face. The shrine's belltower had just begun ringing six bells after noon when Huguenin's eyes finally opened.

"That should do it," he said with satisfaction. "The spell is called the Banishment of Regret," he explained. "Old family recipe. It's nuanced, but this gentleman will find when he wakes up that he has absolutely no memory of what has transpired in his own life in the last six months. It's gone, erased like ink sanded off a page. Which is a pity, because that was one of my finer performances of the Black Duke." He sighed, rising. "It deserves remembering."

"He won't remember the book?" Atopol asked, surprised.

"Not you, nor me, nor anything he's learned since Yule," Huguenin promised as he straightened. "Ironically, the spell is based on one that the Censors are fond of using. But he will not remember where he is or why, when he awakes. He cannot truthfully say anything about his history for the last half-year. I imagine he will be quite confused.

"Now we should leave," Huguenin said, sheathing his sword. "I don't doubt that he has reinforcements on the way here, and I'd hate to provide them with easy prey. Back to the inn, kitties, where we can take a catnap while the world whirs with activity."

"Why did you come for us?" Gatina asked curiously as they prepared to go.

"Because I was here," Huguenin admitted. "And I felt it was my duty to the family. Your lovely parents were off doing brave, heroic things to rescue my people, and I felt obliged to return the favor. Besides, I've grown fond of my kitties," he said with a smile. "I thought an unexpected appearance might prove decisive. Or at least entertaining."

"I cannot fault your reasoning, cousin," Atopol agreed. "How did you get so good with a sword?"

Huguenin shrugged. "I was raised a Coastlord. Like all young gentlemen of noble birth, I have studied swordplay since I was younger than you. I dislike bloodshed, but I do enjoy the activity," he admitted. "Besides, it prepared me for the stage and the rigors of portraying battles in front of an audience. My masters all thought I was quite good at it, in my youth."

"It certainly surprised Captain Stefan," agreed Atopol.

"And two of his guards which I had to, unfortunately, convince to see a physician after they proved less adept at swordplay than I," revealed Huguenin. "They were Vichetral's men, left behind from the pursuit to secure the empty castle. Bit players," he condemned. "He needs to find himself a better class of henchmen."

"But aren't we still in danger from Vichetral's men?" Gatina asked worriedly.

"How so?" countered the mage. "The only one who had knowledge of our participation in the conspiracy was Captain Stefan and his little book. The Censorate is jealous of its secrets. But now the book is burned and Stefan's mind is wiped of that knowledge. The conspiracy is, for the moment, safe," he declared.

"And what about your people? Your players?" Gatina asked.

Huguenin smiled wistfully. "Well, the season is ruined; of that I have no doubt. The theater in Falas will be closed for renovation for a while, I believe. And while I cannot say for certain, I predict that the nascent theaters in Inmar will see a rise in popularity and talent for the next year or so. Do not worry about my players; they understand that sometimes, it's best to go on tour when your hometown audience has grown bored by your show."

Gatina considered that as they walked slowly and calmly back over the east bridge to the Wayward Turtle. The inn was bustling now as even more travelers arrived and departed in anticipation of the next day's festival. Indeed, there was a crowd in the street in front of the inn as a flood of revelers began the celebration of Midsummer early. They seemed to pay no attention to the battle across the river, nor even the smoke still pouring forth from the smoldering Relian Tower on the skyline.

"Wait," Huguenin cautioned them as they came to the crossroad on the other side of the bridge and the hundreds of celebrants moving along the roadways, or merely drinking and singing on the roadside. "Always read the crowd before you plunge in," he cautioned. "Take their measure and their mood, lest you distinguish yourselves in unfortunate ways. Read them like a book and determine whether they are a happy bunch of drunks . . . or an angry mob about to erupt in a riot."

"They seem to be unworried," Gatina said after watching the people move by her in a mass.

"They're not even paying attention to the fight that happened," Atopol agreed.

"Exactly." Huguenin nodded. "Even though there are dead men cluttering up the crane yard, and smoke on the horizon, they are more concerned with their own revels than what is going on around them. So, adopt a similar demeanor," he advised, smiling broadly. "In such a crowd, a single disgruntled man will call attention to himself. Anyone watching for an aberration in the crowd—say, a couple of sneaking thieves—will spot them like a goat in a herd of sheep. So, smile, laugh, and move through the throng with an easy heart."

"Then what?" Gatina asked.

Huguenin sighed. "A nap—a short nap—until nightfall. Then you kitties and I have an appointment to keep back in Falas Town. The Shadow Council meets tonight to discuss today's busy schedule and report on the results of its efforts. You may be required to report your own success. And after that?" he asked whimsically. "Well, it's Midsummer. Huin's Day. The solstice is a time for celebration and merriment. There's no telling what the gods may have in store for you next."

CHAPTER THIRTY

A MIDSUMMER INITIATION

Father was right. Palomar Abbey, indeed, is a special place.
— from Gatina's Heist Journal

"The danger from the Censorate is—temporarily—abated," Shadow pronounced as his masked face looked around the table. It was near midnight, and the council room of the House of Shadows was filled with those invited to hear the results of the rescue and heist. "Three of our cells were spared arrest and interrogation as a result."

Gatina and Atopol had resumed their position behind their parents' seats, clad in their feline masks and working blacks. Gatina felt exhausted after the last few days' activities, and a few hours of sleep had only reminded her of just how tired she was. Yet she could not miss the opportunity to attend the session. She had worked too hard and endured too much danger to enjoy a proper rest.

"Are you certain the danger has passed?" asked Lord Ram skeptically. "The town continues to be full of Censors. Word from the palace is that they will be granted positions in the court of the Council of Counts."

"There is little we can do to halt that," Gatina's mother said apologetically. "But the immediate danger is done. The Censorate's chief investigator has been neutralized, his mind cleansed of all knowledge of our activities by one of our finest Blue Magi."

"And all records of his investigations have been destroyed," assured Gatina, speaking up about her own role in the operation. "I saw the book burned, personally."

"That . . . is a comfort," admitted Lady Gull. "And a credit to the skills of your House. But it is clear that Vichetral is continuing to gather allies, while we struggle to survive, much less make progress in our efforts."

"We knew this would be a long game, and we are but at the beginning of it," Lord Hound reminded her. "We are moving carefully in pursuit of our goal. There will be setbacks," he warned.

"Setbacks? There will be defeats as well as victories," agreed Minnureal. "We managed to avert a dreadful defeat today. If we had not prevailed, then we would be forced to regroup and reconsider our course. But our goal remains: the usurper must not be allowed to take the coronet and crown himself Duke. To achieve that aim, we must ourselves gather allies."

"We have most of the Coastlord Houses that feel strongly about the matter already recruited," Lord Ox reported. "Thankfully, it is a number that rivals the Count of Rhemes' support. But without sufficient Vale Lords and Sea Lords on our side, I see little hope of a decisive victory. As long as the Narrows and the Straits of Sinjar are in the hands of his allies, Vichetral controls Alshar."

"For now," agreed Hance with a sigh. "As Lord Hound has said, it is yet early in the game, and there are many more throws ahead of us before it is decided. The Vale Lords are largely ambivalent to the politics below Falas. And the Sea Lords . . ."

"Aye, the Sea Lords, alas, have proven favorable to Vichetral's policies," Lady Gull said, shaking her head sadly. "They see the prospect of piracy and slavery as an opportunity to return to their days of glory. War at sea is seen as noble, compared to honest commerce. Too many of them are willing to cooperate with his council in exchange for his blessing to raid without restriction."

"But not all Sea Lords," Lord Ox pointed out. "There are many havens that despise the practice and see Vichetral as another opportunistic Coastlord, fighting over the inlands instead of directing the commercial affairs of the duchy properly. We may yet have some allies among them."

"Enough to take the Straits?" countered Lord Wolf doubtfully. "I admire your ambitions, but Vichetral's fleet is growing in the Great Bay. The Castali hold Farise now, and most of the havens see that as a threat, a threat that only Vichetral seems to stand up to."

"We can approach those havens who might consider joining us," proposed Lady Gull. "I move that we send secret emissaries to those havens and invite them to quietly join us. Or at least resist the temptation of piracy and slavery. Not all of them are eager to fight against the Castali in Farise."

"It is not just the Castali in Farise," reminded Lord Hound. "There are good Alshari there, as part of the occupation. And Remerans. On the morrow, Duke Rard will crown himself king, it is said, and bind those forces together against us."

"Not against us but against Vichetral, who rebelled against the proper heir," Lord Ox corrected. "Anguin has been declared Duke of Alshar by the Coronet Council. Rard recognizes him as the rightful lord of the duchy."

"At the point of a sword," sneered Lord Wolf under his mask.

"Regardless," Minnureal said, shaking her head, "we will have to navigate these waters carefully for the next few years. Duke Lenguin was always popular with a portion of the Sea Lords despite his antipathy to slavery. I am hoping that his son can be persuaded to come to Alshar and raise his loyalists against Vichetral's traitors in due time. The lad is no older than my son, after all, and may yet take his place as a true leader."

"Speaking of betrayal," Lady Gull murmured, "I cannot help but notice that our numbers are lacking in this council. Where is Lady Wind?" she demanded. "Why isn't she here to represent her House in such an important meeting?"

Hance sighed. "You are not wrong, Lady Gull. We have determined that some element of Lady Wind's House has been secretly collaborating with Count Vichetral and the Censorate. Indeed, it was she and her family who provided the initial information to the Censors that began this attack against us. It is all but confirmed. I move that Lady Wind and her House be removed from the Shadow Council as a result and that they face the consequences." There were nods of regretful agreement around the table as each representative of each House approved.

"Lord Hound," Hance said quietly, "you know what is to be done."

"I shall see it so, Lord Shadow, though it gives me no comfort," agreed Lord Hound. "It will take a little time, however. I lost four good men in this fight. I will need sufficient time to reconstitute my forces before I move against the traitors."

"We all lost some good people," agreed Lord Wolf. "Two of mine fell at the bridge."

"They fought bravely and kept the foe from pursuing our folk," reminded Minnureal. "You are to be commended for your leadership and the valor of your warmagi, Lord Wolf."

"Yet how many more will I lose if the Censorate remains in Vichetral's control? And wields irionite?" asked Lord Wolf. "I despise the man, but I will not see my House decimated, fighting a losing war. We must see some progress."

"We are making progress!" countered Hance. "Vichetral's grasp on power is tenuous. He is finding it is easier to conquer than to rule, and we have ensured that will continue. He may have armies in the field and fleets in the bay, but the Game of Whispers knows no frontiers. We build our strength. We gather our allies. And when the time is right, we will strike so decisively that he cannot hold the duchy."

"That is our plan," agreed Minnureal. "Unless someone has a better one, that is how we will proceed. Is there any other business before this council?" she asked, looking around the table. "No? Then we are adjourned. Enjoy the Midsummer holiday. Do nothing out of the ordinary that would call Vichetral or the Censorate's attention to you."

As the various masked Coastlords filed out of various exits from the chamber, the four members of House Furtius came together, doffing their masks as soon as the last council member left.

"I wanted to take the moment to commend you both," Hance said once his face was exposed again. "You did an excellent job on this mission, with very little time to prepare. Indeed, you seem to excel at improvisation."

"Thank you, Father." Atopol nodded, clearly pleased with the praise. "I only wish it hadn't been necessary."

"As do I," Hance agreed. "But when one of our most powerful conspirators has decided that they prefer to betray us in an effort to support our foe, there is little that can be done save to retreat, regroup . . . and plot retribution. Lord Hound will contend with them," he promised. "Indeed, we will be paying a personal visit to Lady Wind, I foresee."

"And while we are seeing to that," Minnureal said, smiling at her children, "you two will continue your studies in your apprenticeships. Your father and I have discussed it, and we feel that the situation has eased enough for you to resume your education. There is still much you need to learn about magic, thievery, and the other arts that are your legacy. But be assured we are proud of you and how you performed in this crisis," she added. "You are becoming fine members of Furtius and a credit to our House."

"Does that mean that we can finally get some sleep?" asked Gatina, a hint of a whine in her voice. "I feel like I've been beaten and dragged behind a mule for days!"

"You may sleep," conceded Hance, glancing at his wife, "but it will be in a carriage. Huguenin has volunteered to drive you. He finds that recent events have encouraged him to seek the fresh air of the countryside over the busy activity of city life for a while. Without his players, his theater is useless for now."

"Drive us?" Gatina asked, confused. "Where? Back to the country estate?" The idea of retiring to Cysgodol Hall sounded luxurious to Gatina after such a long absence.

"Perhaps eventually," conceded her mother. "But you have a few stops to make first and some further work to do. For one thing, you must relate all of this into your heist journals," she reminded them. "Then you must refresh yourselves and prepare for your next mission. But first, there is more pressing business to attend to."

"What business?" Atopol asked warily.

"Cousin Huguenin has collected your borrowed carriage from the orphanage and will be outside shortly. Traditionally, we adopt a quiet manner after so much excitement, but under the circumstances, we felt at least a bit of celebration is in order. After all, you two have some unfinished business to attend to," she said knowingly. "If the Cats of Enultramar are to prosper, they need their accomplishments acknowledged."

"What do you mean?" Gatina asked, even more confused.

"You'll find out in the morning," she promised.

THE BELLS OF PALOMAR ABBEY'S SPIRES FINISHED RINGING THE NOON HOUR as the long line of Nocturns assembled in front of the Chapel of the Stars. Nightbrothers and Dawnsisters warded them, shushed their whispers, and tried their best to keep them from distraction as they prepared for the important ceremony.

Gatina and her brother quietly joined them, their old disguises freshly applied. They had ridden all night from Falas after the successful raid, trying to sleep in the back of the carriage they'd borrowed from the abbey. Gatina found her cell and slipped in behind them as the line began to move forward into the chapel.

Midsummer was a sacred day in all of Alshar, of course; Huin's Day was the sacred feast day of the Holy Tiller, the god responsible for the abundant grain harvest. Though he was a Narasi divinity, even the Coastland communities celebrated the triumph of the Tiller and the beginning of the fruiting cycle. Across the duchy, peasants and serfs flocked to the chapels and temples of Huin, where his brown-clad monks blessed their agricultural implements, gave benedictions over crops, and sanctified the holy work of those who grew the grain that became the bread and ale upon which everyone depended for sustenance.

But the Saganites also revered the day for their own reasons. Midsummer was the summer solstice, the longest day of the year, and the beginning of summer. It had distinct astronomical importance, as well as agricultural significance. It marked the midway point of Callidore's annual journey around the sun, and, as such, it was seen as the appropriate day to advance the station of those Nocturns who had completed the first portion of their training. Midsummer was the Saganite's day of initiation.

Gatina was thrilled to be there, though she had missed the preparations for the ceremony that took place in the days before. She had worked hard on her studies despite the distractions of the summer: the Censorate, the trip to Inmar, and the emergence of her *rajira* and her monthly courses.

She felt as if Avorrita deserved some acknowledgment of that hard work, though it was quite possible her alias would disappear forever after the ceremony. The prospect of fulfilling her vow to the temple was important to her, regardless of the name she had used. Despite all of the problems, she had found quite an education at Palomar Abbey—and that wasn't even including her lessons in shadowmagic and swordplay.

"Avorrita!" came a surprised whisper from ahead of her. Dina and Mathilde were side by side as the line moved slowly forward into the chapel. "When did you get here?" the girl asked, confused.

"Just a while ago," Avorrita whispered back. "Dain and I wanted to at least show up and take initiation," she explained. "Are there any Censors about?" she asked worriedly.

"Not since the night you left," Mathilde answered, giving her a pleased smile. "We were so worried for you!"

"I'm certain it will all get straightened out," Avorrita said unconvincingly. "Did that one Censor—Lantripol—did Lantripol come back?" She made certain there was a bit of fear in her voice. Gatina didn't mind that it wasn't entirely feigned.

"No!" Dina assured her. "They found his cloak and sword at the top of the cliffs! Everyone thinks he jumped off into the stream, but they never found a body!"

"Nocturns!" Sister Nimandi said angrily, approaching the commotion. "This is a sacred ceremony of a most hallowed nature! Silence is best—"

She stopped short when she saw with whom her students were speaking. "Avorrita! You've returned!"

"Apologies, Sister," Avorrita said humbly. "I just came back for the initiation," she explained. "My fellow Nocturns had questions, so I . . ."

The nun looked at her thoughtfully. "Yes, well, I'm certain that many of us have questions. But the proper time for answering them is after the ceremony. This is a time for solemn reflection and meditation, not gossip . . . however intriguing."

"Yes, Sister." Avorrita nodded. "I will speak with them afterward."

"That would be best," agreed the nun, giving Avorrita a long stare. "Welcome back, Nocturn." She returned to her place warding the line.

Dina and Mathilde each gave her a smile, then turned back to the procession. Ahead of them, Arryn and Leonna both turned to see what the fuss was about and did a double take when they saw their missing companion. Avorrita gave a shy wave and then bowed her head.

"You do realize that this is all just a bunch of superstitious nonsense, don't you?" Leonna hissed. "All that stuff about planets and moons as little worlds? Circling the sun? The stars are suns themselves? It's just a bunch of mystical rubbish they made up to fool a bunch of gullible nobles into giving them donations!" she said, scowling.

"Oh, do shut up, Leonna!" Mathilde said, rolling her eyes. "This is a solemn occasion. You are completely useless!"

"She's actually been quite useful," Avorrita said softly, "in her way." That produced a skeptical look from her friend.

Avorrita did truly try to contemplate the infinite expanse of the Sacred Cosmos as she walked. She had come to see the stars as almost living things, not mere lights in the nighttime sky. Palomar might be an unusual abbey, but the Saganites had an otherworldly perspective that the other temples just did not manage.

While the religion of the Huinites, the Luinites, the Tryggites, and even the Brigadine Orders were concerned with the spiritual elements of earthly existence, the Saganite Mysteries had exposed her to concepts beyond mere daily living. The complex interplay between gravity, mass, velocity, and time were now familiar to her, even if she could not understand their intricacies without studying far more mathematics. The orbits of the moons and the other planets around the sun provided compelling wonder at the complexities of the universe in ways that mere agriculture or menstruation or legal theory did not.

The Saganite Mysteries were possessed of a unique beauty, in her estimation, combining the spiritually intriguing elements of celestial observation with the truly sublime knowledge of how the mechanics of the Sacred Cosmos might work. Within the Blessed Darkness, Avorrita—and Gatina—understood the true mysteries of the universe lay.

A special bell tolled, high overhead, and Gatina looked up to watch the belltower. It was a silver bell with a particular tone and ancient manufacture, rung only four times of year. It marked the solstices and equinoxes with absolute precision, tolling out the exact moment when Callidore changed from one season to the next.

Just like she was changing, she realized. She was no longer a little girl, and not yet a woman. The summer of her life was just beginning for her, and there was no avoiding it. The stars waited for no man, the Saganites said. They would not wait for a young woman, either.

Gatina found that she was fine with that. Her childhood was over now that she had her courses. She had her apprenticeship, her family duties to attend to, and the struggle against Count Vichetral ahead of her. Foes like the Brotherhood of the Rat, the Censorate of Magic, and Darkness only knew what other forces would try to stand in her way. She was dedicated to restoring the duchy to its proper rulership as passionately as she was dedicated to mastering the art of thievery, the craft of magic, and whatever else her interesting life threw at her.

Avorrita may never return to Palomar again after this ceremony, she knew. There was a certain sadness associated with the alias—bucktooth prosthetic and all. The gentle-hearted girl that Gatina had worn like a concealing cloak would be in too much danger there and would have to be abandoned as Kitten found new adventures. But she had served her purpose and served it well.

And Gatina was fine with that.

Terry Mancour is the *New York Times*–bestselling author of more than thirty books, under his own name and various pseudonyms, including *Spartacus* (Star Trek: The Next Generation Book 20) and the Spellmonger series (twelve books and counting), among other works. Terry was born in Flint, Michigan, in 1968 (according to his mother) and in 1978 wisely relocated to North Carolina, where he embraced Southern culture and its dedication to compelling narratives and intriguing characterizations. He attended the University of North Carolina at Chapel Hill, majoring in religious studies.

Emily Burch Harris grew up reading Nancy Drew and Susan Sand mysteries before diving into fantasy and horror novels. Born in Maryland and raised there as well as North Carolina and West Virginia, she has a knack for finding cold spots in rooms, legends about witches, lost objects, and folks who like to talk. She worked as a journalist before deciding fiction was far more fun than the stark reality of the news. Emily and her husband have one son, two cats, two dogs, and a few fish. She is the editor and writing partner of Terry Mancour.

CONNECT WITH TERRY MANCOUR

Get updates
http://spellmongernewsletter.com/

Check out the Spellmonger series
https://spellmongerseries.com/

Join the Spellmonger Discord
https://discord.gg/68txXKR

Follow him on Amazon
https://www.amazon.com/Terry-Mancour/e/B004QTNFOO

Like his Facebook page
https://www.facebook.com/spellmongerseries/

CONNECT WITH EMILY BURCH HARRIS

Visit her website
https://emilyburchharris.com

Follow her on Amazon
https://www.amazon.com/Emily-Burch-Harris/e/B017Y87Q7U

Like her Facebook page
https://www.facebook.com/avalonschoice/

Follow her on Instagram
https://www.instagram.com/emilyburchharris

Follow her on Twitter
https://www.twitter.com/emilydbharris

Sign up for Terry's newsletter for the latest musings, updates, and release information from the Archmage himself!

Head to the link below and enter your email to stay connected.

http://spellmongernewsletter.com/

DISCOVER
STORIES UNBOUND

PodiumAudio.com

www.ingramcontent.com/pod-product-compliance
Lightning Source LLC
Chambersburg PA
CBHW021538110726
47902CB00004B/934